A JIM HIGG[INS]
DRIFTLESS MYST[ERY]
NOVEL

Driftless INSURRECTION

SUE BERG

LITTLE CREEK PRESS®
AND BOOK DESIGN
MINERAL POINT, WISCONSIN

Little Creek Press®
5341 Sunny Ridge Road
Mineral Point, Wisconsin 53565

Book Design and Project Coordination:
Little Creek Press

April 2024

Follow Sue on Facebook @ Sue Berg/author
To contact author: bergsue@hotmail.com
To order books: www.littlecreekpress.com

Library of Congress Control Number: 2024906518

ISBN-13: 978-1-955656-71-9

Cover photo: Hazy Hills, La Crosse, Wisconsin © **Phil S Addis**

This is a work of fiction. References to real places, events, establishments, and organizations in the
Driftless area are intended only to provide a sense of authenticity. They are used fictitiously
and are drawn from the author's imagination to enhance the story being told.

ACKNOWLEDGMENTS

My heartfelt thanks:

To Alan for allowing me the creative license I need to write.
Love you always.

To Kristin Mitchell, my publisher at Little Creek Press: You always
produce a book that makes me look better than I am.

To my children and grandchildren: You keep it real. Love you all!

To my loyal fans who follow me on Facebook: Thank you for
buying my books and telling others about the series. Thanks to the
many who have encouraged me with personal notes, emails, and
conversations in and around my community. Writing is a singular,
and sometimes lonely, occupation and your encouragement, which
is so needed today but so rare, has lifted me up and kept me going.
Thanks for refueling my tank!

To librarians everywhere: You are the unsung heroes who keep
information and learning at the forefront of our democracy.

... give thanks in all circumstances.
Test everything. Hold on to the good.

—I Thess. 5:17&21

Praise for the Jim Higgins
Driftless Mystery Series:

DRIFTLESS GOLD

"… an irresistible tale of lost treasure and
the scoundrels who will do anything
to get their hand on it."

~Jeff Nania, author of the Northern Lake Mystery Series

DRIFTLESS TREASURE

2021 Finalist Award in The Independent Author Network

"… Descriptive scenes and well-drawn
characters in a story of crimes with
international implications."

~Greg Peck, author of *Death Beyond the Willows*

ACKNOWLEDGMENTS

My heartfelt thanks:

To Alan for allowing me the creative license I need to write. Love you always.

To Kristin Mitchell, my publisher at Little Creek Press: You always produce a book that makes me look better than I am.

To my children and grandchildren: You keep it real. Love you all!

To my loyal fans who follow me on Facebook: Thank you for buying my books and telling others about the series. Thanks to the many who have encouraged me with personal notes, emails, and conversations in and around my community. Writing is a singular, and sometimes lonely, occupation and your encouragement, which is so needed today but so rare, has lifted me up and kept me going. Thanks for refueling my tank!

To librarians everywhere: You are the unsung heroes who keep information and learning at the forefront of our democracy.

… give thanks in all circumstances.
Test everything. Hold on to the good.

—I Thess. 5:17&21

Praise for the Jim Higgins
Driftless Mystery Series:

DRIFTLESS GOLD

"... an irresistible tale of lost treasure and
the scoundrels who will do anything
to get their hand on it."

~Jeff Nania, author of the Northern Lake Mystery Series

DRIFTLESS TREASURE

2021 Finalist Award in The Independent Author Network

"... Descriptive scenes and well-drawn
characters in a story of crimes with
international implications."

~Greg Peck, author of *Death Beyond the Willows*

DRIFTLESS DECEIT

"... Berg creates a smorgasbord of subplots with characters confounded by real-life issues from family loyalty and faith to forgiveness and love, both lost and found.

~Patricia Skalka, author of the Door County Mystery Series

DRIFTLESS DESPERATION

"An honest portrayal of the crime and rural poverty that exists beneath the bucolic veneer of this unique landscape."

~John Armbruster, author of *Tailspin*

OTHER BOOKS BY SUE BERG

Solid Roots and Strong Wings—A Family Memoir

The Driftless Mystery Series:

Driftless Gold

Driftless Treasure

Driftless Deceit

Driftless Desperation

FOREWORD
THE DRIFTLESS REGION

The name *Driftless* appears in all of the titles of my books because this region of the American Midwest where my novels take place is a unique geographical region, though relatively unknown. The Driftless Region—which escaped glacial activity during the last ice age—includes southeastern Minnesota, southwestern Wisconsin, northeastern Iowa, and the extreme northwestern corner of Illinois. The stories I write take place in and around La Crosse, Wisconsin, which is in the heart of this distinct geographical region.

The Driftless Region is characterized by steep forested ridges, deeply carved river valleys, and karst geology, resulting in spring-fed waterfalls and cold-water trout streams. The rugged terrain is due primarily to the lack of glacial deposits called drift. The absence of the flattening glacial effect of drifts resulted in land that has remained hilly and rugged—hence the term *driftless*. In addition, the Mississippi River and its many tributaries have carved rock outcroppings and towering bluffs from the area's bedrock. These rock formations along the Mississippi River climb to almost six hundred feet in some places. Grandad Bluff in La Crosse is one of these famous bluffs.

In particular, the Driftless portion of southwestern Wisconsin contains many distinct features: isolated hills, coulees, bluffs, mesas, buttes, goat prairies, and pinnacles formed from eroded Cambrian bedrock remnants of the plateau to the southwest. In addition, karst topography is found throughout the Driftless area. This landscape was created when water dissolved the dolomite and limestone rock resulting in features like caves and cave systems, hidden underground streams, blind valleys and sinkholes, and springs and cold streams.

About eighty-five percent of the Driftless Region lies within southwestern Wisconsin. The rugged terrain comprising this area is known locally as the Coulee Region. Steep ridges, numerous rock outcroppings like the Three Chimneys northwest of Viroqua, the classic rock formations of Wisconsin Dells, and deep narrow valleys contrast with the rest of the state, where glaciers have modified and leveled the land.

The area is prone to flooding, runoff, and erosion. Because of the steep river valleys, many small towns in the Driftless Region have major flooding problems every fifty to one hundred years. Farmers in the region practice contour plowing and strip farming to reduce soil erosion on the hilly terrain.

Superb cold-water streams have made the Driftless Region a premier trout fishing destination in the country. A variety of fish, including brook and rainbow trout, thrive in the tributaries of the Mississippi River system. The crystalline streams are protected by Trout Unlimited, an organization that works with area landowners to maintain and restore trout habitat. In addition, abundant wildlife such as deer and turkeys provide excellent hunting for the avid sportsman.

La Crosse is the principal urban center that is entirely in the Wisconsin Driftless Region, along with small cities, towns, and numerous Amish settlements. Cranberries are grown and harvested in bogs left over from Glacial Lake Wisconsin. At one time, cigar tobacco was grown and harvested throughout the Coulee Region, but foreign markets decreased the demand for Wisconsin-grown tobacco. However, tobacco barns or sheds are still found throughout the landscape and are an iconic symbol of a once-thriving industry. The region is also home to Organic Valley, the nation's largest organic producer of dairy products, organic vegetables, and fruits, particularly apples. Winemaking and vineyards have popped up in recent years, and apple production continues to be a staple in the Driftless economy.

After describing the area's geographical features, you can see why Wisconsin is the perfect setting for a mystery series! It's a wonderland of unparalleled geographical beauty, impressive wildlife, and friendly, memorable people. Enjoy!

SUE BERG

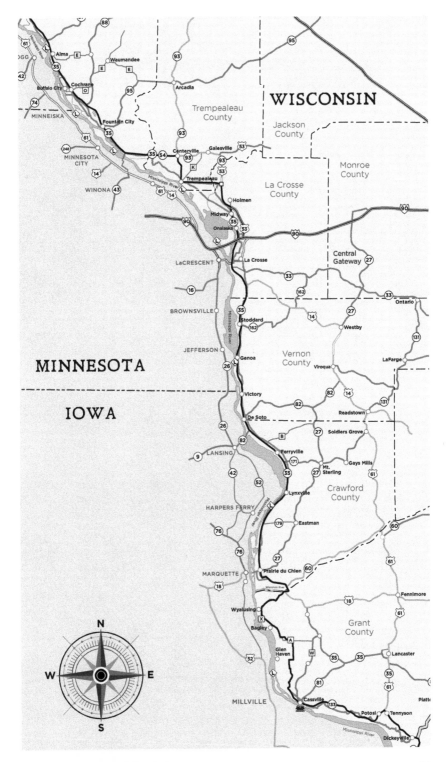

1

WEDNESDAY, MARCH 20, 2019

The blizzard blew in with a savage wallop out of Alberta, Canada, and scoured the countryside of western Wisconsin like a Brillo pad. Its fierce arctic winds and blinding snow squalls growled and hissed and screamed until small trees on the bluffs and hillsides bent to the ground like subjects prostrating themselves before a cruel taskmaster. The drifts behind the Tip Your Hat tavern in Genoa, Wisconsin, seemed like something from a make-believe fairy tale, frozen hard as rocks, the tops hissing with windswept pellets that blew in frenzied swirls. Across from the tavern beyond U.S. Highway 35, the Mississippi River seemed to disappear when whiteouts reduced visibility to zero. When the wind blew, the dark shrouded bluffs hunched on the Minnesota side of the river became invisible across the two-mile-wide expanse of water.

Jed Klumstein, the proprietor of the Tip Your Hat tavern, was huddled under a heap of quilts in the bedroom of the apartment above the bar. The howling of the cold wind outside his window woke him when it was still early; the blue light of a false dawn barely penetrated the frosted window next to his bed. He lifted his head wearily from his pillow and listened to the tapping of frozen snow pellets on the weathered siding. He ducked back underneath the quilts like a turtle hiding in his shell. *Another storm*, he thought disgustedly. *The third one this month. When are we gonna get a break?* He drifted back to sleep, nestled in the warm pleasure of his bed and the cocooning quiet inside the apartment.

By seven o'clock in the morning, the roads throughout the Mississippi River valley were drifted over with more than sixteen inches of fresh snow, making travel virtually impossible. Schools and businesses were closed throughout southwestern Wisconsin. Davy Jones, the La Crosse County sheriff, asked citizens to remain at home and refrain from travel until the plow crews could get a handle on the record snowfall. Most La Crosse businesses closed until noon while the streets were cleared and the snow was hauled away. U.S. Highway 35, the Great River Road, was the only highway that had been kept open throughout the night in an attempt to make it accessible for any emergencies that might occur. Still, road crews found the task difficult in the blinding snowfall. Their work seemed pointless; the snow continued to fall, hampering any travel.

At seven-thirty, an urgent pounding on Jed's upstairs apartment door rousted him from his warm bed. Sitting on the side of his mattress, he slapped his feet on the icy floor, then instinctively snapped them upward toward his chest. Squinting, he scanned the bedroom in the dim morning light and grabbed a pair of wool socks from a pile of clothing that had been haphazardly dropped near his bed the night before. Stuffing his feet into the socks, he stood and stumbled toward the door. The pounding continued unabated.

"Yeah, yeah. I'm comin'," he muttered under his breath as he walked through the dark living room. Dressed only in a t-shirt, boxers, and the wool socks, he pushed off the security chain and whipped the door open.

"What?" he yelled at the figure standing in the hallway. "What's so damn important that you have to beat my door down in the middle of a friggin' snowstorm?"

"Sorry, Jed. I didn't mean to bother you," the young teenager said, his brown eyes apologetic. He scanned Jed's get-up from head to toe and smiled to himself.

"Bobby?" Jed asked, softening his tone, squinting in confusion. The cold wind whipped up the stairway, and he opened the apartment door wider. "Don't you have school today?"

The young man was sensibly dressed to meet the elements in a stocking hat, ski jacket, insulated ski pants, and boots. "No, we don't have school today. Haven't you looked outside? It's a real live blizzard!" he said with an enthusiasm about inclement weather that only the young possess.

"Come on in. It's freezin' out there," Jed said begrudgingly. "I'll make you some hot chocolate."

Bobby pushed past Jed and walked into the chilly apartment.

"That'd be great," the teen chattered.

"If you're lookin' for your dad, I don't know where he is," Jed said, shutting the door. "He hasn't shown up the last few nights."

"Oh, that's okay. I guess you didn't hear. My dad's at the Tomah VA. He's getting dried out in the detox wing. He left the beginning of this week."

Jed's eyes softened with pity. "Sorry, Bobby. I didn't mean to bark at you. I didn't know about your dad."

"Don't worry about it," Bobby said sadly. For someone so young, his eyes reflected a worry that seemed to age him beyond his years. "I hope it'll stick this time. Did you know it takes an average of seven interventions before an alcoholic can finally come clean?" He watched Jed stumble around the kitchen in his comical get-up.

"That's a fact a kid your age shouldn't know," Jed said as he ran his hand through his thick brown hair. He fussed around in the small kitchenette, getting a pan out of the cupboard to heat milk. Setting it on the stove, he flicked on the burner. He turned to face Bobby, who'd found a chair by the small kitchen table.

"So who's watching out for you while your dad's in the hospital?"

Jed asked. He poured some milk into the pan and reached into the cupboard for a can of Nestle's chocolate mix and a bag of marshmallows.

"Nobody," Bobby said, dropping his eyes to the floor. "I can take care of myself."

"I can believe that," Jed said with resignation. "You've had enough practice." He stumbled into the bedroom to retrieve some clothes. When he came back into the kitchen, Bobby continued his litany.

"I'll be fourteen in May. I know how to clean, and I can cook some basic stuff ... eggs and pancakes and hamburgers. Laundry's a breeze. I don't need a babysitter, but I do need a job, and I was hoping you could give me one. I wanna start saving for a car."

"A job? What makes you think you can work at a bar?" Jed asked, scowling. "You're not old enough. Besides, you're too smart to engage in the kind of activities that go on in my establishment."

"I know that, but I thought I could shovel snow out front and out back by the dumpsters. And I could clean the bathrooms in the morning before I go to school," he suggested.

Jed made a wry face, turning over the proposition in his mind. "Well, I guess that would be helpful. It won't pay much. How's seven bucks an hour sound?"

"Eight and we'll call it a deal," Bobby said confidently.

Setting the hot chocolate in front of the teen, Jed lifted his eyebrows. "What? You're negotiating your salary already? Maybe you should be a lawyer."

"Nope. I'm gonna be a cop," Bobby said proudly.

"God in heaven! Drink your hot chocolate," Jed said, looking out at the swirling white snow beyond the window. It seemed to be letting up some.

Realizing Bobby had probably not eaten, Jed decided to make breakfast. While they ate, he did a quick inventory of the teen. Bright brown eyes looked out from a ruddy, scrubbed face that was just beginning to be shadowed with facial hair. His dark mop of hair lay thick and straight and hung almost to his chin. He had grown over the last year, and now his body had taken on a distinctive masculinity— one that would eventually produce a strapping man— strong, tall, and athletic.

Jed knew the last few years had been rough for Bobby Rude with an emotionally absent alcoholic father, a mother who abandoned her family a couple of years ago, and hours spent by himself worrying and fretting over his drunk dad. *The kid's a survivor. That's for sure*, he thought. But he knew Bobby's haunted look came from too many years of responsibility that his father refused to shoulder—a father who had flushed his life down the toilet.

After they wolfed down eggs, bacon, hash browns, and toast, Jed stacked the dishes in the kitchen sink.

"So, you want to start work today?" he asked, feeling more human with some food in his gut.

"Sure. You just tell me what to do," Bobby said enthusiastically.

"Come on, then," Jed said as he grabbed his outdoor gear by the door and began descending the stairs. "We'll start with the snow shoveling. That'll take you a while. You can wear off some of that breakfast."

The bar was dark and smelled of smoke and whiskey and spilled beer. Jed walked behind the long counter and flicked on the overhead lights. The bar was an oak monstrosity that featured carved gnomes in various poses intertwined with leaves and acorns. Jed had picked it up on an online auction. It had cost him more to haul it than what he'd paid for it. Opposite the bar, several booths lined the wall, and toward the back of the building, he'd installed a couple of round tables with chairs for the snack food and pizza he served during happy hour and the Packers games. A large pool table also filled the center of the back room.

Jed turned and went toward the back entrance, where a small vestibule held a collection of tools neatly stacked on shelves, a broom and dustpan that hung on a hook, and a snow shovel that stood in the corner waiting to be used. Grabbing the shovel, he handed it to Bobby.

"Here, you use this, and I'll fire up the snowblower. We'll clean out the dumpsters first," he said.

Bobby grabbed the shovel, adjusted his gloves, and followed Jed outside. The wind had switched to the west; the cold took their breath away. The world had become a white wonderland of sculpted snowdrifts. The sharp features of the rock outcroppings along the limestone bluffs above the tavern had softened with the snowfall, and the edges of trees and houses and roads blurred in the intermittent bursts of arctic wind. Between gusts, everything was hushed as if someone had laid a huge white blanket over the scenery. When Jed slammed the back door, snow came loose from the roof and plummeted off the edge, just missing them. Bobby grinned happily.

"Ain't this somethin'!" he said with a lopsided smile. "It's beautiful!"

Jed shook his head. The innocence of youth. "Beautiful to a poet, maybe. But you probably won't be saying that in another hour," he said sourly.

Jed walked to the utility shed and removed the snowblower. After numerous attempts pulling the starter cord, the machine finally coughed to life. Bobby was already scooping out the snow by the back entrance. They worked for a while and were making good progress when Jed noticed a darkened area beneath a snowdrift next to one of the dumpsters. Frowning, he stopped the snowblower, letting it idle as he walked up to the mysterious hump. He kicked at it, thinking it might be a dead animal, possibly a deer or a coyote or a dog that had been hit on the road and crawled here to die, or a sack of garbage that had missed the dumpster and gotten covered by the snowfall. When he kicked the lump, the sole of a hiking boot revealed itself.

Jed stepped back in horror. After a moment, he leaned forward and, with his hand, swept away some of the snow that covered the body. A red ski jacket and blue jeans lay lumpy and frozen beneath the drift.

"Oh, my God!" Jed whispered. He began digging energetically, brushing and scooping snow frantically into a heap next to the body. By this time, Bobby had joined him and was standing by his side.

"What're you doing?" Bobby asked, peering over Jed's shoulder. "You find something?"

"Yeah. Somebody's buried under here. Help me. Maybe he's still alive," Jed said panic-stricken.

"Are you kidding me?" Bobby asked. His eyes widened with shock.

Jed looked back at him over his shoulder. "Do I look like I'm kidding? Come on. Help me!" he said, his voice edged with desperation.

They continued to uncover the body. Jed's stomach turned over at the thought of someone dying in a drift in subzero temperatures only a few feet from the door of his tavern. When they tried to turn the victim over, he was already stiff with cold. Jed realized the man was dead. He flipped his cell phone out of his pocket and dialed 911.

"What is your emergency, sir?" a detached voice asked.

Jed identified himself. "I found a dead person buried in a drift behind my bar down on Highway 35 in Genoa," he said. He'd forgotten about Bobby, who stood next to him and was listening intently to the conversation.

"Holy moly," Bobby whispered. "First a blizzard and now a murder."

Jed covered the phone with his hand. "We don't know that yet," he said impatiently, his eyes blazing with frustration. "Don't be jumping to conclusions."

Bobby Rude's brown eyes hardened, and he met Jed's angry gaze with one of his own. "How many people have you found in a snowbank with their skull caved in?" he asked. "If that isn't murder, then tell me what is."

2

Lieutenant Jim Higgins, chief investigator for the La Crosse Sheriff's Department, stood on his front porch underneath the overhang of the roof and gazed at the driveway. Drifts as high as his waist lay in pristine mounds. The hardwood trees and evergreens scattered throughout his ten-acre property along Chipmunk Coulee Road south of La Crosse, Wisconsin, were weighed down with snow. Everything lay silent in the frigid air like a whitewashed tomb. A cardinal, whistling a low song, landed in the arborvitae bush next to the house, his bright, beady eyes alert with energy. A tapping on the window caught Jim's attention.

His seven-year-old daughter, Lillie, still in her pajamas, waved excitedly at him. He lifted his hand and smiled, squinting against the white snow. He stepped off the porch and began plodding through the deep snow to the pole shed beyond the double garage. Opening the service door, he stepped into the quiet gloom of the shed with its smells of gasoline and motor oil. He hit the automatic garage door opener. As the door yawned open, the brilliance of the white world outside spread its light into the interior of the shed like the sun barreling over the horizon.

Jim primed the snowblower and pulled the cord. The machine sputtered briefly, then fired up filling the shed with the smell of exhaust. Plowing into the nearest drift, he began blowing the snow from the blacktopped driveway, working steadily for an hour until his wife, Carol, stepped out onto the front porch and waved at him, holding her hand to her ear. He shut the snowblower off so he could hear.

"You're supposed to call Jones at the sheriff's department," she said loudly. "From the tone of his voice, it sounded urgent. Besides, aren't you getting cold? I just made a fresh pot of coffee and some egg and bacon sandwiches."

Jim left the snowblower and trudged to the house. He stepped into the foyer and stomped off his boots. A gust of frigid air blew in after him.

"I *was* getting a little cold," he said, throwing his gloves on the bench under the coat rack.

Three-year-old Henri stood in the dining room off the foyer in his pajamas and gazed wide-eyed at Jim. His coat was covered in blown snow, and the fur around his hood was brittle with frost.

"Hey, Henri. It's Daddy," he said, removing his outer clothes.

The little tyke's face lit up, and he ran to Jim, who enthusiastically picked him up and hugged him. At the same time, he fished his phone out of his pocket and speed-dialed Sheriff Davy Jones. They'd been friends since their college days at UW–La Crosse and had served together for over thirty years in the La Crosse law enforcement community. Their relationship was cordial and easy despite the tension of their jobs.

"Sheriff Jones."

"Davy, what's up?" Jim asked when he heard the familiar voice.

"Trouble down on the river. The owner of the Tip Your Hat tavern in Genoa called a half hour ago. He found a dead man behind his tavern buried in a snowdrift this morning about eight o'clock. Questionable circumstances. We need somebody down there, but the roads are impassable. Since you're the closest cop to the location, I thought maybe you could get there on your snowmobile and check out the situation, secure the premises, and see if you can figure out who this guy is."

Jim grunted, then said, "Yeah, my snowmobile will make it, but it will take me at least an hour before I can get there. It's about ten miles from my house to Genoa. I'll get my gear on and head out. Call the bar and let them know I'm on my way, will you?"

"One more thing," Jones continued. "Apparently, the guy has a massive head wound. No other injuries were reported by the owner of the tavern."

That was one thing Jim didn't want to hear. His stomach turned over with the familiar angst he always felt when someone's life had been snuffed out and he was called to the scene. Was it another act of senseless violence or an unfortunate accident?

"Jim? You still there?" Davy asked anxiously.

"Yep. I'll head out in ten minutes. I'll keep in touch after I assess the situation," he promised. Hearing the conversation, Carol caught Jim's eye. He held up a finger to her.

"Sounds good," Davy continued. "I'm working on getting a team together so we can travel in one vehicle and follow the snowplow down 35, but I'm not sure how long that'll take. Everybody will need to get here first, and the city is hunkered down. We should have someone there in an official capacity as soon as possible. You can get there quicker than we can. At least it isn't dark, and the snow has let up, but be careful. It's treacherous out there," he said. Jones clicked off.

"What's going on?" Carol asked, her brown eyes curious.

"Somebody down in Genoa found a body. I'm the closest, so I'm taking the snowmobile down."

Suddenly, Lillie appeared at Jim's side wearing a frown. Little Henri watched his precocious sister pose her compact body in front of Jim in a face-off. Henri's brown eyes were wide with curiosity as Lillie started in.

"Bapa, you promised we'd build a snowman. You know what they say about parents who don't keep their promises?" She tapped her foot on the hardwood floor—a habit that reminded Jim of her determination and iron will. Her blue eyes held his stare. *She's got confrontation down to a science*, he thought.

Jim knelt in front of her. "You will not hold me hostage with your threats, young lady," he said in a serious tone. "You know that when the sheriff calls, it's my duty to go. We've talked about this many times before. We will build a snowman later, or ..." Jim looked up at Carol, "... you and Mommy and Henri can surprise me with your own creation. Your choice," Jim finished, standing up.

"It won't be the same without you," Lillie whimpered.

Seeing her pout turning to tears, he said, "I'm sorry, toots, but tears will get you nowhere. I have to go."

Lillie stomped her foot, turned, walked down the hall, and slammed the door to her room.

"Seven going on sixteen," Jim lamented, rolling his eyes. "God, help us!"

Carol stood before him with a sandwich and a piping hot cup of coffee. Her eyes radiated sympathy.

"Don't feel sorry for me," Jim said, noticing her expression. "You're the one who's going to have to deal with her." Then his voice toughened. "And don't let her get away with any sass. She has to learn some limits, and now's as good a time as any."

Carol saluted, straightening her posture into a soldier-like pose. "Aye, aye, sir. Your orders will be followed to the letter of the law." She giggled infectiously, then relaxed. "I can handle her, don't worry. We'll take a girlie bubble bath and do our nails and hair. She'll forget all about the snowman. And if all else fails, she can practice piano."

Jim chewed on his sandwich between gulps of coffee. Finally, he handed the cup to Carol, leaned down and kissed her, and began dressing for the trip—first his polar fleece vest and then his other winter clothing. As he turned to leave, Carol sidled up to him with a couple more sandwiches wrapped in tin foil and a small thermos of coffee. "Just in case you get stranded somewhere."

"Thanks, babe. I'll see you later," he said. "Remember, I love you," he whispered huskily.

"The proof's in the pudding," she teased, lifting her eyebrows.

"No, the proof will be later tonight when I get home," Jim said, winking.

□

Jim had forgotten how rough a snowmobile ride could be. His shoulder began aching after jostling and bouncing over the first five miles. The shoulder injury happened last fall in a confrontation with a drug lord who'd abducted his older daughter, Sara. In a standoff in a gravel quarry near Viroqua, Jim was shot, but the infamous Maddog Pierson had been arrested and was currently sitting in the state prison at Boscobel awaiting trial for murder and kidnapping. After surgery and a long bout of therapy, he'd recovered—somewhat. The throbbing in his joint reminded him that his age (54) was betraying him. Healing just didn't come as fast or seem to be as complete as when he was twenty years younger.

The wind had died down, but the cold that was sweeping down from Canada stung his lungs and took his breath away. He pulled his neck warmer over his mouth and nose. No one else was on the roads. Driving down the middle of Chipmunk Coulee Road, he reached U.S. Highway 35 in twenty minutes. Crossing the wide road, he began driving along the shoulder, the snow blowing in white clouds behind him.

The river was silent and imposing, but it still had a particular beauty in the winter months. The trees looked like frozen skeletons reminiscent of a frosty tableau in a Currier and Ives print. Sitting in a bare oak tree near the river's edge, a regal bald eagle scanned the snowy landscape for any sign of life, impervious to the bone-chilling temperatures. Out on the ice, a convocation of the majestic birds gathered near an open spot, eating fresh fish they'd caught that morning, the ice bloody with entrails.

Stoddard, a small river town south of La Crosse, came into view, and Jim slowed his machine as he drove down the deserted main street. The River Road Café was shuttered, the closed sign still hanging in the door, although the Kwik Trip gas station across the street seemed to be open. Cars and trucks along the street were snow-covered bumps, still and mute. Jim wondered how these small-town businesses hung on, especially during the off-season. When he reached the outskirts of town, he gunned the engine and barreled down the highway.

During his ride on the sled, Jim pondered the changes in his daughter, Lillie. After living on the street with her grandmother and being adopted by Jim and Carol over three years ago, she'd shown a marvelous resilience in adjusting to normal family life. She was a precocious child, advanced in language development and her school studies. Constantly challenging them with questions and an insatiable desire to learn, they had been brought up short more than once. Jim chuckled to himself. *We'll just have to rely on wisdom from God to raise her*, he thought.

Recently, they'd learned of her exceptional musical ability. Sister Agnes at St. Ignatius Catholic School in Genoa had spoken of Lillie's talent at parent-teacher conferences last fall.

"Her musical ability is really quite remarkable. I'm quite sure she has what is called relative pitch in the music world, which means that she can identify notes by comparing them with other ones. For instance, if I play a middle C and a G, she can tell me there are five steps between them, and she uses the one note to identify the others by comparing them. She has shown a strong desire to learn to play piano. In fact, I was in my office one day, and I heard these beautiful chords. I wondered who it might be, and when I peeked around my door, Lillie was experimenting on the keyboard.

"So what are you suggesting we do as parents?" Carol asked, concern etched on her face.

"Get her a piano and start lessons. I can recommend some very good teachers at the university," Sister Agnes said.

That had been six months ago, and currently Lillie was breezing through the paces of a very rigorous program of classical piano performance and basic music composition. They never had to tell her to practice. Usually she spent at least an hour per day playing, and if she was composing, the time could stretch to three hours. Her powers of concentration were formidable. Mozart, Bach, and Brahms were often heard floating down the hall from the piano they'd placed in her bedroom.

Jim put his thoughts about Lillie on hold as the little fishing village of Genoa appeared on the horizon. Slowing the engine, he coasted up the vacant street until he came to the Tip Your Hat tavern. The outside stoop had a definitive sagging look. The front door seemed ready to fall off the hinges, and the siding was faded to a dull gray. With the snow-covered roof and frozen landscape, it looked forlorn and deserted, like a haunted house out of a movie set.

Jim dismounted from his sled and stomped up the steps of the creaky porch. Opening the door, he hollered, "Anybody here?"

From the recesses of the dark interior, he heard two voices conversing in soft, low tones. Then someone yelled back, "We're back here. Come on in."

Jim crinkled his nose at the saturated scent of cigarette smoke, booze, and stale air. Walking briskly to the back of the bar, he approached a middle-aged man he presumed was the owner and a teenage boy. The boy pushed his hood away from his face, and Jim was surprised when he saw Bobby Rude.

"Hey, Lt. Higgins! How ya doin'?" Bobby asked, thrusting his hand toward Jim. "I was hoping they might send you down." His warm smile made Jim forget about his cold toes and fingers.

"Bobby Rude! Nice to see you again," Jim said, pumping his hand enthusiastically. Bobby had been instrumental in providing crucial eyewitness testimony that helped identify the killer of a puzzling double murder in La Crosse a few years ago. In addition, he'd helped the police locate the murder weapon. As a result of his observations and testimony, Jim and his team were able to solve the crime.

Jed Klumstein leaned toward Jim, exchanging a handshake.

"You the owner?" Jim asked.

"Yep. Have been for eighteen years. Jed Klumstein," he said seriously.

"Okay. So tell me what happened here," Jim said, still standing.

"I was in bed this morning, and Bobby knocked on my door about ..." Jed started.

"It was about seven-thirty," Bobby finished his sentence.

Jed frowned at him for interrupting. "Whatever. I invited Bobby in for breakfast, and then an hour later, we decided to start cleaning out the snow in the back by the dumpsters. I was using the snowblower, and Bobby was using the shovel. I noticed something dark near the dumpster under the snowdrift, and when I kicked at it, a boot appeared. Bobby and I dug this guy out of the drift, but he was already dead."

Jim turned to Bobby. "How'd you get here, Bobby? You live around here somewhere, don't you?" he asked.

"I just live up the hill. I got out my plastic toboggan and rode down the hill this morning through the drifts," he told Jim.

"You don't lock your tavern at night?" Jim asked Jed, his blue eyes shifting to the owner.

"It was so dead last night—I think I served my last customer about eleven-thirty—that I just locked the front door and left the back open. It was snowing so hard I figured no one would be out traveling, so I put my day's proceeds in my safe upstairs and went to bed. Besides, Bobby has a key. Sometimes he's alone, and he comes and stays over if his dad—" Jed stopped talking and looked at Bobby, embarrassed.

"If my dad is too drunk to get home or he's been somewhere drinking and doesn't want to drive," Bobby explained, finishing Jed's sentence. "Jed lets me sleep on the couch if I need someone to talk to."

"I understand," Jim said, nodding with empathy. He was aware of Bobby's rough home life. After a moment's pause in the conversation, Jim asked, "Where is this person you found?"

"He's back by the dumpster. We didn't want to move him too much in case you had people coming who'd need to look at the scene," Jed said, turning and waving to Jim over his shoulder. Jim and Bobby followed Jed to the back door of the bar.

"Bobby, I know you helped find the man," Jim said, turning toward the teenager, "but I don't allow minors to be present at a crime scene, especially one that might involve a murder victim."

"I'll wait in the bar if that's what you want me to do," Bobby said. His dark eyes and hair made his skin look particularly pale. Jim didn't know if that was his natural coloring or if he was feeling queasy about viewing the dead man again.

"I think that would be the best. We'll visit when I come back inside," Jim explained. "Could you make a pot of coffee?"

"Glad to," Bobby said, feeling important.

Jim went to the dumpster and snapped on a pair of blue latex gloves. He knelt down beside the dead man. Even in the cold temperatures, decomposition was setting in; the victim's complexion had a waxy look, the skin a light shade of blue. He had dark curly hair, and Jim guessed he was about one hundred seventy-five pounds.

He was wearing an expensive L.L. Bean ski jacket, pricey designer jeans, a Rolex stainless steel wristwatch, a soft extravagant cashmere sweater that Jim guessed cost several hundred dollars, and Salomon hiking boots. *He's not a blue-collar worker*, thought Jim. He rolled the victim toward himself to get a look at the back of his head and noticed the crushed skull with a wound about the size of a baseball. There was little, if any, blood in the surrounding snow. *Probably killed somewhere else and dumped here.* He let go, and the victim gently rolled face up again.

"Was this man in your bar last night?" Jim asked, looking up at Jed.

"No. I've never seen him before in my life," he said.

Jim carefully felt the man's pockets and found a wallet, which he laid in the snow next to the body. The victim carried no vehicle keys, which Jim found odd, but he did find his cell phone in the inner pocket of his jacket. "Do you have a blanket or tarp we can drape over the body until the crime scene personnel get here?" Jim asked.

"Sure. Just give me a minute," Jed said as he turned and went back into the bar. While he was gone, Jim inspected the man's fingers—a simple gold band but no other jewelry except the watch. Soon, Jed returned with a woolen army blanket, which Jim carefully draped over the body. Then he pushed snow around the edges to keep the blanket secure. Jim dropped the dead man's wallet and phone in a ziplock bag and walked back into the tavern.

Bobby had made a fresh pot of coffee, and he carried three steaming cups to the booth along the wall where Jim and Jed sat talking quietly. He plopped down next to Jim and began to talk.

"My dad's been real sick this year. He finally agreed to get dried out at the Tomah VA. They say he has advanced alcoholism—something called cirrhosis of the liver."

Jim's heart sank when he heard about the trials the young teen was facing in his life, but he knew it was all too common these days. Alcohol, painkillers, and meth addictions were wreaking havoc on families all over Wisconsin. Jim wished it wasn't so, but the truth was painfully clear as he listened to Bobby retell his latest family saga.

"Well, let's hope this time your dad can get sober. Maybe then he'll start to feel better," Jim said, his face tender with emotion. "So how's school going? You're a freshman now, right?"

"Yep. Going to Logan, and so far it's been good. I made the 'B' honor roll last quarter, and I'm working real hard to make the 'A' next semester. I played basketball, too, but I wasn't very good at it. But they recruited me for the junior varsity baseball team, so I'm looking forward to that." Bobby's eyes reflected the pride he felt in his accomplishments. "How's Miss Higgins doing?"

Jim swallowed hard. He paused, not wanting to dig up unpleasant memories, but he realized his daughter, Sara, had had a big influence on Bobby's development, particularly in reading. "Well, she's had a hard time of it. She's actually going to grad school now in the Twin Cities—St. Thomas."

"I was sorry to hear about what happened to her. I followed it in the *Tribune*. She was my all-time favorite teacher," Bobby said wistfully.

"Yeah, I know," Jim said, sipping his coffee. Memories of the trauma his daughter, Sara, had endured at the hands of Maddog Pierson did nothing to ease the anxiety bouncing around in his chest. He always felt this way when the topic of her abduction came up in conversation.

"Not to break up your reunion or anything," Jed interrupted rudely, "but who's the guy in the snowbank? Was he carrying a wallet?"

Jim nodded, then took the supple leather wallet he'd found in the dead man's back pocket out of the plastic bag. He removed his driver's license, social security card, a federal ID, and a host of other credit and business cards. Tucked in an inner pocket was two hundred dollars in cash. That was it.

"Looks like his name is LeMar Burke from New Orleans," Jim commented, studying the driver's license. "Forty-six years old. His business card says he's a financial consultant for Hathway Industries—real estate acquisition. Long ways from home." Jim felt his stomach lurch when he thought about another set of mysterious circumstances that may have been the result of murder. As he looked at the business card, he thought the name Hathway Industries looked familiar.

"Why would anyone want to come here in March during a snowstorm?" Jed asked, lighting a cigarette.

"He might have been here on business. Or maybe he was visiting family. Who knows?" Jim shrugged. He didn't have a clue—yet. *He might have been followed by someone who had a score to settle*, he thought. "Whoever whacked him on the head didn't steal his money, so robbery doesn't seem like an obvious motive."

"How'd he get here?" Bobby asked. "There isn't another car in the lot except Jed's old Ranger pickup."

"I thought I was supposed to be asking the questions," Jim said, grinning. Turning to Jed, he asked, "You didn't hear a vehicle last night, a snowmobile, or anything like that?"

Jed shook his head. "Nope. When I hit the hay at midnight, the parking lot was empty. I slept like a rock until Bobby hammered on my door this morning."

"Bobby? You hear or see anything?" Jim asked, turning his attention to the teen next to him.

"No, sir. I got up a couple of times to look out the window at the snow, but I can't see the parking lot of the bar from my house."

The front door opened, and the sound of stomping boots alerted them that the investigative team from La Crosse had arrived. Sheriff Davy Jones led the procession as they trailed in.

"So—what's going on?" Jones asked, stopping at the booth. He was dressed like an Eskimo, but beneath the navy ski coat and fur-lined hat, his tan uniform was crisp, his gun clipped on his belt, and his star pinned to his shirt.

Luke Evers, La Crosse County coroner and medical examiner, looked over Davy's shoulder and asked, "Where's the body?"

"I'll show you," Jim said, scrambling out of the booth, motioning them toward the back entrance.

The investigative team trooped through the tavern and gathered outside around the army blanket. Once the blanket was folded back and removed, they began to inspect the surroundings while Luke knelt by the body. Sheriff Jones watched the crew working, then turned to Jim and said, "Who's the kid?"

"He lives close by. Bobby Rude. Remember? He helped us on the double funeral home homicide. He lives just up the hill, and Jed helped him out this morning. His dad's at the VA getting dried out," Jim said.

"He see anything?"

"Nope. Neither did the owner. I have the victim's wallet and phone. I'll get online when I get to the office and see what I can find out. First, I'm going to head home. By the time I get there, the roads should be somewhat cleared. I'll come into the office as soon as I can."

"Sounds good. There's not much else we can do at this point until we get some results back from Luke and the crime scene people," Jones commented.

"My thoughts exactly," Jim said brusquely.

3

By noon, Higgins had arrived back at his home on Chipmunk Coulee Road, had a quick bite to eat while he warmed up, listened to one of Lillie's piano compositions, and headed back to the office in the Suburban.

The roads were slick and snow-covered. In some places, hard drifts across the road made the truck lurch like a bucking bronco when he drove through them. The bluffs along the Mississippi River were hunched in a gray shroud, their dark shapes barely visible through the tapering snowfall and icy frosted air. It was like driving in a deep freezer.

South of La Crosse along Highway 35, shops and businesses were still closed, although a few owners had braved the cold and were blowing or shoveling their way out of the insulated safety of warm buildings. Schools were dark and unoccupied. Traffic was minimal.

Jim drove slowly through town, slowing at the yellow caution lights that were flashing at most intersections. Some numbskull, driving way too fast for conditions, slid through an intersection and almost sideswiped him. Jim grimaced and tightened his grip on the steering wheel, waiting for impact, but the guy was able to pull it out of the skid at the last moment. With his heart in his throat, Jim pulled into the parking lot of the La Crosse County Law Enforcement Center on Vine Street, thankful he'd avoided a fender bender.

The building was an eyesore on the city landscape, devoid of any aesthetic beauty, silent and imposing, its tan presence and dark windows melting into the gray of the winter storm. Jim parked the Suburban, walked toward the architectural behemoth, and pushed his ID through the slot on the secure doorway.

Taking the elevator to the third floor, he wasn't surprised to see Emily Warehauser, his secretary of fifteen years, sitting poised and alert at her desk. The woman was a secretarial phenomenon not to be messed with. He thought of the postal oath: Neither snow nor rain nor heat nor gloom of night stays these couriers from the swift completion of their appointed rounds. *That would be Emily*, Jim thought. Her efficiency and energetic approach to her job frequently left Jim speechless. It was almost as if she could read his mind, superseding any plans or orders he might have had for her. Who wagged the tail of the dog when it came to the office? *It sure isn't me*, he thought.

"Good morning, Jim," Emily chirped as she began her recitation. Her auburn hair was neatly coiffed in a professional cut, her makeup was flawless, and her attire distinctly businesslike. Professionalism oozed from her pores. Jim lifted his eyebrows, stopped at her desk, and waited for her clipped narrative of the staff's whereabouts.

"Sam and Leslie are on their way in. DeDe is still reeling in shock from the amount of snow and the cold temps, but Jude will drop her off when he gets dug out. Apparently, neither one of them has ever seen a blizzard in real time, but being from New Orleans, that's understandable. Paul is here. He's in his office." Finishing her update, Emily looked at him for direction. Getting nothing but a blank stare, she continued. "I left some paperwork for you to complete on your desk."

She's done it again, he thought. *The epitome of efficiency and administrative brilliance.*

"Sounds good. Carry on, Emily," Jim said as he turned down the hall and strolled to Paul's office.

Paul Saner had worked with Jim for over five years. Trusted, capable, and even-tempered, Jim relied on him in countless ways during an investigation. They had a history; Paul was shot three years ago in an ambush that went bad, and Jim had suffered a couple of gunshot wounds in his tenure, the most recent in October of last year. They were both seasoned veterans, and unfortunately, they had the scars to prove it. And they both agreed—getting shot was vastly overrated.

Strolling into Paul's office, Jim knocked lightly as he passed through the door.

"Hey, I didn't think you'd be here yet," Jim said, pulling up a chair in the tiny space. Paul looked up. Always the consummate gentleman, today he wore black dress trousers and a blue dress shirt under a casual gray polo sweater. His face glowed from a recent shave, and his dark hair was combed away from his face.

"I've only been here about half an hour. What's happening in Genoa? I heard chatter on the scanner." He leaned back and listened as Jim told him what they knew so far.

"We don't have a handle on what killed him other than a wicked blow to the head." Jim grimaced as a vision of the dead man lying in the snow reappeared in his memory. "All I know is that half his head is caved in."

"A hammer? That's sometimes a weapon of choice," Paul commented laconically.

"Too early to tell." Jim reached into his pocket and retrieved the wallet he'd recovered. He flipped through the cards inside and handed Paul the business card labeled Hathway Industries with LeMar Burke's name printed across the top in bold capital letters. "I want you to start some research on this company. Seems to be where the guy was employed. We need to get some paper on this guy. From his clothing and expensive Rolex watch, I'd say he might be an executive or a leader of some kind at the company. See what you can come up with."

"Sure. What kind of car does he drive?"

"Wasn't driving one. He must have been killed elsewhere and dumped behind the tavern," Jim told him.

"Whoever dumped him must have counted on him being found."

"Yep. I agree. The killer is sending a message, although I have no idea what that might be yet. There didn't seem to be any effort at concealing the body." Jim stood up, extending his arms to his sides in a kind of yoga stretch. "How's the new little guy doin'?" he asked. He rolled his neck in circles as he listened.

"Well, Maximilian is a good baby, so far. Slept through the night Saturday, which gave Ruby a reprieve so she could get some sleep."

"Are you really going to call him Maximilian?" Jim asked, rubbing his jaw.

"It's already been shortened to Max."

"How's Ruby doing?"

"Oh, you know. You can't keep a good woman down." Paul grinned, folding his arms behind his head.

Jim wasn't quite sure about the implications of that statement, so he didn't ask. In the pause that followed, Jim turned to leave. As he walked toward the door, he said over his shoulder, "Let me know what you find out about our mystery man and Hathway Industries."

As Jim walked down the hall, his cell buzzed. He looked at the caller ID. Luke Evers, the coroner.

"Yeah, Luke. What's up?"

"Can you meet me downstairs in the morgue in a few minutes? We're just rolling up to the entrance," Luke said.

"Sure. See you there." Jim scanned the papers on his desk that Emily had left there earlier in the morning, flipping through them randomly. *More bureaucratic bullshit*, he thought, *but this is the stuff that energizes Emily. She lives for this.* He shook his head and threw the papers on his desk.

He left his office, walked to the elevator, and stepped out on the first floor, which was strangely quiet. He strolled down a long, narrow corridor devoid of artwork to the back of the building. The secretary at the desk buzzed him in.

Jim's wife, Carol, was currently the head secretary of the morgue and had worked for Luke for about ten years. She was well-known throughout the law enforcement center, having been employed there for almost twenty-five years. When Lillie was adopted and Henri—their surprise baby—had arrived all within the same week, she continued working on a part-time basis, devoting more time to their family and children. Audubon Griffin had been hired to fill in two days of the week.

"Luke's expecting you," she said. "How's Carol these days?" She snapped her gum noisily and ran her fingers through her curly red hair. Without waiting for Jim's response, Audubon rushed on. "You know, trying to quit smoking really sucks. Gum just doesn't cut it," she commented, her face frozen in a sour expression.

"Thanks for asking. Carol's fine. The kids keep her hoppin'." He strolled past the desk. "Good luck on quitting. Hope it sticks."

"You and me both. Theatre Two," she said, pointing to the room where Luke was unloading the victim. Jim mumbled his thanks and proceeded through the door.

When Jim walked in, the stringent scent of antiseptic gave him a vague sense of discomfort. The white sterile conditions did nothing to soothe his memories of the violent ways people exited the world. You couldn't bleach out the bloodthirsty tendencies in the human soul. *Thou shalt not kill*, Jim thought. How many people today even knew it was a commandment—arriving hot off the press from Mount Sinai?

Watching Luke step into his white suit, Jim wondered how many times he'd been here and observed the gruesome power of hatred— hatred that bludgeoned, burned, stabbed, strangled, and shot victims to death. Too many to count. He sighed loudly. Here he was in the morgue again.

Luke looked up as he unzipped the black body bag that had been rolled in on a gurney from the coroner's van. He gave Jim a silent nod. Jim walked up to the metal cart and stared at the victim's blue shadowed face, his bloodless features ominously still and ashen, frozen in time. The brilliant light overhead created a halo around the cart that seemed harsh and disparaging, capturing Luke and Jim in its sphere, like two deer who had stepped into the headlights of an oncoming vehicle.

"Do you know anything yet?" Jim asked, feeling slightly queasy, raising his eyes to meet Luke's.

"A few things. The victim died from a powerful blow to the head. The blow crushed his skull and penetrated his brain tissue. The wound is like nothing I've ever seen."

Luke was not easily surprised, and Jim found his response intriguing. "Really? Why's that?" he asked.

He handed Jim a pair of blue latex gloves from under the cart. Jim proficiently snapped them over his large hands.

"We found what we think is the weapon. It was buried underneath the snow about five feet from the victim. The crime scene crew let me take it so I could show you how the wound and the weapon match almost perfectly." From inside the body bag, Luke pulled an item from a large ziplock bag and carefully unwrapped it. Jim drew in his breath when he looked at the weapon, which still had bits of blood and bone clinging to it.

"What is it?" Jim whispered, leaning in to get a closer look.

"I don't know. I've never seen anything like it, but I have a feeling it's old. Possibly ancient."

The weapon, although grisly in intent, nevertheless had a beauty of form and design that was mesmerizing. Elegant, yet deadly. Refined, yet efficient. Its fourteen-inch narrow wooden handle curved slightly toward the ball of the club, which was clenched in the jaws of a mythical animal that resembled an otter. An embedded metal spike protruded about two inches from the wooden ball. A triangular hole near the bottom of the handle probably once held a quiver of feathers. Jim shivered when he thought about the damage that could be done with such a weapon, and yet, he felt a certain dreadful awe at the consummate beauty of the object. A superior craftsman had fashioned the club from the finest grade of ash, patiently carving and shaping it into a fearsome instrument of deadly force.

"Native American?" Jim questioned.

"You got me," Luke shrugged, "but you're probably right. It'll take some research," Luke said. "Get Leslie on it. She'll figure it out." Jim nodded in agreement.

Leaning over the victim, Luke rolled him toward the wall to reveal the wound in the back of the head. Taking the club in his hand, he held it next to the wound. "See how the size of the ball and the indentation in the skull match almost perfectly. Plus, the hole that penetrated the brain tissue matches the spike that's sticking out of the ball. I'm expecting to find metal slivers in and around the brain tissue. I would say right now—unequivocally—that this is the murder weapon, but without official tests, that's a preliminary conclusion. However, I'm very sure that's what the physical evidence will show."

Jim groaned at the implications. How did this stuff always seem to fall in his lap? He could just imagine his team struggling to solve another mysterious death. His shoulders slumped under the weight of this latest discovery. He realized he'd been holding his breath, and he let out a whoosh of air.

"Well, that's a start," Jim speculated. "Crime scene can try to get some latent fingerprints off the weapon, but I doubt they'll find anything." He opened his cell phone and took several photos of the weapon. "Leslie will need these to get started on her research, but eventually, she'll want to examine the object itself. Is that a problem?"

"Shouldn't be. I'm sending it back up to crime scene as soon as I'm done with it. And I agree with you. I doubt there'll be any prints." Luke replied. He looked up and gave Jim a piercing gaze. "I don't envy the job you've got ahead of you, Jim."

"I don't know too many people who do," he said, sighing loudly again.

4

By four o'clock that afternoon, the investigative team had gathered in a small classroom on the third floor that was equipped with a whiteboard, a few hard metal chairs, and a long white plastic table. They'd ordered sandwiches from Subway, and now they were discussing the facts about the murder and the victim. The whiteboard helped them track victims, suspects, evidence, and motives. It was already filling with a plethora of documents, photos from the crime scene, and photos of the weapon that Jim had taken earlier. An enlarged photo of the victim was centered on the board, his name written in caps underneath. The effort to get on top of the gruesome murder before too many hours and days slipped away could often be swallowed up in bureaucracy and legal entanglements. *The tyranny of the present*, Jim thought as he looked at his young cohorts.

Sam Birkstein, the most impulsive of the team, sat slouched in a chair and studied the board with a look of puzzlement. He was known for his theory-building, sometimes letting his imagination get ahead of facts and evidence. But he was becoming a dedicated and patient investigator. His dress, however, was another matter. Today he wore baggy yellow sweatpants, which hung loosely on his lanky figure. A red Alabama hoodie with the words *Alabama: The Crimson Tide* stamped across the front in bold black lettering was bunched around his chest. Sam was known for nabbing high-end clothes at low-end prices during his regular visits to the Goodwill stores in south La Crosse and Onalaska. Paul glared at the shirt.

"What?" Sam said in an accusing tone. "You don't like my sweats?"

"What's wrong with wearing something with Wisconsin Badgers on it once in a while?" Paul said, bristling. "Or the Packers? Or how about looking professional like the rest of us?"

"I can't find any Badger stuff at Goodwill. They're always sold out, or it's not in my size. My deepest apologies for offending your high sense of fashion," he said dramatically, slouching in his chair a little farther. "Besides, I was going to contact some of my drug informants, and I didn't have time to change. A three-piece suit and tie can stifle communication with the lowlifes. Know what I mean?"

Jim eyed Sam's get-up with animosity.

"Could we get to it, guys?" Jim asked impatiently.

Sam returned Jim's stare with an innocence that incensed him further. DeDe Deverioux, the newest member of the investigative team, watched the exchange with a suppressed sense of humor. She caught Leslie's eye and smiled shyly. Being the newbie on the team, she was still getting familiar with the peculiarities of each member of the staff. Leslie rolled her eyes at her husband's choice of clothes, irked at his decision to dress like a homeless vagrant.

"Yeah, let's get started," Paul suggested. He grabbed a yellow legal pad from the table and began referring to his copious notes. "The murder victim, LeMar Burke, was one of four vice presidents at Hathway Industries in New Orleans, Louisiana. He was in charge of real estate acquisition. Hathway Industries is a huge conglomerate that specializes in the building of high-end conference and business meeting facilities that ..." Paul used air quotes and referred to his notes, "enhance and build business ethics, innovative thinking, and creative commercial endeavors to meet the challenges of the global market in the twenty-first century." Paul looked up. "That includes everything from hosting conferences for major corporations and companies to sponsoring think tanks for those who specialize in new and innovative business ideas—all in posh, lush accommodations. We're talking saunas, tennis courts, golf courses, gyms with the latest in fitness equipment, stables for riding, gorgeous swimming pools, top-of-the-line restaurants, and of course, nothing but the most luxurious rooms that you and I could only afford in our dreams. The kind of facility I'm talking about is similar to Whistling Straits over in Sheboygan. Although that might be considered second-rate to Hathway's establishments." Paul looked at each one of them as he paused in his narrative.

"Okay. Did you learn anything about Burke's personal finances?" Jim asked.

"Not yet. I'll dig into that tomorrow. But I'm sure he's worth millions. This company is one of the top fifty companies in the world that specialize in this type of service, and they are very good at what they do," Paul said. "They have facilities in eighteen states, most of them in the South, but they're looking to expand into the Upper Midwest and Canada."

"According to who?" Leslie asked.

Paul glanced at his notes. "A Ms. Gabriella LaMont, executive secretary to LeMar Burke. She's in charge of all public relations, which includes websites, radio and television ads, and numerous trade publications that deal with the hotel and service industry. All of them tout the excellence of their lavish facilities. I scanned a number of them. Very impressive."

"Excellent," Jim commented. "That's a good start. Anybody else have anything to add?"

Leslie looked up and leaned forward, resting her elbows on the table in front of her. She tucked her blonde hair behind her ear and began. "Yes, I examined the photos of the murder weapon. I discovered the club had been associated for two to three hundred years with different tribes of Native Americans who lived in the Northeast and the Great Lakes region. Clubs of this kind also appear in paintings of distinguished Europeans during the 1700s. It must have been a weapon of status. Although we may have never seen one, they are quite popular with collectors today, and there are even organized leagues that hold annual club-throwing competitions."

"You mean like the tavern downtown that has ax-throwing competitions?" Paul asked.

"What? Are you kidding?" Jim asked incredulously. "And these people have been drinking?" His blue eyes flashed at the idiocy of the idea.

"So far, nobody's gotten axed," Paul said, scratching his nose.

"I'd like to see that," Sam said, glancing over at Leslie. "We should go down there, have a brew, and watch that sometime."

"Not," Leslie said, shaking her head.

"That sounds like a train wreck waiting to happen," DeDe said.

There was a slight pause, then Leslie redirected the conversation.

"There are also websites which give specific instructions on how to build one of the ball clubs," she said. "And I found a number of makers in the Tri-State region, the closest being a guy in Black River Falls."

"Do you think the weapon used at the crime scene is old, or is it a reproduction?" Sam asked.

"Without looking at the actual object, I'd say it's an authentic ancient artifact, probably at least one hundred years old, maybe more," Leslie answered. "But that would have to be confirmed by someone who's more of an expert than me."

"Does anyone around here make them? What about the Ho-Chunk Nation or other Native tribes in Wisconsin?" DeDe asked. "Where do people get them?"

"Don't know yet. Those are all questions I had, too. I've got some emails out there to local makers, but I haven't gotten any replies back yet. Maybe tomorrow," Leslie said.

"Motive for the crime? Anyone have any ideas other than the typical ones of money, sex, or power?" Jim asked.

"Those are the three big ones," Sam said. "But with the tie-in of his role at the corporation, I'm wondering if this Burke guy was looking at real estate. He was in charge of land acquisitions. We can check his cell to see if he'd been in contact with any local real estate agents."

"Good thought," Jim said. "You can start on that tomorrow, Sam. Anything else?"

"He did make some local calls," Paul said.

"Well, if you find any real estate contacts, filter that stuff over to Sam," Jim directed. He waited a moment for any other thoughts, and getting none, he said, "All right, then. Tomorrow we'll plow forward."

Chairs scuffed against the discolored linoleum tile, and the team broke up. Outside the weather had calmed, and the sun was sinking toward the horizon. As Jim walked through the parking lot, he deeply breathed the fresh, clean air. The world was a wonderland of white, the temperatures had warmed up, and he was looking forward to dinner. Then he thought of the frozen man beneath the snow. Who killed him? *The million-dollar question*, he thought. Then another. *Why was he here in La Crosse in the first place?*

☐

That evening after supper, Lillie came and stood by Jim's favorite black swoopy chair in the living room as he read the *Wisconsin State Journal*. The trees that bordered Higgins' property were dark gray, and their thick trunks cast long blue shadows on the sculpted snowdrifts in the yard. Dusk was descending. The rosy afterglow in the evening sky hinted at a promising change to less turbulent weather. Jim could hear Carol in the kitchen loading the dishwasher. The logs in the Franklin stove in the corner of the living room crackled and sent up a shower of sparks.

"Bapa?" Lillie said, gently pushing the newspaper away from Jim. "I learned about Chief Blackhawk yesterday in Social Studies." Lillie had been promoted to the third grade for some classes, Social Studies being one of them.

Jim laid the newspaper aside and looked into her azure, blue eyes.

They were wide with the wonder of some new piece of information she had learned. Her blonde curls were still damp from her bath, and her small hand rested on Jim's arm. He was sure some burning question was on the tip of her tongue. The way she intensely studied Jim's face left him edgy. He tried to keep his expression open, downplaying the serious countenance shadowed on her face.

"Can we go to that place on the river where his people were killed?" she asked.

"Sure. I know right where it is, down between Victory and Desoto at a place called Battle Island. There's a marker there that tells the story. What did you learn about him?" Jim asked. He was something of a Wisconsin history buff, and he'd been collecting arrowheads and other small Native tools for most of his adult life. His first wife, Margie, had gathered an impressive collection of Native baskets that were displayed in Jim's study at home and on his shelves at work.

"I learned that sometimes people do some pretty mean stuff," Lillie said seriously, her little mouth turned downward in a pout. Jim calmly watched her and waited for her to continue. "Blackhawk tried to lead his people away from trouble, but the army caught up with them, and they shot and killed them in the river when they were trying to run away. Why did they do that, Bapa?" she asked, tilting her head, waiting for an answer.

Jim sighed. Why *did* they do that? He had no answers, but he attempted an explanation that he hoped a seven-year-old would understand. "I don't know why the army did what it did. Nowadays, those things would be considered unfair, cruel, and inhuman." *Now we just shoot each other in malls and movie theaters and schools. For reasons that defy human explanation. Sometimes for no reason at all.*

"Did little girls like me die in the river?" she asked. Her squeaky voice seemed out of keeping with the weighty topic. Her question stabbed at Jim's conscience. *Leave it to Lillie to make history living, intimate, and personal,* he thought.

Jim laid the newspaper aside and invited Lillie onto his lap. She cuddled against his chest, and he stuffed his nose into her mass of golden curls and took in the innocence and goodness of her. Wrapping his arms around her, he answered, "Yes, many children and babies died with their mothers in the river that day. I'm sure it was very sad."

"People like Henri and Mommy?"

"Yes." The silence after Jim's response stretched on for many moments. The topic fired up Jim's imagination. In his mind's eye, he could see Henri and Lillie and Carol struggling in the river, gunshots ringing out around them, other people being shot, the water turning bloody, people screaming and dying.

"That would be very scary, Bapa," Lillie said quietly with wisdom beyond her age.

Jim felt like someone had rattled his cage. A shiver ran down his spine, and it had nothing to do with the cold, snowy weather. "Yes, it would be very scary, wouldn't it?" he said. Jim rested his chin on the top of Lillie's head as she snuggled deeper into his chest.

He jumped when Carol walked into the room and held out her hand. "Bedtime, Lillie," she reminded her. Noticing their somber demeanor, she asked, "What's going on? You two look like you've had the pants scared off you."

"We have ... sort of," Jim said.

"Bapa, will you listen to my prayers?" Lillie asked, her eyes moist and tender.

"Sure," Jim said, leaning forward and standing up, thankful for a reprieve from his waking nightmare. Carol gave him a look of wide-eyed concern. "I'll explain later," he whispered as he led Lillie to her bedroom.

After Jim had read to Lillie and she had recited her prayers, he turned off the bedside lamp, but Lillie continued to wear a wounded expression. In the glow of the night light, Jim attempted to ease the hurt that had crept into his daughter's eyes.

"Listen, toots," Jim began in his best parental voice, "you're just beginning to learn about history. You know what that is, right?"

Lillie rolled her eyes and sighed dramatically. "History is the things that happened in the past."

Jim leaned over her small body and softly stroked her hair. He looked down at her as she cuddled in her quilts. "Sometimes history is messy. People did things they shouldn't have, and many times things weren't always fair or right."

"Like the way we treated Blackhawk and his family?" she asked.

Jim cringed at the word *we*. "Yes. Blackhawk was treated unfairly, even though he was trying to defend and protect his people."

"Well, that stinks," Lillie said emphatically, folding her arms across her chest.

"Yes, it does." Jim knew from experience that Lillie could stretch this conversation way beyond any realistic boundaries. "And we'll talk about it again, but right now, it's time to go to sleep."

"That stinks, too," Lillie pouted. "I don't wanna go to sleep. This is unfair ..."

"Don't even go there," Jim said as he leaned down and kissed her cheek. "I love you. See you in the morning."

"Parents have way too much power."

"That's life in the Higgins' household. You better get used to it." Preparing for a verbal battle, Jim was surprised when Lillie yawned and rolled over on her side.

"Night, Bapa," Lillie whispered.

"Night, baby," Jim said as he pulled the quilt over her shoulders and tiptoed out of the room.

He walked to the bedroom down the hall and kissed Henri, who was sleeping soundly. Then he retraced his steps to the kitchen, where Carol was preparing a pot of tea. This was their nighttime ritual when they both managed to be home at the same time.

Banging a cupboard door shut, she turned to Jim and said, "That conversation with Lillie sounded pretty serious. You two looked like a couple of scared rabbits. What's up with that?"

SUE BERG

"The reality of historical events does not line up with Lillie's moral compass," he said, shaking his head. "She learned about Chief Blackhawk and what happened at Battle Island back in 1832, and she's upset because his people were chased down and shot and drowned in the river."

"They were?" Carol said, loading a tray with a teapot and mugs.

"Yeah. Didn't you study that in Wisconsin history?" Jim asked, leaning against the counter.

"Maybe, but I honestly don't remember it. Apparently, it didn't make as big an impression on me as it did on Lillie."

Jim followed her into the living room. "Well, I'm sure we haven't heard the last of it. She wants me to take her down to the river and show her where it happened."

"Oh, boy," Carol said, pouring the tea. "That might be trouble. It could trigger things that might cause her some discomfort and generate questions you probably won't have answers for."

"Yeah, it could, but let's not panic—yet."

Over the last three years since Lillie had come to live with them, she had displayed an uncanny ability to visualize and predict events—call it premonitions, intuition, or a feeling in her bones. Whatever it was, Jim and Carol believed it was a God-given gift. More than once, Lillie has accurately *seen* things that had not happened yet. Sometimes, she could perceive a person's intentions by their look—a dark glance or a radiant smile. At first, Jim and Carol were leery, chalking it up to luck or chance or the silly ramblings of an undisciplined child. But as the years went by, they realized her abilities were genuine. They'd become fiercely protective of her and, so far, had been able to fend off any undue attention she might have gained from it. They wanted to keep it that way.

Later, as they got ready for bed, Carol asked, "Jim, this weapon that was found next to the murder victim. That doesn't have anything to do with Chief Blackhawk, does it?"

Jim frowned, puzzled by the question. "I don't know how it could, honey. That's ancient history around here. Lillie's comments about Blackhawk tonight were purely coincidental."

Carol harrumphed to herself. "That's what you think," she said.

They climbed into bed. Jim propped his pillow against the headboard and picked up his latest C. J. Box mystery novel from his nightstand. Carol gently pushed the book out of his hand and leaned over on his bare chest. Jim knew that look. Those brown eyes were anticipating pleasure.

"No reading tonight, honey," she whispered as she kissed him seductively. "It's cold and snowy outside, and I've been giving the kids my attention all day long ..." She slipped her nightgown over her head and threw it on the floor.

Jim's hands wandered down her shoulders to her hips. Her skin felt warm and smooth and velvety. "And you're in need of a little attention yourself. Am I reading this right?" he said, grinning as his dimple dented his cheek.

"Mmm, my, my. You are a good detective."

He returned her ardent kiss, enjoying her warm, moist lips and the feel of her body pressed against him. "I aim to please, baby."

"You always do," Carol said, her breath quickening.

Later, he did pick up his novel and tried to read, but his mind was still mulling over the odd set of circumstances surrounding the murder victim found in the parking lot behind the bar. And Carol's question wouldn't leave him alone either. Could an ancient ball club, a murder victim, and the history of brutality against Natives in the area be connected? The Blackhawk War was fought back in 1832, he reasoned to himself. How could this murder have anything to do with Blackhawk, the warrior of Sauk fame? No way. That was too strange. Impossible. But somehow, the thought refused to back down, and he wondered at its implications. Was Lillie's fascination with Blackhawk the result of a history lesson, or was she unknowingly trying to tell him something?

He grumped under his breath. Carol stirred beside him and rolled to the other side of the bed. Staring at the ceiling, his book askew in his lap, he reviewed all the other strange cases that had been dumped on their department over the years. Despite his uneasiness, he chalked up his jitters to the unknown players and circumstances that always accompanied new cases. His team would figure it out. They always had before. They'd do it again.

5

THURSDAY, MARCH 21

Thursday morning at Sam Birkstein's apartment on Cliffwood Lane had started out chaotic. Leslie, his wife, and their black lab, Paco, had gone out for an early run, but the trails below Grandad Bluff in Hixon Forest were so packed with snow, they were back in less than half an hour.

Leslie glanced at the *La Crosse Tribune* lying open on the kitchen table and the headline of the murder in Genoa. So far the murder weapon had been kept under wraps, but that wouldn't last long.

"I told you the trails would be closed, honey," Sam reminded her, sipping on his first cup of coffee.

Leslie crinkled her nose. "Yeah, I know you did, but Paco needs his exercise, and I thought I'd chance it. Guess we'll have to run the city streets for a few weeks 'til the snow melts a little."

Paco was Leslie's faithful black lab who had served with her in the U.S. Army in Iraq, sniffing out IEDs. They had both come home with some residual effects of serving in a war zone, Leslie with symptoms of PTSD and Paco with shrapnel in his hip. More than once since returning home, Paco had come to Leslie's defense in sketchy situations. His fierce, protective nature ruled in the Birkstein household without challenge. Despite the canine's obvious symptoms of age—a graying muzzle and an occasional limp—he continued to demand regular vigorous workouts. Sam had been reluctantly invited into their inner circle when he'd married Leslie two years ago, and he had become unjustifiably fond of the big black brute.

Now Paco waddled up to Sam and nuzzled his hand, seeking some affection. Sam turned in his chair and ruffled his ears and thumped his side. Paco swiped his pink tongue across Sam's face in a gesture of affection.

Sam glanced at the clock. "I need to get to the office," he commented. He leaned over Leslie, who was still sitting at the kitchen table, and kissed her on the cheek. "See you in a while," he said.

Leslie nodded absentmindedly and said, "Later."

☐

A half hour later at the office on Vine Street, Sam's phone buzzed on his desk. He flipped the La Crosse phone book shut and mumbled to himself. "Over eighty real estate agents in the La Crosse area. How am I supposed to find out if LeMar Burke was in contact with any of them?" He groaned to himself at the legwork it would take to come up with an answer for Higgins. "Well, I might as well get started."

"Sam Birkstein. La Crosse Sheriff's Department. How can I help you?"

"Do your clothes match your professional cell phone etiquette today?" Paul teased.

"Actually, yes, they do. My threads are up to snuff. What's up?"

"Come to my office a minute. I've discovered something, and I'm not sure what to do about it," Paul said.

"Right. Be there in five."

Sam punched off his phone and wondered about Paul's request. Among the close-knit team of detectives, Paul was the professional who played by the book. Despite the antagonism that sometimes erupted between them, they had each other's backs. Paul wasn't stumped very often. Sam minimized the screen on his laptop, got up from his desk, and strolled down the hall to the cramped office. He walked in as Paul was finishing another call.

"So, what's bothering you?" Sam asked. He noticed the picture of Paul's new baby boy on his desk.

"Who said I was bothered?"

"You didn't, but I could tell. What's up?"

"There was a cell number on the back of LeMar Burke's card. I called it. I got Jude Delaney's voicemail."

"Say what?" Sam's jaw hung open. Jude Delaney was married to Detective DeDe Deverioux. He was a renowned New Orleans chef, and his new restaurant, Si Bon, was scheduled to open on the south side of La Crosse on May 1. "Boy, that could be a conflict of interest for DeDe. Does she know that yet?"

"No. Neither does Higgins. But I want you to go with me to check it out," Paul said.

"So it went to voicemail?"

"Yep. The sooner we talk to Jude, the better."

"Agreed. Let me grab my coat."

☐

Si Bon, the upscale dining establishment that Jude Delaney hoped to put on the map in western Wisconsin, was still under construction. Almost a year ago, Jude purchased a large timber frame barn on the outskirts south of La Crosse at the edge of the city limits and designed the restaurant to be a model of energy efficiency and alternative construction methods using a variety of recycled materials. His wife, DeDe, was skeptical about the whole design concept, but she had since become an enthusiastic fan of this new ethos that used architectural salvage and capitalized on energy efficiency. When Sam and Paul arrived, the construction crew was in full swing.

In the peak of the timber frame barn, electricians were hanging wooden wagon wheel chandeliers that dangled from hay ropes and pulleys. Plumbers were laying tile and installing bathroom fixtures downstairs. Sorting through huge pine beams, carpenters selected several that were being used to divide up the cavernous space. A couple of guys were inspecting piles of tobacco shed boards that would cover the inside walls of the barn. On the east wall of the restaurant, stone masons were sifting through piles of limestone, carefully selecting and fitting them into a huge fireplace. Banks of windows on the west wall let in warm light, accentuating the beautiful view of the Mississippi River and the craggy limestone bluffs on the Minnesota side. The noise and frenzied activity of the place reminded Sam of a beehive.

From the depths of the barn, Paul spotted Jude talking to a red-haired woman on the north end of the building. They were hunched over a worktable on which a set of architect's plans were being reviewed. Paul tapped Sam's arm, and they walked toward the table. Sunlight was pouring through the large patio doors to the south, dust motes floating lazily in the chaotic atmosphere. A terraced stone deck outside was topped with a skeletal framework that would eventually become a pergola. Approaching the table, Paul and Sam waited while Jude finished his conversation.

"… so you're saying the cabinetry for the kitchen will be delayed at least a week?" he asked the woman, his face wrinkling in disapproval.

"I'm afraid so. The Amish contractor is a little behind, but he promised me that he'd have them done in two weeks." Seeing Jude's panicked look, she patted his arm reassuringly. "Don't worry. Remember, we built two extra weeks into the entire schedule for delays. You can't avoid them in construction—something always goes kerflooey—but I think we'll still be in good shape for May first as the target date for opening."

Jude looked up, finally noticing Sam and Paul. His face creased into a friendly smile.

"Hey, guys. What do ya think of the place?" he asked, spreading his arms as if he were blessing the building.

"It's starting to take shape. It'll definitely be a unique venue, but the food is what I'm waiting for," Sam said, pointing his index finger at Jude. "And you're da man for that."

"We're wondering if there's someplace we could talk. We've got a few questions for you," Paul said seriously, shifting on his feet.

"Sure. My office isn't quite finished yet, but it's quiet. Follow me. It's just down this hall," Jude said as he turned from the architect and led the way.

Once they had settled in the office, Paul got right to it.

"Do you know a man named LeMar Burke from New Orleans?" he asked.

Jude's eyes suddenly clouded with suspicion, and his friendly disposition seemed to fade.

"Yeah, I know him," Jude said carefully, leaning his elbows on his desk. "He used to come to my restaurant on Canal Street down in New Orleans at least two or three times a week. He's a big roller. He's in charge of land acquisitions for Hathway Industries. He told me he travels all the time, mostly in the U.S. but also in Europe and Japan. Why are you asking?"

"He was found murdered, and his body was dumped behind the Tip Your Hat tavern in Genoa yesterday morning," Sam said.

Jude's expression remained stoic, although his eyes widened considerably when he heard the news. After several moments, he said, "I didn't know he was in town." Then, another pause. "Murdered? Wow! That's pretty unbelievable. Why *was* he in town?"

"We have no idea—yet," Paul said. "We wondered if he'd been in contact with you. Your number was written on the back of his business card."

Jude nodded perceptively. "When I was closing on the sale of my restaurant in New Orleans last fall, we had a conversation about business stuff at my restaurant. When he found out I was relocating to Wisconsin, he asked me for my cell number in case he ever got up this way. That was the last time I talked to him." Jude calmly folded his hands over his stomach and leaned back in his chair as . studied the two detectives.

"So you'd categorize your relationship as just a casual acquaintance?" Sam asked.

"Yeah. I guess that about covers it. He was a good customer, and we chatted occasionally, but we really didn't socialize in the same circles," Jude said.

"And you have no idea why he would have been in the La Crosse area?" Paul asked.

"Nope. None whatsoever. Although I'm assuming he was probably on business for the company. He did mention Hathway was looking to expand in the Midwest." Jude shrugged. "But that's just a guess."

Sam looked out the small office window at the winter scenario where traffic was tentatively creeping along on the slippery, snow-covered roads. He thought about Jude's number on the card. He guessed it was probably a coincidence, but something about it didn't sit right with him. Still, his estimation of Jude Delaney was that he was an upfront, honest sort of person. Was he hiding something?

"So you're familiar with Hathway Industries?" Sam asked.

"You'd be hard-pressed to find someone from the South who didn't have some knowledge of Hathway. They have a huge presence in many southern states. Their business retreat centers are spectacular. Some of my chef friends have worked for them, and their establishments are notoriously upscale with all the latest amenities you could imagine."

"That's what we found out when we did our initial probe into the company," Paul said. "They seem to be the gold standard for business retreat centers."

"Yep. They're the top of the heap in that category, no doubt about it." Jude said. "They have tremendous leverage—lots of money and relationships with some of the most powerful Fortune 500 companies in the world. Their influence shouldn't be underestimated."

"Any ideas why LeMar would be in the La Crosse area?" Sam asked again.

ie'd been in Madison or Minneapolis and was passing

de speculated. He held up his hands and shrugged. "No

_ visibly frustrated. Standing up, he reached for Jude's hand. "If you think of anything else that might be helpful, we'd appreciate a call. No hard feelings, I hope, but the coincidence of your number in LeMar's wallet was something we couldn't ignore."

"Hey, no problem. Remember? I'm married to a cop. I totally get it. Let me know if there's anything else I can help you with."

Paul turned to leave, but Sam stopped at the door of the office. "Good luck with the restaurant. We're all waiting for your opening, man." He smiled, and Jude returned a wide grin. "I'm sure Lez and I will be regular customers."

"Thanks. I appreciate it, and I'll expect to see you here a lot."

In the quietness of his office, after the two detectives left, Jude pondered the news of LeMar's death. He was sure it wouldn't take long for DeDe to discover his connection with Burke. In the last year, he'd worked hard at reconciling with his wife. They were both stepping back from the precipice of a possible divorce—still holding their breath that their marriage would work. They'd come a long way in their relationship, and he was learning to become more transparent and open about his past.

This latest piece of news seemed incredible. Someone from New Orleans, someone he knew fairly well, had come to Wisconsin and been murdered. He cringed when he thought of DeDe's skeptical nature. How was he possibly going to explain his phone number on LeMar's business card to his wife? He'd have to downplay it, but she'd probably freak out anyway. And what would have caused LeMar's death? He shivered when he thought about the possible reasons. He was thankful when a carpenter down the hallway hollered his name. He got up and walked back into the construction area, all the while wondering what questions DeDe might ask about LeMar Burke.

6

By eleven-thirty Thursday morning, the weather had turned nasty again. Jim stared out of his narrow office window at the law enforcement center on Vine Street as huge snowflakes filled the air. The wind picked up from the north, pushing the precipitation into slanted curtains of white. The temperature dropped like a rock, and the roads looked slick with a coating of dull black ice. *So much for a break in the weather*, Jim thought. He turned back to his desk, sat down at his laptop, and began his perusal of Hathway Industries' website. After an hour of reading and clicking on various tabs, he leaned back, reviewing the full page of notes he had jotted on his yellow legal pad. He reached for his phone and dialed Paul.

"Has Hathway Industries been notified about LeMar's death?" Jim asked.

"I checked with Davy. He officially informed them this morning," Paul said.

"And what was their reaction?"

"Shock and then anger. They're talking about getting the FBI involved."

Jim groaned. "I was afraid of that. Who's your contact at the company?"

Jim heard some rustling of paper. Then Paul said, "A Mr. Teddy Rosswell, LeMar's executive secretary. He's the one I'm supposed to contact with information when it becomes available."

"Okay, keep me in the loop, and don't give them too much information yet. I'm heading back to the crime scene," Jim told him.

"What for?"

"To see if I can figure out how the perpetrator dropped off the body in a raging blizzard."

"Sounds like a long shot," Paul said dismally.

"It is a long shot, but what else can we do?" Jim hung up and slipped his cell in his pocket. Getting up, he reached behind the door and threw on his wool navy overcoat. Looping a plaid scarf around his neck, he walked down the hall and stopped at Emily's desk in the lobby.

"I'll be out of the office for a while. I'm going back down to the crime scene in Genoa. I probably won't be back in the rest of the day, depending on what I find."

Emily stared up at him from her perch. "Right, Chief, but you should check in with Sheriff Jones before you go. He wants an update."

"I'll talk to him right now on my way out. Thanks," Jim said as he approached the elevator.

Sheriff Jones' office was located on the first floor. Jim made his way into his office after greetings had been exchanged with his secretary. For about an hour, he filled Davy Jones in on the details of Hathway Industries and the information Leslie had discovered about the weapon.

"Boy, this is a crazy deal. Where you headed now?" Jones asked, noticing Jim's coat.

"Back down to Genoa. See if I can get a handle on how the body ended up behind the tavern. Maybe somebody saw something or left something behind." Davy looked doubtful.

"In a raging blizzard? Good luck with that," he said sharply.

"Something might come up," Jim said, turning to leave.

"Keep in touch," Jones brusquely said as he picked up his ringing phone.

Jim headed to the Vine Street parking lot and made his way through erratic traffic to U.S. Hwy. 35, where the traffic returned to a normal pace. He made good time to the little town of Genoa along the Mississippi River. Turning into the parking lot of the Tip Your Hat tavern, he parked next to the dumpsters where the body had been found. The tavern was set against a hundred-foot limestone bluff. In the foreground, a hillside leveled out above the tavern. Jim sat in the truck and studied the terrain. He noticed an overgrown, weed-infested lane that ran along the top of the hillside and decided to start his investigation there.

Turning the truck out of the parking lot, he wound his way down a side street until he came to the beginning of the lane, which had probably been an old logging trail, now unused and covered in deep snow. Birch, maple, and oak trees grew along the edge of the seldom-used track, which gradually rose to the top of the hillside that overlooked the tavern.

Jim parked along the street, hopped out, and opened the rear window of the Suburban. He took out his snowshoes and belted them on over a pair of insulated boots, exchanged his expensive wool overcoat for a ski jacket, and donned a tossle hat and warm insulated gloves. Before he began hiking the unused trail, he got down on his knees and observed at ground level. The reflection of light at this position changed what Jim was able to see from the surface. He grunted with satisfaction when two slight dips in the snow revealed themselves. *Someone's used this lane in the last few days. Could it have been the killer? Was this the path he used to dump the body behind the bar?*

Jim began snowshoeing along the trail, the sounds of his feet making little swishing noises in the afternoon air. Clumps of dehydrated bluestem grass and bottlebrush grew along the edge of the old road, and they poked their heads out of the deep snowfall. The set of binoculars around his neck ticked against his coat as he huffed up the incline and approached the crest of the hill overlooking the tavern.

When the lane flattened out on top, he stopped to catch his breath. An opening in the undergrowth gave a perfect view of the rear entrance to the Tip Your Hat tavern. From this vantage point, things looked different. Jim noticed the logging trail went higher up the bluff. The killer had probably waited for the activity at the bar to quiet down before he made his descent with the body. He looked around in the snow, hoping for something the killer may have left behind—a match or cigarette or food wrapper or beverage can of some kind. No such luck. If anything had been left, it was covered by the deep snow now.

Jim looked down the hillside toward the tavern and saw broken twigs and branches on the small shrubbery that populated the slope. The killer must have dragged the body behind him as he struggled to deliver his cargo near the dumpster. Eyeing the pattern of broken twigs, Jim could discern the path he'd used to move the body. Once again, Jim got down at ground level and looked up the hill. The tracks continued up and around a sharp corner heavily shaded by a stand of evergreens.

He continued hiking upward, noticing more broken twigs. He stopped next to them. The twigs were bent in a downward direction toward the tavern. He was breathing hard when he came around the bend and discovered a city street, paved and recently plowed. He stood there for a moment thinking. He looked back at the broken shrubbery. *The killer drove to the top of the blacktopped city street and came down the unused trail, stopping at the flattened area above the tavern. Then he dragged the body downward into the parking lot.*

Jim removed his snowshoes and walked down the wet blacktop street. There were only two houses on the paved street. Jim stopped in the driveway of the first, a small ranch-style home from the sixties with a combination garage workshop tucked behind it. He went to the house and rang the bell at a side door. Getting no response, he approached the workshop after seeing a wispy curl of smoke ascending from the chimney. He knocked and heard someone shout, "Come on in!"

A small, diminutive man sat at a wood lathe, shavings scattered on the arms of his sweater, on his worn bib overalls, and on the cement floor. The sharp smell of the wood chips and wood smoke from the stove filled Jim with nostalgia. He thought of his dad and the woodworking they'd done together when he was a kid on a dairy farm in Blair, Wisconsin. The little man pushed his protective goggles to the top of his bald head, shut off the lathe motor, and peered intently at Jim when the door slammed shut.

"Help you?" he asked, his chisel resting on the lathe.

Jim fished his ID from his pants pocket and held it out to the man. He looked at it briefly, then zeroed in on Jim, waiting for him to continue. Jim supposed he looked rather odd in a dress shirt and tie and sporting huge boots on his feet.

"Lt. Jim Higgins, La Crosse Sheriff's Department. I'm investigating the discovery of a body we found behind the Tip Your Hat tavern yesterday morning," Jim said.

"Harold Stubbins," the man said, holding out his hand to Jim. Jim felt the hardened callouses on his hand. "I've lived in Genoa most of my life. The whole town's talkin' about it, I can tell you that much." Jim wasn't so sure what he meant by "it," but he supposed he was referring to the murder.

"I'm sure. Did you see or hear anything the night of the storm?" Jim asked. He leaned against a workbench under the window and crossed his boots in a casual pose, enjoying the cozy atmosphere in the little wood shop.

"Well, that was a damn tough storm," Harold began. He had a way of stretching out his words that forced Jim to listen carefully to his delivery. "It started out with those little pellets in the afternoon. I knew then we'd get a wallop of snow. Big snowfalls always start with those little hard pellets. The wife's been dead now a year, so I holed up in the house during the storm. Didn't even attempt to shovel out 'til today. But I do remember hearing someone drive past the house about ten. It wasn't the snowplow—I know what that sounds like—but I couldn't tell you what kind of vehicle it was. I just wondered who'd be stupid enough to be out in a storm like that.

Jim nodded in agreement. "So … other than a vehicle at ten, you saw or heard nothing else?" Jim asked. "Is that right?"

"That's right."

"Does that street continue upward, or is it a dead end?" Jim asked, pointing up toward the bluff.

"No, it hooks up with Fisher Lane a little higher up the bluff. It's a steep street with a hairpin curve at the top that becomes Fisher. Not easy to drive on, especially in deep snow."

"I can believe that," Jim commented. "Do you remember anything else about Wednesday night?"

"Nope, nothing stands out in my mind other than the storm. Sorry," he said apologetically.

Jim was disappointed but not surprised. "Well, thanks for your time anyway. Here's my card if you think of anything else." Harold took his card, tucked it in his bib overall pocket, then turned on his lathe, dismissing Jim with a flick of a switch.

Jim stepped out onto the snow-covered driveway and headed down the street to the only other residence on the road—a small mobile home with an attached porch. It looked vacant, but Jim again noticed a wisp of smoke rising from the chimney vent. He went up to the porch, knocked on the rusting metal door of the trailer, and waited.

Eventually, a young man with shaggy brown hair pulled the door open. He was dressed in a maroon UW–La Crosse sweatshirt and a gray pair of jogging pants. His feet were bare, and he grimaced as the brisk, cold air swept into the room. He had a heavy, unshaven beard and looked like he'd just crawled out of bed. The young man stepped aside when Jim stepped into the trailer. The place smelled of fried onions and the stale odor of an unkempt house.

Jim flashed his ID. "I'm from the sheriff's department, and we're looking into the body we found behind the Tip Your Hat tavern on Wednesday morning. Did you notice anyone drive by here the night of the storm?" he asked.

"What night was that?" the young man asked, squinting and scratching his stomach, still groggy from sleep.

"Wednesday," Jim said. When the man still looked confused, he reminded him, "Yesterday."

"Wednesday?" He propped his hands on his hips and thought for a moment. "That was the night of the big storm?" Jim nodded. "Nah, my vehicle isn't that reliable, so I stayed in La Crosse at my girlfriend's place that night. I wasn't even home," he said. "Sorry."

"Can your girlfriend verify that?" Jim asked.

"Absolutely." He found a sticky note on the kitchen counter, scratched a name and number on it, and then handed it to Jim.

"Thanks. So you were in La Crosse all evening on Wednesday? Is that right?" Jim asked.

"Yep. Didn't get home until late this morning when 35 finally got plowed," the kid told him.

Jim handed him his card. "Call if you hear anything, you know, like talk in a bar or around town. Sometimes, the smallest detail can give us a direction in our investigation."

"Sure," the kid answered, laying the card on the counter. Jim slipped the note with the telephone number in his overcoat pocket, turned, and pulled the door shut behind him.

As he walked back to the Suburban, the afternoon was beginning to slip into dusk. The icy river had taken on hues of green and dusky blue, and against the backdrop of the deep snow, it was beautiful. The sun was a diffused yellow ball behind the cloud cover. Its light seemed like a flickering candle in a thick blue fog. It was already five-thirty, so Jim decided to head home. He suddenly remembered the phone number the young man in the trailer had given him. He fished it out of his coat pocket and dialed. After a brief conversation, the young woman confirmed that her boyfriend had spent the night at her apartment in La Crosse during the blizzard.

Driving up Hwy. 35, the late school bus was just dropping off Bobby Rude by his driveway. Jim slowed down when the red lights of the bus began flashing. He pulled in behind the bus and rolled down his window.

"Hey, Bobby. Hop in. I'll give you a ride up the hill," Jim yelled.

Bobby turned and walked back to the Suburban, opened the door, and threw his backpack on the seat as he climbed in the front.

"How have you been?" Jim asked, watching the kid out of the corner of his eye.

Bobby stared out the windshield. "Oh, I'm fine. Just had my first baseball practice tonight. Coach Helwig is going to let me play shortstop."

"Great. How's your dad doing?"

Bobby shook his head as if he were trying to forget his formidable problems. "It's tough. I rode over to Tomah with Jed last Saturday, but Dad was having a rough day, and we didn't stay too long." Bobby squirmed in his seat, and his waterproof jacket made a crinkling sound when he moved.

"Sorry to hear that," Jim said. "Sickness changes people. I know. My first wife died of breast cancer. Sometimes it's hard to remember what they were like when they were healthy. But underneath it all, your dad is still in there. Eventually, if he can stick out the treatment program, he might begin to feel a little better. Maybe things will begin to change," he said.

But even as he counseled Bobby, privately Jim knew the battle of getting sober was just the beginning. The treatment was long and hard and exhausting, and it would take vigilance and a life-long commitment to stay sober—a rough, steep road for anyone. He pulled up in Bobby's front yard. They talked for a while about school, his classes, and what he was reading.

"Before you go, do you remember anything more about the morning when you and Jed found the body behind the bar? I've been asking around, but nobody seems to have seen anything."

Bobby nodded. "Nope. Like I told you, I was home that night, but I didn't go outside for anything. With the snow and all, I just watched TV and went to bed about ten-thirty. In the morning, I got up and rode down the hill on my sled to Jed's. We found the body when we started clearing out the snow. I have no idea how it got there."

"I believe you. But if you hear anything or remember something, let me know, okay?" Jim handed Bobby his card. "My home phone number is on the back. Are you managing all right by yourself?"

"Oh, yeah. When I get lonesome, or I get sick of my own cooking, Jed watches out for me. I stay with him quite a bit. Thanks for the ride, Lt. Higgins." Bobby climbed out of the Suburban and trudged up the steps. He turned and waved to Jim before he disappeared into the house. Inside, the kitchen light flicked on, and the house became warmer and less stark.

Jim sat in his car, saddened that this polite, intelligent young boy was, for all practical purposes, an orphan just like his daughter Lillie had been. But now Lillie had a stable, happy home because someone had cared enough to get involved. What about Bobby? What would happen to him? Did anyone really give two hoots about the kid? His mother had disappeared, his father was sick with alcoholism, and the only person who really seemed to care at all was a bartender who occasionally made the kid a meal and listened to him talk.

Jim knew he should report the situation to Social Services, but he also knew about the red tape of government agencies. Bobby Rude had certainly been cheated out of a happy childhood, but nowadays that wasn't uncommon. He supposed for some children, there was no other choice but foster care, especially if they were very young, but Bobby seemed capable of caring for himself. And his father was still alive, although incapacitated at the moment. Bobby seemed confident in his independence, and so far, it appeared he'd made good choices.

When Jim's daughter Sara had taught at St. Ignatius Catholic School in Genoa, she'd watched over Bobby, encouraged him in his academic studies, and made sure his physical needs were met. But Jim wondered about Bobby's heart—his emotions and inner life. Who was helping him develop the crucial qualities of love and kindness, empathy and sensitivity—qualities that are the framework of a successful life.

Jim shifted uncomfortably as he steered the Suburban down the long, steep hill. He took a lingering look at the lonely weather-beaten house on the bluff overlooking the river. The wheels of the truck crunched loudly on the cold, frozen driveway. He turned onto the wide highway that bordered the river and slowly drove home, unable to get Bobby Rude off his mind.

☐

Leslie Birkstein sat at her easel and dabbed splotches of paint on the canvas: black, brown, a little purple here, a little maroon there. The form of the painting had taken shape. Now she just needed to add the details. She'd been painting with intense concentration for the last hour. Her brushstrokes had been confident, but now she hesitated.

Up to this point, the painting had almost composed itself. Suddenly, it was as if someone leaned over her shoulder and whispered a cautionary critique in her ear. She jerked and made a huffing sound, realizing she was trying way too hard.

She leaned away from the canvas, evaluating the portrait, trying not to be too critical. But as always, she struggled to be objective about her own work. Anyone who knew anything about art knew that in any portrait, it was the eyes that told the story. She was pleased that the emotion in the deep-set eyes of her trusty black lab expressed his warm, loyal sentiment. Tough yet tender. The regal, broad head suggested an innate intelligence. Paco could discern the very nuances of Leslie's feelings and emotions. His deep, wide chest held a heart whose devotion to her was unquestioned—his bravery in defending and protecting her from harm was legendary.

So why was she uneasy? Why the feelings of disquiet and agitation?

Paco lay faithfully at her feet. As she sat poised with her paintbrush in hand, he lifted his brown eyes to meet hers and whined. Then he rose to his feet and extended his legs out in front of him in a graceful elastic stretch. He laid his great head in her lap. He'd been doing that a lot lately. Did he sense her anxiety? Probably, but she had no idea what had triggered his concern.

She rinsed her paintbrush and gently laid it on the easel. "Hey, boy," she said quietly, stroking his ears. "What's wrong, huh? Something bothering you?"

Paco snuffled and licked her face as she leaned down toward him.

She heard a rustling at the door and soft footsteps approaching the easel. Sam laid his hands gently on her shoulders and leaned down, brushing her long blonde hair back, kissing her neck tenderly. Paco lifted his majestic head from Leslie's lap and stared at Sam as if he were intruding.

"It's after ten, honey. Are you coming to bed pretty soon?" he asked.

"Yeah, I think I better quit while I'm ahead," she said.

"The portrait looks great. You've really captured the essence of Paco." Sam folded his arms across his chest, studying the painting. "The trick is to know when to quit, isn't it?" he commented.

Leslie grumped. "Yes. That's the key to any great painting. As soon as you start rescuing it, it's too late. You've already ruined it."

Leslie had been painting for about a year, and she'd shown a natural facility for this recent form of therapy. After a bout with pottery and a futile attempt at quilting, Leslie had finally found her niche. At the encouragement of her art instructor, she was preparing a painting for an art show that would benefit the local chapter of the

Humane Society. And she was nervous. And scared. And afraid of what others would say about the depiction of her loyal canine friend.

She stood up suddenly, walked across the small room, and turned to get some perspective. "Do you think they'll like it?" she asked, tapping her index finger against her lips.

"Does it matter?" Sam asked.

"Well, of course it matters." She parked her hands on her hips. "Someone has to like it enough to bid on it, and I certainly don't want to get some ridiculously low bid and stand there embarrassed as hell," she said with a vehemence that surprised Sam. Her shoulders slumped, and she suddenly realized how tired she was. "Besides, a low bid is like a judgment on the worth of Paco ... and he's priceless."

"You're going to do fine," Sam said, walking up to her and placing a kiss on her cheek. "You're always your toughest critic. Just roll with it, or better yet, if you think it'll bomb, don't show up. Or, at the appropriate moment, visit the bathroom."

"That's your advice?" Leslie looked at him with a disbelieving stare.

"I think I better shut up," he said. He grabbed her hand, flicked off the light, and led her down the hall. "Besides, I'm your biggest fan, you know that. If nobody else bids on it, I will."

Walking into the bedroom, Leslie noticed the Bible lying open on the bed. After getting into her pajamas, she folded the sheets and thick quilt back and crawled in. Sam shut the Bible and laid it on the nightstand and got into bed.

"Paco's been acting weird lately," Leslie said, burrowing her head beneath Sam's chin.

"Whaddya mean?"

"Well, he hovers around me and just seems so protective. I can't figure out what's bothering him."

"He does have a sixth sense when it comes to your safety. That is kinda strange."

"Well, I guess we'll find out what it is in due time," Leslie said, leaning over and turning off the light on the nightstand. Sam pulled her close again, then whispered in her hair, "Behold you are beautiful, my love. Behold you are beautiful."

"Is that Shakespeare?" Leslie asked sleepily.

"Nope. Song of Solomon, Chapter 4, verse 1," Sam said.

"It's lovely. Night, Sam."

"Night, love."

7

Jim twirled a pen between his fingers, wondering when spring was going to arrive in earnest. His desk was piled with paperwork, which seemed to pale in insignificance compared to the investigation they were conducting. The drug busts, petty thievery, domestic abuse calls, and financial shenanigans of the residents of the city never ceased to amaze him. But then he thought of the majority of the population who minded their own business, took care of their families, and never committed so much as a parking violation. *There are still good people in the world. Plenty of them,* he thought. *Don't forget that.*

Jim got up from his desk and walked to Paul Saner's office.

"So, have you found out where LeMar Burke has been the last week?" Jim asked, glancing at Paul.

Paul looked up from his notes. "Yep. He spent some time in Indianapolis, then he traveled to Chicago and Milwaukee, and then the two days before he was murdered, he was here in La Crosse."

"Do we have any idea what he was doing in those cities?"

"Still workin' on that, but he used his business credit card, so obviously he was working for Hathway Industries."

"How about his phone records? What do those show?" Jim asked.

"In the cities I mentioned, he was in contact with some larger realty firms. I have some calls in to them, still waiting for responses. Sam's workin' on the La Crosse contacts."

"Where'd LeMar stay when he was here?"

"The BonBon."

"Down on State?"

"Yep. Stayed there Tuesday and Wednesday."

"Get down there and talk to their staff. Go through the room. See if anything turns up."

Paul nodded. "I'll finish up these loose ends and get on it, Chief," he said.

Jim took a few phone calls in his office, then made his way down the dim hallway to Sam's cubicle. Knocking lightly on the door, he pulled up a chair. Presently, the sunshine was burning in a golden stream through the small, narrow office window, revealing dust motes floating in the air. The snowbanks out on Vine Street had shrunk significantly since the temperatures had rocketed up to forty degrees. Commuters' vehicles splashed unceremoniously through the potholes, swishing sludge on the wet roads.

When Sam hung up, Jim said, "Tell me about the calls LeMar made while he was in La Crosse." He leaned back in his chair, crossed one leg over his knee, and waited.

Sam noticed Jim's crisp baby blue shirt, the red and blue striped Salvatore Ferragamo necktie, the charcoal gray Haggar dress slacks, and the lightweight navy wool suit coat of exceptional quality. *How does he afford those clothes?* thought Sam.

"Sam? The phone records?" Jim asked again, looking irritated by Sam's lack of a response.

"Oh, yeah. Let me find them." Sam paged through a pile of papers on his desk, finally pulling out a yellow legal notepad. His eyes scanned the list he'd made.

"Tuesday. He called the Bluff Management Group. They specialize in commercial listings. And he called another one—Tri-State Realty and Appraisals."

"Good. Follow up on that. Any other interesting calls?"

"Not really. Some calls to the Hathway home office in New Orleans and one to his wife, but other than that, nothing's standing out." Sam hesitated for a brief moment, watching Jim with a pensive stare.

"What?" Jim said, running his fingers through his hair. "You know something. What is it? Tell me," he demanded.

"Did Paul mention the phone number he found in LeMar's wallet?" Sam scrunched down in his chair in an evasive move and tipped his chin toward his chest, eyeing Jim carefully over his coffee cup. Jim blinked and shook his head. "No, he never said anything. What'd he find?"

"A number was on the back of one of LeMar's business cards. When he dialed it, he got Jude Delaney's voicemail."

Jim sat up straight. "What? Did you check it out? Confront Jude?"

"Yep. We talked to him yesterday about ten o'clock. He says LeMar was just a good customer at his restaurant in New Orleans. He came into the restaurant a lot, but they were only casual acquaintances."

"Does DeDe know about this?"

"I don't know. Probably not. Unless Jude told her yesterday," Sam said, swirling the coffee in his cup.

"I'll talk to her this morning."

"Better you than me," Sam said.

Jim went on. "We also need to find out if Burke visited La Crosse previously. I have a hunch he made contact with someone earlier who may have resented him or the company he represented. Maybe that was the impetus for the crime." Jim stopped and shrugged his shoulders when Sam gave him a dubious glance. "Maybe he offended someone or made an offer that he wouldn't back away from. I don't know. It's all a crap shoot right now, but it's a place to start."

Sam stretched his arms to the ceiling. "Well, it's a theory, and we need one soon, but the facts are what will ultimately build a framework. I'll check it out. What about the weapon? Do you think there might be a Native American connection somewhere?"

"Yeah, that's possible, but like I said, it's hard to tell this early in the investigation. Do what you have to do and see where it leads. Follow your instincts." Jim got up and headed to DeDe's office, but it was empty. Hearing voices coming from Leslie's lab, he headed that way.

Leslie and DeDe were hunched over the murder weapon, inspecting it under a large, suspended magnifying glass and an exceptionally bright, high-intensity lamp. Their backs were to Jim. He stood behind them, waiting for them to notice his entrance. They were talking quietly, and when they failed to notice him, he spoke up.

"Hey, ladies! Anything interesting?" he interrupted loudly.

Leslie jumped and straightened up suddenly, whipping around to face him.

"Jeez, Chief! You scared the wits out of us," Leslie scolded. Her pale face seemed washed out, and she looked like she hadn't had much sleep.

"You sure are good at sneakin' up on people, sir," DeDe said, her hand resting lightly on her neck. She laid her hand on Leslie's arm. "You okay?" she asked, her voice laced with concern.

Holding up his hands as if he were in a stickup, he said, "Sorry, ladies. I thought you heard me." He lowered his hands and pointed to the counter where the weapon lay bathed in brilliant light. "Let's start over. What have you found out about the weapon?"

"Have a look," Leslie said, stepping back from the counter, "then tell us your thoughts."

Jim sat on the upholstered stool next to the counter and bent over the weapon. A shiver of apprehension ran down his spine as he studied the ancient club. It was a fearsome weapon capable of inflicting excruciating damage to human flesh. He could almost hear the crunch of bone that the impact of the club made when it connected with the skull. Jim was sure LeMar Burke never knew what hit him.

He noticed some details on the club he'd missed before. An intricate beaver was carved on the ridge of the weapon, and a series of wavy lines were etched along the entire length of the handle. The craftsmanship that had gone into the object was truly remarkable. The exquisite detail and pride were evident in the selection of the beautiful ash wood with its superior grain and strength. The careful attention to the selection of icons used in the piece demonstrated the maker's deep understanding of Native American history, lore, and culture. *No detail was left undone*, Jim thought. *If I were a collector of ancient weapons, this would be an artifact I'd want in my collection.*

"Wonderful details and well made," he commented. Straightening up, he turned on the stool and looked at the women. "If it hadn't been used to kill someone, I'd say it's a thing of beauty."

"Yes, it is. Since studying it, we've been doing some research online. We think we may have found the maker," DeDe said. "An artisan named Ryan Blake from the Black River Falls area. On his website, he has many examples of his work that look almost identical to this one. He specializes in replicas of ancient weapons used by the Sauk, Fox, and Winnebago tribes. This one is representative of clubs that were designed and used in the early 1700s. He has a studio, and we're headed up there this afternoon. We have a one o'clock appointment with him," she explained.

"Excellent. Let me know the upshot of your meeting," Jim said, standing up. "Maybe he can give us a lead on who may have owned this one. Before you head out, can I see you in my office, DeDe?"

"Sure. I'll be there in five minutes."

Fifteen minutes later, Jim pointed DeDe to a chair, walked over, and closed his office door. She was dressed in a black, gray, and cream-colored silk blouse in a geometric pattern, black dress slacks, and a gray cashmere sweater that hung gracefully over her generous figure. Despite her fashionable attire, DeDe seemed on edge. Nervous.

Unsettled. Jim sat down behind his beat-up desk and faced her. He was still getting to know her on a personal level. She met his stare with a wary expression.

Breaking the tension in the room, she finally spoke. "You wanted to talk to me, sir?"

"Yes. Something's come up in the investigation that I wanted to ask you about—something Paul found among LeMar's possessions."

She visibly relaxed. "Sure. How can I help?" she asked. Her expression remained neutral. No confusion. No guilt. No indication that she knew what he was going to ask.

"There was a phone number on the back of one of LeMar's business cards—the number was Jude's. Would you know why LeMar would have had Jude's number?" DeDe's face looked like stone, deep and silent.

It was quiet for several moments. Jim waited. His chair creaked loudly as he leaned back and studied the traffic outside his window on Vine Street. Swiveling back to face her, he noticed her expression had changed to confusion and, underneath, fear.

"DeDe? Would you know anything about that?" Jim asked again when the silence in his office had become painfully prolonged. Finally, DeDe huffed and pulled in a breath, and in that moment, her cheeks became pink, suffused with embarrassment.

"I'm sorry, sir. I was just thinking. This is rather embarrassing. You've put me on the spot, I guess. I really don't know why Jude would have had his number. It's possible that he was just a good customer at Jude's restaurant in New Orleans. JuJu had a way of establishing exceptional relationships with people who visited his place regularly. He always took the time to walk through the dining room each evening to ensure that everyone was happy with the service and cuisine. That's what earned him a five-star rating—that and his exceptional cooking abilities. That's the only thing that makes sense to me on the spur of the moment."

Jim smiled, his dimple denting his cheek, and DeDe felt a little twinge of relief. "Well, that's exactly what he told Paul and Sam yesterday," Jim said. "I guess you know your husband better than you thought you did, huh?" he said, leaning forward, resting his elbows on his desk.

"I guess so, sir." DeDe's eyebrows raised tellingly, whether from surprise or irritation, Jim wasn't sure. "I hope so," she whispered under her breath.

As she sat there, DeDe's thoughts raced. Jude had promised he was through with secrets, and she was finally beginning to relax in the security of that promise. He'd shared many painful memories about his childhood, and in the retelling of his heartaches and insecurities, he'd become more open and vulnerable in their relationship. Now this—what did it mean? Was he hiding something from her? Again? Or was it just a quirk of fate that his number happened to be in LeMar Burke's possession? Did Jude have something to do with his murder? *What a nightmare that would be*, she thought. Then another thought. *No, that's not possible. He was with me the whole night of the blizzard.* Her cheeks flushed pink when she recalled the lovemaking they'd indulged in during the storm,

She waited for Jim to say more, but his phone buzzed. "I'll ask him about it tonight," she promised, getting up from her chair and heading to the door.

"Sounds good," Jim said, ignoring his buzzing cell phone. When she reached the door, he called after her. "DeDe, wait."

She turned and looked at him. "If you're really wondering where Jude was on the night of the blizzard, well, he was with me the whole time." She blushed again. "You'll have to trust me on that, sir." He stood up behind his desk and said, "In this job, trust is crucial. I know that's hard sometimes because the very nature of a detective is maintaining a healthy skepticism. Still, when it's all said and done, you need to trust your team, you need to trust your instincts, you need to trust your gut, and … you need to trust your husband. You can't survive in this profession without trust."

"Yes, sir," she mumbled, nodding thoughtfully. She walked down the hallway and drifted into Leslie's office.

"You ready to head out?" DeDe asked tersely.

"Yeah. Everything okay?"

"Not really, but I'll tell you about it later," she said sourly. "Let me get my coat and boots. I'll be back in five minutes."

Leslie stared after DeDe, wondering what had transpired in Higgins' office. She sighed and grabbed her coat off the hook behind the door, trying to imagine what had put DeDe in such a foul mood.

□

Paul and Sam rolled up to The BonBon Hotel on State Street next to Riverside Park after lunch.

"Jeez, if I'd known we were coming here, we could have had something from their lunch menu," Sam said breezily.

"Not. You couldn't even afford a crust of bread here on your salary," Paul said as he wove his way around the sculptured shrubbery outside and into the gleaming lobby. With its reclaimed maple floors, exposed wood beams, lofty ceilings, and touches of original red brick, it was easy to see why it was one of the top-rated hotels in the area.

"I could afford it," Sam said, feeling rebuffed. "Remember, I save hundreds of dollars on clothes at Good Will. Bargains you wouldn't believe. That makes splurges on nice meals within reach once in a while."

"Yeah, right. All I can say is your savings show in your choice of threads, buddy. I brought Ruby here for our second anniversary, and that one night just about broke my poor policeman's budget. My savings account is still in recovery." Paul's eyes softened. "But it was a memorable night. Well worth it, especially when Ruby revealed her purchases from Victoria's Secret."

Sam watched Paul's face change from serious to dreamy. "Don't you mean when she took off the Victoria's Secret?" he asked, glancing around the luxurious lobby. "Was that the night Max was conceived?"

"I don't know. Probably. Anyway, it was a night to remember," Paul chuckled, the heavy front door swishing closed behind them.

They approached the main desk, where a young woman dressed in a sleek black dress looked up from her laptop and flashed them a friendly smile. "Hello, gentlemen. May I help you?" she asked politely, rising from her chair to stand behind the opulent granite counter.

Sam and Paul displayed their police IDs, and her smile faded away. "We certainly hope so," Sam said. "We understand that Mr. LeMar Burke from New Orleans was a guest at your hotel this past week. We'd like to see his room, please," he explained.

The young, dark-eyed clerk continued to gaze at Sam, her eyes pools of uncertainty. "I … I can't do that. We're not supposed to allow any unauthorized people to enter another person's room. I'm afraid I can't do that," she repeated emphatically. "I'm sorry."

"I understand. Then we'd like to see the manager," Paul said, his tone brusque. Squirming under their gaze, she dialed a number and began explaining the detectives' request to the manager.

Hanging up the desk phone, she looked up. "Mr. Lofton will be right down. You can wait over there," she said, pointing to the plush couches and chairs in the lobby. "He'll be right with you."

The manager appeared fifteen minutes later. He was a tightly wound little man with a meticulously trimmed mustache and a four hundred dollar haircut. His suit was black, his shirt a dark burgundy, which was set off by a black Stefano Ricci crystal-trimmed bowtie. He approached the detectives and stood before them, eyeing their IDs like they'd been picked out of the nearest dumpster. Sam bristled at his high-handed attitude.

After introductions, Mr. Lofton asked, "It's my understanding you would like to search Mr. Burke's room. Is that right?"

"Yes, we need to get into his room. We have evidence that suggests a crime has been committed, and we don't want any physical evidence lost or destroyed if the room is thoroughly cleaned," Sam said.

"All right. I guess that would be okay," he said, but his look of uncertainty about the legal aspects of a room search did nothing to convince him that Sam's emphasis on physical evidence was important.

Sam continued, trying to get his point across to the hesitant manager. "We could get a search warrant, but we're well within our legal rights as police officers to investigate the room without a warrant. We'd appreciate your cooperation, sir," he said, although he spoke it through clenched teeth. "It'll save us a lot of time and hassle."

The manager paused for a moment, then nodded. "Come with me," he said, heading through the lobby. Paul and Sam followed him to the elevator.

When they reached the third floor, Mr. Lofton led them to the Luxe River Vue King Suite. According to Mr. Lofton, LeMar Burke had failed to check out, so his room had not been thoroughly cleaned yet, nor had his possessions been removed. Walking into the luxury suite, Paul picked up the faint smell of men's cologne—something expensive, no doubt. In the en suite bathroom, some toiletries had been left on the counter, and a high-end leather suitcase lay open on the luggage rack. It was filled with neatly arranged piles of boxers, T-shirts, and socks.

The manager nervously watched as Paul and Sam put on blue latex gloves and began conducting the search. What they were looking for was unclear to him, but they took their time. Sam wandered out on the attached porch, which overlooked the Mississippi River. The air was balmy, and the view from the room was enticing. In the distance, the river flowed, deep and mysterious, and the blue-gray bluffs were mottled with snow on the opposite shoreline. There was something comforting about them. Joggers and bikers enjoyed the promise of spring in the air at Riverside Park, just across the street from the hotel, and a few mothers pushed strollers along the tree-lined sidewalks.

Two cocktail glasses on a tray were still sitting on the metal outdoor table. Beneath the table, a crushed cigarette stub lay smashed into the concrete. Sam picked up the stub and dropped it in a ziplock bag, along with the cocktail glasses. He wandered back into the room and began going through the closet.

Finally, Mr. Lofton asked, "What exactly is it that you're hoping to find?" His mustache twitched with a false sense of indignity. "We're really not in the habit of allowing police to search through the contents of our guests' luggage and personal belongings."

"Even if the guy's been murdered?" Sam asked, holding up an expensive shirt he'd taken out of the closet.

"Mr. Burke was … murdered?" Lofton repeated, the words catching in his throat.

Sam looked around the shirt at the shocked face of the manager, then switched his gaze to Paul. "Jeez, you see these labels on this guy's clothing. This is stuff I've only seen from very exclusive makers online—Ralph Lauren, Lorenzini, Battistoni. I'd love to find some stuff like this at Goodwill."

"Leave it to the Italians to give the world some class," Paul remarked dryly.

"When did this happen?" Mr. Lofton asked, pale with shock.

Probably thinking about the PR fallout, Sam thought as he watched his face change.

"Wednesday night, sometime during the snowstorm," Sam said. "When did Mr. Burke leave the hotel Wednesday? Do you know?"

"I personally don't know, but I can check with the staff on duty that day and see if anyone recalls his movements," Lofton said, suddenly more cooperative. He whipped out his cell, turned his back for privacy, and began making calls.

Paul continued shuffling through the briefcase that was on the top of the desk, along with a laptop. He'd stopped digging and sorting and was reading something intently. Sam noticed and sidled up to him, looking over his shoulder.

"Find something?" he asked.

Paul continued to read, absorbed in the text of a tri-fold brochure. "Hmm. A brochure from a group called the Driftless Native Consortium."

"Never heard of them. What do they do?" asked Sam.

"Says here that they respect the land and animals and try to live in balance with nature while protecting the inalienable rights of Native American tribes in the Driftless Region to secure and maintain the ancient lands of their people for future posterity." Paul made a face and said, "Sounds reasonable, I guess."

"Boy, that could be taken to vigilante excesses, don't you think? Why does Burke have something like that in his possession?" Sam questioned, still inspecting the quality of the Italian shirt. "Look at the stitching on these cuffs. Superior quality."

"Will you get off the shirt, for Pete's sake! Why does Burke have a brochure like this?"

Sam shrugged his shoulders. "You got me. Bag it and take it with," Sam said, walking over and replacing the shirt in the closet. "We'll have to investigate the group's activities a little closer," Sam said. "Any contact names?"

Paul ran his finger along the printed pages, then shook his head. "No, but their headquarters is in La Farge. We'll have to go down there and check it out."

Sam held up a key ring he'd noticed on the desk. "He must have rented a car at Enterprise. I'll call crime scene and have them go over it. Maybe they can get some DNA or fingerprints from it." Then he turned to the manager. "We'll be sending a crime scene crew over to go through the room and the rental car."

The manager groaned and rolled his eyes upward toward the ceiling. "The negative press is going to kill us," he muttered, punching a number into his cell.

"Yeah, getting crime scene over here is a good idea," Paul said distractedly, still reading the brochure. "We'll be able to pick up DNA from Burke and any other people he may have had as guests."

Mr. Lofton cleared his throat. "Gentlemen, I just talked to the front desk. You're in luck. The girl you met downstairs, Shelby Lewis, was on desk duty during the snowstorm. She'd be glad to tell you what she knows about Mr. Burke's movements during the day on Wednesday."

"Would she know that?" Sam asked.

"Oh, absolutely. Our staff is trained to develop relationships with all of our customers. We aim to provide the best possible service for everyone who stays with us. And Shelby is very charming and accommodating," Mr. Lofton said with a distinctive snap in his voice. "She's one of our best employees."

"Great. We'll talk to her before we leave," Sam said.

They finished their search, opening drawers, looking under the bed, and checking the closets once more, but they found nothing else other than the brochure and Burke's personal laptop that might be pertinent to their investigation. They thanked Mr. Lofton and took the elevator back down to the main lobby. While they rode down, Paul said, "Why don't you question Shelby since you're obviously the most charming." Sam waved him off. Paul snickered and said, "Women warm up to you when they see those thick curly locks and those sultry hazel eyes."

"Aw, shut up. You're so full of it," Sam said, but he was grinning.

Approaching the main desk, Shelby looked up from her computer. She was a pert size three, her dark hair coiffed in a casual pageboy style, her bangs feathered over her forehead, making her intelligent brown eyes seem especially luminous and inviting. She gave Sam a closer look, and suddenly he felt like a bug under a microscope, but it wasn't an altogether bad feeling. She stood before them in a practiced pose that suggested polite and efficient customer service. But underneath, she radiated a smoldering sexuality that wasn't lost on the two men.

"So, Shelby, what can you tell us about Mr. Burke's movements on Wednesday?" asked Sam. *Those eyes*, he thought. *Very sexy.*

"He had breakfast in the dining room about seven o'clock. I'm not sure where he was until ten o'clock, maybe in his room. But another man met him in the lobby at ten, and they left together. Then they came back about one o'clock and went upstairs. I only worked until two, and I didn't see him leave again by the front entrance in the afternoon. I came back on duty at six—you know, that was the day of the storm—and ended up staying until Thursday morning."

"Do guests have to use the front entrance, or are there other exits from the hotel?"

"For security purposes, all visitors use the front entrance, but guests staying with us have key cards for the entrance to our parking lot," she said succinctly.

"So Burke met someone at ten and returned with the same gentleman at one o'clock? Is that right?" Sam asked.

"Yes, that's right," Shelby answered.

"What did the other gentleman look like? Do you remember?" Sam questioned. He leaned over and rested his elbow on the front counter.

"He had dark hair, kind of a longer style—like yours but straight." Her eyes drifted to Sam's loose locks, and he squirmed uncomfortably. "He was tall—over six feet—and he wore a jacket that looked Western." She stopped and looked away as she thought about it. Then she shook her head. "No, not Western, but kinda like those Indian blankets. Some kind of Native American design. Black with a red geometric pattern on it."

"Really?" Paul said, impressed with the details of her memories.

"Really," she reiterated, nodding her head, looking at him as if he were an idiot. "A very unique jacket."

"Did he appear to be a Native American?" asked Sam.

"Could have been, I guess," she said hesitantly.

"But you're not sure?"

Shelby pursed her lips and shook her head. "No, I'm not sure of his ethnicity. Sorry."

"That's okay. You've given us some good information," Sam said. "Anything else you can remember?"

Shelby nodded, then said, "Nope. That's about it."

Sam slid his card across the desk. "Just call if you think of anything else."

She smiled shyly, and her eyes locked with Sam. "I'll be sure and do that," she said. Sam felt a sudden warmth on his cheeks as Shelby resumed her position at her computer, her fingers racing over the keys.

They walked out into the March afternoon, which had warmed up considerably. The bank clock down the street registered forty degrees. Sam inhaled deeply, the fresh air making him think that spring might be just around the corner. The buds on the maple tree looked fat and round, and beneath the melting snow along the edge of the sidewalk, little tufts of grass were greening up and poking their stalks toward the warm sunlight. Of course, in Wisconsin during March, that could all go to hell in about an hour. Sam recalled the fickleness of the month—full winter one day and a spring thaw the next. The college kids hadn't started sunbathing yet—too much snow—but that would happen as soon as temperatures hit the seventy-degree mark.

On the way back to the office, Paul and Sam discussed the stranger who had met Burke in the lobby of the hotel. Sam believed whoever it was had probably also had a drink with Burke on the patio attached to his hotel room. They were still discussing the possible implications when they stepped out of the elevator on the third floor of the law enforcement center. A familiar, if somewhat obnoxious, voice was coming from Higgins' office, drifting down the hallway. Sam and Paul looked at each other in disbelief.

Emily Warehauser looked up as they approached her desk.

"Recognize that voice?" she asked the two men, her eyebrows raised.

"Are you kidding me? I thought he was gone for good," Paul remarked, glancing down the hallway. "When did he roll in?"

"About fifteen minutes ago, and I'm sure Higgins is already sick of his verbiage," Emily said as the men turned and made their way to Jim's office. "Tread lightly," she warned.

"... and listen, Chief," the voice continued. "I've met some of these insurgents that live on the fringe of our culture. They do have a point, after all. Taking away the Native's land was a terrible miscalculation on the part of the United States government, and we've been paying the price for it ever since."

Sam and Paul walked into Higgins' office. "Ever since what?" Sam asked.

Jim looked up, thankful for the interruption. The young man occupying a chair near Jim's desk turned and popped out of his seat. His obvious enthusiasm and excitement at seeing Sam and Paul was evident as he pumped their hands energetically. His curly brown hair and baby face were familiar. Intense hazel eyes hinted at a razor-sharp intelligence and a boundless curiosity. He'd grown a couple of inches since they'd seen him, and his clumsy social skills seemed to have leveled out somewhat. He was wearing a pair of khaki pants, a tan long-sleeve T-shirt, and a camo vest with an MVAC logo over the pocket.

Three years ago, Jamie Alberg, archaeological savant and treasure hunter, had helped Higgins and his team solve a one-hundred-fifty-year-old mystery involving a cache of gold coins stolen in 1866 from Fort Crawford near Prairie du Chien. In the process of tracking down the hidden treasure, he'd almost met his Maker when he'd been thrown into the Mississippi River, miraculously surviving in spite of his abysmal swimming skills. His mild autism could grate on the nerves, and his intensity when collecting information was over the top. Truthfully, Higgins had been delighted to escort him from his office three years ago. Now, like Arnold Schwarzenegger, *he was back.*

"Hey, guys. Wow! I haven't seen you in quite a while. Lt. Higgins tells me you have another murder on your hands," Jamie said excitedly.

"Yeah, and it sounds like you've got some kind of opinion about that," Paul commented, ignoring Jim, who was waving him off in the background, gritting his teeth in a show of frustration. "So what brings you back to La Crosse?" Jim swiped his hand across his neck in a "don't go there" warning.

Jamie settled back in his chair and crossed one leg over the other. The enthusiasm in his voice bubbled over and filled the room. "Oh, I'm back working at MVAC for a while until my applications to some east coast universities come back. Then I'll decide where I want to go to pursue my doctorate."

"You mean you can get a doctorate in forensic archaeology?" Sam asked.

"Absolutely. Several universities offer programs, but I'm hoping to study out East somewhere—possibly Yale, Dartmouth, or Harvard. In the meantime, the powers that be at MVAC are sending me out to the caves around here to document the rock petroglyphs and do a comparison study of the images. I'm cataloging them and writing accompanying text that explains the subject matter of the pictures in preparation for a possible guidebook. Doesn't pay much, but it's beer money."

"That sounds like it's right up your alley, Jamie," Sam said, noticing Higgins' conspicuous scowl, which only seemed to deepen as the conversation went on. "You're pretty good at exploring caves." Jim rolled his eyes and rested his head on his closed fist.

"A good source of mine was telling me that you found a very interesting weapon at the scene of the murder. A ball club? Is that right?" Jamie asked. His face glowed with feverish anticipation as he waited for someone to share the clues about the case.

Sam noticed Jamie's deep-set hazel eyes burning with interest. He'd changed very little. His ability to irritate Higgins hadn't seemed to change either. He leaned forward, resting his hands on the arms of the chair, waiting for one of them to spill information about the crime and the ancient weapon.

Jim suddenly came alive and sat up straight. "Any information about this current case is confidential and needs to be kept under wraps until we have a better handle on the situation, especially the weapon. We're still not sure of its origins, age, or maker," Jim said. "Or who may be the next target." Jim remained calm, but the distinctive authoritarian tone in his voice was not lost on anyone in the room, especially Sam and Paul. "So everyone needs to keep the weapon information under their hat until further notice—that includes the press."

Jamie's eyes flicked from Sam to Paul and finally came to rest on Jim's stern face. His expression jolted the young archaeologist's memories of earlier conflicts he'd had with Higgins.

"Absolutely, sir. I completely understand," Jamie said with exaggerated seriousness. "I've learned a few things since I left La Crosse, you know."

"Great. Glad to hear it," Jim said, his voice tinged with a cool civility barely noticeable over the underlying sarcasm.

Jamie continued babbling as if Jim were not there. "We have the same policy when we're working at digs. I wouldn't think of jeopardizing your case by blabbing information to the press," he said defensively, directing his comments to Jim. "Although I know I did do that one time. As I recall, you weren't very happy with me." Jim dipped his chin and locked eyes with him. Jamie rose from his chair and grabbed his ski jacket. "I've been working on my people skills, too. Can't you tell?" When no one answered, he rushed on. "I can see you're busy, so I won't hassle you. I'm staying with my mom if you need to contact me. Any information pertaining to caves, rock art, or Ho-Chunk culture, just let me know. I'm not an expert, but I do know a lot about those topics, and I have some contacts," Jamie said as he backed out of the office into the hallway. "Good to see you guys again." He waved, turned, and walked down the hallway.

In the silence that followed his departure, the three seasoned detectives exchanged perplexing glances.

"Don't even go there," Jim said grumpily, holding up one hand. "We cannot afford to have Jamie involved in another case. Remember the last time he tried to help? He almost got himself killed!"

"Well, he's extremely enthusiastic, and he is quite knowledgeable about certain subjects," Paul said tentatively, knowing he was trying Jim's patience. "And, to his credit, he did locate the cave where the gold stash was hidden." Jim flashed him a chilly glance. "Besides, he seems to have grown up some," Paul finished hurriedly.

"In your dreams, buddy," Jim said sourly, tapping his finger loudly on his desk. "There is no way that kid is getting tangled up in this investigation. Just so we're on the same page."

Paul crossed his arms over his chest. "Okay, okay. I've got it, Chief."

Switching topics, Jim asked, "So, did you find out anything at The BonBon?"

"Yeah, we did." Paul started explaining the brochure outlining the mission statement of the Driftless Native Consortium.

"Huh. Interesting. Never heard of them," Jim said as he scrutinized the colorful pamphlet that Paul had handed to him. He read for a few moments and then said, "So their mission is to keep current Native lands in the hands of Natives?" he asked. "Is that right?"

"Yep, in a nutshell. They're some kind of PR group between the Ho-Chunks and the general public, from what I can tell. I'm not sure if that includes buying back land or preventing it from falling into the hands of the non-Native population, but we'll find out more when we go to talk to them," Paul said.

"They're headquartered in La Farge?" Jim asked.

"Yep, but the brochure says their jurisdiction covers the entire Driftless Area. They're located in the old Organic Food facilities. I know where that is. Sam and I are going to drive down there and check it out."

Sam spoke up. "Another thing. The desk clerk saw Burke with a man who was wearing a distinctive Native American jacket of some kind on Wednesday afternoon, the day of the storm. Might have been of Native descent. We think he may have had a drink with Burke on the outdoor patio of his hotel room. Found a cigarette butt, too."

"Really? Was anybody able to identify the man?" Jim asked.

"No one at the hotel recognized him," Sam said. "Burke rented a car from Enterprise. Crime scene is going to go down and take it apart. Plus, they'll go through the room to see if they can find anything."

"Good. That's good. What about the two realty agencies? Anything there?" Jim continued, zeroing in on Sam.

"Gotta check my emails. Haven't gotten any return calls yet. Playing phone tag, but I'll buzz them again and see what I can uncover," Sam explained. "Where are DeDe and Leslie?"

"Up at Black River Falls paying a visit to a …" Jim scanned his notes, "Ryan Blake, some artisan who specializes in reproductions of ancient weapons. Leslie discovered his website online. They think this guy might have made the weapon found at the murder scene. They're not back yet."

"Anything more from the coroner?" Paul asked.

"Yeah, he called just before you came in," Jim said, scratching his ear and referring to his yellow legal pad. "He found shards of metal in the victim's wound that matched the metal peg that was protruding from the club. The indentation of the wound and the profile of the weapon are an exact match. The ball club's our weapon, without a doubt." Everyone thought about that for a moment. Jim bowed his head, deep in thought.

"How hard will it be to track down the owner of the weapon?" Sam asked, breaking the silence.

Jim looked up. "There are no latent prints on the weapon. Whoever killed LeMar was smart enough to wear gloves and must have thoroughly cleaned the handle of the club. It was expertly wiped down after it was used, according to crime scene," Jim told them. "If we can establish a maker of the weapon, we may be able to trace the owner that way."

"If it's ancient, then ..." Paul's voice trailed off.

"It'll be a lot harder to trace, but not impossible," Jim finished. After a few moments of silence, he squared his shoulders and said, "So I guess we've got our work cut out for us, guys."

"I guess so, Chief," Paul said as the two men exited the office.

8

"**S**o you're saying this ball club is really old—like hundreds of years old?" DeDe asked as she stared at Ryan Blake.

Blake was tall, ramrod straight in his posture, proud, and slightly arrogant. His skin was the color of brushed leather. His dark eyes met DeDe's with self-assurance. A ponytail hung down his back and shone with a blue sheen, and a small silver hoop in his right ear reflected the sunlight. In both his personality and his formidable skills as a maker of replica weaponry, he radiated confidence. He was dressed casually, wearing a dark blue sweater and a pair of blue jeans, which were dusted with a smattering of sawdust.

"Yes, this ball club is really old," Ryan said, tapping the counter next to the murder weapon. "And if you'd studied projectile points and the materials used that are indigenous to the area like I've done, then you would know that this ball club is authentic. The head was carved from the root ball of an ash tree, and its shaft is about fourteen inches. These ancient weapons almost always had shorter shafts than ones made in the last fifty to seventy-five years. My replicas have shafts that are at least sixteen, sometimes seventeen inches long. It's similar to mine in that it includes familiar Native iconography like the beaver, but I can assure you this is not one of my reproductions." He stood behind the counter in his small shop and waited for the two detectives to ask more.

"How can you be so sure?" Leslie asked. "To me, it seems impossible to tell."

"Experience. And a certain level of knowledge that can only be gained by working with similar materials over many years. It all adds up to what you call being an expert, I guess," Ryan said, shrugging nonchalantly. He continued explaining.

"Sometimes I get a certain feeling about a piece that I can't really put into words. Not bragging, but I've been doing this since I was about seventeen, and I'm fifty-one now. I have a collection of about four hundred weapons, some of which are on loan to museums throughout the country, so I've worked with pieces like this for a long time. After a while, you develop an eye for the ancient—a certain expectation in your mind of what an artifact should look like. When you've seen as many weapons as I have, you kinda develop a library of images stored in your brain. Plus, I've made about that many reproduction weapons myself. So in the field of antique weaponry, I'm considered the go-to expert in the Midwest, although I've evaluated weapons throughout the United States and Europe."

He stood behind the display case and eyed the two detectives with an air of impassivity. Beneath him in the glass showcase, several knives and hatchets lay in gleaming rows, their edges razor sharp, their handles expertly carved to fit the human hand. Deadly but beautiful at the same time.

Leslie appreciated the effort it took to identify the source of the artifacts and to assess their age. She had an eye for ancient Middle Eastern art, particularly pottery and sculpture. She'd honed her skills during her years in the United States Army studying under Dr. Rachel Drummond, a U.S. Army archaeologist and antiques recovery expert. Once again, Leslie took in the essence of the man: his tall, strong physique, his ebony hair and brown eyes that radiated intelligence, and a certain smug assurance that he was right. Leslie understood

Blake's mindset and respected his expertise knowing it was well-earned over years of careful, astute observation.

"So if this weapon is ancient, do you recognize it? Is it one from your collection?" Leslie asked.

Ryan smiled, but the pleasure did not reach his eyes. "I wondered when you were going to get around to that. All of the weapons in my collections are marked on the bottom of the handle with a bullseye—a point with an arch over the top—like an eyebrow over an eye or a fermata in music." He snapped on a pair of latex gloves and reached for the weapon that was lying on the counter. Turning it over, he pointed to the bottom of the shaft. There in the lamplight, DeDe and Leslie could see the faint but distinct marking.

DeDe looked up into Ryan's face. "So this weapon is from your collection?" she asked, carefully watching his reaction.

"Yep, but it's not one I made. It came from my collection of ancient weapons. I can probably trace the owner. I keep records of all my sales. But it will take me a while to search through the computer images to find this particular one."

"What would a weapon like this cost?" Leslie asked.

"Over five thousand dollars. This one dates to the late 1700s. The older the weapon, the more it commands on the market," Ryan explained.

Another thought came to DeDe. "Can some of these weapons be attributed to certain Native leaders or tribes?"

"Now you are pushing the envelope," Ryan said, his eyes wary. "The only way it could be attributed to a certain leader would be through the oral tradition of the tribe. And in some instances, if the family stories have been kept alive, a weapon can be traced to a figure in history. But it doesn't hold much weight with historians in the traditional sense. Without a written record of ownership, there's no paper trail, and its authenticity is usually dismissed. It's really word of mouth, possession over a period of many years, and a certain trust between the owner and buyer." Leslie nodded in understanding.

It was much the same with ancient artifacts that she'd studied.

"But it still holds a place of honor among the family and tribe? Right?" DeDe asked.

"Oh yes. Very much so," Ryan said, pushing back some loose hair.

Leslie looked around the workshop. The smell of wood and beeswax permeated the place. Along one wall, Blake's craftsmanship was displayed on a corkboard: handcrafted axes, bows and arrows, and clubs. They gleamed with a patina that begged you to touch them, and the hand-carved figures on them were exquisite. The wood stove crackled as burning logs gave off a shower of sparks and made a popping sound. Ryan walked over and opened the door to the stove, throwing in a few birch and oak logs. Flames sprang to life, and the wood burned with a rasping hiss filling the room with the pungent smell of smoke.

"Is this weapon attributed to anyone that you know of?" Leslie asked as Ryan walked back to the counter.

"I believe it's probably a Sauk weapon made somewhere in the upper Mississippi Valley, and it probably dates to the early 1800s. The beaver is a typical choice for a carving, but this beaver has a number of interesting details. The tail is laced with crosshatching, and the claws on the front paws are an interesting detail. The wavy designs in the handle suggest waves on water, perhaps representing a river." He hesitated for a moment.

"Yes? Is there something else?" DeDe asked.

Ryan thought, pursed his lips, and then let out a sigh. "You probably didn't notice this. It's slightly discolored." He placed his thumb against the shaft near the end and rubbed gently. When the women leaned in, they could see a round circle of metal about the size of a pencil eraser embedded within the wood. Leslie lifted her head, a quizzical expression on her face.

"What is it?" she asked.

"Lead. The Sauks were well-known for their smelting expertise and frequently spent time in the ore mines in southern Wisconsin, where they extracted lead, which they used to trade for supplies they needed from white men. One leader in particular encouraged his tribe in this endeavor."

Leslie's blue eyes sparkled with fascination. "Really? Who was that?"

"Blackhawk. He was active in the corner where Wisconsin, Illinois, and Iowa meet. And, of course, he is famous for the conflict named after him down near Victory on the Mississippi," Ryan said.

"But what makes you think this weapon belonged to him?"

"The oral legends of the Sauk say he always marked his weapons with inlaid lead. Near the base of the handle." Ryan shrugged. "It comes down to trust in the oral traditions of the family. That's all I know."

"But do you believe it?" DeDe asked.

"It's all a matter of interpretation. Belief in the traditions of the tribe is an individual thing."

He hadn't really answered the question, but she had a feeling this was as far as Ryan would go.

"Why would anyone leave something so important at the murder scene? That seems contradictory to everything you've told us about the reverence that these items had in the family and tribe," Leslie commented.

"This is just a guess, but leaving it behind suggests a powerful message of some kind—one that someone was willing to sacrifice for." Ryan held the two detectives' stare, his brown eyes smoldering with conviction.

"Do you know a Mr. LeMar Burke from New Orleans?" Leslie asked, watching Ryan's face carefully.

Ryan frowned. "Isn't that the name of the guy you found murdered behind some bar down on the river?"

"Yes. Do you know him personally?" Leslie asked.

"No, never heard of him until I read about it in the *La Crosse Sentinel*. Mind if I take a few pictures?" Blake asked. "It will make tracing it a little easier."

"Be my guest," Leslie said.

Blake removed his cell phone from his shirt pocket and snapped several photos. He looked up when he was finished and politely thanked Leslie.

Leslie reached for the weapon, wrapped it back in the bubble wrap, and carefully laid it back in the cardboard box. "Well, Mr. Blake, you've been very helpful. You've given us a lot to think about. Thank you." She shook his hand and tucked the box under her arm.

"I'll get back to you after I've traced the sales record on my computer," he said. DeDe handed him their cards, and they walked out into the sunshine. Before she started her Prius, Leslie glanced over at DeDe, thinking about all the information they'd been told.

"Whaddya think?" she asked casually.

"The guy knows his stuff. The question is—how does it tie in with the murder of LeMar Burke?" DeDe looked back at the small, yellow home with black shutters. To the north of the house, a border of blue spruce was weighed down with the recently fallen snow. DeDe could see the shadow of Ryan Blake watching them from the front window.

"He says he doesn't know who bought it? That doesn't ring true to me. The guy's a walking encyclopedia." She hesitated for a moment. "I think he knows who bought the weapon—he's just not saying at this point. I mean, what are the chances that this weapon would be in his collection? Is he involved, or is someone he knows involved in this? Hard to tell at this point."

"Well, he knows more than he's admitting. So far, we've got a lot of information but not a lot of answers," Leslie said as she leaned over and turned the ignition.

Inside the workshop, Ryan Blake stood behind the front window and watched the detectives head south to La Crosse. Outwardly he appeared calm, but his guts were rolling with apprehension at the news of LeMar Burke's murder. He had to make some phone calls to follow up on his suspicions. It pained him to do it, but he had no choice. It had to be done. He'd been afraid of something like this since a group of young, spirited Native men had broken away from the tribe and joined forces with other insurgents in the area. *How had his son ever gotten involved with those hoodlums?* he thought. *And why was one of his most prized clubs used in a murder?*

He felt the sweat rolling down his armpits. He turned away from the window and pulled out his cell phone, his heart hammering in his chest.

☐

Sam broke off a piece of candy bar and popped it in his mouth, the chocolate sweetness delivering a satisfying rush. He was waiting for a real estate agent at Bluff Management Group to come to the phone. He was about ready to hang up when a female voice perked up at the end of the line.

"Hello, Detective Birkstein? This is Tanya Cadwallader returning your call. How can I help you?" Her voice had the sound of a heavy smoker, husky and deep. Sam swallowed and cleared the chocolate from his throat.

"This is Detective Sam Birkstein. We're investigating the business dealings that your agency had with Mr. LeMar Burke from New Orleans. His phone records show that you or someone at your office had several conversations with him over the past few days. Could you tell me about that? About his interests in the La Crosse area?" Sam tipped his chair backward until he could comfortably put his feet on his desk.

"What do you want to know?" Ms. Cadwallader asked in a suspicious tone.

"Mr. Burke was found murdered near Genoa early Thursday morning. We're investigating his business dealings here in the La Crosse area, trying to make some connections."

He heard a sharp intake of air, then a gushing apology followed. "Oh, my gosh! That's horrible! I didn't know. I apologize," she said, sounding sincere. "I didn't mean to put you off. How can I help?"

"We'd like to know about any business he was conducting in the area, particularly in the area of real estate acquisition," Sam said, reminding her of the original question. "Anything you can tell us would be very helpful."

"Can I meet you somewhere?" she asked. "My schedule is extremely busy with showings for the next several days, but I can squeeze a little time out this afternoon. It may take me a while to explain Mr. Burke's interests around here."

Sam could almost imagine her checking her cell. *Typical real estate agents, always wheeling and dealing, rushing around meeting prospective clients ... and gossiping,* he thought. *I bet she's got some interesting information.* But, in all fairness, he realized the market *was* hot. Every agency in the area was working overtime trying to capitalize on the advantages of the bull market. Agents who didn't jump on buyers' and sellers' interests in real estate offerings right now weren't doing their jobs.

"Fifteen minutes? Drugan's on Third?" Sam suggested.

"That's just around the corner from our office. Make it a half hour. I'll get a booth." The phone clicked off.

☐

Sam didn't make it in a half hour; instead, it was more like forty-five minutes since traffic was congested downtown. Everyone was getting out of work and heading home. *I should've walked,* he thought testily. *In the time it took me to find a parking space, I could've been sitting in a booth.*

He rushed into the restaurant and inhaled the aroma of freshly baked bread. His stomach growled, the smell overwhelming his senses, and he rubbed his belly absentmindedly. Scanning the downstairs for the real estate agent, he realized he was clueless since he'd never met Tanya and didn't know what she looked like.

"Excuse me," he said to a bustling teenage waitress, a tray piled precariously high with food. "I'm looking for a Tanya Cadwallader." She looked at him wide-eyed and pointed to a gal at the entrance.

"Check with her. She's the hostess," she said. She lifted the tray over her shoulder as she hurried away. Sam walked over to the woman at the entrance. When she looked up, he explained his dilemma, and the hostess led him right to the booth where Tanya Cadwallader was checking messages on her phone.

Tanya Cadwallader was a forty-something heavy-boned woman with medium brown hair that had a dramatic, platinum streak across her front bangs, which partially hung over one eye. She wore heavy makeup. Loop earrings with inset turquoise stones dangled in her ears, and a silk scarf in a swirled design accentuated her black dress. Knee-high black leather boots with two-inch heels peeked out from under the table. Her expression was one of detached disinterest, although when her eyes scanned Sam from head to toe, her demeanor subtly changed. Sam noticed the change, filed it away, and turned to the hostess. "I'll have a mocha cappuccino. You?" he asked Tanya, pointing to her.

"An Americano and a raspberry-filled long john, please," she said politely.

Sam slid into the booth and reached inside his jacket for his notepad and a pen.

After introductions and small talk, Sam began asking questions. "What can you tell me about LeMar Burke's activities with your agency?" he began.

Tanya leaned toward Sam, suggesting she had valuable information. In a hushed voice, she said, "LeMar Burke was a big player. His familiarity with high-powered Fortune 500 companies was well-known. He dropped a lot of big names in conversation, and when I looked him up on his website, I realized none of it was exaggerated. He really was a major player in the field of real estate. I guess *tycoon* is a label that would fit his personality."

The realtor's assessment of Burke piqued Sam's curiosity. "If he's such a high-roller, his interest in La Crosse seems unusual," he commented. "I mean, this is a small college town. Not exactly hicksville, but certainly not his normal playing field."

"Yes. You're right about that. But when he explained his specific real estate needs, I had no doubts about why he was looking for property here. Real estate offerings in our area are reasonable compared to those on the East and West coasts. His company was hoping to expand into the Midwest, and La Crosse's natural beauty is a great asset for the type of facility he was hoping to build. La Crosse is centrally located with access to several surrounding states, not to mention Canada." Tanya shrugged nonchalantly. "Made sense to me, and if a deal would have been successful, the entire La Crosse area would have benefited from his company's investment in our community. Believe me, the staff at my agency was rooting for the deal. It would have provided several hundred jobs. He was the best prospect I've ever dealt with, certainly the richest—and now he's dead." She made a disgusted face. "Story of my life."

"Sounded almost too good to be true, didn't it?" Sam asked.

"Yeah. I guess maybe it was, considering what happened to Burke. What's with this murder deal, anyway?"

"The investigation is just getting started," Sam said evasively, avoiding specific facts about the crime. The waitress delivered their orders, and Tanya took a bite of her long john while she waited for Sam to continue.

"I'm wondering if his probe into the real estate market here triggered a reaction from someone or some group that was opposed in principle to his company's interests. Can you tell me what tracts of land he was looking at?" Sam asked.

"Yes, I can," Tanya said. She reached into her humongous leather bag next to her on the seat, pulled a file folder from it, and opened it. "I met with him several times last fall, once in January and twice in February. He was interested in two specific properties, one of which was on the market and one of which was privately owned and not for sale." She gave Sam a meaningful look. "However, just because a property isn't for sale doesn't mean you don't pursue the owner and make an offer. On the contrary, I think he looked at the owner's refusal as a challenge, and Burke was a man who did not back away from a challenge."

Sam's eyebrows lifted at this revelation. He cocked his head to the side and said, "And the old real estate axiom was at work: 'Any property can be for sale at any time if the price is right.'" Sam watched Tanya's reaction.

She smiled warmly. "Absolutely. We're never shy about approaching people who have prime real estate that is not for sale. Sometimes you get lucky and hit the jackpot."

"So—back to this land. Where was it? Who owned it?" Sam asked, staring at his notepad scribbled with bits of sporadic notes. He took a sip of his cappuccino.

"One piece of property was out toward Valley View Mall. It actually was within the city limits of Onalaska." Tanya took a sip of her coffee as she scanned her papers and moved her finger down the photocopied fact sheet. "It was a one-hundred-acre piece for sale by an investment group from Minneapolis. But Burke wanted access to the river and its charm, which that property did not have. So I approached the private owner south of La Crosse. Burke had been here earlier in January and had spotted the acreage. The property is actually across from Blackhawk Park along U.S. Hwy. 35. Easy access to the river, gorgeous views of the surrounding bluffs, a creek that empties into the main channel of the Mississippi, almost one hundred acres of natural beauty, and a couple of caves which supposedly have ancient Oneota petroglyphs—all things that got the attention of Burke in a big way. His visionary prowess came completely alive. He was smitten big time."

"Owner?" Sam was taking fastidious notes now, his pencil racing across his notepad.

"A Mr. Terry Waite—with an 'e' on the end of Wait—a professor at the university. Inherited the property from his bachelor uncle back in the sixties when he was just a kid. Over the years, its value increased, and now it's a gold mine of a property. Although we didn't talk price when I introduced Burke to the professor, a million dollars would be a steal for a guy like Burke who had an impressive budget."

"What was this guy's reaction when he met Burke?"

"Well ... I met the professor first to try and break the ice, and believe me, it was icy. Waite made it clear he was not interested in Burke's offer, whatever that might be. But as I talked, he softened somewhat and agreed to at least meet with him."

"You must have the gift of persuasion. How'd it go?" Sam asked, his hazel eyes holding her gaze.

"Okay at first. They skirted around each other for a while, but when the topic shifted to the care of the land, environmentalism, a carbon footprint, and all that stuff, Waite found out what Burke's real intentions were. Their environmental philosophy wasn't even close to lining up. They were on opposite ends of the spectrum. Waite worshiped at the feet of Mother Nature and believed in a hands-off policy; Burke was an opportunist who looked at the environment as something at his disposal—a means to an end—the raw material to make his dream resort a reality. After a heated discussion, Waite totally clammed up and refused to discuss any negotiations that might lead to a sale. It pretty much went dead in the water."

"Burke's reaction?"

"Not good. He was terribly disappointed, but he was determined. He insisted I continue to try and convince Waite to come to the table."

"Did you?"

"Several times over the course of the last few months."

"Did Burke contact Waite?"

"I don't know. He might have, but I wasn't aware of any communication they might have had."

Sam made a note to check LeMar Burke's phone records again to see if Terry Waite had been called in the recent past.

"We've learned that Burke met with someone at The BonBon Hotel on the day he was murdered. Tall, longish dark hair, wore some kind of Native American style jacket. Sound familiar?" Sam asked.

Two little frown lines creased Tanya's forehead. "Not to me. Do you have a photo?"

"No, we're workin' on that."

"Sorry, I can't help you," Tanya said. Sam believed her.

"Well, you've given us some valuable information. I'll email you a photo of the guy in the lobby as soon as we can get one. Here's my card if you think of anything else that might be helpful." Sam slid his card across the table.

Tanya gave him a puzzled look that made Sam suddenly uncomfortable.

"What?" Sam asked, his eyes widening with discomfort.

"Are you free? You know—playing the field? I have a daughter who's—"

Sam reddened and interrupted, waving one hand in front of him. "No. No. I'm very happily married." He started to get out of the booth.

"Sorry. I had to ask. No harm done?" Her smile was soft and shy. Sam wondered if she really did have a daughter. Then he thought about Paul's comments earlier at The BonBon. *Were women really attracted to him?* He doubted it.

He smiled. "No offense taken. Thanks for the help."

9

SATURDAY, MARCH 23

Jim sat at the dining room table chewing a second piece of whole wheat toast dripping with raspberry jam. He'd already eaten two poached eggs and two strips of crisply fried bacon. Carol sat opposite him, studying him. She worried about the stress of his job on his health and how he might react to the news she had to tell him. She took a deep breath and started.

"Jim? Honey?" His eyes drifted away from the *La Crosse Sentinel* lying next to his plate. The headlines about the murder in Genoa had galvanized his attention since they'd sat down to a quiet, early breakfast together. Lillie and Henri were still asleep.

"Yeah, babe. I'm listenin'," he said absentmindedly, but he really wasn't. He felt an irritation at being interrupted while skimming the article about the murder. He was still racking his brain about possible motives and, of course, the unique murder weapon.

"Really?" She tilted her head. "Listening is an act of love. It requires a response," Carol reminded him, leaning over the table toward him. "And eye contact."

Jim thought she sounded just like her sister, Vivian Jensen, the psychologist.

"What's your point, hon?" he asked, looking up at her. Even without makeup, her smooth complexion and dark brown hair made him sit up and pay attention. Her large brown eyes had fascinated him since the first time they'd dated. Nothing had changed about that. After three years of marriage, he'd learned to appreciate the mind and will behind the eyes, and now, when he saw the steely determination in them, he wondered what Carol had on her mind.

These sessions had become more frequent lately. They popped up every couple of months since he'd been seriously wounded by Maddog Pierson in a confrontation last fall in a gravel quarry. *Not this again*, he thought. Irritated that Carol had disrupted an opportunity to review the facts of the current murder on his agenda, he reined in his tongue and answered politely, "We seem to be talking past each other." He pushed the paper farther away from his plate in an attempt to placate her.

"I'm worried about you," Carol said, reaching over and taking his hand in hers.

Jim sighed and rubbed his eyes with his other hand. *Here we go again*, he thought.

"What are you worried about? I'm fine. What's going on now?" Jim asked, his irritation growing. His hair was wild, sticking up here and there, but it was pleasantly appealing. "What's wrong now?"

"I think you should have a really good physical checkup. After all, you are fifty-five, and your dad died of a heart attack when he was just sixty-one." Carol's eyes moved over his face, looking for signs of resistance.

"So?" The reference to his age pushed his buttons, and he fought down the urge to level Carol with the facts of his optimal health. He patted her hand and leaned back in his chair folding his arms across his chest, focusing his attention on her.

"I just want to be sure that you're healthy," she said, her brown eyes serious.

"Well, after our little romp in bed last night, you should know that I'm totally on my game." A look of triumph crossed Jim's features, and his blue eyes sparkled. Then, seeing Carol's worried look, his face softened. He sat forward and leaned his arms on the table. "Honey, you're only as old as your mind says you are, and my mind is sharp as a tack. You cook healthy meals, and we watch our weight. My blood pressure has always been good, and I take very little medication. A statin. Big deal," he finished. He took another bite of toast and a sip of coffee.

"I know, but an active sex life isn't always an accurate indicator of good health, is it?" she said.

"It is in my book," he commented casually, looking back at the paper. "You can start worrying when I can't get it up anymore."

"Age creeps up on you, Jim." Carol continued. "The kids are a handful, and I know when we got married, you didn't expect to be a father again. Now you've got two children under seven. It's like starting all over," Carol said. She sipped her coffee, her brown eyes pensive.

When is this litany going to end? Jim thought.

He paused in an effort to appear rational and in control. He calmly began building his case. "I did start over. And have I ever complained once about the kids? Jeez, Carol, I love them and you with all my heart. I know what my life would be like without you. I lived it. Remember? I was lonely and isolated and becoming bitter. And believe me, I'm thrilled with the way things have worked out. I wouldn't trade one thing about my life." He hesitated a moment. "Well, that's not totally true. I'd change what happened to Sara, but—" He blew out a breath of frustration. "You know what I mean." His blue eyes seemed to darken whenever the subject of his estranged daughter from his first marriage was mentioned.

"Yes, I do know what you mean." She watched Jim return to the newspaper, his eyes scanning the article about the murder. "Anything being reported that's wildly speculative, or are all the facts about the case accurate so far?" She sipped her coffee and ate some oatmeal.

"It's pretty much accurate. We're trying to keep the news about the unusual weapon under wraps, but rumors are circulating on Facebook, Twitter, and Snapchat. The tweeters are rumbling along in their naive misinformation and dramatizing everything, which is pretty typical these days," Jim said sourly.

"How do you know that? Do you keep up with all those sites? I thought you hated social media."

"*I* don't keep up with them, but Leslie and DeDe do. They're my go-tos when it comes to social media. And Emily's no slouch either when it comes to that."

"Well, I guess you haven't seen the latest Twitter post from Sara then, have you?" Carol asked, dreading the reaction Jim might have when he found out the latest news.

Sara had abruptly quit her teaching job at St. Ignatius Catholic School in Genoa after her abduction. When she left the area, she'd enrolled in graduate school at St. Thomas, a reputable Catholic college in the Twin Cities, and pushed the restart button of life without the counsel of her father or her fraternal twin, John. Both of them had been frozen out. It was a sore subject all around.

Jim looked up, apprehension crossing his face. "I knew it. She's gone over the edge, hasn't she?" His eyes were wide with suspicion. "What's happened now? She join some hippy commune in California?"

"Jim, really? You need to settle down," Carol warned, staring across the table at the growing trepidation shadowing his face. "She has to find her way back on her own terms. We've talked about this more than I care to remember."

"So what's going on now?" he snapped, ignoring the paper, his attention finally focused on Carol.

"It seems Father Knight is no longer a priest, and your daughter is no longer unattached and playing the field." Carol leaned back waiting for the verbal blast.

"Whaddya mean?" Jim asked quietly, swallowing hard. His face paled, and he lowered the newspaper to the table.

"Sara and Jerome are engaged, Jim. She announced it on Facebook and Twitter last night. Big diamond, romantic dinner at a posh French restaurant in St. Paul overlooking the glittering lights along the Mississippi. All very proper." Carol's face was pinched, but then her features softened as she looked wistfully at Jim, remembering the day they'd become engaged. "They looked extremely happy. Remember how happy we were?" She watched him carefully as a deafening silence descended in the dining room. Jim's face was frozen in disbelief. Carol waited and waited.

"Jim, say something."

He sat stone-faced, looking out the dining room window. He seemed to be a thousand miles away. "There are no words," he said quietly. When he looked back at Carol, the hurt in his eyes made tears well up in her own.

"I'm sure she'll call and let you know. Just be patient. It'll all work out," Carol said, but the reassurance she tried to deliver sounded cheesy and fell flat. "What do you need? How can I help?" she asked desperately.

Jim shook his head and pushed the newspaper away from his plate. He stood up and went to the bedroom, where he dressed in blue jeans and a sweatshirt. In the back hallway to the garage, he slipped on a pair of socks and his athletic shoes. He was putting on his old ski jacket when Carol appeared.

"What are you doing?" she asked.

"Goin' to see Sam. I'll be back later," he told her curtly. Seeing the concern in her eyes, he leaned over and brushed her cheek with a quick kiss. "I'll be back by eleven. Let's take Lillie and Henri to Battle Island this afternoon, okay?" he said softly. He zipped his jacket. Carol felt a stab in her heart when she looked into his blue eyes.

"That sounds great. I love you, you know," Carol whispered.

"I know."

☐

Jim wandered the aisles of the Onalaska Home Depot, killing time before he met Sam. Scrutinizing the products on the display racks, he picked up random home improvement supplies that he really didn't need: a box of wood screws, a package of fine grit sandpaper, some cheap paintbrushes, and some LED light bulbs. Not exactly his idea of retail therapy. *Let me loose in a men's shop in Paris—now that's retail therapy*, he thought. While he aimlessly shopped, he thought about his daughter and the latest change in her life.

He was hurt that she'd chosen to tell the world about her engagement before she'd even bothered to call him. It was just another painful reminder of the changes in their relationship throughout the last year.

After Sara's abduction by Maddog Pierson, nothing had been the same between them. Jim had tried to give his daughter the space she needed to make her own decisions, but it seemed like all the years of trust and companionship they'd enjoyed had gone up in smoke when the criminal world knocked down the door of her life and stomped on her trust. Sara hadn't called in over two months. Their last conversation was stilted and awkward, something that had never characterized their interactions before. A relationship that had once been loving and close had now gone sour. So many things between them had changed. Jim hated it. *That damn Maddog*, he fumed.

He grabbed a pliers and threw it in his cart. A guy down the aisle looked at him with alarm and quickly walked away.

Jim stood impatiently in line, leaning on his cart behind an obese woman with three kids on the fat side who were clearing the shelves of candy and chips, tossing them in the shopping cart, oblivious to her ranting. The longer Jim listened to them, the madder he got. She finally gave up and let the kids have what they wanted. *Spoiled brats*, he thought grumpily.

While he waited in line, he texted Sam, but not before he'd checked the time. He knew Sam and Leslie enjoyed the relaxed atmosphere of Saturday mornings with time for an extended run with Paco, a decent breakfast, and an extra cup of coffee—things that never happened during the hectic rat race of the work week. *Just wait until they get kids*, he thought.

Sam texted him back and agreed to meet him at Sharon's Diner for coffee at nine-thirty. The retro establishment was a popular north side eatery complete with red leather booths, a black and white linoleum tile floor, waitresses who wore frilly, white aprons, and good, home-cooked food and wonderful baked goods.

By nine-thirty, Jim had slipped into a booth and ordered a coffee and a gigantic cinnamon roll. *So much for my healthy diet*, he thought. His mood had smoothed out somewhat. The place was bustling with families out for Saturday morning breakfast, and although it was on the noisy side, the diner had a good buzz and a friendly atmosphere. Sam breezed through the door ten minutes later. He ordered coffee and listened to Jim rattle off the facts about his daughter for ten minutes.

"Sara's engaged to a priest?" Sam asked, his eyes wide with shock. "*The* Father Knight who used to be at St. Ignatius in Genoa? Her former boss … *and priest?*" Sam let out a huff of air. "Sounds like something straight from a soapie. How does that work?"

"Yeah, I know. Tell me about it. I couldn't believe it either when Carol told me." Jim's face crinkled in confusion. "That news came right out of the blue and slapped me upside the head. I never saw it coming."

"When's the wedding?" Sam asked.

"How would I know?" Jim snapped angrily. "I just found out about it thirdhand from Carol, who saw it on Facebook." Jim leaned over the table, supporting his head with one fist, his eyes downcast. His cinnamon roll sat untouched. "Talk about a kick in the teeth."

"Are you gonna eat that cinnamon roll?" Sam asked, pointing at it.

Jim pushed it toward him. "Help yourself."

Sam hungrily tore off a piece of roll and stuffed it in his mouth while he had an argument with himself about giving any kind of advice. When Jim stayed silent, Sam decided to wade in. "Listen," he said, unsure if his suggestions would be accepted, "I'm making some assumptions, but you asked me here for advice. Am I right?"

Jim nodded. "I guess so. Am I going to like what you have to say?" he asked, a frown perched over his blue eyes, which were flashing with anger.

"Maybe. Maybe not, but here goes," Sam said, leaning toward Jim and pushing his coffee cup aside. He chewed on the cinnamon roll, the white gooey frosting coating his lips.

"Women who've been traumatized can go through some strange phases. It's all part of forgiving themselves and eventually forgiving their abuser. Their emotional equilibrium takes a major hit, and it takes time for them to find a new norm." He stopped briefly to lick the frosting from his lips. "Sometimes they lash out at the people they love the most. Their trust levels are incredibly low. Believe me, there are times when I come home, and I'm not sure which Leslie is going to greet me. She still has nightmares and can't sleep sometimes, and it's been over three years since Wade tried to kill her. And God help you if you ever startle her. She might deck you or flatten you against the nearest wall, which she's more than capable of doing."

The image of Leslie's startled face yesterday in the lab came back to Jim.

Sam continued. "All I know is this—you've got to be steady and be there. It's tough, but you have to roll with the punches, Chief."

"Punches? I'd be glad to get a few. I get nothing," he ranted in a hoarse whisper. "In case you didn't know it, Sara's pretty much shut me out of her life. And since she's in the Twin Cities, I never get a chance to take her out for a sandwich or a cappuccino. We used to do that all the time."

"She'll come around. It just takes time."

"That's what I was afraid you'd say. And I've given it time. It's been at least six months."

"I know."

"So?"

"Give her more time," Sam concluded. "You can't rush these things. Believe me, I know. I've lived it."

Jim sat silent, absorbing the challenges that lay ahead. He didn't know whether he should thank Sam for his advice or get up and walk out the door.

"So Father Knight is no longer a priest?" Sam asked after a few moments of silence, still trying to wrap his head around the news.

"You can't be married and be a Catholic priest," Jim said flatly, looking at Sam with hooded eyes. "But I'll give him credit. At least he didn't choose the alternative."

"What alternative?" Sam asked.

"Having an affair and knocking up my daughter."

"That's true," Sam said. "See? You're starting to see the positive side of things." He smiled widely. "Wow! Just think. He must really be crazy about Sara to be willing to set aside his calling as a Catholic priest. That takes some balls."

Jim made a wry face and snickered softly. "Bad choice of words, buddy, but I guess his sacrifice is another positive, huh?"

"I'd say so," Sam said. He held up a finger. "Remember, time and patience. You gotta be in it for the long haul. Isn't that what parents are supposed to do?" His hazel eyes seemed to plumb the depths of Jim's parental commitment.

"Yeah. That's what parents do," Jim said flatly.

☐

Bobby Rude stared at the doctor, unwilling to believe the devastating news he'd been told about his father. His face was paler than usual, and sweat had broken out along his hairline. He felt his heart ramp up until it was banging against his rib cage.

"So, you're telling me my dad is going to die. Isn't that what terminal means? He's not going to live long, right?" Bobby asked, gripping the wooden arms of the chair. His brown eyes were liquid pools of grief.

To Dr. Westphal, Bobby seemed much older than thirteen. His eyes told the story—this kid was wise, but not by choice. *Life has taught him some hard lessons*, the doctor thought.

Dr. Westphal glanced at Jed Klumstein, who'd brought Bobby to the Tomah VA hospital. *God, I hate this*, the doctor thought. He fixed his eyes back on the tragic teenage boy and began his explanation.

"I'll keep this simple, Bobby. Your dad has what is called hepatic cirrhosis of the liver, brought on by years of chronic alcoholism. He gets very fatigued—you might have noticed that the last couple of months—and he's lost a lot of weight. His abdomen is quite swollen, and he bruises easily. A few days ago, he started bleeding from his rectum. I'm going to recommend that he enter our VA nursing home. With some intensive nursing interventions, he may be able to come home in a few months, but ..." The doctor sighed audibly, not wanting to deliver the final blow. "... the other possibility is that he will gradually slide into a coma and at some point, pass away." Dr. Westphal stopped talking, trying to let Bobby absorb the stark facts about his father's condition. Bullshitting the kid now wouldn't work. He'd had way too much real-life experience. The office was so quiet he could hear the ticking of the clock on the wall above his desk. Finally, Dr. Westphal asked, "Do you have any questions?"

Despite his stoic expression, he could see that Bobby was struggling to accept this latest update. After all, the kid was only a teenager.

"How much time does he have?" Bobby asked quietly, bowing his head, avoiding eye contact.

"It's hard to say. Your visits mean a lot to him, Bobby. I'd encourage you to keep coming and spending as much time with him as you can. That will have a huge effect on his mood," Dr. Westphal said. "Do you have anyone you can lean on for support?"

Bobby looked at Jed, his eyes like those of a lost child. "My mom left almost four years ago now, and I don't have any other family, but Jed's been good to me. He's my neighbor, and I go to his place a lot. And Lt. Higgins checks on me every once in a while."

"I'm sorry to be the bearer of bad news, son. If there's anything else I can do for you, please let me know, okay?" Dr. Westphal said. "We have counselors here who can help you."

"Sure. Thanks for all you're doing for my dad. I know he appreciates it," Bobby said as he stood up and walked toward the door of the office. "I'll try to come back again next weekend," he said as he left the office.

Jed followed Bobby into the hall. He wrapped his arm around the boy's shoulders. When he looked over at the teenager, tears were glistening in his eyes, and a few escaped down his cheeks. They walked silently to the car and climbed in.

"Bobby ..." Jed started.

"Don't say anything, Jed. There's nothing to say," Bobby said softly, wiping his tears on his sleeve.

At that moment, Jed was sure he'd never seen a sorrier sight. And Bobby was right; there was nothing he could say that would improve the situation. Jed started the car and headed back to Genoa.

☐

By Saturday afternoon, the air had warmed. The sun's beams produced more energy each day as its angle to the earth increased. The sixteen-inch snowfall from Wednesday's storm had shrunk rapidly as the temperatures rocketed up. The creeks and rivers were swollen with melt-off. As fickle as Wisconsin weather could be, Jim felt spring in the air, but being the practical person that he was, he braced himself for a capricious rollercoaster ride of variable weather over the next couple of months.

After meeting with Sam at the north side diner Saturday morning, Jim and Carol packed up the kids and headed for the river in the afternoon. Jim parked at a traffic turnout along U.S. 35 just south of Victory near Blackhawk Park along the Mississippi River. He and Lillie got out of the truck and read the historical marker about the fighting at Battle Island between Blackhawk and the United States Army. Lillie solemnly stared at the vast wideness of the river where the Indian mothers and children had been shot and drowned. Jim wasn't sure what thoughts Lillie was having, but her solemn face suggested she understood the serious nature of the conflict despite her young years.

In the distance, they watched a bald eagle zero in on a fish in open water. The huge bird shoved off a branch that was as thick as a man's arm and swooped downward from the gnarly oak tree along the shoreline. As it picked up speed, Lillie slapped Jim's arm in excitement.

"Look, Bapa!" She pointed at the majestic bird as it hurtled toward the water like a rock flung from a slingshot.

"Keep your eye on him, Lillie. He's goin' after a fish," Jim said, amazed by the drama unfolding before them.

The eagle dive-bombed the water in a spectacular lunge, its talons extended. Splashing the surface with dramatic expertise, the bird came up with a fish clenched in its razor-sharp claws. Lillie's eyes widened when the eagle landed on the shore just a hundred yards from them, where he tore the fish apart with its golden hooked beak, blood and guts spreading on the frozen, snow-covered ground.

"Boy, that eagle was fast," she whispered, looking up at Jim with an innocence that made his heart trip. "And he was really hungry."

"They're awesome predators," Jim commented casually. They continued to watch the eagle tearing at the fish, swallowing hunks of flesh.

"Bapa, I'm so glad you brought me here. This is a very special place," Lillie said seriously, slipping her little hand into Jim's.

"Yes, it is. That's why there's a park named Blackhawk and a marker telling his story."

"We should always remember how many people died here," Lillie said reverently. Jim anticipated a question bubbling to the surface. "Does that make this a holy place?" she asked.

The Catholics must be getting their message across, he thought.

"Well, normally *holy* is a word we use to describe God and believers. But some people might describe this place as sacred."

"Is that the same as holy?"

"Pretty much."

They were silent for a while. The noise of the traffic rumbling along the highway seemed like an intrusion in the beautiful setting. But in the silent moments between the incessant whining of wheels on pavement, Jim could sense the deep imprint of history on this place—the conflict and bloodshed that had soaked into the soil and water and the unanswered questions that would never be adequately explained or rationalized. This was a place of human drama. A place of triumph and disaster. A place of birth and death. A place of love and hatred. A place of damnation and salvation. He hoped someday Lillie could appreciate the layers of human experiences and the chronicle of struggle that had seeped into the land and river.

"Jim? Some hot chocolate?" Carol asked, holding out a mug.

Startled, he realized he'd gone off on some deep philosophical tangent into the past. Lillie looked at him expectantly and dropped a couple of marshmallows into his cup. Henri toddled innocently in the parking lot, picking up rocks and throwing them toward the moving traffic. Jim took the mug of hot chocolate and sipped it.

"The kid's got a good left hook," Jim said, smiling, watching Henri's throwing antics. "Might be a pitcher hidden somewhere in there."

"Henri. Stay over here," Carol warned, crooking her finger at him when he wandered toward the steep bank next to the highway. She was bundled up in a hooded ski jacket and heavy snow boots. Her brunette hair was mussed, and her skin had turned a rosy pink color in the cold air. Jim thought she looked beautiful. She turned back to him. "I'm glad we came, aren't you?" Her smile was wide and lovely.

"Definitely. There's a lot to see around here, even in the winter, and the weather today is gorgeous," Jim said, breathing the crisp air. "Before you know it, we'll be back on the river in the *Little Eddy* fishing and camping." They finished their cups of hot chocolate, and he said, "How about a trip to Culver's for hamburgers and ice cream?"

"Yeah! Let's go," Lillie shouted, punching her fist in the air, heading for the Suburban.

"You're gettin' by cheap, buddy. Just wait 'til they're sixteen," Carol grinned. "They'll be eating us out of house and home and asking for twenty-dollar bills to fill the gas tank."

Jim chuckled and grabbed Carol's hand. "Bring it on," he said, smiling.

10

D'Marius Blake, a.k.a. Little Hawk, pried his eyes open and squinted at the ceiling of the winter lodge. The light of dawn was just creeping over the Kickapoo Valley Reserve where the Ho-Chunk camp was located on a 1,200-acre piece of land, which was part of over 7,300 acres set aside in a nature reserve managed by the Wisconsin DNR. The traditional Ho-Chunk shelter felt snug and safe, its branches covered with a birchbark roof and insulated by deep snow.

Gray shafts of smoke curled toward the vent hole in the roof. The slumbering figures of his compatriots were hunched and quiet in their sleeping bags. Someone farted loudly, and Little Hawk smiled. He sat up, leaning back on his elbows as the sleeping bag fell away from his bare chest. Chunks of blackened logs in the firepit still glowed with radiant heat.

Little Hawk quietly rose from his sleeping bag, slipped his well-worn jeans over his long underwear, and stepped outside the shelter to relieve himself in the snowbank. Coming back in, he tugged a sweatshirt over his head and grabbed a few birch logs from the stack of wood next to the door. He walked to the firepit, stirred the coals, and laid the logs on the glowing embers. Almost immediately, they crackled into yellow flames that licked upward toward the smoke-stained ceiling.

At twenty-two, D'Marius Blake had inherited many of his father Ryan's traits—in particular, his impressive physique. He was strong and tall with a deep chest, raven black hair, and dark brown eyes set in an aristocratic face. His brown skin glowed like polished bronze, and he had long, fine-boned fingers like those of a craftsman—like those of his father. He was known among the insurgents for being headstrong, impatient, and outspoken. There was nothing meek or timid about Little Hawk.

He was proud that he could trace his lineage back to Blackhawk, the famous or infamous warrior, depending on your opinion of historical events. In fact, he credited his feisty temper and unwillingness to compromise to his ancient progenitor.

Blackhawk, the Sauk warrior, protected and defended his land and family from white settlers and marauding soldiers, but he was eventually defeated in a series of skirmishes in 1832 that culminated in intense fighting with U.S. soldiers at Battle Hollow and Battle Island on the Mississippi River near Victory, Wisconsin. After his ignoble defeat, Blackhawk was relegated to embarrassment and scorn. Taken to prisons out East, he was paraded as the vanquished warrior before thousands who wanted to see the spectacle of a humiliated, captive savage. Eventually, he returned to the Rock River Valley, where the members of his family gradually faded away, decimated by illness, starvation, and poverty.

Despite the hundreds of years separating Little Hawk from his tribal hero, he still identified deeply with the pain of losing their Native lands and the humiliation and disgrace his people had endured from white men. That was the whole purpose of the insurgent movement—to reclaim and protect those lands that had been taken away from them in the treaty cessions of the mid-1800s. It seemed like a lost cause, but someone had to keep the dream alive.

Their beloved homeland in southern Wisconsin and northern Iowa and Illinois had been swallowed up by white settlers. Now it was filled with every conceivable luxury of modern life. Its woods, fields, creeks, and rivers were tainted with pollution, paved into submission, and degraded by modern life. To Little Hawk, it seemed like a deep, dark scar cut across the land and water of their sacred home.

"Hey, what're you doin' up so early?" a voice behind Little Hawk whispered, startling him out of his daydream.

"I didn't drink as much as you did last night," Little Hawk admitted, grinning, still sitting on his haunches before the fire, poking the coals with a stick. He gazed over at his friend. "You don't look so hot."

"I feel even worse than I look," Tommy said sullenly. "God, that vodka can creep up on you, and then it's too late. I feel like I've been hit between the eyes with a sledgehammer." Tommy DeFlorian did look terrible—pale and withdrawn. Sitting cross-legged before the fire, he asked, "What did you think of the meeting last night?"

"Bright lightning, loud thunder, dark clouds, no rain. That's what I think," D'Marius said sarcastically. Tommy seemed puzzled by the saying. Noticing his confused look, Little Hawk explained.

"This group is nothing but a bunch of weekend warriors who want to do a little camping and drinking and club throwing. They have no idea how to achieve their goals. They just keep rutting around in the muck. Me," Little Hawk poked his chest, "I've got plans. I know what I'm doin', you'll see." His eyes glowed with a kind of fervent intensity that scared Tommy right down to the soles of his shoes.

"You better be careful," Tommy warned, looking sideways out of the corner of his eye at Little Hawk. "Your dad is pretty worried about you, you know."

Little Hawk's head jerked up, and he stared at Tommy with hard, glittering eyes. "How do you know that? Who you been talkin' to?" he snarled.

"My neighbor, Tim."

"That windbag?!" Little Hawk spat with indignation. "He gets his latest information at McDonald's from a bunch of old guys who've got their heads up their asses and farts in their pants. Not exactly stuff you can rely on," he said caustically.

"Whatever." Tommy shrugged, trying to defuse the spark of anger in Little Hawk's face.

"What'd he tell you?" Little Hawk asked in a hoarse whisper.

Tommy smiled subtly. "He told me he saw a couple of women leave your dad's place Friday. They were at his shop for about an hour poking around. Tim went over later and found out they were detectives from the La Crosse Sheriff's Department. They're investigating the murder of that big shot from New Orleans they found down by the river. You hear about that?"

"Ya, I heard about it. So what?" Little Hawk stared into the fire and thought Tommy seemed uncharacteristically focused for somebody who had a roaring hangover.

"They found one of your dad's clubs next to the victim." Little Hawk felt his insides turn to water. Tommy watched him carefully, then repeated, "Like I said, you better be careful."

"What's that supposed to mean?" D'Marius snarled. Sometimes Little Hawk made no effort to disguise his arrogant disposition.

Tommy got up and moved to the other side of the lodge, leaving Little Hawk brooding in front of the fire. After several moments, Little Hawk stood up and began packing up his belongings. He'd get no support for his plans from this group. *Bunch of wussies*, he thought.

He had dreams of restoring Native land to its rightful owners. A place where ancestral lands could once again be fruitful, where Natives could occupy places of dignity and honor. The words of Blackhawk sprang into Little Hawk's mind. "We always had plenty. Our children never cried with hunger. Our people were never in want. Rock River was a beautiful country. I loved my towns, my cornfields, and the home of my people. I fought for it."

D'Marius felt his heart stir with resolve. "I'll fight for our people and our land, Blackhawk. You'll see. I will never give up," he whispered as he walked resolutely to his pickup. Throwing his gear in the truck box, he got in and roared along the snow-packed trail in the meadow until he came to the gravel access road. *Time to move on*, he thought. He spun the gravel and floored the accelerator on the truck, his mind whirling with possibilities.

□

Jamie Alberg slouched behind the wheel of his Jeep. He was parked on a steep ridge above the Ho-Chunk campsite. Far below in the valley, the young Natives' camp was silent and snow-covered. Despite the night temperature of twenty-four degrees, Jamie had kept warm. The zero-degree rating of the Kelty sleeping bag he'd purchased at REI had proven accurate. Still, he had only slept a few hours toward morning on the front passenger seat of his vehicle.

His overview of the camp was a bluff above the Kickapoo River, dubbed the most crooked river in the United States. It lay silent and frozen like a white winding snake as it zigzagged through the bottom of the valley. A hoary frost had crept in during the night and left the landscape looking like something out of *Grimm's Fairy Tales*—a lacy milieu of white frost that clung to the trees and grass. This morning he'd spotted several herds of white-tailed deer among the thick stands of pines, and squirrels scampered among the oaks and maples, leaping athletically from branch to branch despite the freezing temperatures. Two scarlet cardinals in survival mode fed on seed pods near his vehicle and nibbled on baneberries clinging to their stalks.

He lowered his binoculars, resting them on his down-filled vest. Pouring a cup of coffee from his thermos, he wrote a few notes in the tablet he'd flipped on the dashboard during the night. *My archaeological note-taking skills have come in handy during this surveillance*, Jamie thought. *I lucked out when they didn't notice me outside the shelter last night.* He realized the information he'd discovered about the group's plans would be invaluable in the investigation of the murder of

LeMar Burke—if he could get Higgins and his team to listen to him. Thankfully, the young men in the bark-roofed shelter had been more concerned about getting drunk than in keeping their agenda hidden. *That may come back to haunt them*, he thought.

His foray into the valley on his snowshoes in the bright moonlight had been a perilous gamble, but he wasn't stupid. He'd been in other scrapes during his short lifetime, and they'd taught him that anything of value entailed a few risks.

Jamie watched Little Hawk burn up the road, heading back to the main highway toward La Farge. He reached over and started the Jeep. Cautiously, he backed away from his lookout over the river, followed a camp road through some scrubby brush out to the main road, and headed toward La Crosse, hoping for an opportunity to relay his information to Lt. Higgins at the law enforcement center.

11

MONDAY, MARCH 25

The wailing cries of baby Max pierced the silence of the early morning hours at the Saner home on Market Street. Paul groaned and felt Ruby's side of the bed. Cold. She must already be up. Baby Max had fits of colic. Although Ruby was exhausted, she never complained. He sat up at the edge of the bed and glanced at the time—5:10 a.m.

Gazing out of the second-story window to the street below, he knew he should offer to walk the little guy. Instead, he stumbled to the bathroom and stepped in the shower, letting the hot rivulets of soapy water beat on his shoulders. Afterward, he slipped into a T-shirt and boxers and descended the stairs to the living room, where Ruby was feeding their son.

"I thought I'd relieve you," Paul said softly.

"Well, seeing he's nursing, I don't think that's going to happen unless there's something you haven't told me," Ruby teased. "You're not thinking of a sex change, are you?" She grinned wickedly. Her auburn hair was gathered in a chaotic swirl, the curls collected in a clip on top of her head. Sitting in the Amish rocker in her plush blue bathrobe, she crossed her shapely legs and watched as Paul sprawled on the couch and clicked on the TV. After several minutes, she stood and walked over to him.

"Here, you can burp him while I take a shower," she said, handing him the baby.

Little Max made squeaking noises as Paul rhythmically patted his little back, hoping the wailing wouldn't start up again. An image on the TV screen caught his attention. He quit patting his son's back and leaned forward, balancing Max in his arms while he turned up the volume on the remote.

A local news reporter from WKBT, one of two local La Crosse television stations, began talking as he stood in the early morning darkness in front of the law enforcement center:

"The murder of a New Orleans man found behind a bar in Genoa during the recent snowstorm on Wednesday has become a challenging mystery to law enforcement officials. According to sources close to the investigation, an unusual murder weapon was found near the body. A ball club from the 1700s, a weapon known to be used by Sauk and Fox Indian tribes in the Upper Mississippi Valley region hundreds of years ago, was discovered at the scene of the crime. There is no word yet on a motive for the murder, but the weapon has left La Crosse County investigators scratching their heads. I'm talking this morning with Jamie Alberg, an employee of the Mississippi Valley Archeological Center, who has a broad knowledge of local Native American culture."

Paul grimaced and stared at the ceiling. *Higgins is going to go ballistic*, he thought.

"Can you tell us where someone might find a weapon such as the one used in this crime?" the reporter asked.

The camera panned toward Jamie, who swelled with the confidence of an expert in his field. Paul cringed at the thought of Higgins watching the newscast. *He's going to blow a gasket*, he thought.

"These weapons are known to have been made and used by Sauk warriors in the Upper Mississippi Valley since the early 1700s.

Nowadays," he brandished a photo of the club, "a weapon like the one found at the murder scene would most likely have come from someone's private collection. Many are in museums around the country, but they're very rare, and this unusual weapon creates an interesting twist to the investigation the police are conducting." He lowered the photo to his side.

Jamie rambled on for a few more moments until the reporter interrupted him and ended the interview. Paul muted the TV volume then began texting Higgins. *Not good,* he thought. *Not good at all, especially for a Monday morning.*

□

Jim stood in his boxers and T-shirt in his bedroom, scrolling through his texts on his phone until he eyed one from Paul that had arrived at 5:32 in the morning. He scrunched up his face in confusion and opened the text: "Have u seen the AM news? WKBT? See you @ the office. P"

"Oh, brother. I wonder what that's all about?" he muttered under his breath.

"Who're you texting?" Carol asked, walking into the bedroom and drying her hair with a towel.

"Paul. Something was on the morning news he thinks I might be concerned about."

"Well, don't watch it. Just go to work and deal with it there."

"Ya think?"

"Yes. I'm positive." Carol stood in front of him, her hair in a tousled mess, her brown eyes serious. "Remember, Jim? You promised that you'd try to keep your police concerns at work and not let them spill into our personal lives. We don't want any more confrontations in our driveway with criminals like the murderers we had a couple of months ago."

Jim groaned to himself. "Easier said than done." He scowled at his phone still clenched in his hand.

She kissed him quickly on the lips. "Take it somewhere else. I'll appreciate your efforts more than you know."

After a noisy breakfast in which Lillie and Henri argued about almost everything, and Henri spilled his orange juice all over the *Wisconsin State Journal*, Jim grabbed his navy wool overcoat and scarf, kissed everyone goodbye, and headed into the law enforcement office on Vine Street.

Entering the elevator at the center half an hour later, Jim held the door for Sam who was also just arriving.

"I see Jamie made the news this morning," Sam said cautiously.

"We've got bigger fish to fry than Jamie Alberg," Jim said brusquely. He'd watched the brief interview on his phone before he'd left for work. "I'll deal with Jamie, but Leslie and DeDe's information about the maker of the weapon could lead us in a whole new direction. We'll meet later this morning and see where we're at."

Waving briefly at Emily, Jim stopped at his office door, his hand resting on the doorknob. Sam continued down the hallway. "By the way, where's Leslie?" Jim asked.

Sam stopped and turned. "She said something about an appointment. She probably meant her counseling session. She usually has them on Monday mornings once a month. I don't know. I don't keep track. She'll be here later this morning."

Strolling into his tiny office cubicle, Sam noticed the air was a stuffy mix of dust and old coffee. He began straightening his desk. During his mini cleaning spree, his cell rang.

"Detective Birkstein."

"Hello, detective. This is Shelby Lewis. I talked to you on Friday when you came to The BonBon. You told me to call you if I remembered anything else about Mr. Burke." A picture of the elfin clerk with her dark hair and eyes swam into Sam's memory. *Hmm*, he thought.

"Yes. I remember," Sam said. He leaned forward in his office chair and propped his elbows on the desktop. "Go ahead, Shelby. What other information do you have?" he asked, pulling a yellow legal pad and a pen across the desktop.

"I asked around about the guy with the Native American jacket. You know, the guy who met Mr. Burke Wednesday afternoon?"

"Yeah. Go ahead," Sam said, clicking his pen, ready to take notes.

"Remember I told you they went out and came back about one o'clock? When they returned to the hotel, the bartender sent drinks up to Mr. Burke's room. We checked the credit card that was used for the purchase. The guy's name is Trent Willow. He used his VISA card to buy the drinks that were delivered upstairs to Mr. Burke's suite."

Sam felt a tiny spark of excitement. "Excellent, Shelby. This is really important information. Do you have his address?"

"The address assigned to the VISA card is 3479 Pammel Creek Road. I think that's over in Morman Coulee somewhere. Anyway, it's on the south side of town, back by the bluffs."

"Fantastic, Shelby. Thanks so much," Sam said sincerely.

"No problem. Glad to help," she said, and the line went dead.

☐

Meanwhile, Paul had arrived and was wading through a compilation of LeMar Burke's financial records that had arrived via a warrant request. Trying to uncover another person's personal finances and how they tied in with a crime seemed to be his strength, although he took no pleasure in it. He huffed impatiently. The attachment in his email from the Crescent City Credit Union in New Orleans was several pages long.

Paul groaned noisily and scrolled through the records, getting a handle on their complexity. His early morning was already catching up with him, and it was only 9:15. He yawned and turned back to his computer.

"Might as well get to it," he muttered, hitting the print button. Leaning back in his chair, he watched the financial spreadsheets spewing out of the printer in front of him.

☐

That same morning, Leslie stood in the cramped bathroom of

the duplex on Cliffwood Lane and stared at the pregnancy dipstick submerged in urine in the plastic cup. She fidgeted nervously, waiting for the tiny screen to indicate the results. Paco, ever watchful, whined at her feet, his big brown eyes looking at her forlornly. Finally, he lay down on the bathroom floor, releasing a pent-up groan.

Leslie leaned against the wall, her arms across her chest, staring at the ceiling, waiting for the results.

How could I forget to take my birth control pills for a week?

It was that stupid art show for the Humane Society. *That's how I forgot*, she thought. She'd gotten so distracted painting Paco's portrait that she put everything else on hold. That was a screwup of major proportions, and she had no idea how Sam would take the news. How would she tell her husband she was pregnant? What would he say? She squeezed her eyes shut as she imagined his response. Holding the dipstick, Leslie focused on the symbol that appeared in the tiny window. She blinked her eyes in disbelief, and her heart felt like it stopped beating. *Oh boy*, she thought. *This news is going to rock Sam's world.* Paco nuzzled her hand, and when she bent down, she could almost feel his empathy reaching across space to enfold her. He licked her across the cheek as if to say: *I'll love you no matter what.*

□

"What part of confidential do you not understand?" Jim asked, his voice rising in volume as the conversation began. He stood at his desk, his cell phone pressed to his ear. Emily heard the crescendo in his voice, the irritation in it. She peeked in, but Jim waved her off.

For reasons unfathomable to Jim, Jamie Alberg set his teeth on edge. Maybe it was his know-it-all attitude, his cockiness, his youth, his social awkwardness. Who knew. The kid was smart— probably brilliant in his field—but when he messed in police business, Jim overreacted and became unreasonable.

"I was asked for my professional opinion about the weapon, Chief, and I gave it," Jamie said coolly with a level of conviction that surprised Jim. He sounded confident and sure of himself, leaving Jim feeling like a cantankerous old crank who'd climbed out on a limb that was cracking and threatening to break.

"You don't speak for the police department, need I remind you? Number one. You are not an officer of the law. Number two. You are not actively involved in this investigation in an official capacity. And number three. You stood in my office a few days ago and promised me you would keep a lid on any information you might have about the case, particularly the weapon." Jim was on a roll. "And what did I see this morning? You waving a photo of the weapon on the morning news for everyone to see. Well, so much for promises, Jamie," he spat rudely. "Your interview on the morning news has social media buzzing. That seems to be a unique talent of yours."

"That's not true, Chief. In this day and age, you can't stop social media. It has a life all its own. Besides, don't you rely on citizen tips in cases like this? Don't answer that because I know you've previously asked for the public's input to help solve crimes. Furthermore, I have quite a bit of knowledge about ancient weapons that your team could benefit from. I also have important connections to people in the Ho-Chunk community who could lend some perspective and cultural insight into the mystery of the ball club that you found at the scene of the crime. So before you chew me out, you might want to think about being a little more proactive with the press. Maybe a press conference once in a while might solve some of your PR problems, especially with those who use social media," Jamie said reasonably.

Jim choked back his outrage and sputtered, "PR problems? You think the sheriff's department has PR issues with the community?" He was thunderstruck at the cool composure of this upstart. That the department needed to rely on Jamie Alberg to improve its relationship with the media was beyond belief. *Where does this kid get off?* Jim thought. But before he could respond, Jamie continued.

"That's the way it appears to me, but that's for you to evaluate. I'm not goin' there. But I will tell you that I know who makes authentic weapons like the one at the scene of the murder," Jamie offered.

Jim felt like a rabbit greedily hopping after a dangling carrot. His jaw muscles rolled with tension as he struggled to maintain his sense of decency and fair play. His chest felt tight, and he briefly thought of Carol's admonition about getting his health checked out. Was he toying with a heart attack? *Better calm down, bud,* he thought. He was about to respond when Jamie offered more tidbits.

"The guy who makes the weapon replicas is Ryan Blake. I've been a huge fan of his work, and I follow him on social media and check his website frequently." He cleared his throat conspicuously. "His son, D'Marius Blake, also known as Little Hawk, is a member of a group of young Natives who have pulled away from the tribal traditions and teachings of the Ho-Chunk Nation and have formed a loosely organized group. They have some interesting goals. Whether he's involved in the murder is beyond my capacity to assess. After all, I'm not a detective."

"Ya got that right," Jim snarled. Then he checked his attitude, realizing he was being petty and bullheaded. In a more civilized tone, he said, "And I'm sure you'd be more than willing to share your insights," he continued. *Swallow your pride,* Jim thought. *Maybe the kid can actually help.*

"I think my information could help you," Jamie said.

Jim sighed and ran his hand through his hair. He parked his fist on his hip and said, "Okay, Jamie. Be here at one o'clock in my office. We'll listen to what you have to say."

"You got it, Chief. I'll be there," Jamie said.

Jim disconnected and slipped his phone into the pocket of his suit coat. A pile of file folders teetered at the edge of his desk. He straightened them into a neater pile, but he was too keyed up to work on the contents. He hoisted himself out of the chair and walked rapidly down the hall to Sam's office.

When Jim walked in, Sam was intently studying something on his laptop. Jim leaned over his shoulder and began scanning the information on the screen.

After several minutes, Jim asked, "Who's Trent Willow?"

"That big guy that LeMar Burke met at The BonBon. The desk clerk did a little investigating of her own and traced his credit card. We've got his address. I was about to head over there."

Jim felt a shiver of satisfaction. "Good. I'm coming with. Maybe we can find something out about this guy before Jamie Alberg arrives at one o'clock and makes us all look like complete, incompetent idiots."

"You fighting with Jamie again? I heard some yelling down the hallway. So when is he going to impress us with his astounding knowledge?" Sam's stare left Jim feeling exposed.

Jim fidgeted and straightened his tie, then stared back at Sam, clearly uncomfortable with Sam's question. "He claims he has valuable knowledge that he's uncovered that will help move the case along." He held his hands up, palms out. "I decided to roll with it. He's not *always* wrong … I guess," he said weakly.

The concession by Higgins left Sam wondering. "Let's get movin' then," Sam said, grabbing his coat from the hook behind the door. "We've only got three hours to discover something that will advance our cause … and render Jamie, the impresario, speechless."

☐

Paul concentrated on the financial spreadsheets in front of him, trying to glean information and possible motives from columns and columns of numbers. As he looked over LeMar Burke's financial statistics, he realized the guy was a numbers whiz and a financial genius. *It takes money to make money,* he thought, *and Burke had plenty of it.*

At forty-six, Burke was worth over fifty-two million dollars, much of it tied up in real estate in and around the city of New Orleans. His 401K showed a current balance of over fifteen million dollars, all of which would now be transferred to his wife, Natalie, when the probate procedures were completed. His other investments were valued in the millions, and his current checking account balance was $34,956.

Paul spent some time online reviewing Burke's current real estate holdings. His home was a classic southern charmer, complete with a state-of-the-art kitchen, five bedrooms and five bathrooms, double sets of French doors leading to the rear landscaped portico, a front porch with soaring Corinthian columns, heart pine flooring throughout, and of course, a generous sized swimming pool. A few blocks from Audubon Park and the Mississippi River, it was assessed at over four million dollars. In addition, he owned a number of high-end apartment buildings and three condominium complexes in the Canal and South Peters area of downtown New Orleans. LeMar Burke was a high-end roller, just like the real estate agent from Bluff Management had told Sam.

But it wasn't the real estate or even the impressive bank accounts and 401K that caught Paul's attention. Instead, he noticed several large withdrawals from Burke's personal checking account within the last three months: one on January 15 for fifty thousand dollars, another withdrawal on February 23 for seventy-five thousand, and one for one hundred thousand dollars on March 15. That's about a quarter of a million dollars withdrawn in less than three months. Unless he or his wife had a terrible out-of-control spending issue, which was possible, that was a lot of money going somewhere. But where?

Paul reached for his landline and dialed the number of the Crescent City Credit Union in New Orleans. After identifying himself and the purpose of his call, he was directed to Mr. Boyd Williams, one of the senior financial consultants at the bank.

"How can I help you, Officer?" Mr. Williams asked, his classic southern drawl laced with concern. "I understand you have some questions about Mr. Burke's finances."

"Yes, I do. I received Mr. Burke's financial statements from your institution in my email this morning. I'm wondering if you can help me understand three withdrawals that took place within the last three months. They were quite sizable," Paul explained.

"Just a moment while I pull up his accounts," Mr. Williams said.

Paul heard the clicking of a computer keyboard in the background. After a couple of minutes, Mr. Williams said, "Did you say checking?"

"I didn't, but yes, his checking account is the one I'm referring to," Paul said.

"Hmm. Yes, I see what you're talking about. Are you referring to the cash withdrawals in January, February, and March?"

"Yep. Do you have an explanation for that?" Paul asked.

"No, not really, but I will say it was unusual behavior, especially for someone as astute in finances as Mr. Burke."

"So the withdrawals were taken in cash?" Paul asked, wanting to confirm the information.

"Yes, they were cash."

"Doesn't that raise red flags on your end?"

"Well, yes, it does. We're obligated by the Bank Secrecy Act to report any transaction to the IRS over ten thousand dollars, either withdrawals or deposits, and we must ask for identification from the person withdrawing or depositing the money, even though we may already know them."

"So, what was your reaction to these large withdrawals?"

"Well, I'm afraid our reactions really don't come into the equation. What people do with their money is not really something we're allowed to question, although it certainly raises questions about their activities. However, Mr. Burke was a highly skilled money manager, and we assumed he had a good reason for doing what he did. He was, after all, a millionaire many times over," Mr. Williams said in a rather snippy tone.

"Yeah, and unfortunately, he's dead, isn't he?" There was a long pause.

"You have a point, Officer," Mr. Williams said.

They talked a while longer about Burke's investments, IRA accounts, and annuities, but the conversation really didn't tell Paul any more than what he'd already gleaned from the records himself.

"Thanks for your time. I appreciate it," Paul finally said, ending the exchange.

He placed the phone back in its cradle and leaned back, thinking. Trying to find out where $225,000 cash went wasn't going to be easy. In fact, it might be impossible. Payoffs in a crooked land deal? Blackmail of some kind? Gambling? High-end call girls? The list went on. But it did clarify one thing: LeMar Burke's financial activities were not as lily-white as the banker made out. The large withdrawals were suspicious at the very least—certainly not within the normal banking activities Burke had demonstrated in the past. Even the senior bank official at Crescent City Credit Union had admitted that. What activities had Burke been involved in that demanded over two hundred thousand dollars in cash? That was the question that begged for an answer.

□

Leslie Birkstein walked hurriedly toward the law enforcement building on Vine Street, dodging a few conspicuous puddles of melting snow, and swiped her badge through the secure entry. The morning was almost gone. It was cloudy and cold, and the sky was the color of gray slate—typical March fare.

Her mind churned at the discovery of her pregnancy. The news threatened to launch her into a full-blown anxiety attack, but she pushed the immediacy of the situation out of her mind for the moment. She breathed deeply as her therapist had taught her and repeated her mantra, "One day at a time," under her breath. Walking to the elevator, she thought about the assignment Higgins had given her and DeDe Deverioux—interviewing Professor Terry Waite.

Leslie stepped off the elevator and briefly greeted Emily. Then she walked briskly down the hall to DeDe's office.

"Hey, sorry I'm late," she said, slightly out of breath, standing in the office doorway. "I had an appointment. Are you ready to interview Professor Waite?"

"Yep. Let me grab my coat."

The UW–La Crosse campus was only about ten minutes from the

law enforcement center, and they had almost reached the visitor's parking lot on La Crosse Street when Leslie's phone buzzed.

"What? A robbery? Where?" Leslie asked rapidly. A brief pause. "Yeah, we're right in the neighborhood. We're on our way." Turning to DeDe, she pointed to a side street. "Turn right and head to the Kwik Trip on West Avenue. Apparently, there's a robbery in progress. Chief Pedretti alerted any law enforcement officers in the vicinity to report to the scene. I guess that's us."

DeDe's face paled as she spun the car around the corner and accelerated down the street. The back of the convenience store loomed ahead. She roared into a vacant spot in the rear of the store that was used to unload merchandise and slammed the car into park. Reaching for the glove compartment, she unlocked it and grabbed her pistol.

"You got your vest and gun?" she asked Leslie.

"Nope. I'll cover the back of the store. If the back door is open, I can get inside and maybe talk him—" she said.

"No, no," DeDe interrupted. "Don't go in without your weapon or vest. Just stay at the back entrance. I'll cover the front."

"Okay, but be careful," Leslie warned, her eyes wide with apprehension. In the distance, they could hear sirens blaring. Other police units were racing through the busy midday traffic heading to the convenience store.

DeDe ran around the front of the building. Leslie felt the adrenaline pumping through her system, her senses on heightened alert. She approached the back service door and turned the knob. At that very moment, the door swung open hard, knocking her to the pavement. A man with a ski mask pulled over his face burst into the small unloading area behind the store and began sprinting down the street toward the university campus.

Recovering from the surprise collision with the door, Leslie picked herself off the pavement and began running after the perpetrator, gaining steadily on him as he wove in between parked cars along the campus street. Up ahead, Leslie noticed another cop car screaming toward them, its red and blue strobe lights flashing.

"Stop! Police! Drop your weapon!" Leslie yelled loudly.

The man looked briefly over his shoulder, spotted Leslie chasing him, and continued sprinting across campus, dodging students on the sidewalks, forcing them to step aside as he continued running willy nilly.

Several other officers joined the pursuit, converging on the man from different directions. He crossed another side street, and just as Leslie stepped off the curb, a car appeared out of nowhere. Coming fast, the driver hit her near the front passenger headlight, which sent her flying up onto the snowbank that bordered the street. She landed roughly on her right side, hitting her head hard on the frozen ground. She briefly looked up at the naked trees lining the snowy street, and things started fading away. Little white stars appeared, then everything went black. Her eyes rolled back in her head, and she passed out.

☐

Leslie felt like she was underwater. She hovered on the edge of reality like a diver who'd gone too deep and now had to struggle upward toward air at the surface. She gasped with shock when the scream of the ambulance siren finally penetrated her consciousness. The deafening blast compounded the ache in her head. A sharp pain in her shoulder throbbed with intensity. She felt the comfort of a warm blanket being draped over her body as she was hoisted into the waiting ambulance. She heard a familiar voice and opened her eyes. DeDe knelt beside her on the floor of the vehicle while she talked on her cell.

"Right, Chief. She was chasing the perpetrator, and when she ran out into the street, a car hit her. I caught up with her just as she flew up over the snowbank and landed on her side. She hit her head pretty hard. We're on our way to the St. Francis ER." DeDe listened, then answered, "Meet you there."

When DeDe realized Leslie had gained consciousness, she leaned over and grabbed her hand, pushing her cell phone back in her pocket. "You got hit by a car. Do you remember?" she asked. The ambulance siren screamed as the driver maneuvered through the city streets to the hospital.

Leslie turned to look at DeDe, then grimaced in pain at the goose egg forming on the back of her head. "So that's what it feels like." She smiled weakly through her confusion.

"We'll be at the ER in a few minutes," DeDe told her. "Just stay quiet."

By the time the ambulance crew had unloaded Leslie and wheeled her through the door of the ER department at St. Francis Hospital, Jim and Sam had screeched into a parking space and were jogging toward the entrance. They'd been on their way across town to interview Trent Willow when DeDe had called.

Sam felt the panic rising in his chest like a bubble, threatening to cut off his breathing. He hurried into the ER and jogged to the admissions desk.

"My wife. Leslie Birkstein. Is she here yet?" he asked, his voice raspy with urgency. Jim came up behind him and laid a hand on his shoulder. The admitting nurse looked at the two men.

"Who are you, sir?" she asked calmly.

Sam whipped out his ID. "My wife was hit by a car. Leslie Birkstein. She's a police officer. Has she come in yet?" he repeated.

Another nurse, who was standing farther away from the desk in the center of the ER's receiving area, turned when she heard the commotion and said, "The ambulance just arrived. Let them come through."

The two men hurried through the swinging admittance doors and watched the gurney come down the hallway.

The same nurse pointed to the ambulance attendants and said, "Room three. Dr. Lawrie is the attending physician. He'll be in right away." Then, turning to Sam and Jim, she raised her hands in a protective gesture. Pointing to Jim, she asked, "Are you the husband?"

Her eyes were steady and her voice calm—a picture of unflappability amidst the chaotic clatter of carts, jostling equipment, and scurrying medical personnel.

"No," Jim said and nodded at Sam. "This guy is. I'm her boss."

"Just wait right here," she said to Jim. She turned to Sam. "When they get her settled, I'll come and get you," she said. "In the meantime, the admitting clerk will give you some paperwork to fill out."

"This is bullshit! I need to be with her! Now!" Sam said loudly. Jim laid his hand on Sam's arm.

"Easy, tiger. Just let them assess her," he said. "We'll just be in the way. They're good. Let them do their job." Sam locked eyes with Jim. His nostrils flared, and his eyes were wild with panic. "It'll be okay. Come on, let's sit over here," Jim continued in a fatherly tone. The nurse caught Jim's eye, winked, and silently mouthed, "Thanks."

Jim led Sam to a set of chairs against the wall. They plopped in them and watched as a portable X-ray machine was wheeled into the examining room. Nurses and medical technicians crowded around Leslie. Sam leaned his elbows on his knees and raked one hand through his brown curls, his pent-up energy setting his foot jiggling.

A half hour later, Sam had completed the hospital admitting forms. Dr. Lawrie stuck his head out of the examining room and said, "Mr. Birkstein." When Sam stood, he crooked his finger at Jim.

"Just the husband for now," he said, holding up his hand when Jim rose out of his chair to accompany Sam. Sam was ushered into the room. DeDe came down the hallway and quietly sat next to Jim, explaining the account of the robbery at the convenience store.

In the examining room, Sam stood by the side of the gurney. He looked down at Leslie, who was white and unusually quiet, her eyes half-mast. Her long blonde hair was spread out on the white pillow. She seemed dazed and confused. Taking her hand, he said softly, "Lez, I'm here."

Leslie's eyes slowly drifted to his face. It took all her effort to focus on him.

"What happened?" she asked. "Everything hurts ... tired."

"Shhh. You were hit by a car. Don't talk. Just rest," Sam said. Leslie drifted off.

Dr. Lawrie looked at Sam and began giving his diagnosis. "I've given her something for pain. That's why she's so sleepy. She's experiencing some amnesia, which is typical of a concussion. There's a pretty big goose egg on the back of her head. I'm ordering a CT scan in order to rule out a possible brain bleed. Thankfully, the X-rays indicate nothing's broken. Her shoulder will be sore for a week or two. She has some ugly contusions on her right side where she landed, but they'll disappear with time. She may experience some nausea and dizziness in the weeks ahead, but I think the baby is fine. Sometimes these kinds of falls can cause a spontaneous miscarriage, so if she starts to bleed in the next couple of days, you need to bring her in immediately. Otherwise—"

"Whoa, whoa, whoa!" Sam interrupted loudly. Dr. Lawrie stopped talking, his eyes wide with surprise. At the sound of Sam's loud outburst, Leslie's eyes popped open. Sam froze in disbelief, his hands poised in front of him as if he could hold back the reality of the words he'd heard. "Baby? What are you talking about? Back up the train, Doc." The confusion on his face caused Dr. Lawrie to lock eyes with Sam and reassess the situation.

"I'm sorry. I thought you knew. Your wife is in the early stages of pregnancy."

Sam's hands flopped to his sides, and he felt Leslie reach for him. She wrapped her fingers around his. He looked at her and noticed her eyes were misty with tears. "I'm sorry, Sam. I just found out this morning. This was not how I planned to tell you."

Sam leaned down and kissed her tenderly. "It's okay, baby. You rest. We'll talk later," he said softly. "It's okay," but he wasn't sure if he was trying to comfort Leslie or himself.

"I'm needed in the next room," Dr. Lawrie said, picking up his clipboard. "I'd like to keep her overnight for observation and get that CT scan immediately. Then you'll be able to take her home. How's that sound?"

"Fine, fine," Sam muttered, waving at the doctor in an absentminded gesture, but his mind was reeling with thoughts of a baby.

"Congratulations. She had a close call," Dr. Lawrie said softly, "but I think she'll be all right." He patted Sam's arm, turned, and left the room.

Alone now, Sam watched Leslie sleeping. He brushed her blonde hair away from her face and kissed her again on the cheek. Suddenly the panic he'd felt in seeing Leslie on the gurney and the news of the pregnancy caught up with him like a perfect storm. He eased himself into the chair in the corner of the small room, willing his heart to slow down. *Holy moly. I'm going to be a dad.*

☐

When Leslie had finally settled in her room with Sam by her side, Jim called Paul and filled him in on the details of the robbery and Leslie's accident.

"So she's going to be all right?" Paul asked, his voice tight.

"Yeah, but she's banged up," Jim told him. "There's nothing broken. She has a concussion and some bruises. Sam'll take her home sometime tomorrow, but she'll be hurting for a while."

"Damn! How does she always get in these situations?" Paul said, letting out a breath of frustration.

"The girls were in the vicinity of the robbery, so they responded and did what they were supposed to do. Goes with the territory, I guess. She's tough. She'll be fine," Jim said, reassuring Paul. "Listen, I want you to head over to the university this afternoon and interview Professor Terry Waite. That's where DeDe and Leslie were headed when Leslie got hit. He's in the Humanities building. He teaches American history and Native American culture. Find out where he was on Wednesday, the twentieth. Also see if he knows anything about the Driftless Native Consortium. Question him about the meeting with the real estate agent that Sam interviewed—I forgot her name—but she's at Bluff Management Group."

"Sure. I've got some financial stuff on Burke that we need to look at, too," Paul said.

"Sounds good. Talk to you later."

Jim tucked his phone in his jacket while he continued walking across the parking lot of the hospital to his Suburban. DeDe climbed into the front seat and turned to him.

"So what are we doing?" she asked.

"Heading over to interview this Trent Willow guy. He's over on Pammel Creek Road."

"What about Jamie? Sam told me he's coming at one o'clock?"

Jim started the engine and began backing out of the parking space. "I forgot about that. Call Emily, will you? Tell her what's happened and see if she can reach Jamie before he makes a trip over to the office. Push the meeting back to tomorrow morning."

As Jim drove across town, he reviewed the questions he wanted to ask Trent Willow, the man who'd met Burke at The BonBon Hotel the day of his death. Traffic was light. They drove through several residential neighborhoods, finally coming to Pammel Creek Road. Willow's property was set against a limestone bluff. The large split-level home sat among the rolling wooded hills. Jim guessed it was about ten acres, similar to his property in Chipmunk Coulee.

The gray ranch house was set back from the road with a dramatic limestone outcropping as a backdrop. Jim drove up the winding paved driveway, which was accented with blue spruce, clumps of white birch, and soft maples. The lawn had been meticulously landscaped with attractive shrubbery. Large rocks were arranged in manicured flower beds throughout the property.

Pulling up to the house, Jim noticed the stacked limestone chimney and gently curved sidewalk that led to the porch and the massive front door. An attached three-car garage was at the east end of the house, and beyond, to the west, was a horse barn and a fenced-area for riding. A curtain moved discreetly in the large front window. Someone was home.

Jim and DeDe got out of the Suburban and walked up the sidewalk to the front entrance. DeDe rang the doorbell and waited. Eventually, a petite woman of Asian descent opened the door. She stood in front of them, her dark hair pulled up into a ponytail. She wore blue jeans, a pastel yellow sweatshirt, and gray sneakers. Although she wore no makeup, her olive skin glowed with the blush of good health. Her dark eyes looked at them inquisitively.

"Yes? May I help you?" she asked politely. Jim recognized the Hmong accent in her speech.

"We're looking for Mr. Trent Willow. Is he in? We'd like to talk to him if we could," Jim said.

"Do you have an appointment?" the woman asked, tilting her head slightly.

Jim and DeDe briefly flashed their IDs.

"I'm sorry, we don't," Jim explained, "but it's important that we speak to Mr. Willow."

A look of anxiety crossed the woman's face when she saw the IDs, but it disappeared quickly, replaced by a friendly smile. She stepped aside and swept her hand to her side, indicating they should come in.

"Just wait right here. He's in his office," she said as she walked down a long hallway.

The interior of the house was impressive. To the left was a formal living room. Oriental rugs were tossed on dark, gleaming walnut floors. Dark brown leather couches and chairs were placed in a casual arrangement facing a massive fireplace. Above the fireplace, an oil painting of a morning river scene tugged at Jim's art sensibilities. Wisconsin artist Hayley Klum was well known throughout the Midwest for her vibrant color pallet and vivid portrayal of wildlife along the Mississippi. The spacious room had a distinct style, with pastel walls covered in fine art and dark walnut shelves displaying

Native American artifacts and basketry. In one corner near the front bay window, a baby grand piano sat. Jim wondered if it had ever been played.

To the right of the entrance was a library with an impressive collection of volumes arranged in pristine order on dark bookshelves. Thick carpeting and heavy drapes on the windows gave the room a dark mood of serious reflection. But even with all the amenities of a comfortable life, the home felt cold and impersonal to Jim—a showplace that existed to impress guests but one that was not lived in.

The woman who had shown them into the house returned. "Please follow me," she said with a flick of her hand.

Jim and DeDe followed her into the rear of the house past a gleaming modern kitchen and down a long, wide hallway until they came to the door of an open spacious room that was obviously a large working office. Two burgundy upholstered chairs were positioned in front of a large oak desk that sat in the center of the room. A bank of wide windows filled one wall of the office. Beyond that, a couple of horses grazed on a large round bale of hay. Behind the desk was a wall of bookshelves that held collections of photographs, mementos, awards, medical and historical reference books, and biographical selections. Several gray filing cabinets stood along another wall. In one corner, a wood carving of John Wayne as Rooster Cogburn added a unique flair. This was a room alive with action; it was clear that this was the heart of the impressive home. While they waited for Trent Willow to finish his conversation on the phone, Jim scanned the titles on the bookshelves.

"I'm sorry. I didn't mean to be rude," Mr. Willow said pleasantly, pointing to the two chairs, "but that was a call I had to complete. Please sit down."

After introductions, Jim and DeDe made themselves comfortable and looked expectantly at Willow. The Hmong woman offered them refreshments, but they declined.

Willow was a large man with broad shoulders and a pot-belly stomach. At one time, he'd been fit and strong, but now he was leaning toward flabby. His dark hair was professionally trimmed. He was clean-shaven, and his dark eyes reflected a sense of curiosity. A long scar ran across his forehead over the bridge of his nose. His complexion was the color of walnut shells, and high, well-defined cheekbones suggested Native American descent. Wearing a white shirt that was open at the collar, he gave an impression of friendliness and hard work, and his genial expression invited trust.

"So, what can I help you with?" he asked them, folding his thick hands on top of the desk in front of him.

"We're investigating the death of LeMar Burke. He was found behind the Tip Your Hat tavern in Genoa early Wednesday morning," Jim began. "We understand from various sources that you knew Mr. Burke. Is that right?"

Willow's demeanor shifted subtly, and the optimism in his eyes changed to a shadow of regret as if clouds had blocked the sunshine. "I read about his death in the *Tribune*. I really liked him. The article hinted that foul play was suspected. Was he murdered? Because that's what's circulating on social media."

Jim noticed his evasion of the original question. "Unfortunately, that's true. Did you know him?" he asked again.

"We became acquainted when he attended a forum on real estate development at the Radisson in January. It was a joint effort by the La Crosse Tourism Board and Tri-State Realty Association. We were introduced and got to talking and found out we had a lot in common."

"Like what?" DeDe asked, analyzing him with her serious brown eyes. Jim thought Willow suddenly looked like an insect wriggling under a microscope. Some of his friendliness seemed to seep away.

Willow frowned at the abrupt question and blew out a noisy breath. "Well, we both loved people. And we were enthusiastic about bringing real estate opportunities and development to La Crosse

County. Both of us have refurbished century-old buildings into loft apartments and office buildings, so we exchanged a lot of ideas we'd used in past projects. You may be familiar with the Gund Brewery Loft apartments over by the hospital. Those were designed by an architect friend of mine, and my agency rents them to prospective clients. Anyway, getting back to LeMar, we had several dinners together and became good friends in a short time. I was really upset to hear about his death. What can I do to help you?"

Mr. Willow leaned back in his office chair, the leather creaking noisily under his weight. Jim glanced at DeDe, who was taking meticulous notes.

"On Wednesday, March 20, you were at The BonBon Hotel down near Riverside Park. Is that correct?" Jim asked.

Willow leaned forward and pulled an appointment calendar toward him from the corner of his desk. He flipped backward a few pages and nodded. He found the date and read his notes in the calendar square.

"Yes, I was there. I met LeMar at about ten. We went and looked at some land he was interested in and then came back to his hotel room and had a drink."

"When did you leave the hotel?"

Willow thought carefully. His eyes drifted to the horse barn outside, then he gazed back at Jim and DeDe and said, "I think I left about two o'clock. Somewhere in that time frame anyway." He referred back to his appointment book. "I had another meeting in Onalaska at three, so I'm sure I left around two."

"Can you tell us about the content of your conversation with LeMar?" DeDe asked.

"Like I said, we looked at a piece of land, discussed the plans that his company had in mind for the area, talked about the real estate market—mostly shop talk."

"Where do you work, Mr. Willow?" DeDe asked.

"I'm an independent realtor and developer, and I operate here out of my home office. In addition, I serve on a number of advisory boards."

"Are you married?" Jim asked.

"Twice. Didn't seem to work for me. I'm unattached right now," Willow said, eyeing DeDe cautiously.

"Did Mr. Burke mention his wife or anything about his personal life that might have been troubling him?" DeDe asked.

"Aren't trouble and wives mutually exclusive?" Willow asked, smiling broadly.

"We're talking about a murder, Mr. Willow. I don't find anything humorous in that," DeDe cautioned him. Jim looked down and rubbed his chin. *You go, DeDe,* he thought.

Willow's smile disappeared, and he became serious. He drummed his fingers on the arm of his chair and sat up straighter.

"Believe me, Ms. Deverioux, I would never take murder lightly." His dark eyes held DeDe's for a moment, and then he continued his evaluation of LeMar Burke. "He mentioned his wife briefly, in a good way. Other than that, he seemed fine—optimistic and friendly. Always looking for the next deal. He was a mover and shaker, that's for sure."

"Obviously, not everyone appreciated his personality like you did," Jim commented. "Do you know of anyone else who might have met with him while he was in the La Crosse area?" Willow sighed but stayed silent.

"The reason I ask," Jim continued, "is that we found a brochure in his hotel room." Jim slid the sleek tri-fold brochure of the Driftless Native Consortium across the massive desk to Willow. "We were wondering where he might have gotten it." Willow picked it up and looked through it.

"I gave it to him," Willow said, locking eyes with Jim. "I'm on the board at the consortium, and I try to educate people about their mission and work throughout the region. Most people don't realize that the entire Driftless Area was an important part of the Fox and

Winnebago lands. In fact, Pammel Creek was one of the original village sites of the Oneota people. MVAC has found bison horn cores just about three blocks down this road," Willow said, pointing to the west. "Many Ho-Chunk Natives consider the entire La Crosse River Valley sacred ground. So when developers come in, I give them this brochure and encourage them to get Natives' input before they begin their real estate development plans instead of running into trouble later. I encourage them to be proactive."

"Makes sense," DeDe said, nodding in agreement with Willow. "So you're Native?"

Willow nodded. "Fifty percent. My father was Ho-Chunk, and my mother is American with Norwegian ancestry."

DeDe continued. "How did LeMar view the consortium? Did he understand their concerns?"

"His environmental philosophy was in direct conflict with the aims of the consortium. He was surprisingly out of step with current environmental thinking. On a personal level, he claimed global warming was a bunch of hocus-pocus and a colossal eco myth, although I'm sure that wasn't the attitude of Hathway Industries. I tried to convince him to rethink his position, but that didn't go too well," Willow explained.

"You parted friends?" Jim asked.

"Oh yes," Willow said, shaking his head vigorously. "LeMar was a professional; he wasn't interested in holding grudges or butting heads over political differences. But he did enjoy a rousing debate, and I provided one for him."

"So who else would have had a reason to hate him enough to kill him?" DeDe asked.

"That's the million-dollar question, I guess," Willow said. He lifted his hands in a futile gesture. "I have no idea."

"Where was this land you went to look at?" Jim asked.

"There's a one hundred-acre farm south of La Crosse across from Blackhawk Park on 35 that really had LeMar excited. It's owned by some professor at the university. We went down there to look it over—a roadside appraisal—and he filled me in on the company's plans for their exclusive business resort. It was impressive, I have to admit. But I could see where the Ho-Chunk Nation would be opposed to such a development, plus the owner had no interest in selling."

"Really?" DeDe asked, scrunching up her face. "The Ho-Chunk opposed it? Why? Don't they basically do the same thing when they build and develop a property for their casinos?"

"They develop the land where the casino sits, but LeMar's plan involved much more than a typical casino. Besides the multi-level hotel and restaurant, the place he envisioned included a nine-hole golf course, tennis courts, riding stables, and access to the creek and river. And there are caves with ancient petroglyphs on that farm. Those are considered sacred by the Natives. I know the landowner was committed to keeping the public away from them. LeMar had no such intentions. In fact, he wanted to use the caves as a drawing card for tourism. It was a sore spot between us."

DeDe looked up, alarmed. Willow hurried to explain.

"Don't get me wrong. The DNC is committed to keeping ancient Indian sites intact, and Waite's property is just one example they're concerned about. They monitor those sites regularly, and whenever possible, they try to work with the landowner to preserve them. The petroglyphs are very susceptible to erosion, humidity, and building construction. They degrade rapidly when they're exposed to human activity, and the fragile sedimentary rock can flake off. To be preserved, they need to be protected from human and environmental influences. We disagreed about that, but it wasn't important enough for me to kill him," he said. "You don't kill someone over painted pictures in a cave."

"Well, maybe you don't, but somebody else might," DeDe said.

"So who else would be upset enough about Hathway Industries' plans to kill Burke?" Jim asked. "Do you have any ideas?"

"No, I don't. It could be a personal vendetta that has nothing to do with his work at Hathway, although I doubt it. I wish I could be more helpful. I don't envy your job trying to figure that out," Willow concluded.

13

Paul walked through the university campus toward the Mead Humanities building. Snowbanks lined the broad sidewalks, and bleary-eyed students crossed the campus on their way to classes bundled up against the cold and loaded down with clumsy backpacks. Farther across the expansive grounds, a group of students threw snowballs at each other. Professor Waite had agreed to meet Paul at three o'clock in his office on the second floor. Paul glanced at his phone—2:30. He had plenty of time.

Arriving at the Mead building, Paul decided to catch the tail end of the class Waite was teaching—Wisconsin History with a Regional Emphasis. He found the lecture hall, quietly opened the door, and slipped into a seat in the very back row. Students were listening intently and taking notes.

"… so as we conclude this lecture about the Native Americans' attitude toward the white man's encroaching settlements and the acquisition of Native lands in the late 1700s, I close with a quote from Chiksika, a Shawnee chief. 'The white man's race is a monster who is always hungry, and what he eats is land.' Think about that. Be prepared to discuss the quote next time. We'll continue this lecture on Wednesday. Your reaction papers about today's discussion will be due at our next session. No more than one hundred fifty words, please."

Professor Waite closed his notes that were lying on the podium and talked briefly to a couple of students who had come forward with concerns. Other students packed up their belongings and hurried toward the exit, a low buzz of conversation trailing into the hallway. After finishing with his student exchanges, Professor Waite picked up his briefcase, pushed the door open, and walked rapidly down the hallway. Paul got up and followed him to his office. He knocked on the open office door. The professor looked up and set his briefcase on the floor.

"Detective Saner, I presume?" he said, holding out his hand without a smile.

They exchanged handshakes, and Paul sat down in a chair against the wall.

Professor Waite was a tall, thin man whose clothes hung on him like a scarecrow. He was so thin, Paul was sure a brisk wind could topple him over. His beakish nose sat below a pair of probing, green eyes, and a pronounced Adam's apple bobbed conspicuously when he talked or swallowed. His salt and pepper hair was combed away from his face, which gave him an austere, severe appearance. He sat down in an office chair behind his desk, his body folding up like an accordion.

"Enjoy the lecture?" Waite asked, resting his elbows on the desk.

"Oh, I just heard the last few minutes of it," Paul said. "I'm afraid the content of your lectures isn't why I'm here."

"So what brings you here, then?"

Paul noticed the irritable tone as if he'd insulted the professor, although no insult was intended.

"We're investigating the death of LeMar Burke. He was found in a snowbank behind a tavern in Genoa Thursday morning after the snowstorm. We understand you knew Burke. Is that correct?" Paul asked.

Waite hesitated a moment and said, "Actually, I only met him once, and believe me, that was enough." The bitterness in his voice was not lost on Paul.

"You didn't hit it off?"

"Hardly."

"Explain," Paul demanded, feeling his temper flaring, antagonized by the professor's curt manner and brisk condescension.

The professor's eyes hardened. "He was interested in my property, though it wasn't for sale. He struck me as a typical money-grubbing real estate tycoon who saw something in someone else's sandbox and wasn't going to give up until he got what he wanted. I found him to be thoroughly and disgustingly greedy and opportunistic. A classic specimen of a bully."

Paul asked, "Did he make an offer on your property?"

"Tried to. I wouldn't listen, although that Cadwallader lady from the real estate office continued to call me several times after I'd met with Burke." Waite's lips curled in a sneer. "She's not much better than him." He threw a pencil on the desk that he'd been twirling in his fingers.

"What kind of offer did he make?"

Waite leaned forward aggressively. "How could that possibly be official police business?" he asked angrily. His long pencil-thin finger firmly tapped the desk as he talked. "That is private information that I fail to see is any of your concern."

"This is an official police investigation. You would be wise to cooperate, sir," Paul said brusquely. "In my experience, money and property are often strong motives for murder. I am well within my rights as an officer of the law in asking you that question, and I expect your full cooperation." He paused, stared at Waite, then repeated his question. "What kind of an offer did Burke make on your property?"

After several silent moments in which Paul was sure the professor was weighing his options, he answered softly, "Two million dollars."

Paul studied his face and swallowed uneasily. "And you refused?" If looks could kill, then at that moment, Paul should have been dead.

"Please, Officer. The least you can do is grant me the moral high ground," Waite said, his thin voice dripping with resentment. "My property is sacred. It is one of several sites in the area where prehistoric Oneota villages were located. Pottery shards, buffalo horns, and petrified seed corn have been excavated from my property in archaeological digs conducted by MVAC. Riley Creek, a Class One trout stream, runs through my land. In addition, there are two caves on my land that have exquisite Oneota petroglyphs, which I plan to preserve for posterity. It is not now, nor shall it ever be, for sale as long I live and breathe. You cannot buy something that is sacrosanct."

His recitation had been delivered in a quiet but determined voice, his green eyes boring into Paul. He appeared calm, but Paul noticed as he spoke his breathing had increased, and his nostrils flared. Beneath all his self-righteousness, anger simmered and threatened to boil over. Clearly, Paul had struck a sensitive nerve.

"Your land sounds like a paradise, Mr. Waite," Paul said calmly. "How did you acquire it?"

"I inherited it from an uncle back in the 1970s."

Paul decided to switch gears. "Where were you on Wednesday evening, March 20?" he asked.

Without referring to a calendar, Professor Waite said, "Well, since we were being pummeled by a sixteen-inch snowstorm with fifty-mile-an-hour winds and roads that were impassable, I was at home where most people who have any common sense should have been."

"Are you always this disagreeable, sir?" Paul asked, folding his arms across his chest. He could feel a hot flush coloring his neck and traveling to his cheeks.

"Sometimes more so," Waite answered, a slight grin on his lips.

"I can't imagine. Can anyone testify to your whereabouts the evening of the snowstorm? Perhaps your wife?" Paul asked.

"I live alone. I'm not married, nor have I ever been," Waite snapped.

"A partner, then?"

"I am not gay. Single people without conjugal relationships do exist in our culture, detective."

"I'm sure you'd know about that," Paul said, gritting his teeth. *Who the hell could get along with you, anyway?* he thought. Changing direction, he asked, "Are you familiar with the Driftless Native Consortium?"

Waite frowned as his eyes wandered up toward the ceiling in a show of innocence, but Paul recognized the evasive tactic when the professor refused to meet his gaze. "No, I've never heard of them. Who are they?"

"A group devoted to maintaining ownership of lands currently held by the Ho-Chunk tribe in the Driftless Region. They hold nature in high regard, and they try to respect and protect it."

"Sounds like a group that has found a cause worth fighting for."

"Fighting's not mentioned in their aims and goals. Do you know something I don't?"

"Like I said, I've never heard of them," Waite repeated, his eyes steely with rancor.

I'm getting nowhere fast, Paul thought. He stood up abruptly. "Thanks for your time, professor. Here's my card if you think of any other pertinent information about LeMar Burke." Paul slid his card across the desk and turned to leave. When he got to the doorway, he stopped. He turned to Waite and said, "I'm wondering about something."

"Yes?"

"'The white man's race is a monster who is always hungry, and what he eats is land.' That's what you said this afternoon. Is that what you think about LeMar Burke? Was he a monster who wanted to eat your land?"

Waite stared at him in silence, although Paul could see his mind spinning.

"Because if he is," Paul continued, "then I think you're a prime suspect in his murder."

Before Waite could respond, Paul was walking rapidly down the hallway. Behind him he heard the professor yell, "Detective, I resent your implications! They are unfounded and unabashedly false!" Paul kept walking and waved his hand over his head. He gritted his teeth and loosened the tie around his neck. Somehow Paul had gotten under the skin of the crotchety professor, and he had no intention of relieving his discomfort.

14

Toward morning on Tuesday, Jim had a dream.

In the dream, he sat in his deer stand at the far border of his ten-acre property along Chipmunk Coulee Road. Hunched against a tree in a little swale surrounded by mature woods, he watched for signs of wildlife activity. The morning light was just coming over the eastern horizon, the pink and gold blush of the sky filling him with a sense of wonder.

He reveled in everything outdoors: the musty smell of rotting leaves and the raucous calls of a pair of bluejays wheedling at each other from a grove of white pines. A pair of red fox pups roughhoused under the overhang of a rock formation that sprang from the ground like an ancient fortress at the back of Jim's property. A huge white oak stood like a primordial sentinel, its mottled gray trunk cracked and weathered in the light of the approaching dawn. Acorns lay scattered on the ground, and a chipmunk scurried among them. His beady little eyes took in Jim's presence. The varmint raised his tail and chirred a warning.

Jim sensed the old man's presence before he actually saw him. The hair prickled on the back of his neck, and a shiver of alarm ran down his spine. When he turned his head, the ancient warrior appeared as if out of a fog, materializing slowly, turning into flesh and blood. Tall and impressive in stature, the figure watched him from beneath a low-hanging branch of a giant white pine. His dark, liquid eyes studied Jim with the arrogant expression of someone who finds an adversary lacking. He moved carefully into the open, his steps silent. Jim glanced at his feet—moccasins. No wonder he hadn't heard him.

Jim remained seated and tamped down a sense of trepidation. He flicked on the safety of the 30-30 deer rifle, laid it carefully against the trunk of the oak where he'd been sitting, and pulled his knees up to his chest, resting his arms on top of them. Jim considered himself to be a good hunter and an even better detective, but he was embarrassed at the amount of noise he made in the woods compared to the old man. He felt immature and clumsy in his presence. Leaning against the trunk of a gnarled oak, Jim watched as the Indian silently sat down in front of him on a bed of fallen leaves and acorns. The old man crisscrossed his legs and leaned forward, studying Jim in silent scrutiny.

Several moments passed as the two men regarded each other. The whole scenario reminded Jim of interrogations he'd conducted where each participant sized up the other. The old man eyeballed Jim from top to bottom as if he could see to the bottom of his very soul. The Indian had a regal quality about him—the mark of a born leader. As the moments ticked by, Jim realized he'd never met anyone like him.

The Native's bronze face was the color of brushed suede, lined and wrinkled with age. Despite his years—Jim guessed he was in his late fifties—his body seemed younger, still strong and supple with broad, long, well-muscled legs and lean, beautiful hands that were surprisingly soft yet powerful. A wedge of hair stood in a stiff bristle on the top of his bald head. If protruding ears could be considered a distracting fault, then Jim conceded his ears were his worst feature, but he was still distinctly handsome in an arresting manner. Both ears were pierced, and bangles of very fine beads hung in loops from them. Around his long, aristocratic neck, another set of multi-colored beads lay gracefully on a buckskin tunic that was open at the neck and fringed on the sleeves and lower edges. His breeches were tanned deerskin, and he carried a magnificent handmade tomahawk that hung at his side from a belt.

Jim wondered about him. What did he want? How had he found him? Why was he here?

The warrior's dark eyes were deep pools of mystery, sad but, at the same time, fierce and unrelenting. His nose was long, and his wide nostrils flared above a sensitive mouth. Brooding silently, he gazed at Jim with hooded eyes, his lips full and pink.

Jim held out his hands in a gesture he hoped was amiable. "This is my land," he finally said, pointing down to the ground as if he needed to explain his presence.

The man nodded briefly. "You are on sacred ground," he said slowly. "My reason tells me that land cannot be sold. No one owns it. We must all care for it."

Now, it was Jim's turn to nod. "I can agree with that," he said slowly with seriousness. He waited, wondering what would happen next.

The ancient warrior seemed comfortable in the silent woods. In fact, he reveled in the silence, absorbing it, worshiping it. *He's content,* Jim thought. *Peaceful. Unperturbed. He's on familiar turf. This is his ancient homeland.* But it was clear from his proud but sad demeanor that he had seen battle and witnessed death. Jim noticed a deep scar on his neck as though a razor had slashed him. He'd fought for this land; he'd paid a price for his presence here. They sat in silence for several minutes, nature speaking a language that needed no words.

"You have children?" the old man finally asked. "A daughter?"

"Yes." Jim held up four fingers, then felt stupid about the gesture when the man was obviously adept in the English language. "Twins who are grown, and a younger girl and boy."

"A woman?"

"Yes, I have a beautiful wife. I love her very much," Jim said, tears filling his eyes, surprised at the sudden emotion that swept over him.

The old warrior gazed at him. "I am alone now. Asshewequa has left and gone to the clouds," he said sadly, his hand waving in an upward motion toward the brightening sky. "But she gave me children." Jim nodded in understanding.

They sat in silence again, listening to the waking woods. Jim heard the rustlings of unseen creatures around him, the birds flitting from tree to tree, the skitterings of chipmunks in the leaves. The night was over, and the day had come.

"Who are you?" Jim asked quietly.

"Your daughter called me in the night. I heard her voice and came. The Great Spirit has given her a gift," the old man said.

"Yes, He has," Jim said. He waited, unwilling to believe that Lillie had anything to do with this.

"You doubt," the old man said softly, "but you would be wise to believe her. Her sadness for my people has moved me."

Suddenly, Jim realized who the warrior was. His eyes widened in amazement. His throat felt parched, and he swallowed uncomfortably.

"Blackhawk?" he croaked hoarsely.

A slight smile crossed the lips of the old man. "I must go. Listen to your daughter. I have given her a message." Blackhawk rose to his feet in a graceful, lithe motion, turned his back, and disappeared into the woods, vaporizing like a mist.

"Wait! Wait!" Jim yelled loudly, awkwardly struggling to get up from the ground. Suddenly, he felt someone tugging at his arm.

"Jim, honey," Carol said sleepily. "You're dreaming."

Jim's eyes fluttered open, and he sat up abruptly, the quilts falling away from his chest. Carol sat up beside him, the swell of her breasts visible beneath her sheer nightgown.

"Are you okay?" she asked, her face puffy from sleep.

"No. No, I'm not okay," Jim stammered. He turned toward her

in a sudden movement that made her pull away from him. He was sweating, and his hair was disheveled. His wild-eyed stare alarmed her.

"Have you ever had a dream that was so real you'd swear it really happened?" he whispered intensely.

"Not lately, but from the looks of it, you must have had one." She brushed his cheek softly with the back of her fingers. "Jim, you're scaring me." She rubbed his arm gently, trying to comfort him.

He plopped backward on the bed, his head hitting the pillow with a *poof*. "Am I losing it?" he asked.

"I don't think so," Carol said, hovering over him, her brown eyes sympathetic. "But I can see this dream has rattled you."

"God, it was so real, honey. I could've almost touched him."

"Touched who, Jim?"

"Blackhawk. He came to me in my dream."

Carol was fully awake now. "Jim, this is getting weirder by the minute. Blackhawk came to you in a dream? Seriously?"

"Yeah. It was Blackhawk," Jim said matter-of-factly, his heart still thumping in his chest.

"Maybe you are losing it," Carol whispered.

□

Sam heard the rumble of a machine being rolled down the hospital hallway, its wheels clattering on the ceramic tile. He breathed deeply and opened his eyes. He was lying in a hospital recliner near Leslie's bed. He stretched his legs, unwinding from his cramped position, then walked to Leslie's bed, being careful not to jostle her and cause her any pain. Studying her face, he felt an intense desire to protect her and the life that grew inside her.

Leslie moved and grimaced, then let out a long, soft groan. Her headache had eased somewhat, but her shoulder and side were turning a deep ugly purple. She opened her eyes and looked at Sam.

"I feel like I've been hit by a Mack truck," she complained softly. "Even my teeth hurt."

"If you'd been hit by a Mack truck, you wouldn't be alive to tell about it," Sam said, smiling sadly. "They caught the guy who tried to rob the Kwik Trip. He was tackled by a couple of city cops, arrested, and hauled downtown to jail." He reached for her hand and held it firmly. "As soon as you feel up to it, we're going home, and I'll make you a breakfast fit for a queen."

A trim, friendly nurse swished into the room, her stethoscope swinging rhythmically against her chest as she came up to the bed.

"Get some sleep?" she asked, smiling, attaching the blood pressure cuff to Leslie's arm.

"A little bit. When can I go home?" Leslie asked.

"As soon as Dr. Lawrie does rounds and looks at your CT scan. Then, and only then, will he release you. Can I get you anything?" the nurse asked.

"Maybe some ice water. That's all," Leslie said. After the nurse had left the room, Leslie looked at Sam, her blue eyes somber. "How are you feeling about everything?"

"You mean the baby?" he said, staring past her into the hallway.

"Yeah, the baby."

Sam lowered his eyes and studied his wife. He took in her Scandinavian beauty: the fair skin, the long blonde hair, the arresting blue eyes. "Hey, I'm fine with it. No, actually, I'm really thrilled, but I think I'm a little bit scared," he said softly. Soft curls framed his unshaven face, and his eyes welled up with tender emotion. "Is that normal?"

"Perfectly normal, I'd say." Leslie paused a moment. "I'm a little scared, too. I was worried you'd be furious when I screwed up, but I should have known you'd take it in stride. You always do."

"You're going to be a beautiful pregnant lady and a great mom." Sam leaned over and kissed her mouth, lingering for a moment. He pulled back and said, "I figured out why Paco's been so protective of you lately."

"Oh, yeah? Why's that?" Leslie asked.

"He knew you were pregnant," Sam said.

"Sam. Get serious," Leslie said, dipping her chin slightly, dubious about his conclusion. "Dogs do not have the ability to do that. That's impossible," she chided, watching his face.

He looked at her intently. "Paco does," he proclaimed.

Leslie shook her head. "He's special, but he's not *that* special."

"What about pheromones?" Sam asked. "You do know, don't you, that dogs can smell substances that we could never detect in a hundred years? Their noses are thousands of times more sensitive than ours."

"So now you're telling me that I stink?"

"No, no, no. I'm just saying it's possible that Paco detected a change in the pheromones you give off, and when you got pregnant, he became more sensitive to that, tuned into the change in you, and then became more protective. A dog's world revolves around smell, honey."

"Highly questionable reasoning on your part," Leslie said laconically. "And I'm not sure I want more attention because of the way I smell." She crinkled her nose.

"Well, you always smell good to me, so go ahead and be a doubting Thomas if you want, but that's what I think."

"A what? Who's Thomas?"

☐

DeDe Deverioux heard water running somewhere and finally woke up and realized Jude was brushing his teeth in the bathroom that adjoined their bedroom. She hadn't talked to him yet about the phone number found on LeMar Burke's business card.

"JuJu?" she called softly.

"Uh-huh." Jude stuck his head around the frame of the bathroom door, his toothbrush in his hand. "Whaddya need?"

"When you're done, will you come in here? I need to talk to you about something," she said.

"I already know what it is," he said, disappearing into the bathroom.

"You do?"

"Yeah," he answered. "My phone number on the back of LeMar's business card. Right?"

Several moments passed. He walked into the bedroom and looked at DeDe: her dark eyes, her black glossy hair, and her large, voluptuous body. He'd been waiting for her to ask him about the phone number. Why she hadn't, he wasn't quite sure. He hoped it wasn't some test he'd already failed.

"How come you didn't mention it to me?"

"I didn't think it was that important, I guess. I barely knew LeMar, although I appreciated his patronage at the restaurant. But seriously, honey, that phone number was just a quirk of circumstance. A one-off."

He walked over to the bed and sat down next to his wife. DeDe had propped herself up against the headboard with a couple of pillows. Her expression was mysterious. Was she mad? Suspicious? He didn't know. He thought by now he'd be able to read her moods a little better. He'd really been trying, but the more he tried, the worse he got at interpreting her nonverbal cues.

DeDe said, "I just wanted to make sure we discussed it. I believe you, by the way, but it's because of something Higgins told me."

"Oh, yeah. What was that?" Jude asked, surprised.

"He said without trust, life can get pretty hard. I think he's right. So I decided to trust you on this." She lowered her chin and looked up at him with hooded eyes. "Don't disappoint me, baby."

He leaned over and kissed her. She placed her hands on his chest and returned the kiss, softly at first, then more urgently.

"We've got some time before breakfast," she said, pulling her nightgown over her head.

Jude's eyes softened with desire.

"I always have time for that," he said huskily.

▢

At breakfast that morning, Jim was exceptionally quiet. He was still spooked by the dream about Blackhawk, wondering about its meaning. His gullibility in believing that messages could be delivered to him in a dream left him questioning his sanity. Since when had he started believing people could materialize from thin air? Or that people who appeared in dreams could give him advice about some real situation in his life? *Only in a dream, bud,* he thought. *Or in the Bible.* Still, never in his adult life had he had a dream that seemed so amazingly real. The *Wisconsin State Journal* lay next to his plate, untouched and unread. He sat like a zombie, staring out the dining room window, watching the cardinals and chickadees at the bird feeder.

"Honey? Your waffle is getting cold," Carol reminded him. "Are you feeling all right? You don't look so good."

"Just trying to figure out the significance of my dream. What did it mean?" he said softly. "It was so real I felt like I could reach out and touch him."

"It might not mean anything, Jim," Carol said flatly, trying to distract him. "Dreams are just dreams, aren't they? The subconscious running across the movie screen of your mind?" She stood across the table from him and pointed to his plate. "Your waffle's getting cold."

Jim looked down at his food. He didn't even remember Carol setting the waffle in front of him. *Come on! Snap out of this,* he thought, irritated at his blockheaded stupor. *Who believes in the validity of dreams in everyday life anyway? Isn't that just some New Age hocus-pocus? Some Freudian mumbo- jumbo?* He groaned loudly. "You're right, honey. I don't know what's wrong with me."

He began pouring syrup over his waffle. Carol dumped his cold coffee in the sink and refilled his cup. She leaned down and kissed him on the temple.

"What's that for?" he asked grumpily, chewing on a chunk of waffle.

"Just because," Carol said, still carefully watching him while he ate. "Maybe I should call Vivian and ask her about dreams. She might have some suggestions."

Vivian Jensen was Carol's psychologist sister who had a burgeoning counseling practice in Holmen, a small city fifteen miles north of La Crosse. She'd given Jim many valuable insights into human behavior during several of his previous investigations.

"How 'bout if I call her today?" Jim offered. "I'd rather tell her about it and get it straight from the horse's mouth."

"Are you saying you don't trust me to relay your thoughts?" Carol asked, annoyed.

"No, not at all," Jim said, picking up on the change in her voice. "But you work today, and you've got to get the kids up and off to school and daycare. You've got a lot on your plate. I've got time. I can call her," Jim said.

Carol visibly relaxed. "You're right. I am kinda busy today."

"How 'bout if I cook tonight? Shrimp Alfredo with Parmesan? Salad? Breadsticks?" Jim asked. "Do we have some good wine?"

"Yeah, we do. Some cabernet and some edelweiss," Carol said, her voice returning to normal.

"Frozen shrimp in the freezer, right?"

"Yes, there's a bag in the freezer. Some breadsticks, too." She smiled at him. "I'll take it out so it can thaw. Shrimp Alfredo sounds wonderful."

☐

By ten o'clock in the morning, the team had gathered in the classroom down the hall from Jim's office. The weather outside was gray and foggy, which depressed everyone's mood. On Vine Street, the traffic splashed through puddles, throwing icy brown sludge on the snowbanks piled against the curbs. Depressed people in a blue funk hunched against the seemingly endless winter.

Paul, DeDe, and Sam stared at the whiteboard where motives, leads, and evidence about LeMar Burke had been collected. Right now, the board had significant empty white spaces intersected by photos of the victim at the crime scene, an enlargement of the ball club that had been used to kill Burke, and scrawls of information they'd found out in interviews. Jim hoped by the end of their session today that a significant amount of new information would help them develop a motive in the case.

"Trent Willow knew Burke," Jim said, drawing an arrow between the two men, "and seemed to like him. I didn't sense any latent hostility between them. On the contrary, they seemed to have become friends in a relatively short amount of time. He acknowledged that he was a big presence on the real estate scene, was well known nationally as a wheeler-dealer, and had actively pursued Terry Waite with the goal of purchasing his property."

"Which isn't for sale—not now, not ever—to quote Waite's own words," Paul added sourly, a sarcastic bite in his voice.

"Tell us about your meeting," Jim said, leaning back in his chair. He crossed his arms over his chest, his light blue shirt and maroon fleur-de-lis tie accentuating his blue eyes. He kicked his feet out in front of him, assuming a listening pose.

Paul rolled his eyes. "Waite is a royal pain, unabashedly caustic and arrogant beyond belief," he said. "I'll be honest. I didn't like him or his style of communication. He didn't hide his feelings of disgust when he talked about LeMar Burke and Tanya Cadwallader. However, Burke did make an offer on Waite's property." Paul paused for effect. "Two million bucks."

Sam whistled. "Holy moly. That's a lot of cash. That'd be hard to resist, especially on a university salary."

"Any other impressions?" Jim asked, locking eyes with Paul.

"After we exchanged insults, he lectured me about the high moral ground. I more or less suggested he was a prime suspect in Burke's death. That got a rise out of him, I'll tell ya," Paul said, frowning. "He practically chased me down the hall and out the door."

Sam scribbled notes on the whiteboard in his distinctive handwriting, a cross between an architectural script and calligraphy.

"So you think this Professor Waite hates Burke enough to have murdered him?" DeDe asked skeptically.

"Maybe. But right now, lots of things are possible. We don't have enough information yet," Paul explained. "But I intend to look into Waite's bank accounts, and I've got a warrant to get a look at Waite's phone records at Verizon to see who he was talking to in the weeks leading up to the murder."

"Good idea," Sam said, his pen poised in mid-air. "He sounds like a nut."

"A sanctimonious nut," Paul added.

Suddenly, Emily appeared at the door of the classroom. She knocked quietly on the door frame and waited.

Jim looked over at her. "Yes, Emily. Did you need something?"

"Jamie Alberg is out in the lobby," she said, shrugging her shoulders. "Do you want to see him now, or should I have him wait?"

Jim glanced at the wall clock. "Have him wait 'til we're done here. I'll meet with him in a half hour or so," Jim instructed.

"So I get to babysit him until then?" she asked, pursing her lips.

"Looks like it," Jim said, scratching his ear.

Emily rolled her eyes, turned, and walked briskly down the hallway, her skirt sashaying to the rhythm of her hips.

After she'd gone, DeDe continued. "We had a very interesting conversation with Ryan Blake at his shop outside Black River Falls. He really knows ancient weapons, especially Native American ones. We both got the feeling he was holding out, though. He knows more than he's letting on."

"I called a number of specialized shops in the area," Jim began. "A gallery in Eau Claire—Blue Earth/Copper Moon—sells originals and replicas of ancient Native American weapons. I've got a call in to the owner. Maybe that's who Ryan Blake sold it to. I'll have the owner of the gallery look up his sales and see if anything pops up."

DeDe nodded. "I'll contact Blake again. He was supposed to call us back, but he hasn't done that yet," she said. "His records are computerized, so you'd think he'd have found out by now who bought the murder weapon. Kinda strange."

"Yeah, it is," Jim said in an irritable tone. "Go see him again, unannounced. See what his reaction is. If we have to, we can get a search warrant to get the records."

"Right," DeDe said. "By the way, Ryan believes the weapon is one that was originally made by Blackhawk—or someone from his tribe. According to tradition, the Sauk people were talented in the extraction of lead from mines around Mineral Point. Apparently, Blackhawk marked his weapons with an inlaid bead of lead near the bottom of the handle. Our weapon has that mark."

"Blackhawk?" Jim repeated calmly, but the alarm bells pulsing through his system made him intensely uncomfortable. Parts of his dream came back to him in amazing clarity. He leaned forward and rested his elbows on his knees, trying to steady the uptick in his heart rate.

"Yeah, you know that Sauk chief who fought somewhere down on the river?" DeDe said. "Being from South Carolina, I'm not familiar with Wisconsin history."

"Well, you are, aren't you?" Sam said to Jim, noticing his deer-in-the-headlights look.

"I'm not an expert, but I do know some of the historical events that have taken place in this area." Jim paused, hoping the answer wouldn't draw attention to his historical knowledge. "I'll get moving on the warrant for the weapon sales today. Take it with you, and if he's uncooperative, you won't have wasted a trip," Jim suggested.

"Gotcha," DeDe replied. "One other thing that Leslie found out. When anyone was successfully killed with a ball club, it was left beside the victim. Kinda like a mark of valor or something."

"So whoever killed LeMar was proud of it?" Jim suggested.

"It appears that way. And it's someone who knows about the tradition behind the weapon," DeDe said.

"Getting back to this Trent Willow," Sam said, addressing Jim. "What were your impressions of him?"

"He seemed like a straight shooter to me. He's on the board of the

Driftless Native Consortium, and he tried to educate Burke about their aims and practices, but that didn't go over too well with him. Apparently, Burke hasn't bought into the global warming theory of the earth," Jim said. "Was that your impression, DeDe?"

"Yes," DeDe said. She leaned forward and tapped her finger on the table. "I think he was being straight."

"Sam, I want you to check out the Driftless Native Consortium. Talk to some people down at their corporate office and see if they know anything about Burke or Willow." Turning to Paul, he asked, "Burke's finances? What's happening there?" Jim asked, glancing at Paul.

Paul shuffled through his notes. "He's a millionaire many times over. Owns significant real estate in the heart of downtown New Orleans. Big 401K and other investments. A checking account that makes my savings look like a kid's piggy bank. But the thing that caught my eye was some significant cash withdrawals he made early this year—over $225,000. It's gonna be hard to trace—maybe impossible. But that's a big chunk of change in anybody's book."

"Have you talked to Burke's wife?" Sam asked.

"Nope. Thought I'd do that today," Paul said, clasping his hands behind his head.

"What about the crime scene? Did the techs find anything?" Sam asked.

"No prints. Whoever committed the murder was careful," Jim said.

They talked a while more, tried out some tentative theories, and ended with assignments for the next few days.

"All right. I think we're all on the same page," Jim said when they'd exhausted all the possibilities. "Take this info and turn over some rocks. Use your own judgment. Shake a few cages. Get your ear to the ground and get out on the street. Somebody knows about this murder. Somewhere there's a connection in this whole ball of information," Jim said, pointing at the whiteboard, which was filling up. "Somebody or something is still in the shadows. I'm leaving it up to you and your contacts on the street to root out something that will lead us in a new direction or tie all of this stuff together into a workable theory." Jim stood abruptly, waving his hand over the team as if he were blessing them. "Are we clear?"

"Got it," Paul said as they stood and walked toward the door. "What about Jamie?"

Jim gave Paul a dubious stare. "You're kidding, right? You're worried about Jamie?"

"Just saying. You never know what he's come up with."

"I'll deal with Jamie," Jim said patronizingly.

"Whatever, Chief," Paul muttered under his breath.

"Chief? Can I talk to you a minute?" Sam asked as he trailed after Jim down the hall.

Jim turned and waited for him to catch up. "Sure. Come on in," he said.

When they'd made themselves comfortable in chairs, Sam started. "I need to fill you in on Leslie's condition," he said. He nervously jiggled his leg up and down. When Jim stared at his jumping leg, he stopped abruptly.

"Yeah. So what's up?"

"Leslie's pregnant."

"Really? Wow! That's great," Jim said enthusiastically, a dimple denting his cheek. Standing behind his desk, he noticed Sam's scowl, and his smile faded. "Isn't it?" he added tentatively.

"Yeah. I mean, I guess so." Sam stopped talking. Jim waited. "Actually, it's fine, although the first I heard about it was when the doc spilled the beans yesterday in the ER. Leslie was going to tell me, but she hadn't gotten around to it yet."

"So it was a major surprise," Jim said, keeping his expression neutral.

"You could say that. But we're fine with it ... I think." His face scrunched up like he had a stomachache. Jim suppressed a grin. "What I needed to talk to you about was her assignments. I don't want her in any situations where there's a possibility of her getting hurt or shot. I've done some online research, and it's not just her health—policing situations can affect the baby, too."

"Sure, that's a valid concern," Jim agreed, nodding his head. "Listen. With Leslie's skills in research, I can easily assign her desk duty, but she may not like that. You're going to have to pave the way if this is gonna work. This conversation we're having right now is for our ears only. I want her to approach me and talk to me personally. If she finds out you're trying to plan her work assignments, she's gonna be ticked." Jim's eyebrows went up a notch. "Understand?"

"Yeah, I hear you, but she's so damned independent. She always thinks she can take care of herself. You know, all that feminist bullshit, but I'll talk to her tonight and try to convince her without letting on that we've talked."

Jim tipped his head to the side in a gesture of doubt. "Good luck on that. She's feeling okay?"

"She's sore from the accident, has some mild headaches. But as far as the pregnancy goes, she seems fine at this point, although the doc said she could spontaneously miscarry from the impact with the hard ground. But each day we get further down the road is a good sign, so hopefully that won't happen."

"Good. Encourage her to come in, and we'll have a conversation."

Sam stood up. "Thanks, Chief. I appreciate this."

"No problem. Glad to help, and congratulations. If you need any advice, been there and done that."

After Sam left, Jim leaned back and thought about the moment Carol had told him of her pregnancy. He'd been fifty-two, she forty-two. They'd been stupid in love and hadn't thought about protection, believing that Carol was menopausal, and the possibility of pregnancy didn't exist. He still cringed at their naivete when he thought about it. That came to a screeching halt when Carol said those two little words: "I'm pregnant." After a few arguments in which each tried to blame the other, they'd adjusted to the reality, and now they had Henri—sweet, brown-eyed, lovable Henri. Another son. Another one of God's precious blessings.

A soft tapping on his outer office door interrupted his thoughts.

"Jim?" Emily asked. "Jamie? You were going to see him?"

"Oh, sure. Send him in."

Jim began straightening his desk and answered a few brief phone calls. Two minutes later, Jamie strolled into the office. He was dressed in a pair of dark brown corduroy slacks, a plaid L.L. Bean wool shirt in soft hues of gold, tan, and brown, and a pair of Doc Marten hiking boots. His clothing gave the appearance of an older, more mature man, but that didn't fool Jim. He still looked like a junior high kid, wet behind the ears. The curly hair, the soft hazel eyes, the chasteness that rolled off him like a fresh breeze. Whether the clothes were a ploy to get the respect he thought he deserved, Jim couldn't tell, but it didn't take long for the familiar assertive attitude to spill from his lips as soon as he came into the room and found a chair.

"Now, Lt. Higgins," he started in, "I think you may be going down the wrong trail with your investigation of LeMar Burke's murder," he said, leaning back confidently, watching Jim's reaction.

Jim took a deep breath, checked his attitude, and decided to let Jamie hang himself. *If I give him enough rope, he'll do himself in*, he thought.

"And what trail would that be?" Jim asked calmly, continuing to straighten a few piles of paperwork. He picked up a pen, signed a form, and threw it in his OUT basket, then absentmindedly tucked the pen behind his ear.

Not getting the response he'd anticipated, Jamie continued. "Mmm ... well ... I think this murder doesn't exactly follow the typical motivational framework you usually use in your detective work."

"And what typical motivational framework are we talking about, Jamie?" Jim's blue eyes sparkled with humor.

"I don't think you're focusing on the underlying theme of this insurgent group I told you about the other day. They have regular monthly events. I'm not sure yet what their credo is exactly, but from my surveillance of this group—"

Sitting forward suddenly in his chair, Jim interrupted. "What surveillance?" he asked brusquely.

"Well, they have a *training camp.*" Jamie made air quotes as he talked and rolled his eyes. "If you can call it that, down on the Kickapoo Valley Reserve. You probably know that twelve hundred acres of the KVR are set aside for the Ho-Chunk Nation. These young upstarts have built a traditional shelter there, and they meet once a month to drink, throw weapons, like axes and ball clubs, shoot their bow and arrows, grill some venison steaks, and bullshit. They had a session there last weekend."

"Wait, wait," Jim interrupted again, waving his hand in the air, trying to keep up with the facts spilling out of Jamie. "How do you know about this group?"

"I have a Native friend who helps out at MVAC. You know, the Mississippi Valley Archaeology Center down on campus?"

"I'm well aware of it," Jim stated briskly.

"We've been on a number of archaeological digs together in the area, and in conversations with him, he mentioned this group. By the way, the tribal elders have tried to discourage their activities without much success."

"So this surveillance you did. Tell me about that," Jim said, interested despite his lack of enthusiasm for Jamie's theories.

"Through my friend, I heard about their weekend rally, and I parked my Jeep up on the ridge overlooking their camp behind a good blind of sumac, of course. My Jeep's brown, so it blended in nicely. Anyway, when they were all thoroughly drunk and acting like idiots, I crept down the hill and listened outside the shelter."

"What'd you find out?" Jim asked with more enthusiasm than he'd meant to show.

"Most of the Natives use the group's activities to escape their everyday lives and have a weekend with the guys. But Little Hawk gave quite an impassioned speech around the campfire. He has a fire and determination about him that I think needs to be taken seriously. He's very passionate about retaining and reclaiming lands that were lost in the Blackhawk Wars."

By this time in the conversation, Jim found himself pulled into Jamie's narrative.

"What?!" Jim said loudly, the annoyance written on his face. "That's ridiculous. He must be some kind of a nut! That's ancient history. You can't change that now. Most of the Native lands have been sold, developed, and paved over. He must have a few screws loose if he believes that."

"Yeah? Well, you tell him that. He's pretty serious. I think the saying "He has a fire in his belly" would apply in this situation." Jamie's hazel eyes had a seriousness that Jim found disturbing.

"So what *is* his plan?"

"Not sure yet," Jamie responded slowly, "but I think you have to consider the fact that he's acting as a lone ranger. He can't seem to move the insurgent group off first base in spite of his fiery speeches. They haven't taken up the cause, and he's pretty disgusted with them. He seems to have the idea that he is carrying on the tradition of his great-great-great-grandfather, fighting to regain the lands that were originally held by his descendants' tribe."

"You're not going to tell me that his ancestor is Blackhawk, the Sauk warrior, are you?" Jim asked, his large blue eyes filled with disbelief.

"One and the same, Chief."

Jim's heart ticked faster in his chest. "And I thought my dream was just a dream."

☐

Jamie left Jim's office in a flurry of self-importance, strutting down the hall and stopping at Emily's desk to promote his agenda. Jim sat in his office chair and thought about what Jamie had told him. Was it possible that Little Hawk had taken it upon himself to get rid of LeMar Burke, who was attempting to buy a prime piece of real estate from Terry Waite that had two caves containing ancient Native petroglyphs and was proven to have been the site of an ancient Oneota village? Did Waite and Little Hawk know each other? It was possible. La Crosse wasn't that large of a city. Waite was at the university, and it was likely that Little Hawk could have had him for some classes. Through conversations, Little Hawk might have exchanged his outmoded, radical philosophy with Waite. Jim was pretty conservative in his politics, but he knew that some university courses could be skewed to the left in a big way, depending on the professor's leanings. Maybe Waite had become a believer in Little Hawk's cause. Something to think about.

Jim shook his head. The possibility still seemed absurd to him, but he also knew that there were plenty of radical fringe elements in and around the Driftless Area—gun rights activists, survivalist groups, social iconoclasts anxious to prove a point, and certain university and clergy who preached a gospel of social liberation from the tyranny of capitalism. And what about Terry Waite? Had he secretly become sympathetic to the cause of Little Hawk? Were the two in cahoots, or was D'Marius acting alone? Little Hawk definitely needed to be investigated, and Terry Waite was suddenly becoming a much more interesting figure in the investigation.

Jim buzzed DeDe. "Can you come to my office for a minute?" Jim asked.

"Sure. I'll be right down."

When DeDe walked in, Jim laid out his plan. "I want you to research Ryan Blake's son, D'Marius, also known as Little Hawk. I know he's part of a Native insurgent group, but I don't know how serious they are about their aims and goals. You might try contacting the Ho-Chunk tribal headquarters in Black River Falls to see what they know about the group. They might have some kind of manifesto, but I get the sense they're not that formal—their goals are probably not in writing. I've decided to head up to Black River Falls this afternoon to talk to Ryan Blake again. Maybe he knows what his son's been doing."

"Good luck. He never mentioned his son when we talked to him," DeDe said. "I'll get on it right away."

After DeDe left, Jim stood, walked over to the door of his office, reached behind it, and retrieved his wool overcoat. Walking out into the lobby, Emily looked up briefly.

"Not too many changes in Jamie. Huh, Chief?"

"Ya got that right," he said, rapping on the counter above her desk. "But you have to admit he always seems to find out stuff nobody else knows."

When the meeting on the third floor broke up, Sam and Paul decided to drive to La Farge, a small village southeast of La Crosse on State Highway 82, to visit the headquarters of the Driftless Native Consortium.

The weather was pleasant, with temperatures in the mid-forties, brilliant blue sky with white cirrus clouds floating high in the air, and sunshine that warmed the cab of the Jeep as the men drove through the rolling hills and quiet farmland. Feeling drowsy from the heat in the vehicle, Sam reached over and flicked the fan off.

"Leslie gonna be all right?" Paul asked.

"Well, I hope so. She's been having some headaches, but that's supposed to disappear in time. Of course, her pregnancy has complicated things a little bit."

Paul turned his head slowly. "Pregnancy? Leslie's pregnant?"

"Yeah. I found out when she got to the ER. She was going to tell me but hadn't gotten around to it, and then, BAM—she got hit by a car. That woman can get in more sticky situations than anybody I know."

"But you're okay with her being pregnant?"

"Well, duh! Since I was a full and conscious partner in the whole conception thing, I guess I better be okay with it." Sam ran his hand through his wavy locks, looking indignant. "Besides, now that I've gotten over the initial shock, I'm actually kind of excited."

Paul sighed. Sam seemed like such a kid, although he was almost thirty. "Just a warning: Parenthood is like no other experience you've ever had."

Sam looked puzzled. "But it's good, right?"

Paul grinned. "Oh, for sure, but it will challenge you on levels you never knew existed."

They drove over a bridge where the Kickapoo River was swollen with melting runoff and threatened to overflow its banks. The village of La Farge was a typical small town with a population of 775, according to the latest village sign. It was complete with a main street that had a number of businesses, including a grocery store, a gas station/convenience store, a small medical clinic, one dentist, a truck repair garage, and a lumberyard. The recession had been tough on other enterprises in the small community, and several storefronts were dark and deserted. Sam turned left on East Penn and drove to the end of the street where an old feed mill had been converted to office space and now housed the DNC's corporate headquarters.

Sam and Paul got out of the car and walked into the entrance of the converted building. The old oak floors creaked as they wandered through the cavernous space, which was now filled with partially compartmentalized spaces where people were working on computers and answering phones.

Eventually, they found a door labeled Driftless Native Consortium Office. Inside, they found a middle-aged Native man behind a desk. He was on the phone and looked up expectantly when the two detectives walked in. He held up a finger as he finished his conversation.

After he hung up, he stood and offered his hand. Paul Loud Thunder was the district director of the consortium, an agency that the Ho-Chunk Nation had established to manage state and federal assistance programs more efficiently, delivering services to the Native residents in the area. Loud Thunder was dressed casually in a button-down blue oxford shirt, a vest with a distinctive Native American design, and a pair of khaki Docker jeans.

Paul began by telling Loud Thunder about the curious circumstances of LeMar Burke's murder.

"Were you aware of the murder?" Paul asked.

"I read something about it in the paper, and I saw a blip on the TV this morning before I came to work." A confused look came over his face. "So why are you here at the DNC? I don't understand," Loud Thunder said. "What could our agency possibly have to do with a murder?"

"We don't know, but we're checking out every lead we can think of. When we were looking through the victim's hotel room, we came upon your brochure. We wondered why Burke would have had one in his room."

Loud Thunder held out his hands and shook his head. "I have no idea. Our brochures are available at various retailers throughout the Driftless Area, so he might have picked it up on a whim."

Sam spoke up. "That makes sense. Do you know Trent Willow?"

A wide smile crossed Loud Thunder's face. "Oh, yes. He serves on our board and does a lot of PR for us. He's a real proponent of what we do here."

"Which is what, exactly?" Paul asked, cocking his head to one side.

"We try to promote an ethical regard and respect for our Native land and nature while encouraging the dignity and self-government of the Ho-Chunk people in the Driftless Area."

Paul asked, "Where do you get your funding?"

Loud Thunder leaned back in his chair, comfortable and confident. "Much of our funding comes from casino profits—a chunk is allocated to us every year—and since 2003, we also receive funding from the federal government through the U.S. Commission on Civil Rights. The funds are used for rural development, food programs, and infrastructure development. In addition, we accept donations from private citizens and some corporations." He got up from his desk and pulled open the top drawer of a gray filing cabinet tucked in the corner. After shuffling through some documents, he handed Sam a copy of their latest financial statement. "This document should help you understand our funding and what we do with those funds throughout the Driftless Area."

"Would that include maintaining and protecting petroglyphs located throughout the Driftless Area?" Paul asked.

"Petroglyphs?" Loud Thunder asked. "You mean cave art?"

"Yes," Sam said.

"No, and I would know if we did. I suppose in a roundabout way we do, but I don't know of specific funds used to do that. We really concentrate our efforts on rural business development, and that includes anything that adds to the strength and vitality of our tribal communities."

Paul sighed. "So your agency is more involved in social programs rather than protecting cultural sites?"

"Yeah, I guess you could say that. Sorry I couldn't be of more help," Loud Thunder apologized.

"No problem. We appreciate talking to you," Sam said.

Walking back to the Jeep, Sam commented, "Well, that was a dry run."

"Not unusual in our line of work. But about the time you don't check something out, it turns and bites you in the butt," Paul reminded him.

Sam reached over and started the engine. "That's for sure."

☐

Little Hawk leaned against the tailgate of his 2008 GMC Sierra 1500 crew cab pickup. He was parked at the Badger Sportsman's Club in Pleasant Valley, just a few miles south of Professor Terry Waite's hundred-acre property. The property was wedged between Mohawk Valley Road and County Trunk K at the southernmost end of La Crosse County. A two-wheeled trailer held a sign that advertised a chicken dinner, which had been held Saturday night. The parking lot was deserted now, which suited Little Hawk just fine.

He leaned down and strapped on his snowshoes. Reaching into the bed of the pickup, he grabbed his knapsack, which he had packed earlier with his cell phone, a first aid kit, a couple bottles of water, a few sticks of venison jerky, and some protein energy bars. He hoisted the backpack over his shoulders, shut the tailgate, and set off across the terrain, his long legs pumping in an easy stride, his poles and shoes swishing in the heavy snowpack.

The day was warm and gorgeous for March, with a hint of spring in the air, the sunlight streaming through the woods. Little Hawk walked for about a half-mile to the top of the ridge. The pines that peppered the hillside glistened with a blue-white sparkle that filled him with awe. Winter birds flitted from tree to tree, and a red-tailed hawk sat in a barren burr oak, calmly surveying the scenery for any sign of movement. When he reached the top of the ridge, Little Hawk looked down at a juncture below him where the two valleys tumbled together. Mohawk Creek cut a curving path through the bottom of the valley floor.

He descended the ridge at an angle, traversing the deep snow until he came to the bottom. The cave on Waite's land was another half-mile west toward the creek. It lay along a limestone outcropping that hugged a hillside. If you didn't know the location of the cave, you'd never believe it existed. It just looked like a depression on the side of the hill with an opening that was camouflaged by gray dogwood and elderberry bushes. A few boulders were strewn around the entrance.

As he approached the cave, he was startled to find another set of tracks in the snow that had come in from the north on Waite's land. He wondered who else besides Waite would know about the cave containing the petroglyphs. He stopped abruptly at the sight of the tracks, staying in the woods at the edge of the valley. He squatted down, got out his binoculars, and scoped the area around the cave opening. Little Hawk knew Waite well enough to know that he'd never let anyone on his land without permission.

He saw movement. Someone was coming out of the cave. A young man with dark hair dressed in winter garb pushed his way through the deep snow into the open sunshine. He wielded a carved walking stick. A large pack was slung over his shoulder, sagging with something heavy. He looked around. Little Hawk flattened himself under the bows of a large blue spruce and watched the young man's movements, particularly his facial expressions. He seemed quite confident, and a smugness moved over his face as he looked back toward the cave. Moving northward through the open field, the intruder took long, determined strides on a pair of antique snowshoes, soon distancing himself from the cave's entrance. The young man disappeared into a grove of mixed hardwoods and pines along the creek. Little Hawk crouched on his knees and watched him depart.

He was not easily spooked, but the young visitor to the cave left him with a sense of uneasiness. He thought he was the only one who knew about the cave. He'd never seen this kid before, and he wondered what he was doing here. He felt a familiar deep-seated suspicion about this situation, something he attributed to the interactions he'd had in the white world. Had Waite sold out and told someone else about the location of the cave? He doubted it, but now he wasn't so sure.

Through years of experience, Little Hawk had learned to negotiate two cultural worlds—the white Anglo culture and his Ho-Chunk Native culture. To be successful as a Native, you had to walk in both worlds. In some ways, he considered himself more accepting and inclusive than many of his white friends and acquaintances. Most of his young years were spent learning the importance of this dual universe from his father, grandmother, and tribal elders. He'd found the white man's motives of greed and materialism were often the pillars of their value system. Little Hawk found that abhorrent. The only exception to that rule he'd ever found was Terry Waite.

When the young man finally disappeared among the trees, Little Hawk stood and moved toward the cave. Reaching the entrance, he knelt in the snow and squeezed through its narrow opening. His flashlight on his phone illuminated the ancient drawings: the wingspan of a stylized thunderbird, a herd of white-tailed deer who raced along the rock wall with a hunter in pursuit, the abstract outline of a buffalo. Beautiful, primitive drawings depicting daily scenes of survival. Evidence of the intelligence, resilience, and staying power of his people who had sustained their way of life over the past several centuries.

He scuttled his way deeper into the cave until he came to a natural chiseled rock shelf. He moved a few large stones that looked as if they belonged there and sighed deeply, relieved at what he saw. The ball club was still there, encased in a weathered deerskin sheath. Apparently, the young man hadn't discovered this treasure—yet. He carefully covered the club and moved the rocks back into a natural-looking arrangement.

This is what he fought for—the preservation of his ancient culture and the dignity and sovereignty of his people. His eyes scanned the petroglyphs, and he breathed in the moist, chalky air as if gaining strength for the tasks ahead. *Remember, this is the evidence of our people's existence*, he thought. *Honor them and preserve what is left.*

☐

Detective Paul Saner sat at his desk since returning from the trip to La Farge. He spent the last few hours calling and badgering anyone who might have an idea where the large amounts of cash from LeMar Burke's bank account had gone.

"So, Mrs. Burke, you have no knowledge about the large withdrawals from your husband's checking account over the last few months?" Paul asked.

"I'm sorry, detective," Mrs. Burke replied. "My husband was the sole caretaker of all financial things." Her voice was soft and had a lilting southern accent. "Whenever I needed money, I just used our debit card. I really have no idea why he would have needed cash in such large amounts."

"Did he have a gambling or an addiction problem that you were aware of?" Paul asked.

"Oh my, no! LeMar would have a drink occasionally, but he wasn't even what I would call a social drinker. And he detested gambling—considered it a weakness not to be indulged." Paul heard some snuffling, and when Mrs. Burke resumed speaking, he could tell she'd started to cry. "He was so good to me. I miss him so much," she said, her voice cracking.

"I'm sorry to have to ask you these questions, but it's really important that we try to find out where this cash went."

"Have you contacted the bank?" Mrs. Burke asked, sniffling.

"Oh, yes. They thought it was highly irregular on his part. Apparently, your husband was a very financially responsible client. They were just as puzzled as I was," Paul explained.

"I'd really like to help. After all, I, more than anyone, would like to know who killed my husband."

"Of course you would. I understand," Paul said soothingly. "Can you think of any other contacts that I might talk to? I'm at a dead end here, and anything you could tell me would really help."

They talked a few minutes more, and Mrs. Burke gave him three contacts, but she seriously doubted that they would have any ideas about the money.

An hour later, after numerous calls to the suggested contacts and a call back to the Crescent City Credit Union, Paul was no further ahead than he'd been two days ago. He'd come up empty, and he was out of ideas.

☐

Ryan Blake stood at the back door of his small house and vigorously shook the rug. Wood shavings and dirt tumbled out into the air and peppered the snow with a coating of fine dark dust. Housecleaning was not his strong suit, but every once in a while, he attempted some cleaning, such as it was. He went back in the house, laid the rug on the freshly scrubbed floor by the door, and walked through his living quarters to his workshop in the front of the house. All morning he'd been working on a ball club replica that had been commissioned by a collector of ancient Native weaponry from Superior, Wisconsin. The club was taking shape. The ash burl, though hard to carve, was beginning to show its grain. The jaws of a bear were becoming defined and sharp. When the final coat of beeswax was applied, the glow of the wood and detail of the carving would be breathtaking.

Using a wood pick and other carving chisels, Blake continued to remove minute pieces of the burl, adding a level of detail not usually found in replicas. But after all, that's what set his work apart from the rest of the crowd—his meticulous attention to detail and an emphasis on the appropriate cultural images, which made his weaponry as good, if not better, than the originals.

The bell above the shop door tinkled softly. The front door opened. Blake looked up from his workbench to see a tall, slim man with grayish-blond hair standing just inside the door. He wore a fine gray woolen overcoat of exceptional quality, a crisp blue pinstriped shirt, a dark tie, and soft gray slacks.

"Can I help you?" Blake asked politely, but inwardly, he thought, *Cop.*

"I hope so. I'm Lt. Jim Higgins, La Crosse Sheriff's Department," he said formally, holding out his ID as he walked toward the counter and stopped in front of Blake.

Blake took in the demeanor of the man standing before him. *More questions*, he thought. He stuck out his hand, and the two men shook. Jim stood by the display counter taking in the atmosphere of the shop. The smell of wood smoke from the small stove along the wall reminded him of his little Franklin stove in the corner of his living room. Along the same wall as the stove, a corkboard displayed various weapons that Blake had crafted.

Jim scanned the artifacts hanging on the wall. "Your weapons are impressive. I'm a fan of Native American baskets. Or I should say, my wife Margie was. The only weapon I have is a hatchet pipe made of catlinite from the quarries over by Pipestone, Minnesota."

Jim watched Ryan's expression. Blake was dressed casually in jeans and a stained sweatshirt. Jim noticed his long fingers and his wary, brown eyes.

"Things made from catlinite are very beautiful. That type of dark red stone has a special quality. I'm glad you like my work. How can I help you?" Blake said, keeping his voice neutral. He gently laid the wood pick he'd held in his hand on the top of the glass display case.

"A few days ago, I believe you talked to two detectives—Birkstein and Deverioux—from the La Crosse Sheriff's Department," Jim started to say. Blake nodded agreeably. "You were going to check your records and find out who purchased the ball club that was found at the scene of a murder victim in Genoa. Did you ever dig up that sales receipt?" Jim's blue eyes reminded Blake of a clear mountain stream. He wasn't normally intimidated by people or the questions they asked, but suddenly he felt a chill of apprehension.

"Actually, I just found it yesterday. Let me go back in my office and get it," Blake said. "Be back in a minute."

Blake turned and disappeared through a door with scuff marks on the bottom and a doorknob that wobbled when it was turned. While he was gone retrieving the receipt, Jim casually walked around the shop. He studied the knives in the display case and the weapons hanging on the wall. The man's skills had obviously been honed and perfected through years of practice. A few minutes later, Blake was back, a piece of paper in his hand. He slid it across the counter toward Jim.

Jim picked up the receipt and looked at it—Blue Earth/Copper Moon Gallery in Eau Claire. "Thanks," he said. "Were you aware, Mr. Blake, that your son, D'Marius, has been associating with a fringe group of young Ho-Chunk Natives?" Jim asked, his stare locking with Blake's.

The weapon maker sighed and looked down in an attitude of defeat. "What's the old saying? 'Youth is wasted on the young.'"

Jim shrugged, waiting for his explanation. "So, is he involved with them?"

Ryan nodded. "Yeah, the last time I checked, he was still hanging around them."

Jim asked, "What do you know about their goals?"

"I'm aware of some of their activities, like the camping they do down on the reserve. I've tried to discourage his participation with them. They seem like a bunch of hoodlums to me, but he won't listen. He says they're of a like mind, whatever that means. I personally don't think they pose much of a threat other than giving the Ho-Chunk Nation a bad name. Alotta bluff, booze, and bullshit, in my opinion. I guess when I think about it, I wasn't much different when I was that age. I drifted and was pretty aimless for a while. It wasn't until I learned the art of making weapons that I really got my life together. My son is like me, idealistic and proud of our Native heritage."

"So you don't think these young men have any serious goals which might involve the murder of a very prominent real estate agent who was interested in land once held by your tribe?" Jim asked, crossing his arms over his chest.

"They don't have enough brains or energy for that. From my understanding, they're a bunch of weekend warriors who like to have a drinking party every once in a while and get away from their wives and kids."

Jim made a wry face. "Fair enough. Do you think your son could be involved in other illicit activities that might involve large amounts of cash—say drug trafficking?" Jim asked. He was thinking about the cash that had disappeared from LeMar Burke's checking account.

Blake made a face of disapproval. "My son is passionate, I admit that. But I don't believe he would bring harm to anyone. He's idealistic at heart. He won't even drink a beer, let alone do drugs."

"Where does your son live? Here?" Jim asked, pointing at the counter.

"No. He has a place on Norwegian Valley Road over by Cashton. When he got his tribal casino check at eighteen, he was one of the few in his senior class at BRF who actually wanted to invest in something that holds its value—a piece of land. He has a real nice little place—a ranchette with forty acres back in the woods. Part of his 'eighteen money' is still in the bank, so he's not typical of most Native kids his age."

"How much money do they get when they turn eighteen?" Jim asked, finding this conversation interesting.

"The casino earnings are put in a trust for them until they're eighteen. They have to finish high school and get a diploma. Then they take a finance class to learn some money-management skills, although most of that goes over their head. All they see is this huge wad of cash. Right now I think it averages anywhere from one hundred fifty to two hundred thousand dollars."

Jim whistled and his eyes grew large. "That's a lot of money for a kid to handle."

"Yeah, and a lot of the kids get themselves in trouble. They spend it like water, and then they've got nothing left. Fast cars, trips to Disney for their entire family, clothes and shoes at the mall, paying off bills that their parents have accumulated over the years. Pretty soon, it's all gone. A lot of hard-earned lessons and long-time regrets."

They talked awhile longer, and Blake gave Jim directions to Little Hawk's cabin.

Jim reached out his hand again, grasping Ryan's firmly. "If you find out anything about your son's recent activities with this group, please let me know. But I'll try and catch up with him in the next few days." He slid his calling card toward Ryan. "My home number's on the back."

Ryan glanced down at the card, then said firmly, "There's no way I'd ever believe my son would be involved in a murder."

Jim held his stare. "I can't tell you how many times I've heard that in my line of work, sir. I sure hope you're right."

Jim turned and quietly exited the shop. He climbed in the Suburban and sat for a minute looking at the unassuming home. Nothing fancy. In fact, for someone as well-known as Ryan Blake, Jim was surprised at the run-of-the-mill building. The roof needed a shingle job, the windows were about fifty years old, and the yellow siding was faded, flaked, and peeling. A collection of dead, rusted-out vehicles were strewn helter-skelter around the property, their metal humps covered by patches of snow. Jim didn't know what he'd expected, but it wasn't this. He turned out onto the highway.

As he drove back to La Crosse in the late afternoon, he had a sense that Ryan Blake really didn't approve of this insurgent group. He seemed to think they weren't capable of anything as serious as murder, but Jim knew from experience it wasn't always the murder that was complicated; it was covering up the deed after it had been done. His intuition told him Little Hawk might be involved somehow. Right now, he sensed that someone else was either covering for him or trying to hide what had already been done.

Despite the efforts of the team, they had little to go on. Unless Sam, Paul, and DeDe uncovered something that would lead them further along the path or give them some new options, they were at a standstill.

15

It was after six o'clock by the time Jim had puttered around in the kitchen Tuesday night making shrimp Alfredo, a salad, and breadsticks. He was late getting home and late getting the evening meal started. Henri and Lillie were not enthusiastic about the shrimp and had pushed their food around the edge of their plates for ten minutes. When it was obvious they didn't like the shrimp, and although it went against their rule about the kids trying new foods, Carol got up from the table and made each of them a hot dog.

"Don't say anything," she reminded Jim, holding up her hand as she sat back down at the table. "I just don't have it in me tonight to force them to finish the shrimp. They tried it. It'll have to do."

"It's not a problem, honey. Bad day?" Jim asked, crunching on a mouthful of lettuce. He noticed her frazzled look, the dark circles under her eyes. There was a sadness about her tonight that told him something bad had happened at work.

"There was an accident up by the Home Depot exit next to Farm and Fleet. A seventy-seven-year-old lady cut someone off. They went onto the shoulder, which was soft, the car flipped, and a middle-aged man was killed. Messy, very messy," she explained. She pushed her plate away. The fatigue on her face reminded Jim of the difficulty of her job.

"Family?"

"Yep. A wife and four teenagers. Not good," she said softly. Jim nodded in understanding.

"I'm sorry, honey," he said, touching her hand. They continued conversing as Jim filled Carol in about his interview with Ryan Blake.

"So this Blake guy is pretty well-known for his skills in weapon-making?" Carol asked.

"From what I've read online, on his website, and in a few trade magazines, the guy's a genius."

Lillie piped up. "Real geniuses are pretty rare, Bapa," she said with authority. "But Mozart was a genius, hands down."

Jim raised his eyebrows and took another bite of shrimp. Lillie followed up with a question. "When is Sara going to come home and see us? I miss her," she finished, her mouth forming a moue. Sara, Jim's daughter from his first marriage, had been their live-in babysitter when Henri was born, and she had bonded deeply with Lillie almost immediately.

Jim sighed. "Well, she'll call one day, and I'm sure it'll be soon." He wiped his plate with a breadstick, noticing Lillie's pout. Carol gave him a ponderous glance.

"Can I call Sara?" Lillie asked, her eyes wide with the appealing idea, her gaze shifting back and forth between her parents.

Carol smiled softly. "Sure, baby. Finish your dinner, and we'll go in Daddy's office and call."

"Really, Mom?" she asked, disbelieving.

"Really," Carol said with a faint smile. "Eat your hot dog and your grapes. You, too, Henri." Henri chomped on a breadstick instead and gulped his milk.

"I can talk, too?" Henri asked.

"Sure, you can talk to Sara, too. Finish up your food first," Carol repeated.

While Carol supervised the phone call to Sara, Jim cleared the dishes from the table, put the extra food in the refrigerator, and loaded the dishwasher. He was relaxing in the black swoopy chair in the living room watching the PBS nightly news when Carol appeared at his side, cell phone in hand. He looked up at her.

"Sara wants to talk to you," she said. "I'm going to get the kids ready for bed."

He muted the TV and took the phone, trying to manage the mix of feelings he was having: irritation that Sara had announced her engagement on social media before she'd had the courtesy to call him, trepidation that the conversation wouldn't go well, and anxiety about how much this wedding was going to cost him.

"Sara, honey. How are you?" he said, faking the cheerful tone in his voice.

"Hi, Dad. How's everything there?" she asked, her voice soft and apologetic.

"Lillie and Henri miss you terribly. So do Carol and I. When are you going to get down here to see us?"

"We've already had our spring break, but we were hoping to drive down on Saturday. Would that work?"

"Absolutely. That'd be great! We'll freshen up the basement apartment for you."

"Sounds good. We'll have a lot to talk about."

"I can believe it," Jim said, working to keep the sarcasm out of his voice. His thoughts raced. *Like why I wasn't informed about your engagement. Like how this love affair happened in the first place. Like why our relationship has gone down the tubes … Like all kinds of stuff I can't even put into words.*

As if reading his thoughts, Sara said, "I'll explain everything when we come. Okay, Dad?"

"That's fine. We'll talk then. Love you," Jim finished.

"Me, too." And the line went dead.

Jim huffed and leaned back in his chair, the cell phone lying in his lap. He stared at the ceiling, trying to come to terms with the changes in his daughter's life. But then, when he analyzed it, he supposed he was the one having trouble adjusting. His little girl married. *Don't be a jerk. Be happy for her and Jerome. Just because she's fallen in love with someone doesn't mean she loves you any less.*

After an extended call to his son John, inviting him to dinner Saturday night, Jim walked down the hall and said goodnight to Lille and Henri. Then he immersed himself in a new C.J. Box mystery, and an hour later, Carol called him from the back of the house. He walked down the hallway into the bedroom, but she wasn't there.

"I'm in here, Jim," she called softly.

Jim laid his book on the nightstand and opened the door to the master bathroom. The scent of something soft and delicate filled the air. Candles had been lit, and the lights were turned down very low. The room glowed with a romantic vibe. Carol's work clothes and underthings were in a pile in front of the tub.

Five years earlier, Jim had built a luxury suite for his first wife, Margie, complete with a deep soaking tub that was centered in the middle of the room. The ceiling opened to the night sky by means of two large skylights. It was one of his favorite things about his house—this bathroom spa that looked up at the stars and his black swoopy chair in the living room. Moonlight glowed on the snow at the back of Jim's property. The shadows of the majestic oaks and maples along the border of the yard cast black shadows that shifted and danced in the moonlight.

"Hey, mind if I join you?" Jim asked. He pulled off his socks and tie, unbuttoned and removed his shirt, and dropped his trousers and boxers on the floor. Carol looked at him longingly.

"I was hoping you'd join me, love," she said in a sultry voice. She was sipping another glass of wine, and the candlelight around the room added a special ambiance that always aroused Jim. He lowered himself into the warm, soapy water opposite Carol, basking in the gentle fragrance of lilac and lavender. He took in her dark hair, her mischievous brown eyes, her shapely arms resting on the edges of the tub, the water and bubbles barely covering her breasts.

He let out a low moan. "Boy, this feels great," he whispered, immediately relaxing.

"After the day we've had, I figured you and I could use a little downtime," Carol said, gazing at the stars overhead.

"Any chance Lillie's going to spy on us like she's done before," Jim asked, his blue eyes twinkling, "and then announce it to the world?"

Carol laughed softly. "Nope. I checked on her fifteen minutes ago. She's out for the count. Henri's dead to the world, too."

Jim took Carol's hand and pulled her toward him. She didn't resist; instead, she planted her breasts on his chest and gave him a deep, passionate kiss. She pulled back and then lightly fingered the scar on his shoulder. She did that sometimes when she was feeling insecure about the dangerous situations he got into. He'd been shot more than once, and Jim knew Carol struggled with the violent characters he encountered in his job. He knew their lovemaking grounded her; it made the nasty shadows disappear, if only for a few passionate moments.

He grasped her shoulders and kissed her again. "Mmm. Now that's what I'm talkin' about," he said huskily.

"Less talk and a little more action," Carol said, her brown eyes soft with desire.

"Sara's comin' home on Saturday," he whispered in her ear as his hands wandered over her naked, slippery body. "That's good news."

"Uh-huh."

"We need to clean ..."

"Shhh, Jim. You're spoiling the mood. Be quiet and kiss me again," Carol whispered fervently.

"I can do that."

☐

Later that evening, the dull *thwack* of an ax embedding itself in a board was immediately followed by the exuberant roar of approval from a crowd standing near the narrow throwing lanes. Detective Sam Birkstein was nursing a beer at The Aimless Ax bar on the corner of Fourth and Jay in downtown La Crosse. Perched on black metal stools, patrons were drinking while others were focused on the ax-throwing competition. The crowd was a mix of college and middle-aged customers. By nine-thirty, the place had filled up with enthusiastic fans. Two regular competitors were having a friendly match, and several more clientele were lining up for their first attempt at throwing an ax at a bullseye.

The bar provided cheap axes sharpened to a razor edge, safety release forms for obvious reasons, and fifteen-foot throwing lanes with a plywood bullseye target at each end of the lanes. Eight lanes were separated from each other by panels of heavy metal fencing designed to keep ax-throwers and spectators safe. A long wooden bar stretched down one side of the establishment. A few tables and chairs were scattered near the front of the tavern, but the majority of the space was set aside for ax-throwing.

Sam was dressed in what he hoped was typical college clothing so he'd blend in with the college-aged crowd: well-worn jeans, a black T-shirt that said "Define Adult," which he wore underneath his Wisconsin Dells letterman jacket. He'd actually been a Dells Chief in high school, participating in track his junior and senior years when his dad was the Lutheran pastor at one of the churches in town. The jacket held good memories for him, and he liked the blue and black headdress on the back. He leaned over to the two girls sitting next to him at the bar. One of them was hefty with wide shoulders; the other had a slender profile.

"You've seen this before, I take it," he said to the girl closest to him.

Both girls grinned and slurped their beers. The heavier of the two looked Sam up and down while she wiped the beer from her lips with her tongue. *God, don't let them come on to me*, Sam thought.

"Yeah, we come here pretty often. The guys who hang out here have a serious male attitude, ya know. No quasi-transgender inclinations here," Wide Shoulders said. Sam noticed her heavy makeup and low-slung blouse. He tried not to stare at her cleavage. "It's hard to find guys who aren't always apologizing for their sexuality."

"Anybody who can throw an ax when they're half lit has got to be on the primal end of things, don't you think?" the other girl commented, sampling a deep-fried cheese curd. Her hair was piled on top of her head in a messy yet attractive topknot. "Kinda turns my crank, you know," she finished, taking another swig of beer. "Always did like the lumberjack type. This ax throwing puts reality TV to shame."

Sam slowly shook his head. "Guess I hadn't thought of it that way before, but this is the first time I've been here, so I'm still getting the vibe of the place. Know what I mean?"

Wide Shoulders nodded, her whole upper body swaying in time with her head. "Oh yeah, I totally understand. It *is* kinda shocking the first time you watch it. Ax throwing is really popular in Canada, I guess. Leave it to La Crosse to come up with something like this. I'll bet the two guys who thought this up are rolling in some big-time money."

Another ax whistled through the air but banged noisily off the board. A groan of disappointment rippled through the crowd. As Sam watched the competition, he noticed a petite, intense blonde sitting at a table toward the front of the pub, nodding in a preoccupied way while she listened to a guy babble in her ear. Her whole body seemed to be taut with tension, not unlike someone walking a tightrope. After a few moments, she got up from the table and walked over to the bar, got an ax, and stood in line by one of the cages.

Sam felt Wide Shoulders tug at his arm. "Oh boy, you're in for a treat. That little blonde gal is really good—I mean, she has exceptional throwing abilities."

"Really?" Sam commented. "I wouldn't think women would find ax throwing very stimulating. Seems like a guy thing to me."

"She's different," Slender Girl said. "I guess she has some Indian boyfriend. He isn't here tonight, but supposedly he has no time for whites imitating Native American's skills."

"You mean Little Hawk?" Wide Shoulders asked, looking at her friend. She waved her hand nonchalantly. "He's the only one who takes himself seriously." She frowned. "But he is kinda scary."

"Little Hawk?" Sam said. "Who's he?"

Wide Shoulders gave Sam a dubious look. "You haven't run into Little Hawk downtown or on campus? Boy, you are sheltered. You need to get out a little more."

"I've been off my drinking game lately," Sam said, but he felt good that they actually thought he was a college student. She lifted her eyebrows and focused her attention back on the blonde.

"Well, you'd remember Little Hawk if you met him. Tall, dark, long black hair. Really good looking, but he's a total lunatic who thinks he's going to reclaim Native lands from white owners. You should hear the arguments he gives some of the professors. What a stupid idea!" Wide Shoulders sputtered. "He must not know how the real world works."

"Hey, look!" Slender Girl pointed toward one of the cages. "The little blonde gal is going to throw."

Sam watched in fascination as the petite woman approached the cage. She checked her grip on the ax, made a few practice passes, planted her feet in a wide stance, then rocked back and forth and, with surprising heft, released the ax. The weapon tumbled end over end, hitting the wooden bullseye with a deafening thud. The crowd, especially the women, cheered wildly. She retrieved the ax and pitched it confidently at the target several more times. She was amazingly accurate, and her poise with the weapon was impressive. It seemed to fit in the hollow of her hand.

As she made her way back to her table amid a congratulatory crowd, Sam got off his stool, set his beer bottle on the bar, and thanked the girls for their company. He walked through the crowd and was jostled on all sides until he stood in front of the blonde's table.

She looked up at Sam with a question-mark expression. She seemed exceptionally intense and focused.

"Your skills with the ax are pretty impressive," Sam said. The guy seated next to her gave Sam a dirty look.

"Just takes practice," she said, shrugging off the compliment. She crossed her legs in a seductive move and ran her eyes over Sam.

"You must have had a lot of that," Sam continued, his hands in his pockets. "Practice, I mean."

"Are we still talking about ax throwing?" she asked, her voice mellow and husky.

The guy sitting with her at the table interrupted. "Hey, look, buddy, we were busy here," he said rudely, flicking his finger back and forth between himself and the blonde. "You're kind of intruding, you know?"

Sam held up his hands. "Sure, no problem." Turning to the blonde, he said, "Congratulations. You lit the place up."

"Thanks," she said simply. She stood abruptly. Someone bumped into her, shoving her against Sam. He caught her arm. "You've got cop written all over you, buddy," she whispered in his ear.

"It's that obvious, huh?"

"Yeah. I think you're losing your touch," she said, brushing past him. "But you are *very* cute."

As she walked through the crowd to the bar, Sam went out the front door and walked to his car. *Must be getting too old for the college scene. Can't blend in anymore*, he thought. His cell beeped in his pocket. He climbed into the car and answered.

"Birkstein."

"Sam, where are you?" Leslie asked sleepily.

"Striking out. I guess my undercover skills are slipping. Somebody spotted me, and I even wore my Dells letterman jacket."

"That's probably what blew your cover. Letterman jackets are way out of style, honey. Very uncool these days." She giggled softly. "Poor baby."

Sam leaned over and started the Jeep. "Are you feeling better?"

"I've got a slight headache, but I'm good."

"Should I be worried?" Sam asked.

"No. I'm fine. I'm going to have a cup of tea and get ready for bed."

Sam smiled at the thought of Leslie sitting with her teacup and protected by Paco, her trusty black lab. He didn't worry when Paco was on the scene. "Well, I'm going to sit here awhile. I won't be home until later, probably closer to midnight."

"If your cover's blown, what's the point?" Leslie asked.

"I might see something that could be useful. You never know," Sam said.

Leslie sighed. "Paco and I are going to bed. You've got your key, right?"

"Yep. I'll be home later."

Sam sat in his Jeep next to the curb in front of The Aimless Ax and watched carousers wandering the streets, jovial and happy as the alcohol buzzed through their systems. When he saw a city police cruiser roll by, he jumped out of the Jeep. The taillights on the squad car lit up as the policeman braked. Sam ran to the passenger window.

He recognized the officer when the window rolled down.

"Hey, Mike. Mind if I jump in and ride with you for a little while?" Sam asked.

"No problem. What are you doin' out here tonight?" Mike asked as Sam crawled in the front passenger seat. Although he worked for city police, Mike Leland was also earning credits toward his detective certification. He had previously assisted Higgins' team in a take-down of a dangerous criminal holed up in Vernon County. The squad car smelled of stale coffee and onions. Sam looked down at the console between the seats where a limp sub sandwich sat languishing in a paper wrap—the source of the onion smell.

"I'm trying to get a handle on a little ax-throwing blonde that I just saw put on quite a show at that bar on the corner of Fourth and Jay," Sam said, buckling his seat belt. He studied the side of Mike's face, noticing the fatigue and weariness in his expression.

"I thought you were happily married," Mike said, frowning, catching Sam's eye.

"I *am* happily married. I'm not trying to put the moves on her. I'm investigating that murder down by Genoa, and my intuition tells me she may be involved. You know the one where we found that ancient ball club in the snowbank," Sam said. His irritation at Mike's comment about prowling for another woman and its implications confirmed the power of the cop gossip mill. Still, Mike was a good friend and an even better source of street information, so he ignored the insinuation. "She was extremely accurate with those axes, and if she can fling an ax, then she can throw a ball club, too."

"Sounds like kind of a weak link. You must have more to go on than that, don't you?" Mike asked dubiously.

"Oh yeah. She also knows Little Hawk."

"Who's that?" he asked, even more skeptical.

"D'Marius Blake. Ever heard of him?" Sam asked.

Mike braked for a trio of drinkers who jaywalked in front of the squad car. The amber hue of the street lights added a garish quality to the revelers on the street. "Name sounds familiar. I've probably given him a D&D – not uncommon for kids in the college bar scene. And now they get to throw axes when they're drunk?" He shook his head disgustedly. "Who's idea was that, anyway?"

"I don't know, but listen to this—D'Marius' dad is a famous ball club maker. And the club we found by the body in Genoa was made by him."

"Still sounds kinda far out to me," Mike said. He reached for the used sub sandwich.

"Don't eat that. You'll probably get salmonella," Sam warned. Mike grimaced and tossed the sandwich back on the console.

By this time in the conversation, Mike had patrolled his way around the vicinity of Third Street and was driving past the back alley behind The Aimless Ax. Sam turned his attention in that direction and noticed the silhouette of two people in the alley who looked like they were arguing. A smaller person was poking a finger into the chest of a much larger person. There was no mistaking the intent; the two were having a disagreement of some kind.

"Hey, stop a minute," Sam said. Mike braked suddenly and pulled over to the curb. Sam hopped out of the car. He leaned down and talked through the passenger window. "Come back and check on me in a couple of minutes. I'm going to investigate this situation in the alley."

"You got your vest on?" Mike asked seriously.

"Nope. I'll be okay. Don't worry," Sam said. Mike looked doubtful, but he promised to check back in a few minutes. The window rolled up as he drove off.

Sam turned away from the cruiser and began walking down the alley toward the two shadowy figures. When they became aware of his presence, they stopped talking and waited for him to approach. Sam walked up to them, planted his feet, and pulled his hands out of his pockets. He was vaguely aware of his SIG Sauer pistol in his holster under his jacket.

"Is there a problem here?" he asked. In the dim light of the alley, Sam recognized the woman, the petite ax-throwing blonde.

"You're like a bad penny. You just keep showing up where you don't belong," she said, turning up her lip in disgust. In the dark of the alley, the woman's face looked tougher, rough around the edges. Her makeup made her face harsh, and her lips were dark red and stretched tight. Since her demonstration in the bar, she'd donned a black leather jacket, and her tight jeans revealed her willowy figure.

"Well, since you already know that I'm a cop, why don't you spare me the sarcasm and answer my question? Is there a problem here?" Sam said assertively, looking from the blonde to the large man.

The man stared at Sam, his eyes black and flat. He was built like a world-class wrestler—hard muscles, jumpy eyes, and apprehensive. But he answered Sam's question with surprising diplomacy. "There's not a problem here, Officer. We were just getting a few things straight.

It's private business."

"Who're you?" Sam asked, pointing a finger at the tall, well-built man.

"Blake. D'Marius Blake. I'm also known as—"

The woman interrupted. "We have some things to discuss, privately," the blonde said, tersely clipping off her last word.

"Your name?" Sam asked, focusing his attention on her. The woman was definitely a package. Her self-important attitude screamed from her pores. *Where do these people come from?* Sam thought.

"Lori Lifto," she said through gritted teeth. "Really, Officer. Could you please just leave us alone so we can settle our differences?"

"As long as you promise not to get physical," Sam said, attempting to relax.

"I wouldn't dream of it," D'Marius said, smiling amiably. "I'll be a perfect gentleman. Thanks for caring."

Sam turned but then stopped and pivoted back to the two. Lifto crossed her arms over her chest.

"Now what? Another sudden revelation?" she asked insolently,

"Have either of you ever met a man named LeMar Burke?" Sam watched their reactions carefully.

Blake and Lifto looked at each other, getting their signals straight.

"LeMar who?" Lifto asked.

"LeMar Burke," Sam repeated.

"Never heard of him," Lifto said emphatically.

"Ditto," Little Hawk said. "Should we know him?"

"I thought you might have heard about his murder down near Genoa. He was killed with an ancient ball club—a blow to the back of the head that killed him instantly. My understanding about the ball club is that it is traditionally thrown at the victim, but I'm sure just braining someone with one would work, too."

"They are usually thrown from a distance. The honor in killing with a ball club is accuracy. One blow. Kinda like one shot when hunting deer," Little Hawk said. He had an odd kind of authoritative aura about him.

"Well, whoever killed Burke was very accurate with the weapon. There aren't many people who could do that," Sam said, watching Lifto's narrow, slitted eyes. "Of course, somebody who throws an ax very accurately might be able to do it," he finished.

Lifto made a sputtering sound. Little Hawk laid his hand on her arm, but she shoved it off. "You're assuming the ball club was thrown, but maybe somebody just snuck up behind him and clubbed him over the head with it," she spat angrily. "Besides, associating my ax-throwing skills to a recent murder is a bit of a stretch, don't you think?" Her lips curled in a sneer. "What about all the stuff about innocent until proven guilty? You cops are all the same! What a bunch of bullshit!"

Sam found her tirade interesting and revealing. "Just saying. It makes a person wonder," Sam said, feeling a tiny bit of triumph with the zing of his comment.

Sam turned once again and followed the alley out to the street. Little Hawk and Lifto watched him walk away, and when he was out of earshot, Lifto turned to the tall Indian.

"So when was this kid at the cave?" she said, her words stabbing the air like staccato pellets.

"A couple of days ago," Little Hawk started. "I really don't know—"

Lifto rudely interrupted. "Listen, you said you had everything under control. Obviously, that's not true." Little Hawk's dark eyes focused on her sculpted face frozen in anger.

"Quit worrying. I've got a handle on it. I know who he is, and I know where he lives," he said, his voice more confident than he felt. Lori always made him feel weak in the knees.

"Then take care of it. This kid could make everything unravel. And that cop is a royal asshole, too." Her eyes looked down the alley again, but Sam had disappeared.

"Don't even go there. Cops are a special breed. You hurt one or kill one, and they will hunt you to the ends of the earth," Little Hawk reminded her.

"Don't talk to me like I'm stupid. This whole plan of yours should have been flushed a long time ago. From now on, I'm in charge." She turned abruptly, walking briskly down the alley with D'Marius close behind, her black boots slapping the pavement.

In the meantime, Sam reached his Jeep. He climbed in and started it, easing carefully into traffic. Cruising slowly, he made a right-hand turn on Cass Street and drove through a neighborhood filled with lumber mansions from another era while thinking about the amazing skills of the female thrower. He arrived at his duplex on Cliffwood Lane about fifteen minutes later.

He turned the key in the front door of the apartment and heard Paco woof a greeting from his bed in the hallway. He spent a few minutes in the bathroom, tiptoed into the bedroom, and dropped his clothes on the floor. Leslie rolled toward him, making a little groaning sound, but she continued softly snoring. He kissed her gently on the cheek, rolled over, and was sleeping before he knew what had happened.

16

Tanya Cadwallader rolled over in bed Wednesday morning and slapped her beeping alarm clock on the nightstand. The alcoholic buzz from last night had faded, and in its place, a roaring headache was marching toward a full-blown hangover. She groaned, peeked at the fluorescent green numbers on the digital clock in the dim light, and rolled toward the wall for a few more minutes of sleep. But that didn't last long. A wave of nausea washed over her, and she bolted unsteadily toward the bathroom and vomited.

Coming back into the bedroom, she sat forlornly on the edge of the bed, her breath hot and sour. Where had she been last night? What time did she get home? Trent Willow's face appeared in her brain like a piece of dirty clothing that had washed on shore after a bad storm. While she vaguely recalled the basic facts about her night on the town, she grimaced suddenly as she remembered the argument she'd had with her daughter, Felicity, when she stumbled into the house at one in the morning.

"Mom, you've got to go back to your AA meetings," Felicity pleaded. "You're going to kill yourself or somebody on the road. I can't believe you drove home as drunk as you are! What's wrong with you? You should have taken a cab! Why didn't you call me?" she railed, her eyes dark with anger.

Tanya stood unsteadily in the kitchen and leaned against the countertop, listening to her daughter's tirade. Raising her right hand in a Girl Scout pledge, she stood tall and said sarcastically, "Hi. My name is Tanya, and I'm an alcoholic." She burped loudly, then slumped in a chair next to the kitchen table and held her head in her hands.

"This isn't anything to joke about, Mom! I'm seriously worried about you." Felicity's eyes were large, and her face reflected the pain and disappointment of the confrontations she'd had with her mother about her drinking. *Like it does any good*, she thought bitterly.

"You're a good kid, and I'm a lousy mother," Tanya slurred, her head resting on one fist. "No, wrong word. I'm a hopeless, lousy drunk. Those are the facts you'll have to deal with, honey."

Felicity walked over to the table and gently helped her mother out of the chair. Thank God for the Alateen meetings that helped her understand the disease of alcoholism and gave her coping skills. Supporting her mom around the waist, Felicity walked her into the bedroom and put her to bed.

"No, Mom, you're a good person who just happens to be an alcoholic," she said, pulling the quilts over her and turning out the light.

Now, in the early light of dawn, Tanya was overwhelmed by yet another slip. How many times had she fallen off the wagon in the last couple of years? Ten? Fifteen? She shook her head in disgust. Maybe she wasn't even really in recovery. Had she ever stopped drinking long enough to experience true sobriety? She didn't know, but she knew she was doing irreparable damage to her relationship with her daughter. And this latest relapse was another reminder of why her husband, Tony, had left six months ago. Tony. Patient, forgiving Tony. Even he couldn't take the drunken binges and the embarrassing public spectacles. Would Felicity eventually leave, too? *If you keep drinking, she probably will.*

Tanya rose from the bed. The room started spinning, and she hurriedly sat down again. Five minutes later, she was in the shower. The hot water pounded over her head and neck, relieving some of her pain. She stepped out of the shower stall, toweled off, and gulped two extra-strength Tylenol with a few swallows of water. Then she brushed her teeth, fixed her hair, and applied a light layer of makeup.

A half hour later, she was dressed in leggings, a long sweater, and knee-high boots. She drove her Chevy Equinox downtown to the Bluff Management Realty office on Main Street, though she was still slightly buzzed.

As she turned on Main Street, St. Joseph the Workman Cathedral loomed in the early morning light like a medieval castle materializing out of a fog. The huge limestone church dominated the downtown area with its tall clock tower and dazzling stained glass windows. The deep peal of its bronze bell was a harbinger of comfort that drifted over the city. Eight gongs floated through the morning air, reminding Tanya of the passage of time. When she stepped out of her car, the sound of the bustling traffic and the church bell assaulted her throbbing head. She stepped up on the sidewalk and stumbled to the front door of the office.

Inside the office, the agency's secretary—some new kid who'd just graduated from Western Tech—was answering the phone. Her work area was plastered with colorful sticky notes. *Wasn't there some program on the computer that eliminated the need for sticky notes?* Tanya thought. The little pieces of paper fluttered when the furnace kicked in, making Tanya's stomach wobble with anxiety.

"Any messages for me?" Tanya asked, leaning on the counter for support.

"Some Willow guy called asking for you. Here's his number," the secretary said, handing her a bright orange note. The young secretary snapped her gum noisily and answered the phone.

"Thanks," she said weakly. "I appreciate it." The secretary backed away from Tanya when she caught a whiff of her breath. Tanya turned and crept down the hall. "I'll return his call a little later," she said over her shoulder.

Sitting at her desk with the office door closed, Tanya gazed at the photo of her only daughter. Her dark hair and brown eyes were traits she'd inherited from her mother, but her empathetic nature and care-giving skills came directly down the genetic pipeline from her dad. She thought briefly of her husband, Tony, who'd tried so hard to make their marriage work. Tanya clucked her tongue with dissatisfaction. *Felicity deserves someone better than me,* she thought. *Why does she still love me? I've done nothing but disappoint her.*

Tanya wondered exactly what she'd told Trent Willow last night that would necessitate an early morning phone call. Did they just talk about real estate? Did she flaunt the extra cash she'd gotten from LeMar Burke? What had she done? Tanya vaguely recalled a lengthy conversation about Burke and a hand on her thigh as she sat at the bar. Would her night on the town cause another major embarrassment for the real estate firm? There had been plenty of them in the past. A nagging uneasiness crept over her when she tried to recall the details of their discussion.

Tanya swiveled in her chair and gazed out the office window that faced a popular city park and shelter. In the spring and summer months, a vibrant farmers' market filled the area with optimism and happy vegetable lovers. Now it was empty. The swings shifted gently in the wind, and patches of green grass stuck out of the receding snowbanks. Tanya's eyes burned, her stomach was doing a nauseous dance, and the headache that had started earlier now spiked into an intense pain that drummed unmercifully inside her skull. She thought about calling her AA sponsor, but she wasn't totally sober yet. *At noon,* she thought. *I'll call Father Schmidt at noon.*

She reached for her day planner, flipped it open, and noticed a number of showings: one at nine-thirty near Black River Falls, another after lunch, and a late showing at four o'clock. A busy day that will be hard to navigate in her condition. *A vodka gimlet would really get me straightened out.* She shook her head and closed her eyes. *When will you ever learn? That's exactly what you don't need.* The voices in her head jockeyed for superiority until she wanted to scream, but screaming would hurt and expend too much energy, which she desperately needed to get through the morning. It was always like this when she woke up with a raging hangover; one voice in her mind threatened to overwhelm her with guilt, and at the same time, the other voice reminded her of the need for another drink, leaving her incapable of accomplishing anything. *Jeez, get your act together. You're the owner of this agency,* she thought.

Despite the intensity of the hangover, she turned her chair back toward her desk and began returning messages that had been left on her answering machine. In half an hour, she was beginning to feel a little better, at least somewhat human again, but a long way from normal. She straightened her desk and opened the lower desk drawer. She frowned in puzzlement at the thick envelope lying beneath the files she'd lifted out. Peeking in the envelope, she gasped in surprise, then hurriedly put the envelope back in the desk drawer as though her hand had been scorched. It was filled with one-hundred-dollar bills. A lot of them. Too many to count. Tanya remembered the night Burke had offered her the money as a reward for her efforts with Terry Waite, even though she barely remembered the incident. Obviously, she hadn't put the money in the bank. *How could I forget to do that?* she thought.

She slammed the desk drawer shut and locked it, loaded her leather bag with the files and information for each property she had to show, and walked back down the hall and out of the office.

Climbing into her Equinox, she programmed the address of the small acreage outside of Black River Falls into the vehicle's navigational system. The computerized voice of the GPS, although impersonal, made her journey north toward the property easier. She didn't have to pay attention—just follow the directions of the idiot voice and drive.

As she traveled north along State Highway 54, she pushed thoughts of the money and LeMar Burke from her mind and reviewed the positive aspects of the property she was hoping to list. Through a conversation with the owner, she knew it included forty acres that bordered Gullickson's Glen State Park. The land featured lush stands of pine and oak savannahs, numerous creeks, and a three-bedroom log cabin that had been lovingly updated with modern amenities without compromising the original integrity of the cabin. *What's not to love?* thought Tanya. *Sounds like a place perfect for a retiree or someone looking for a second home—a getaway for an artist or writer.*

The weather was gorgeous. It was a promising spring day, with the temperatures likely to hit sixty-five degrees. The trees were heavy with pregnant buds waiting to burst into green. Along the highway, a group of bikers were pumping energetically, the sun shining on their shoulders, their heads down in a serious competitive pose. Their multi-colored helmets looked like a necklace bobbing along the side of the road. *I'd probably die if I tried to do that*, Tanya thought sourly.

When the automated voice of the GPS reminded her of the next turn, she slowed the car onto County Road X. She drove through dappled sunshine, avoiding some serious potholes. It felt more isolated and deserted here, and she nervously pushed her hair away from her face. The stands of trees were closer to the road and seemed to hover over her car, making her feel tense and claustrophobic.

A doe leaped across the road about a hundred yards in front of her. She slowed down. She'd hit a deer last year and totaled her car, and she had no desire to repeat the experience. Bauer Road appeared on a street sign, and she made a right turn, following the narrow lane, noticing a few other summer cabins set back from the road.

Driving up to the log home, she saw a dilapidated Ford pickup parked at an awkward angle in the driveway. The cabin sat under a towering white pine. Pine cones were scattered around the base of the tree, and a few had landed on the roof of the cabin. The lawn was sandy, the grass sporadic and thin. But the lot had a nice selection of hardwoods and pines and a garden shed near the edge of the lot.

Tanya called into the office—standard procedure since a number of real estate agents around the country had been murdered or raped in isolated locations recently. She'd insisted on this protocol for all her agents. It made no sense to take stupid chances. She talked to the new secretary and relayed her location.

Tanya unplugged her phone from the charger on the dash and grabbed a yellow legal pad and pen from her leather bag. She stepped out of the car just as a tall, balding, fifty-something man opened the front screen door of the cabin. He was dressed in blue jeans and a red Badgers sweatshirt. The floorboards of the open porch creaked under his weight. His face broke into a friendly smile.

"You must be Tanya," he said, grinning at her from the porch.

"Yep, that would be me. Jack Bishop, I take it?" Tanya said, reaching out her hand as she stepped on the porch. After introductions, he began showing her the interior of the cabin. They surveyed the property, doing a walk around while Tanya asked more questions about the natural area that bordered the lot.

"So that area over there," she pointed north, "isn't part of your property, right?"

Jack told her, "No. That's part of Glen State Park. It's a popular recreational spot in the county. There are some pretty neat petroglyphs and a large cave filled with Native etchings."

Tanya groaned, and her shoulders slumped. "Oh, brother. I've looked at some other properties that had those features, and it didn't go well."

Jack frowned. "What do you mean?"

"Someone down south of La Crosse owns some property with a cave decorated with petroglyphs. He got extremely defensive about the carvings, something about protecting them from human exposure. It caused a lot of animosity with the potential buyer."

"Well, these petroglyphs aren't on my property, but they are within walking distance of the cabin. You can see some of them because they're right in the open along one of the hiking trails. Actually, I think it's kinda neat."

Tanya shook her head. "I wouldn't advertise it in the listing of your property. There's a group out there right now that's on the fringe. They might give you a hard time if they know you're encouraging people to view the caves. Some people in the area are adamant about protecting them from human interference."

"You mean some tree huggers?" He waved his hand in the air as if swatting away a pesky fly. "Well, what can they do?" Bishop asked. "It's a free country, isn't it?" although doubt had crept into his voice.

"Look, can we agree not to mention the caves and petroglyphs?" Tanya asked. "If you want to tell potential buyers about it once they've seen the property, that's your prerogative, but I'd strongly recommend we don't mention it in the property description."

Bishop made a wry face and shrugged at her advice. "Sure, that's fine by me. Where do I sign?" he asked.

As Tanya drove away from the property, the revelation of the cave drawings rattled her. She certainly didn't want to be associated with any more murders like LeMar Burke's. Bishop seemed like a nice guy; the last thing she wanted to do was give some half-cocked radicals a reason to hassle or intimidate him.

Driving back to La Crosse, she realized she needed a bathroom. She gently pounded the steering wheel, silently chastising herself for her stupidity in not using the cabin's toilet. But a few miles down the road, a rest area appeared under a group of large majestic pines, and she turned into the parking lot with a sense of relief. A car turned and followed her into the lot, but in her desperation to use the facilities, she didn't notice. She hurried toward the women's restrooms. As she was washing her hands, the entrance door to the facility squeaked open. She looked in the mirror, a shadow blocking the light from the parking lot. A sense of panic welled up in her chest.

Her face scrunched up in confusion. Unfortunately for Tanya, she saw the club too late. It hit her on the back of the head, and the sound at impact resembled the dull thump of someone splitting a ripened watermelon. Blood and brains splattered on the wall. Tanya fell to the floor, and in the last conscious seconds of her life, she thought, *Oh no. Who's ever going to find me here?* Then, *I love you, Felicity.*

The weapon clattered on the cold cement where it lay next to her, silent and deadly, having fulfilled its purpose. The killer grunted with satisfaction, turned, and walked to the car in the lot, and drove away.

☐

Sam was standing at the stove cooking a mid-week breakfast, something he usually didn't do until the weekend. He flipped the bacon with a pair of tongs and placed some paper towels on a plate to drain it. Then he opened the refrigerator and grabbed a dozen eggs in a cardboard container.

"So you think I shouldn't be out in public working on this murder case because of the pregnancy?" Leslie asked, looking over her coffee cup at Sam. *Like fun, buddy*, she thought. *Think again.*

"Only if it means you won't be put in compromising situations," he answered.

"Isn't that how I got in this condition in the first place?" Leslie asked, hiding a grin that was just below the surface.

Sam ignored her stab at humor. "I've been reading about the effects of stress on the baby in the womb, and policing situations can add to that stress," he explained. Leslie smiled. Leave it to Sam to always have her best interests at heart. "And besides that, I don't want you to get shot."

"What about expectant fathers? Should we worry about them getting shot? Maybe you should be on desk duty, too." Sam remained silent, but his shoulders slumped. Leslie continued. "Just saying. Aren't mothers and fathers equally important in the whole parental scheme of things?" Sam stopped his cooking efforts and stared at her. She continued, "So, when did you talk to Higgins?"

He laid the tongs on the counter. "How do you know I did?"

"I'm a detective ... and a woman with this incredible sense of intuition," Leslie said, giggling. She got up from the table and walked up to Sam, hugging him around the waist. "I appreciate your efforts with Higgins. I'll talk to him today."

"You feel up for work?" Sam asked, his hazel eyes steady. Leslie nodded.

"Maybe in a couple of days," she said. "I still have a nagging headache."

Sam always had trouble concentrating when she was this close. She smelled like peaches and lilac, and her blue eyes could see right through him every time. "One egg or two?" he asked.

Leslie held up two fingers. "Eatin' for two now, so I'll have two," she said. Paco woofed his approval. "Make one for Paco. He's on pregnancy duty, too." She beamed a radiant smile. "Hey, when are we telling our parents about this baby? Gosh, can you imagine your mom? She's gonna go ballistic."

☐

Jim Higgins arrived early at the law enforcement office on Vine Street. The building was quiet, something that wasn't the norm. Emily was already sitting at her desk. *Just once I'd like to beat her at this early morning game*, he thought. He looked at the wall clock—7:20.

"Mornin', Chief," she said cheerily.

"Are you ever in a bad mood?" Jim asked, leaning on the counter and looking down at her.

"Takes a lot to throw me off my game, sir." She looked up at him, her green eyes sparkling with health. Her bold blue dress accentuated her robust glowing complexion, and the cap sleeves revealed a little shower of red freckles on her well-toned arms. Jim's eyes drifted to her hair.

"Did you do something different to your hair?" he asked, crinkling his eyebrows together.

Her smile fell. "Well, yes. Don't you like it?" she asked, her fingers twirling a few curls.

"Oh, it's lovely. It looks great." He breathed a sigh of relief when her smile reappeared. Somewhere in the back of his mind, he remembered the newest office etiquette—refrain from any comments that might draw attention to gender or personal comments about hair, makeup, or clothing. *Well, I just flunked with flying colors*, he thought. *Just another indication of my dinosaur mindset.* "So what's on the docket for today?"

"Your team is supposed to be catching a killer, I guess ... and I'm still waiting for your proposed departmental budget summary," she said formally. "Any progress on that front?"

Jim's forehead creased in a frown. "The budget? No progress. The murder hasn't moved much off square one either, although Jamie provided a few leads. That kid never fails to surprise me."

"He certainly is a nerdy little twerp with a superior attitude, isn't he? What about Leslie? How's she doing?" Emily chattered, some friendliness seeping back into her voice.

"Better, I guess. Maybe she'll be back to work this week. Tell her I want to talk to her if she comes in."

"Yes, I will." Her fingers flew over the keyboard. Jim cringed at the prowess of her word-processing skills, especially in light of the two-finger approach he used in his own unique antiquated hunt-and-peck method.

He walked down the hall to his office, sat down at his laptop, and scrolled through his emails. *The tyranny of modern technology*, he thought. *Whoever said technology frees us to do other things had their head screwed on backward, but you can't turn the clock back now.*

DeDe had sent him a detailed report on Little Hawk's background. An excellent student at Black River Falls High School, he participated in track and wrestling, setting a new state record in the 400-meter dash and the javelin. *Javelin? That took some strength and throwing accuracy. Could be a skill that would readily transfer to throwing ball clubs,* Jim thought.

He had one DUI in high school but had managed to keep his nose clean throughout his college career. He seemed like an unlikely murder suspect, but he was fixated on his ancestor's legacy. Could that passion be enough to murder someone who'd smeared his hero's name? Jim harrumphed to himself. Motivations for murder could include just about anything. Unfortunately, a lot of people were killed for very stupid, random reasons. It would have to be a pretty significant insult to old Blackhawk's reputation to fire up Little Hawk into committing a murder. Then he recalled his dream and the way Blackhawk had looked right through him. *Hmm.*

Jim leaned back in his chair, watching the traffic come to life on Vine Street through the long, narrow window in his office. He closed his eyes and indulged in some serious thinking. But the more he thought, the less confident he felt. What did they really know so far?

Some Louisiana real estate hotshot turns up dead behind a broken-down bar in a tiny Mississippi River town. An ancient ball club is found near the body, the apparent murder weapon. Trent Willow, a casual friend of the murder victim, was with him the day of the murder but nothing points to his involvement, unless you count having a drink with him while he was still alive. His alibi of being at other meetings during the late afternoon and evening had held up under intense scrutiny.

Ryan Blake, the original owner of the weapon, was no longer in possession of the weapon when the murder happened. Did the Sauk tribe really make the weapon under the tutelage of Blackhawk? Maybe. According to Ryan Blake, it was an authentic ancient weapon. So who had the weapon on Wednesday, March 21? Didn't know yet.

According to Detective Paul Saner, LeMar Burke had an unpleasant confrontation with Professor Terry Waite a month before he'd died. And the realtor, Tanya Cadwallader, told Sam that Burke was a mover and shaker who'd seriously offended Waite's strongly held beliefs about environmental activism and the preservation of ancient Oneota culture. From what Paul had reported, Waite seemed like a total jerk, although that didn't make him a murderer. Did Burke demand too much, and Waite snuffed him out? Or was the murder based on some worn-out retribution of a bunch of unruly Natives on the periphery of society? Seemed unlikely. Maybe it was an odd combination of the two. Who knew? He certainly didn't.

Toward nine o'clock, after working at his desk for a few hours, Jim pulled out his cell and dialed the number of Blue Earth/Copper Moon Gallery in Eau Claire. After exchanging introductions, the manager, Dylan Meyer, promised to check into the purchase of the ancient weapon.

"Could you put a rush on that and call me as soon as you know? One person has been killed, and we want to stop any more tragedies from happening," Jim informed him.

Meyer promised to call as soon as he tracked down the buyer. *Another mad chase that will probably eat up time and get us nowhere*, Jim thought. When he hung up the phone, he wasn't at all sure the call would yield anything helpful. That's when Sam walked into his office.

"Hey. What's up?" Jim asked as Sam pulled up a chair. He scanned Sam's clothes. He looked professional, smartly dressed in a pale pink dress shirt, a subtle black print tie, and a pair of decent black dress pants. However, his black and white wingtips screamed ugly and reminded Jim of the saddle shoes that girls used to wear in elementary school forty years ago. He couldn't imagine where he'd found them, and he didn't ask. *Pick your battles*, he thought.

Sam felt Jim's eyes moving over him. He asked impatiently, "Do my threads meet with your approval?"

"Your threads, yes; your shoes, no, but you don't need my approval. You need Jones' approval. He's the one who sets the bar for the dress code. If you don't like that, you'll have to take it up with him."

Switching topics, Sam said, "I met this girl last night down at The

Aimless Ax."

"A girl at the what?" Jim leaned back in his chair, wondering what wild goose chase Sam had been on in the wee hours of the morning while he was cuddled up in bed with Carol.

"The Aimless Ax down on Fourth and Jay. You know, that bar where you throw axes at a target. It's a real legit place."

Jim rolled his eyes. "What possessed you to go there?"

"You said to get out on the street, so that's what I did. Anyway, this girl, Lori Lifto, started throwing axes, and she cracked the place up. She's really good. Very accurate. She threw the ax at least ten times and hit the bullseye every time."

"And how does this relate to our case?" Jim asked, squinting his eyes.

"She knows Little Hawk."

"You mean D'Marius Blake?"

"Yeah. Ryan Blake's son. They were having an argument out in the alley behind the tavern after her ax-throwing display inside, and I happened to see it and interrupted them. I asked them a few questions."

"What'd you find out?" Jim had to admit Sam had a certain tenacity and inventive approach to his job.

"Well, there's some kind of connection between the two of them. Lori claimed they were having a difference of opinion and were trying to sort out their problems. D'Marius was polite enough, but I got the feeling Lori was very unhappy with him about something. I sure wouldn't want to take him on, but that didn't seem to bother her. The guy is built like a WWE wrestler, and I think he could kill somebody if he was cornered."

"Maybe he did kill somebody. What else?" Jim asked curtly.

"If Lori can swing an ax that accurately, then she could also deliver a very accurate blow to the back of someone's head with a ball club," Sam said.

"Wait a minute! You didn't actually accuse her of that, did you?"

Jim asked angrily.

Sam sat back and studied his fingernails. "Not in so many words, but it takes a lot of umph to get an ax to stick in a wooden target. There were plenty of men at the bar who couldn't do it. Whoever threw the club at LeMar knew what they were doing, and they were strong enough to kill him with one blow."

Jim sighed. "You've got a point, but it's weak and based on supposition. That being said, find her. Today." Jim said. "Bring her in for questioning. I want to know where she was the day of the murder. Whatever alibi she gives you, it needs to be solid and verifiable."

Sam stood up and walked to the door. "I'll find her and see what shakes out," he said as he disappeared down the hall.

Jim's phone buzzed again, and he answered in a brisk tone.

"Higgins."

"Jim, are you free right now?" Carol asked, her breath hoarse and raspy. She rarely called him at work, so when she did, alarm bells went off in his brain.

"What's the matter? Are the kids okay?" he asked, standing up behind his desk suddenly.

"Lillie won't go to school until she talks to you, Jim. She's been throwing a fit ever since she got up this morning. Crying, won't eat breakfast, won't get dressed. I can't get a thing out of her. Can you talk to her?"

"Sure. Put her on," he said patiently. *How much trouble can a seven-year-old cause?* he thought. *With Lillie, you'd be surprised.*

"Bapa? I'm scared!" Lillie blurted. She hiccupped, and Jim could tell she'd been crying.

"What's wrong, toots? Can you tell me about it?" He could envision her curly blonde hair, her azure blue eyes, and her ear pressed to the phone as she impatiently told Jim about her crisis. *She's going to terrorize us when she gets in her teens*, he thought.

"Somebody's in trouble, Bapa. A lady's going to get hurt! I just know it. I don't want to know it, but I do. Why do these dreams keep happening to me?" she said, the words tumbling over each other. Jim could hear the panic in her voice and her soft crying over the phone.

He sat down. He'd been hoping the dreams were over. They'd rapidly de-escalated since Lillie had been adopted over three years ago. He'd attributed the waning of the premonitions to a stable and loving home life. They'd been optimistic that as the nightmares diminished, Lillie could enjoy her childhood years without the forebodings and nightmares that had plagued her earlier.

"Tell me about your dream, honey," he said gently, recalling his own feverish nightmare.

"Blackhawk was in my dream, and he told me about a lady who was going to get hurt. She's in a brick building along a highway, Bapa. Someone's after her. You need to stop them!" Lillie ordered vehemently, her voice taking on a desperate tone.

"Okay. Calm down, sweetie. You know I'll do everything I can to help this lady, right?" There was silence on the end of the line. "Lillie?" he asked again, but his emotions were welling up inside as he listened to her quiet sobs.

"What if it's too late, Bapa? Maybe they already found her and hurt her." More crying.

"Sometimes we can't do anything about that, but I'll try, Lillie. Really, I will. Do you believe me?" he asked. By now, his heart was breaking. That his lovely child should be so burdened with such an awful premonition seemed totally unfair.

"Yes, I believe you," Lillie said simply, her voice sounding calmer. "I'm counting on you, Bapa."

"Thank you for telling me about this. I'll do all I can to help. You know that, don't you?"

"Yes."

"Can you give the phone to Mommy now?" he asked. He heard some rustling, and then Carol came on the line.

"What's this all about?" Carol asked impatiently, panic rising in her voice.

"Listen. It's bad enough that we've got a panicked child. Don't you freak out on me, too," he warned, his voice grave and serious.

Taking a deep breath, she said, "You're right," although it took all of her self-control not to bombard Jim with questions. "So what's this all about?" she repeated, her voice calmer.

"Something about some woman being in danger. God only knows who that could be, and I mean that literally—only God knows. I reassured Lillie that I would look into it. I don't know if she really believes me or not, but can you try to get her to calm down and get her to school? She needs to be in her normal environment, not home brooding about some off-the-wall dream."

"I agree. I'll do my best."

"Good. I'll talk to you later," Jim said. He punched his phone off and laid it on his desk, slumping limply in his chair. He leaned forward, his elbows on his desk, his head in his hands. The mature, rational adult inside him wanted to disregard the conversation with Lillie. After all, who believes a seven-year-old's dream about a Sauk warrior who's been dead for over two hundred years? Some woman was in trouble? That could be anyone. But then he remembered how rattled he'd been by his dream of Blackhawk, and suddenly Lillie's apparitions didn't seem so stupid. He said a prayer for her and sent it heavenward.

Emily appeared suddenly at his door, a look of consternation on her face that Jim was all too familiar with.

"Davy Jones wants you and your team in the situation room downstairs right now," she said urgently.

"Why?"

"Not sure, but he sounded pretty agitated."

"Got it. I'll see who else is here and head down."

Jim got up from his desk and walked rapidly down the hall, gathering up DeDe and Paul. Sam had already headed out to find Lori Lifto, and Leslie was on sick leave.

"What's going on, Chief?" Paul asked as they crowded in the elevator.

"I don't know, but the way my morning has been going, it can't be good," he explained, running his hand through his hair.

Paul gave Jim a sideways glance as they stepped off the elevator onto the first floor of the law enforcement center. Higgins seemed distracted and unsettled. The quiet atmosphere of the early morning hours had evaporated, and every city and county law enforcement officer in the building was heading to the situation room, a large room used for group announcements, press conferences, and policing situations that needed immediate attention.

Jim, DeDe, and Paul walked in, found a space along the back wall, and squeezed together elbow-to-elbow. Jim nodded to the La Crosse Chief of Police, Tanya Pedretti. The buzzing rumble of conversation coming from the personnel who were crammed in the room sounded like a hive of angry bees. Sheriff Davy Jones walked into the room and made his way to the front, where a podium had been placed. He opened a few notes, looked up over his reading glasses, and began speaking in a commanding voice.

"Ladies and gentlemen. Could I have your attention, please?" he asked. The scuttlebutt in the room ceased, and it became very quiet. "You're all aware of the murder of LeMar Burke down on the river last week during the snowstorm. The investigation of that crime is continuing under the direction of Lt. Jim Higgins. So far, there are no outstanding suspects, although the investigation has uncovered some people who are acquainted with Mr. Burke. They are being interviewed. The motives are still fluid, but every lead is being pursued. Jim? Anything you want to add?"

Heads turned, and Jim made a brief statement. "We're investigating all leads. Things are developing. We're making some headway, but we've got a long way to go. Keep your ears to the ground and report anything you hear to one of the investigative team."

Sheriff Jones nodded. Jim sensed that something important was about to be dropped in their laps. Jones continued.

"At around eleven this morning, a traveler on Highway 54 south of Black River Falls stopped to use the restroom facilities at a rest area and discovered the body of Tanya Cadwallader, the owner of Bluff Management Realty here in La Crosse. She died from a blow to the back of the head."

Jim grimaced and turned white. He felt sweat break out on his forehead. Was this really happening? How could Lillie have been right? He couldn't believe it. Her dream *was* a warning. The words of Blackhawk came back to him—*I have given her a message.* He crossed his arms over his chest and studied the floor, avoiding eye contact with others. When the buzz in the room finally died down again, the sheriff continued. "Next to her on the floor of the restroom was another ancient ball club, which appears to have been the murder weapon."

Jim glanced at DeDe, then at Paul.

"I didn't see that coming," Paul whispered to Jim, studying his face. "You look weird. Are you all right?"

"No, I'm not. You ever get information that you wish you knew nothing about?" Jim said caustically, closing his eyes briefly.

Paul looked confused. "What do you mean?" he mumbled. An officer in front of him turned around and gave them a sour look.

"Later," Jim replied, throwing the officer a cool glance in return.

Jones continued. "The Jackson County Sheriff's Department has asked for our assistance in the case. I will keep everyone posted as soon as I receive more information. Some of our officers will be heading in that direction. Everyone—and I mean everyone—needs to be alert to this developing situation. We may be dealing with a serial killer. Follow up on any suspicious activity. Use your contacts on the street and report anything you learn, no matter how trivial." Several hands shot up in the air, and Sheriff Jones did his best to answer their questions with the limited information he'd been given. Finally, he shook his head. "No more questions at this time. That's all. Keep your ears to the ground, people. Any contact with the press, refer them to me," he finished. He crooked his finger at Jim, then pointed in the direction of his office. The team headed that way.

SUE BERG

17

While the detective team attended the meeting, Sam headed across town. The beautiful spring weather they'd enjoyed the last few days had turned ugly. The sky was filled with dull, gray clouds, and a misty drizzle soon became a full-fledged downpour. Street gutters flowed with water and raced to the storm sewers. Cars and trucks splashed noisily through the sheets of rain, and Sam shook his head at a biker pedaling along the street. "Get a car, buddy," he said under his breath. The meteorologist on Mix 96 warned of possible flooding in low-lying areas. Sam flicked off the radio as he drove across town to Lori Lifto's residence, a walk-up efficiency apartment on Pine Street about a block from Myrick Park.

Although the apartment building was probably fifty years old, it was well-kept, set back from the street about thirty feet. Sam parked his Jeep in front of the apartment, leaned across the front seat, opened his glove box, and slipped his Glock 22 pistol into his underarm holster, then slipped a windbreaker over his shirt. He still had visions of Lori Lifto throwing an ax with chilling accuracy. Somehow his pistol seemed ineffective against an ax flying through the air.

Everything was quiet. He stepped out of the Jeep, walked quickly up the narrow cement sidewalk, and took the flight of stairs two at a time. Standing under a small eave that extended over the doorway, he knocked loudly. Nothing. He pounded on the door again and waited another few minutes. Finally, he tried once more, beating continually for at least thirty seconds.

"Hey! Do ya mind?" a man yelled up to him. Sam glanced down the stairs. A middle-aged man dressed in a UPS uniform stood under an umbrella gazing up at him.

"Whaddya need?" the UPS man asked. "You lookin' for Lori?" The rain pinged off his umbrella and splashed on the sidewalk, saturating his slip-resistant, rubber-soled work shoes.

Sam flicked the hood of the windbreaker over his head and began descending the stairs. "Yes. It's really important that I find her. Do you know where she is? At work maybe?" Sam asked.

"Nah, she's not at work. She works nights at the Kwik Trip bakery. I didn't hear her come home last night. I can always tell when she's home—the squeaky floors and the slamming cupboards. Then there's the shower and the toilet flushing. I can hear the water running through the PVC pipes. I basically hear everything, and believe me, she wasn't here last night. I would have heard her."

By the time the UPS man finished his story, Sam had come down the stairs. He stood in the downpour, the rain running in rivulets across the hood of his windbreaker.

The UPS man moved the umbrella over Sam's head, and they stood uncomfortably close beneath it.

"Do you talk to Lori once in a while?" Sam asked. "How well do you know her?"

"Oh, I don't talk to her much. With Lori, you gotta be careful about the kinds of questions you ask her. She might tell you to take a friggin' hike, or she might tell you to buzz off, or she might give you one of her beautiful smiles. You just never know," he said, shrugging his shoulders. "She's not the friendliest person on the planet. Know what I mean?"

"Actually, yeah, I do know what you mean." He thought back to her snappy comments in the alley last night. Sam pulled his card from his wallet and handed it to the UPS man. He looked at it, then glanced up at Sam.

"You're kinda young to be a detective, aren't you? Do you kick ass and take names like the detectives in those novels?"

"Occasionally. We come in all sizes, shapes, and ages, just like everybody else," Sam said. He noticed the UPS man studying him. "It is what it is," he said. "Listen, would you mind keeping an eye out for Lori? Call me when she comes and goes?"

"Why? She do something criminal?" The man's eyes were suddenly suspicious, and he nervously rocked back and forth on his feet.

Sam toughened up his voice and leaned toward the man, pushing the parameters of his comfort zone. "What do *you* think?" Sam asked him. "Do you think she's capable of criminal activities? I'm asking you." Sam tapped the man's chest with his index finger.

The UPS man squinted and said, "I think she could be a whole lotta trouble … in a whole lotta ways."

"I tend to agree with you." Sam stepped back and smiled. "Hey, thanks for your help … and the umbrella," he said. He ran toward the Jeep and crawled in. As he pulled away from the curb, he wondered where Lori was and what she was doing. Somehow, he couldn't shake the image in his mind of her throwing axes at a target, striking the bullseye every time.

☐

Bobby Rude's father died late Tuesday afternoon. Jed Klumstein drove Bobby over to the VA hospital in Tomah during the afternoon. The young man was surprised at how death had arrived. He could still hear his dad's last raspy breath. Finally, it became a little wisp of air, a release, an escape from his alcoholic tyranny. Bobby knew he'd never forget his death, the tremulous gasp and final shudder, then the stillness that came over him. Since that moment in the hospital room, a wall of emotion had been bottled up inside his chest like a dam filled with water that was waiting to burst over the top. He'd used up his bravery and courage. Now he was all alone, abandoned in the world without a family. He sobbed quietly at his dad's side for several minutes until Jed tenderly wrapped his arm around his shoulder and led him to the truck in the parking lot.

After making arrangements for his father's body to be sent to the mortuary in Stoddard, Jed and Bobby arrived back at the house in Genoa late Tuesday evening. Jed had insisted Bobby spend the night with him in his apartment above the Tip Your Hat tavern, but for once, Bobby didn't want to be with Jed; he wanted to be alone to think about the life that alcohol had stolen from his father, and ultimately the father who had been stolen from him. How was it that people could stay drunk for years and never claim victory over a liquid that reflected the amber light in the bottom of a bottle? Didn't make any sense to him.

Early Wednesday morning, Bobby crawled out of bed despite the fact that he hadn't slept much. He packed a knapsack with a bologna sandwich, a bag of chips, an orange, and a can of Dr. Pepper. Throwing in some miniature Snickers candy bars, he took his journal, his flip phone Jed had bought for him, and a small flashlight.

Nobody knew about the journal, the one he kept hidden between his mattress and box spring. Lately, it seemed to be his best friend. The lined notebook listened, never judged, recorded his pain and small victories, and allowed him to look back on the crooked path that was his life. Was he wiser for it? He didn't know, and he really didn't care. He just knew he needed a friend, and his pen and journal were always there waiting for him, welcoming him into a world of release, a balm from all the angst he'd experienced in his young, turbulent life.

He walked away from the small, weathered house and traipsed down the steep hill to the bottom of the driveway in the false dawn, his knapsack slung over his shoulder, carrying his father's old wicker snowshoes on his back. In the distance across the highway, the Mississippi River's wide expanse reflected the glow of the early morning light. As the minutes passed, the sky lightened from dark gray to a mustard and scarlet blush along the horizon. *Red sky in the morning, sailor take warning*, Bobby thought. One of the many things Sara Higgins, his fifth-grade teacher, had taught him about weather. A persistent mist continued to shroud the bluffs on the Minnesota side. A flock of Canadian geese bobbed on the river's current near shore while the main channel was peppered with ice chunks that aimlessly floated on the currents.

Striding purposefully along U.S. Hwy. 35, Bobby stuck out his thumb when he heard a pickup truck approaching him from behind. The pickup slowed, its engine winding down. Someone pulled up next to him and opened the passenger door. It was Geoff Hanson from Genoa, a faithful patron of Jed's bar, who was on his way to work at the former G. Heileman Brewing Company, now owned by Stroh's on the south side of La Crosse.

"Where you headed, Bobby?" he asked, glancing over at him. The truck smelled of oil and grease and a faint odor of stale beer.

Brushing his hair away from his face, Bobby lied. "Gonna meet a friend at the Kwik Trip in Stoddard. He's taking me into school."

"Kinda early, isn't it?" Geoff asked, pulling back onto the highway, his gnarled fingers gripping the steering wheel. He wore a City Brewery hat that was tipped to one side, his eyes hooded beneath the brim.

"We've got some studying to do in the library," Bobby said seriously.

"You must be a better student than I was. I avoided the library at all costs," Geoff said as he pulled out onto the highway.

Bobby smiled and continued joking with Geoff. When he let him out at the intersection of Hwy. 35 and Mohawk Valley Road near the Stoddard Kwik Trip, Bobby noticed the suspicious look in Geoff's eyes, but he gave him his best smile and waved him off. The truck putted slowly down the road, its exhaust leaving a trail of puffy blue clouds in its wake.

As soon as the pickup disappeared from sight, Bobby started walking down the gravel road out of town until he came to an open field. He strapped on the old snowshoes and set out across the field, heading south toward the rolling hills. He avoided the most daunting bluffs, sticking to the low-lying valleys until he came to the back gravel roads of Pleasant Valley. He was in no hurry. Jed had informed the principal of Logan High School about his father's death, and he had granted Bobby a week of excused absences to attend his father's funeral and grieve his losses—as if a week was all he'd need to mourn. *People are so stupid*, Bobby thought. *I lost my dad years ago. I've been sad for a long time. A week off of school isn't going to cut it.*

The rain began falling harder, no longer just a misty curtain. Bobby stopped and dug out a cheap Walmart rain poncho from his knapsack and fitted it over his head. It wasn't fancy but would keep him relatively dry. He'd been to the cave many times over the past two years, although Professor Waite wasn't aware of his presence there. Bobby was sure if he knew, he'd have been arrested for trespassing. Waite's reputation preceded him; he was some kind of environmental nut. Bobby steered clear of him at all costs.

The air was hushed and quiet. Birds flitted among the trees and undergrowth, searching for seeds and dried berries. Along a steep hillside, an outcropping of limestone rock created an overhanging ledge, and underneath it, a mother red fox guarded the entrance to her den, licking her lips conspicuously when Bobby stopped and observed her. He worked his way through the wooded edges of the valley until he worked up a sweat.

As he approached the cave, he noticed bootprints in the snow much larger than his own. Suddenly, he became wary and wondered about the wisdom of visiting the cave by himself, but he had his cell phone if things went wrong.

There was something about the isolation of the cave that comforted Bobby. As he gazed at the ancient cave paintings, he forgot his problems, losing himself in the swirl of the images. How many hours had he spent lying on his back, his flashlight aimed at the damp walls, wondering about the artist who had scratched the drawings into the sandstone wall? The stick figures, which seemed crude when he'd first discovered them, showed a resilient people and a noble lifestyle that had disappeared from the landscape.

He walked up to the cave, slid through the entrance hole, and scrambled into the cavity, dragging his knapsack with him. He took his flashlight out of his pack and turned it on. The familiar images on the rock wall brought him a sense of peace and security. He lay on his back for several minutes, focusing the light on different areas of the cave—the thunderbird, the herd of deer, the tiny stick man figures that seemed dwarfed by their circumstances. It was kind of the way he felt right now in his life. In his search, his flashlight flicked against a rock shelf toward the back side of the cavern that he'd never noticed before. He focused the light on the shelf.

Scooting along the floor of the cave on his butt, he made his way to the shelf that protruded from the rock wall. The ceiling of the cave seemed to hang uncomfortably close above his head, and his sense of claustrophobia revved up. A few rocks sat on the shelf, but somehow, they seemed out of place. He reached up and moved them aside. That's when he saw a deerskin wrapped around something. He wasn't sure what was concealed in the hide, but his heart began pounding in his chest as he lifted it from the shelf. He propped his flashlight on a rock nearby and carefully unwrapped the hide package, peering at its contents.

Inside lay a beautiful Native ball club, complete with a protruding nail in the burl head. When he saw the club, chills ran up his spine. He remembered the man who was killed behind Jed's tavern. *Wasn't he killed with one of these?* he thought. His hands began to shake. This one had been well cared for, and it seemed to be a treasured item important to someone. Who would have hidden the weapon here? Had it been lying here for centuries on the shelf, forgotten, or did it belong to someone in the area who'd chosen to keep it hidden within the cave? His memory flashed to the bigger footprints in the snow outside of the cave, and he shifted uncomfortably. He didn't have answers to his questions, but a dread filled his chest.

He sat for a moment, gathering up his thoughts. Murder. Ball clubs. Lt. Higgins.

Working quickly, he folded up the deer hide package and laid it carefully back on the shelf, replacing the rocks where he'd found them. Grabbing his knapsack, he crawled out of the cave and began his hike to the nearest road. He puffed with exertion. He needed to get to a spot where he could get a signal on his phone and call Lt. Higgins. He'd know what to do about the club. After all, he was a detective.

☐

"So you're telling me you have some leads, but there's nothing concrete—nothing solid enough to bring someone in?" asked Sheriff Jones. Jim, DeDe, and Paul were seated in front of the sheriff like a trio of ruffians in the principal's office. Paul shifted uncomfortably in his chair, and DeDe stared at the floor. Although Jim was irritated by the antagonistic barb of Jones' question, he was proud of his team and the efforts they were making in the case.

Sheriff Davy Jones stood behind his desk, hands on his hips. His crisp tan shirt and dark brown tie were immaculate, and the star on his chest glinted when the light bounced off it. His face was haggard with the weight of his responsibilities. He waited for confirmation from the three detectives about any information in the murder case of LeMar Burke—something he didn't already know. "Well? Do you have anything earth-shattering to report?" he asked, his voice hoarse and raspy.

Jim sighed loudly. "Sam's out right now trying to find some girl who flings axes very accurately at a target, but—"

Paul interrupted. "Sam gets these wild hairs, sir. But in his defense, a lot of the time he tends to be right." He looked sideways at Higgins, who gave him an inscrutable glance. Jones rolled his eyes.

"Well, at least he's doing what I asked," Jim said sourly.

"Which is what?" Jones asked, totally confused. *Have these guys really solved some of the worst crimes in La Crosse County history?*

"He's out on the street, trying to find out who might have seen something or knew something about Burke's murder," Jim explained. "I know Sam's theories can be somewhat off-the-wall at times, but he does get us thinking outside the box ... as crazy as that seems," he added begrudgingly under his breath.

"What about D'Marius Blake and this insurgent group of Ho-Chunk Natives? Any possible leads there?" Jones asked.

"We're working on that," DeDe offered. "Little Hawk is definitely a suspect, but I think it's more likely that he and his girlfriend, this Lori Lifto that Sam met, are tied up somehow. They deny ever meeting Burke, but we'll keep at it and talk to them again. We just haven't made any firm connections yet."

"Well, we need to start making some real soon. I don't need apologies; I need evidence, witnesses, and suspects," Jones said, his hands on his hips. "My phone is jammed with texts from people who believe these murders are a threat to their safety. It's panicking the public, and we sure don't need that on top of everything else," the sheriff reminded them. "God, ball clubs flying through the air, women flinging axes! What the hell is going on? And don't get me started on the press." The three detectives sat despondently, their shoulders drooped, their eyes downcast. Waiting for a response and seeing that none was forthcoming, Jones continued his tirade.

"There's one more thing I think you should know. Whether it's related to your case or not, I can't tell you at this point." He stopped briefly and made eye contact with the team. "A group of rabble-rousers have been picketing and protesting at the Scenic Rivers Energy Cooperative headquarters on East Avenue this week after the CEO announced plans to shut down the operation of the coal-generated power plant in Genoa within the next five years. The protestors' issue seems to be the proposed high-power transmission lines that are coming down from Canada, which will be carrying electrical current to our area once the power plant is dismantled."

"Yeah. I've read a little bit about that, but that's not happening for quite a while yet, as I understand it," Jim commented.

"True. But if you want to head off corporate decisions, you have to interrupt plans early and often. It's kinda like trying to stop a barge on the river once it's got some steam up. Not easily done," Jones explained. "The protesters are getting up a head of steam early, from the looks of it."

"What's that got to do with our case?" Paul asked.

"Maybe nothing. But the proposed line is going to pass right next to Terry Waite's farm. Didn't you tell me, Jim, that he was adamant about keeping the public away from some special Indian caves he's got on his land?" Jones asked.

Jim stared at Jones, then exchanged a cryptic glance with Paul and DeDe. "That could be a crucial link into what motivated the killer," Jim said quietly.

"Waite would fight that tooth and nail," Paul said. "His righteous anger would be off the charts."

"Well, it might lead to something important," Jones mumbled. Everyone thought about that for a moment.

"This is big. Really big," Paul said excitedly.

"Don't jump to conclusions yet," Jim said, "but it could be a piece of the puzzle."

Sheriff Jones clapped his hands, startling the detectives. "All right, everybody. Here's the plan. Right now, Jim, I want you to take Paul and get up to the scene south of Black River on Highway 54. See if anything from the murder up there ties to the Burke killing down here," Jones ordered. "The Native American weapon definitely is an interesting link common to the Burke murder, but there might be more that these two crimes share."

In a gesture of frustration, he ran his hand through his graying hair. Then, in a softer voice, he continued. "I knew Tanya Cadwallader. She was our real estate agent when we bought our house in the Seton neighborhood over in Shelby Township. She had a problem with alcohol, but the last I knew she'd been attending AA and was doing better. I liked her. She certainly didn't deserve to be clubbed over the head and murdered." He stopped briefly, thinking. "From what I've been told, the murder weapon is quite similar to the one used in the Burke killing. That's a connection, but there might be other connections, too." He pointed his finger at Jim. "If anybody can figure out this mess, Jim, it's you and your team. So get up there and see what you can do." Turning to DeDe, he ordered, "And you, Ms. Deverioux, get over to Tanya Cadwallader's office and help city police go through it. See if anything turns up. She's tied up with this thing somehow."

Having been dismissed, the three detectives stood, turned, and trailed into the hall. Paul and DeDe scrambled to keep up with Jim as he hurried toward the elevator. When they'd crammed in, DeDe spoke up.

"I guess I'm heading to Tanya's. I'll talk to her office staff," DeDe said.

"You do that," Jim said when the elevator dinged. Stepping onto the third floor, Jim turned to Paul and said, "My office in fifteen minutes. We'll take the Suburban."

"Right. I'll be there," Paul said, going down the hall to his office.

Jim plopped in his chair behind his desk and punched in Carol's work number.

"Jim? What's up?"

"Listen, there's been another murder up near Black River. Same type of weapon." Jim heard a sharp intake of air.

"Jim, does that mean what I think it means?"

"Well, that depends on what you mean." There was a long pause on the other end. "Was Lillie's dream accurate? Is that what you mean?"

"Yes. She was right, wasn't she?"

"Yep, she was."

Carol groaned softly. "That poor little girl. Why does she keep having these premonitions, Jim?" He could imagine Carol's brown eyes filled with sympathy, her face creased with worry.

"I don't know, honey. I wish I did, but she was right on. Tanya Cadwallader, a real estate agent from La Crosse, was killed in a rest area off Highway 54 south of Black River sometime this morning with a ball club very similar to the one that killed Burke."

Jim heard Carol's sharp intake of air. "No wonder Lillie didn't want to go to school," Carol lamented.

"Yeah, it's understandable. Listen, I want you to deflect Lillie's questions until I get home. I still haven't figured out what I'm going to tell her, but right now, I'm heading to Black River with Paul. I'm not sure when I'll be back. It'll probably be late. Don't wait up."

"Okay. What are we going to do, Jim?"

"About what?"

"About Lillie."

"We're going to love her for who she is, premonitions and all. That's what."

☐

Jim and Paul climbed into the Suburban in the law enforcement parking lot a half hour later and began the journey to Black River Falls. Paul offered to drive, and Jim didn't fight him for the privilege. As they left the city and pounded north up State Highway 54, they talked about possible murder scenarios, tossed around ideas, trashed some as ludicrous, and discussed those that seemed more believable.

"Do you think those transmission lines could be a possible motive in the murders?" Jim asked.

Paul frowned and pursed his lips. "Don't know, but any threat like that would send Terry Waite off the deep end."

Jim nodded. "I want you to spend every spare minute in the next few days looking into the connections between these protesters and

Terry Waite. See if he has anything to do with them. Does he support their work? Does he give them money? Also, see if Hathway Industries has used its influence in some way. It might lead us to something that would explain these murders—as crazy as that sounds."

"Maybe that's where all that cash went from LeMar Burke's checking account. Paying off someone at Scenic Rivers for influence with the high-line project?" Paul suggested tentatively. Jim listened as Paul talked, but in the back of his mind, he was thinking about Lillie's strange dream and her chilling premonition. He thought about his conversation earlier that morning with Lillie and wondered what kind of questions she'd ask about the lady tonight. He *knew* she would ask, and he had no idea what he was going to tell her.

"As soon as we get back, I'll start digging," Paul said. More silence. "Speaking of crazy, what do you think of Sam's idea that some ax-wielding female could be the killer?" Paul asked after they'd driven for a while. "Where does he come up with this stuff?"

Jim grunted, and his face reflected disgust. "Well, you should talk. You're the one who defended his harebrained ideas to Jones. And, from what I understand, he got this latest idea at The Aimless Ax."

"The what?"

"The ax-throwing bar downtown. That's where he met this Lori Lifto, female ax-thrower extraordinaire," Jim said, making a rude noise. "Another one of his theories." How could it be that they had sunk to the level of looking for someone whose ax-throwing skills might have been put to use in snuffing out a high-end executive from New Orleans and a real estate agent from a small, midwestern city? *We've hit a new low*, Jim thought.

"Well, we've got to start somewhere," Paul commented laconically.

"Right. Things can only go up from here. Should I give my probable versus possible speech now?"

"Nah, Chief. I've heard all that before."

Jim's phone buzzed.

"Higgins," he said curtly, pressing the phone to his ear.

"Lt. Higgins?" a timid voice said.

"Yes, this is Lt. Higgins. Can I help you?"

"It's Bobby Rude, Lieutenant. I need to talk to you." He sounded out of breath.

"Talk away, buddy. How's your dad doing?" Jim asked. There was a painful silence and heavy breathing that stretched into several seconds. "Bobby? Your dad? How's he doing?"

"He died last night," Bobby said quietly.

Jim closed his eyes briefly and listened to the soft sobs over the phone, embarrassed by his insensitivity. "Oh, I'm so sorry, Bobby. I didn't know."

Paul looked over at Jim and mouthed, "Who is it?"

Jim raised his eyebrows and covered the phone with his hand. "Bobby Rude. His dad died last night," he said softly.

Paul grimaced. He focused his attention back on the road.

Jim continued listening, punctuating the conversation with a few short comments here and there. Suddenly, after several moments, he stiffened and sat up straight. "Whoa, whoa, whoa! Wait a minute. Slow down. Say that again." Paul looked over at Jim, alarmed at the tone of his voice.

Bobby said in a tight voice, "I found a really old ball club in a cave, and I thought you should know about it since that guy behind Jed's bar was murdered with one of those clubs. Right?"

"You found a ball club in a cave? Where is this cave?" Jim asked.

"It's near Stoddard on some professor's land. Up Mohawk Valley Road," Bobby said.

"You mean Terry Waite?" Jim asked.

"Yeah. I forgot his name, but that's the guy."

"How'd you know about this cave, Bobby?"

"I've been visiting it for at least two years. Nobody knows I've been there—"

"Bobby, listen to me," Jim interrupted. "Someone probably *does* know you've been there. You need to be very careful. In fact, don't go there anymore until I can meet with you. The people who are using these clubs are deadly serious in their intent. Promise me you'll stay away from the cave."

"Sure, Lt. Higgins. It takes at least two hours to hike in there. I was just there anyway, so I won't be going back for a while. Don't worry. I'll be fine."

"Well, I will worry about you unless you promise me you'll go over and stay with Jed tonight above the tavern. Is that a deal?" Jim's forehead was creased with a deep frown.

"Yeah. I can do that. When are you going to come and talk to me?"

"Tomorrow morning," Jim promised. "Stay at Jed's until I get there. We'll make a plan then, okay?"

"Okay. Thanks, Lt. Higgins." Bobby's voice sounded relieved like a dam of guilt had broken loose. "I'll see you tomorrow." He abruptly hung up.

"What the hell was that all about?" Paul asked, glancing over at Jim.

"Well, I'm not sure I understand all of it, but Bobby Rude went to a cave on Terry Waites' farm today—apparently, he's been there before—and while he was there, he found a ball club hidden in the cave."

"You mean the cave Waite was having a fit about when I talked to him? The sacrosanct treasure that needed to be preserved for generations to come?" Paul said sarcastically.

"If you keep hanging around all those educated people, your vocabulary is going to grow by leaps and bounds, and we won't be able to communicate anymore," Jim said, grinning. Paul blew through his lips, his dislike for Waite still fresh in his mind.

"But to get back to Bobby ..." Jim started again. "He had enough sense to know the ball club was significant in our investigation, and he wants to tell me about it. And not that we're counting or anything, but that's the third weapon that's come to light in this investigation."

"Yeah, you're right. The Burke weapon, the Cadwallader weapon, and now another one that Bobby discovered in that cave," Paul said.

"I'll run over and talk to Bobby in the morning. But we need to talk to Terry Waite again for a lot of reasons. Finding a ball club on his farm looks suspicious, at the very least." Jim looked at Paul.

Paul pursed his lips, his face reflecting his dislike for the man. "Well, get ready to be humiliated, denigrated for your obvious stupidity, and written off as a joke for your lack of intelligent detection skills," he said sourly. "I'm sure Waite will have a heyday pointing that out to you when you talk to him."

"He's not the first who's ridiculed me, and he won't be the last. Nowadays, cops are either the hero or the heel," Jim grumbled. "I'll talk to Waite tomorrow downtown. He needs a reminder of the consequences of withholding information during a murder investigation." Jim went quiet for a few miles, then he said, "You know, Bobby could be a really good cop someday."

☐

The landscape near Black River Falls changed from brown farm fields lying fallow waiting for spring planting to tall stands of evergreens punctuated by swamp and marsh on either side of the highway. Patches of thick snow still lay along the side of the road, and more patches were scattered intermittently throughout the landscape. Paul and Jim passed a few rusty mobile homes and an abandoned used car lot. The vehicles were lumpy with corrosion, and the sign next to the abandoned lot tilted at a precarious angle, the lettering mostly faded away.

As they got closer to the wayside, the red and blue lights of squad cars and emergency vehicles flashed ominously. The state patrol had cordoned off one lane of traffic for about a thousand feet in front of the wayside in both directions. Paul maneuvered the Suburban along the shoulder of the road, impatiently passing cars and trucks that were waiting to be directed through the bottleneck. Someone in a gray pickup truck flipped him off. As Paul approached the entrance to the wayside, a state patrol officer held up his hand in a stop motion, frowning at his driving antics. Paul pulled up alongside the officer. They flashed their IDs, and he directed them into the parking lot, which was jammed with police vehicles, a Jackson County crime scene van, and the coroner's SUV.

The CSI van was parked in front of the women's restroom, where technicians were busy gathering evidence around the wayside toilets. The place hummed with intensity. A tall, thin man in a tan and brown uniform waved at Jim while he continued a harried conversation with a man in a dark suit. Jim recognized the plainclothes detective from other Jackson County investigations he'd assisted with. *Clayfish? Claybird? Clay something.* He couldn't remember, although he knew he was a member of the Ho-Chunk Nation.

Jim and Paul walked up to the sheriff, who nodded at both of them.

"What's happening, Sheriff Walsh?" Jim asked. "We only know what Jones told us this morning."

"Crime scene found fingerprints, but in a public restroom, that's a crap shoot at best. We know how that goes. DNA is improbable, although we could get lucky," Sheriff Walsh began. "We haven't located any witnesses or other travelers who might have been in the parking lot during the attack. No surveillance cameras, obviously. We're missing on all cylinders, but we're pullin' out all the stops. Can't you tell?" He rolled his eyes in disgust. "We do have the murder weapon." He looked past Jim and Paul to the toilets in the distance. "Just when I thought we were handling everything on our plate, and then this happens."

"Just tell us what you want us to do. We're here to assist in any way we can," Jim said.

Sheriff Walsh started again. "Well, the victim was hit from behind when she was standing at the sink washing her hands. She probably saw her attacker in the mirror, but it came so fast and furious she didn't have time to react or defend herself. The head wound seems to fit the club's profile." He closed his eyes and ran his hand across his face. "It's nasty. Very nasty."

"Yeah. I know. The other victim's wound was bad, too. Mind if we take a look? We'd like to see if the two murders might be related somehow," Jim said.

"If the weapon is any indication, they sure seem to be. Go ahead," Sheriff Walsh said, cocking his head toward the restroom as another police officer approached him. "Let me know what you think when you're done."

Jim and Paul walked down a slight incline and approached the women's toilet. When they reached the small cement block building, they both stopped and put on shoe coverings and blue latex gloves. Jim poked his head around the door frame and flashed his ID.

A crime scene tech looked up from a kneeling position near the victim.

"Can we have a look?" Jim asked.

"Sure. You the guys from La Crosse?" the tech asked. Paul nodded. "Go for it," she said, standing and moving outside. "I'll be right outside."

Paul and Jim walked past the technician and knelt next to Tanya Cadwallader. Her eyes were partially open, and the dullness of death in them turned Paul's stomach. He swallowed hard as Jim avoided the dark puddle of blood near her head. Then Paul noticed the blood and brains spattered on the wall next to the sink. His stomach turned over, and he quickly stood and vomited in one of the toilet stalls. When he came back, Jim rolled the victim toward the wall to get a better view of the wound.

The shattered skull and battered flesh stirred a slow burn of anger in Jim's gut. He swallowed the bile that had gathered in his throat. Nearby, the chalk outline of the weapon on the cement floor revealed its proximity to the body. After a few moments, Jim stood up and pulled off his gloves.

Locking eyes with Paul, he asked, "You gettin' mad yet? Because this pisses me off." He threw his gloves in the trash bin with a flourish.

Paul wiped his mouth on his sleeve and popped a breath mint. "It looks very similar to the Burke murder, wouldn't you say?" Jim recognized the disconnected attitude and the dull gaze that had washed over Paul's features. *We've all got our own way of handling this kind of stuff*, he thought.

"Yeah. That's exactly what I'd say," Jim said, his voice rippling with anger. "Ambushed from behind, hit hard and accurately. No traces except the weapon lying next to the victim," he recited. "In fact, I'd say it's the same killer—one hundred percent. There's too many similarities for it not to be."

"Unless it's a copycat," Paul said laconically.

"There's that, but I don't get that feeling. Whoever it is, they're off their everlovin' rocker."

Jim and Paul left the restroom and went outside, where the female crime scene tech was having a cigarette. Jim stopped in front of her, and through a haze of smoke, he asked, "Did you find any kind of evidence in or around the toilets?"

She stomped her cigarette into the mud and said, "Actually, we got a pretty good fingerprint from the outside door handle and another one farther up on the door where someone rested their hand. Maybe listening before they went in?" she said, hypothesizing. She shrugged her shoulders. "Maybe not. I guess that's your territory, but there aren't too many people who use these restrooms at this time of year. Pretty cold and deserted," she said when she saw the detectives' vacillating expressions.

"Do the fingerprints match?" Paul asked.

"Can't tell yet. We'll have to get them to the lab and check it out. You want a call when we get the results?" she asked.

"Yeah, I'd appreciate it," Jim said, handing her his card. "Thanks."

Paul and Jim walked briskly across the parking lot, weaving their way through groups of law enforcement officers and first responders to get to the Suburban, which was parked close to the road.

"Hey, Jim. Wait a minute," Sheriff Walsh called out when they were almost to the SUV. Jim turned around and walked back. Walsh looked unhinged. The wind tousled his hair, and a light sheen of sweat covered his face.

"One of my officers learned from Cadwallader's secretary that Tanya talked to …" he looked down at his small notebook and moved his finger down one of the small pages. "Here it is. A Mr. Jack Bishop on Bauer Road. He listed his property with the Bluff agency this morning. Thought you might want to talk to him. He's right over there in the red Badgers sweatshirt." Jim looked in the direction he was pointing and saw a tall, balding man who seemed pale and distraught, conversing with a plainclothes cop, probably another detective.

"Thanks. We'll talk to him," Jim said. "Come on, Paul."

"Jim," Walsh said as he walked away. Jim stopped and turned back.

"You'll let me know what you find out, right?" Walsh asked.

"You bet," Jim responded.

They approached Mr. Bishop but waited for him to finish his conversation. Then they introduced themselves.

"This is just terrible," Mr. Bishop said softly, his blue eyes rimmed with tears. "I just spoke to her a few hours ago. I can't believe this. She seemed like such a nice lady."

"We understand you're upset, but can you tell us about your conversation with Ms. Cadwallader?" Jim asked gently.

Mr. Bishop swallowed hard, and his eyes swept over the tall pine trees at the back of the wayside as if that might help him remember the details. "Miss Cadwallader arrived about ten this morning. We spent about an hour looking over my property and cabin. We talked price and worked on the language describing the strong points of the property that a buyer might be looking for. Toward the end of the conversation, I mentioned the cave paintings that are in Glen Park, which butts up to my property on the north." He pointed vaguely north in the direction of the park.

"Cave paintings?" Paul interrupted, scowling, his pen poised midair. "What cave paintings?"

"There are some ancient paintings on an exposed wall in the park. There's also some inside one of the caves. They're not on my property per se, and I wanted to mention them in the description of the property's features, but Tanya advised against it. She told me there's some controversy surrounding these ancient petroglyphs right now, and she advised me not to mention them in my description of the property. She said it might draw negative attention, so I said fine, and we signed the papers. That's the last time I saw her." He looked at them with an expression that begged for an explanation of the senseless violence that had taken place.

"Did she say anything else? Did she mention anyone by name?" Jim asked.

"No, she just made a point about the caves, but I didn't understand exactly why," Mr. Bishop said, still confused.

"It's a long, convoluted story, but thanks so much for what you told us. You've been very helpful. If anyone contacts you about the petroglyphs, please call us immediately," Paul said as he handed him his contact information.

"Be careful," Jim added. "We're not sure yet if this cave art is a factor in the murders, so please be cautious. Call one of us immediately if someone threatens you." Mr. Bishop's eyes widened, and his mouth dropped open.

"Am I in immediate danger?" he asked quietly, fingering a button on his shirt sleeve.

"No, no. I wouldn't say that," Jim explained hurriedly. "We just want you to be aware of the situation and exercise some common sense."

"Okay, I guess I can do that," Mr. Bishop said weakly.

They talked a while longer before Jim and Paul walked to the Suburban and climbed in. Jim turned to Paul and said quietly, "These cave petroglyphs are an ongoing theme running through these murders. Let's head over to the Ho-Chunk headquarters and see what they can tell us about them."

"I agree. We're here anyway," Paul said, "but I need some lunch first."

They drove into Black River Falls and found a small café on the main street that served hot lunches and good coffee—at least that's what the sign advertised. They walked in and found a booth. Jim ordered a taco salad, and Paul ordered a cheeseburger and onion rings. They both ordered black coffee.

While they waited for their food, Jim called Sam. The waitress brought coffee, and it tasted fresh and delicious.

"Any luck finding this Lori Lifto woman?" he asked when Sam answered.

"No. I went to her apartment, but she wasn't there. The guy downstairs said he would keep an eye out for her and call me. But I might have spooked her the other night when I questioned her about the murder."

"From your description, she didn't sound like someone who would be easily spooked. She's around somewhere, maybe with Little Hawk."

"Yeah, that's what DeDe and I thought. Can you text me Little Hawk's address? It's somewhere up by Cashton, right?" Sam asked. "I thought I'd drive up there and talk to him."

"Wear your vest," Jim said seriously.

"Don't you mean a helmet?" Sam asked.

"What?"

"Well, people are getting their skulls smashed in. A vest wouldn't do much good, would it?"

"Whatever. You know what I mean. Whoever is doing the killing is not a person to mess with. I'll text you the address," he said curtly.

Jim and Paul finished their lunches and headed for the tribal headquarters on Airport Road. A wide boulevard led to the two-story modern brick structure. At the main entrance, a prominent, colorful sign above the entry doors featuring an eagle and black bear greeted visitors to the Ho-Chunk Nation. Jim and Paul walked into the building and approached the front desk.

"We're from the La Crosse Sheriff's Department," Jim began. "We'd like to talk to someone who can tell us about the cave paintings in the area. Is there somebody here who could do that?"

The woman behind the desk smiled at Jim, her dark eyes friendly, her manner helpful. She said, "You'll want to talk to our heritage preservation officer, Stephanie Decorah. Let me check to see if she's in the building somewhere."

"Sure. We'll wait over there," Jim said, pointing to a small reception area near the counter. As Jim made himself comfortable on the vinyl couches, Paul browsed through some tourist brochures in a rack near the entrance. Jim's cell beeped.

"Lt. Higgins."

"Chief. I talked to Cadwallader's secretary in the La Crosse office," DeDe began explaining. "She said that Tanya came into the office hungover this morning from a night on the town with Trent Willow. She was supposed to return his call this morning when she got in the office, but apparently, she never did because when I contacted him, he knew nothing about her murder—at least, that's what he told me. I've asked him to come in for questioning. He's on his way."

"That's interesting. What else?" Jim asked impatiently.

"Dylan Meyer from Blue Earth Gallery in Eau Claire called and said the ball club used in LeMar's murder was sold to a collector from Wausau. I'm tracking the guy down now. Not sure where that's going, but I'll keep you posted."

"You do that. Who's helping with the Willow interview?"

"Leslie, if that's all right. She came in early this afternoon. One more thing—when city police searched Cadwallader's office, they found a large bundle of hundred-dollar bills. More than twenty thousand dollars."

Jim sat up suddenly. "How much?" he asked.

"Over twenty thousand in hundred-dollar bills," DeDe repeated. "Where it came from is anybody's guess."

"Has the daughter been interviewed yet?"

"No, but I'll head over there after the Willow interview. I'll let you know what I find out."

"That's good. Listen. When you interview Willow, find out about his relationship with Tanya and his whereabouts this morning. See if he knew anything about the cash. Hear anything from Sam?"

"Nope. All I know is he hasn't found Lifto yet. The last I heard, he was heading to Little Hawk's place over by Cashton."

"Yeah, I know. I talked to him. I hope he's careful. Somebody's killing people with clubs. That's a nasty way to make a political statement, if that's what this is. Next thing you know, they'll break out the axes."

"Axes, sir?"

"Pretend you didn't hear that," Jim said curtly.

"Anything else?" DeDe asked.

"No, but be careful. Call me when you know something." Jim hung up and called Judge Celia Monroe's office and got her secretary on the line.

"Brenda. Jim Higgins. I need a search warrant for two residences, Tanya Cadwallader and Terry Waite, but I'm up in Black River Falls right now and probably won't be back until later. Is the judge in court tomorrow?"

"She's in court until one o'clock, then she'll spend the afternoon in her office, so get everything to me early before nine. I'll see what I can do to speed things along."

"Great. Thanks, Brenda."

"Now what?" Paul asked. Jim told him about Cadwallader and Willow's night on the town and the large amount of cash in Tanya's desk.

"That's a lot of money just laying around," Paul commented. "Sam went alone to Blake's place? I don't like the sound of that."

"He'll be all right if he remembers to wear his vest," Jim grumped, his lips turned downward in disgust.

"We'll get whoever this is, Chief," Paul said, noticing Jim's disgruntled expression. "We always have before. Remember Heather

Lovstad? You got a confession out of her on her deathbed, for Pete's sake."

"Yeah, and the killer got smucked in a plane crash which took the place of a trial. Sometimes God has a way of evening the score."

"That's true. Righteous retribution, huh?"

"Yeah, something like that. 'For the Lord has a day of vengeance.' Isaiah 34:8."

"Lt. Higgins?" the woman at the desk called to Jim. The two detectives stood and walked over to the counter. "Stephanie is in Tomah at the Ho-Chunk Museum and Cultural Center today. She'll be there until four o'clock if you want to drive over and talk to her."

"Thanks. Maybe we'll do that," Jim said politely.

Jim and Paul walked out of the building to the Suburban, discussed their options while they sat in the parking lot, and decided to drive to Tomah and look up Stephanie.

"These cave paintings are such a weird common denominator," Jim said. "They seem to tie things together, but we need to talk to somebody who knows more about their significance. Maybe that will give us a direction because right now, I'm out of ideas."

They drove southeast on Interstate 94 for half an hour. The windshield wipers swished quietly, pushing a fine mist across the glass that blurred the wooded land along the freeway into a brown and tan collage.

Arriving at the museum in downtown Tomah around two-thirty, Paul parked the truck next to the building. Jim knew the museum had just recently opened. The 50,000-square-foot building was divided into sections, each featuring some aspect of Ho-Chunk life and culture. A volunteer at a souvenir counter pointed them to an area where Stephanie Decorah was busy working with the museum's manager on an exhibit of Native Winnebago basketry.

Jim scanned the displays and walked up to her. "Ms. Decorah?" he asked.

The young woman turned to face the men, a basket in her hand.

Her dark eyes glowed with confidence. Dressed in a blue jean skirt and white blouse, her tall, slim frame and dark, shining hair gave her an air of friendliness and trust. Smiling, she said, "Yes, I'm Stephanie. Can I help you?"

"We hope so," Jim said, pulling his ID from his jacket. "We have some questions about the cave paintings that are found throughout the area. Is there someplace we could talk privately?"

"We can use my office," she said, pointing toward the back corner of the building. "Come this way." She gave the basket to another woman, turned, and waved her hand for them to follow.

Once they were settled in the small cubicle, Jim explained the murders that had occurred and the role the cave paintings and ball club seemed to play in the incidents.

"I read about the La Crosse murder in the newspaper, but ... wow! That's quite an unusual set of circumstances, isn't it?" Stephanie asked. "And now another person has been murdered?" Her eyes were wide with astonishment.

"Yes. That's why we need your help. Are you familiar with any Ho-Chunk fringe groups who might be using the cave paintings as a reason to kill someone? Say someone who didn't appreciate their importance or someone who failed to see their historical and cultural significance? Maybe someone who wants to destroy them?"

Stephanie crossed her legs and leaned back, comfortable in the swivel office chair.

"Well, I know there's a group that broke away from our traditional values. They've been meeting down on the Kickapoo Reserve about once a month, I guess. But my husband, who's a tribal police officer, is skeptical about their reasons for forming their own group. He's been to a few of their meetings, in fact. His conclusion is they don't seem to be focused enough to carry out a strategic plan of retaliation. And he says their goals are pretty vague—something about protecting and buying back Native lands. Seems like a moot point in this day and age. His impression of them was that they were just a bunch of weekend warriors looking for an excuse to party and smoke some dope. The problem is they feed the stereotypical image of Natives we're trying to change."

"What do you mean by 'stereotypical images of Natives'?" Paul asked bluntly.

"Come on, detective," Stephanie said impatiently, a sense of indignation just below the surface of her words. She pushed a strand of hair away from her face. "I'm sure you're aware of the commonly held image in white society that Indians are shiftless, lazy, drunken bums who mooch off the government," she said, a hint of defensiveness creeping into her voice. Paul nodded and reddened slightly with embarrassment.

"We've made great progress in teaching our Native children their heritage and the role they have to play as American citizens. We're hopeful that over time, we can restore the vision of our people as unique contributors to the American way of life while still respecting and upholding traditional Ho-Chunk values." Her dark eyes glowed with a sense of purpose.

"Has that been successful so far?" Jim asked.

"We see signs of hope. In reality, our children are our best and most precious resource in changing the stereotypes in people's minds," she said. Jim thought about Lillie's unabashed sorrow of the brutal slaying of Blackhawk's people in the Mississippi River over two hundred years ago. If Lillie was any indication, then there might be hope that things could change for the better.

"I agree with you on that," he said. "So what can you tell us about the Native cave paintings in the area?"

"There are cave paintings throughout southwest Wisconsin and Minnesota, and petroglyphs are scattered in different locations around here, too," Stephanie began. "But I don't think many Ho-Chunks are focused on cave petroglyphs, although they are fascinating. They were drawn by ancient Native peoples—Pre-Columbian, probably Oneota or possibly the Cahokia about eight hundred to one thousand years ago."

"Are paintings different from petroglyphs?" Paul asked.

"Yes. Paintings or pictographs are drawn with charcoal or some kind of natural pigment, whereas petroglyphs are carved or chipped into the rock," Stephanie said. "Anyway, La Crosse, Vernon, and Jackson counties have a number of sites that feature deer, bison, birds, boats, and humans interacting in different scenarios. Historians estimate that most were made with quartzite tools. Over near Friendship, the Roche-A-Cri State Park has an awesome landmark that rises about three hundred feet above the land. That specific butte outcropping was probably used as a navigational guide for travelers down through the ages. It's covered with petroglyphs. Really fascinating."

"My daughter Lillie would love it," Jim said. "But getting back to my question. Do you think these petroglyphs could be a factor in these murders?"

Stephanie stared at the floor for a few moments, lost in thought. She shook her head. "I just don't see it. Who would kill over some ancient carvings in a cave? It just doesn't make sense to me."

"Even if it was done to preserve and defend an ancient cultural record? Or an ancient cultural hero?" Jim asked. *Like Blackhawk*, he thought.

Stephanie tilted her head to one side. "Maybe, but that's a stretch, don't you think? You'd have to be pretty radical to do that. It just doesn't seem justifiable to me." She stopped short, her eyes popping open, surprised at the incongruous nature of her comment. "Of course, murder is never justifiable, is it?" Her eyebrows lifted slightly.

"You've got a point there," Paul said prudently.

Jim's eyes hardened, and the muscles in his jaw tightened. When he looked at Ms. Decorah, she noticed his determined look and his perceptive gaze.

"Somebody is killing people with an ancient ball club," Jim said sternly. "There must be some kind of significance in their choice of weapon."

"Maybe they chose the weapon to deflect attention from their real motive," Stephanie said.

"I see what you mean," Paul said. "Use the weapon to detract us from the real reason behind the killings."

"Yes. Is that possible?" Stephanie asked.

"Anything is possible, but is it probable?" Jim asked. Stephanie looked confused.

"That's the million-dollar question," Paul said.

□

Sam gunned the Jeep when the red light on Losey Boulevard turned green. In the distance, he could see Grandad Bluff soaring six hundred feet in the air, its limestone profile familiar to every La Crosse resident. He traveled a couple of blocks, then turned onto Highway 33 and drove in a southeasterly direction toward Little Hawk's property near the small town of Cashton.

As he climbed out of the La Crosse River valley and up onto the ridge, the weather changed, and though the sky was a slate gray, at least it wasn't pouring buckets. The snow that had carpeted the ground just a week ago was spotty. The green grass, dried brown vegetation, and lingering pastiches of snow created a variegated landscape like a patchwork quilt. Farmers had let their cows out of the barn, and they stood clumped together in barnyards, sloughing off the confinement of the winter months.

The pastures sloped steeply into deep valleys where small streams were swollen with melting snow. Weathered barns and tobacco sheds in various states of disrepair dotted the rural landscape. A flock of turkeys pecked for acorns on a hillside, and deer browsed at the edge of a wooded area.

Sam drove into the small town of Cashton, turned right off Main Street, and continued on Hwy. 33, which dipped into several valleys. Gravel roads branched into more rural terrain—roads with names like Johnson Coulee, Hinkst Hollow Road, and Buckeye Ridge.

Sam wove through the countryside for about five miles, then turned on Norwegian Hollow Road, and meandered across the valley floor. Gradually, the road climbed toward the top of the ridge in a series of steep hills and hairpin curves. On the crest of one of the hills, he spotted the fire number Higgins had given him. Turning cautiously onto the gravel driveway, he rolled his window down and breathed the cool mist that saturated the atmosphere. The skeletal trees in the woods were damp with moisture, mystical and claustrophobic—like something out of a spooky movie.

The driveway ended, and in the clearing a prefab log cabin squatted on a patch of overgrown brown grass. The home was square with a green steel roof and triple pane windows whose frames were the same color. A simply constructed covered porch ran across the front of the cabin. A few oaks, maples, and large white pines were sporadically scattered throughout the property. Next to the cabin, four Adirondack chairs were arranged at the edge of a fire pit, and a couple of forked sticks for roasting hot dogs and marshmallows leaned against one of the chairs. About a hundred feet back from the cabin, toward the edge of the cleared land, sat a white metal pole shed. A few chickens pecked the ground nervously, their beady eyes darting.

Sam sat in the Jeep, getting a feel for the place. He'd learned the hard way that nosing around somebody's property could result in a bite in the ass by a dedicated guard dog. He didn't want to go there again. He grimaced when he recalled the stitches he had gotten in his rear end when he'd entered a large industrial shed guarded by some kind of medieval mongrel who took his guard duties seriously. His cockiness and beginner investigative enthusiasm had gotten him into a world of hurt.

No one seemed to be around. It was very quiet except for the chattering of birds in the trees. A red and white Sierra 1500 crew cab pickup was parked on one side of the driveway, and Sam assumed the vehicle was Little Hawk's. He continued to wait, watching the cabin for any signs of life. He'd discovered that most people, if they were home, couldn't resist looking out the door or a window when someone drove up on their property. Five minutes later, Little Hawk stepped out onto the front stoop of his cabin. He gave a tentative wave. Sam got out of his vehicle. Little Hawk wore a gray flannel plaid shirt with a red T-shirt underneath, a pair of rugged Carhartt tan jeans, and a pair of rubber garden clogs with no socks despite the cool temperatures.

Little Hawk walked down the steps toward the Jeep, stopping about five feet from Sam. In broad daylight, his physique was more impressive than the night Sam had met him in the dark alley behind The Aimless Ax on Fourth Street. His wide shoulders, narrow hips, and bulging biceps made Sam feel inadequate on some subconscious adolescent level. Sam forced himself to remain calm and friendly, smiling and relaxed. Little Hawk's dark eyes held an odd combination of curiosity and confrontation, but his physical presence alone was enough to ward off the unaware. *You'd have to be stupid to take on somebody his size*, Sam thought. Still, he sensed some kind of challenge was being formulated, but he stayed quiet, hoping Little Hawk would fill in the silence.

"You lost, Officer?" Little Hawk asked with a grin. "You're a long way from the big city, aren't you?"

"I could say the same about you," Sam said, leaning against the grill of his Jeep, crossing his arms over his chest. "I didn't think you'd remember me. Quite the place you've got here. I like it, but then, I like the country."

"I bought the land right out of high school with my eighteen money from the casino," Little Hawk began explaining. "Had the cabin delivered a year later. The Amish built it. Never regretted locating here. The people on the ridge are friendly without being too nosy. Know what I mean?" He cocked his head to one side, his black hair shining with a blue hue. He waited patiently for Sam's response, but he was in no hurry to be drawn into an argument. Sam continued the friendly chat.

"Actually, I do know what you mean. Right now, my wife and I are renting a duplex over by Grandad Bluff. Our neighbors are friendly enough, but nothing beats having something you can call your own."

"Yeah, taxes and upkeep are all my own, too," Little Hawk said tersely. "Part of being a red-blooded United States citizen, I guess."

Sam nodded in understanding. "Have you seen your friend Lori today or talked to her?" Sam said, suddenly changing the subject. "I went to her apartment, but she wasn't home."

Little Hawk's face tightened. "Nope, I haven't talked to her today," he said. "She works nights and sometimes weekends, so we don't get together for weeks at a time. It's either feast or famine with Lori. If she shuts you out, it could last for months." Sam noticed Little Hawk's eyes traveling over him, stopping at his feet. "Where'd you get those shoes?" he asked sarcastically. "Looks like something you'd wear when you're ghetto cruisin' in Milwaukee."

Sam ignored the comment. "After your argument the other night in the alley, I wondered how it went after I left. Has Lori shut you out?" he asked, keeping the pressure on.

Little Hawk crinkled his nose conspicuously. "She was ticked, but that's not unusual for her." He chuckled softly. "She *does* have a temper."

"She seemed pretty hostile when I talked to her in the alley. What made her so mad?"

"Like I told you, it's a personal issue between us." His voice had hardened; he didn't want to be reminded of Lori poking her finger into his chest.

"Fair enough," Sam said, "but you do know we're investigating the ball club murder in Genoa." Sam leveled his gaze at Little Hawk. "And now, this morning, another murder took place near Black River Falls. A woman realtor from La Crosse was killed with the same type of weapon—a ball club. Realty. Clubs. Murder. Seems to be a pattern, wouldn't you say?"

Little Hawk shrugged his shoulders, but beneath his calm exterior, Sam sensed panic.

"I'm not a detective," Little Hawk said, "so I wouldn't know about things like that."

"The woman who was killed in Black River was Tanya Cadwallader. Do you know her?"

"Nope. Never heard of her," Little Hawk said curtly. He looked away from Sam's direct stare, focusing suddenly on the woods surrounding his property. His eyes drifted back to Sam, and he shuffled nervously on his feet.

"What about Professor Terry Waite? Do you know him?"

"Sure. I've had a couple of his classes at the university."

"Are you actively engaged in activities with a Ho-Chunk insurgent group that meets occasionally at the Kickapoo Valley Reserve for weekend warrior retreats?"

"Used to be. I dumped those guys. They're a bunch of losers."

"So tell me about your hero, Blackhawk," Sam said, backing off a little. "I understand you're named after him."

Little Hawk burred at the question. "What's to tell?" he smirked, his lip curled in disdain. "He was beaten into submission by a bunch of soldiers who ran his tribe into the Mississippi and shot the women and children like sitting ducks. As if that wasn't enough, he was taken captive and humiliated in front of crowds of white men out East who wanted to see what a defeated Indian looked like. Then he came home to his cornfields and village to watch his people die in poverty, sickness, and starvation."

"That's a sad story. Should I apologize?" Sam asked, not trying to be funny. Little Hawk's body tensed with agitation.

"It's more than sad. It's a travesty of people everywhere who are trying to fulfill their destiny." By now, Little Hawk's eyes were dancing with anger, and beneath his brown skin, his cheeks were flushed bright pink.

Easy, buddy, Sam thought. "So Blackhawk is your what? Great-great-great-grandfather?"

"You need a few more greats. I'm the seventh generation who descends from his line."

"Wow! That's something," Sam said, truly impressed by the DNA of the whole thing.

Sam thought about the answers Little Hawk had given during their conversation. It didn't fly that this guy could be so clueless about the murders that had taken place yet know that he was the seventh generation who descended from Blackhawk and could spout off his oral history at the snap of a finger. And what about his famous father, who was known for his amazing replicas of ancient weapons? And what about that little ax-flinging girlfriend of his? Sam sighed, put his questions on hold, and reined in his skepticism, knowing they had absolutely no proof of his involvement in either murder. All they had were assumptions, and you couldn't arrest somebody on that and expect to get a conviction. Instead, he addressed Little Hawk calmly.

"You know, Little Hawk," Sam said, straightening to his full height, "I don't believe anyone as smart as you could be so unaware of these murder victims, especially when the weapon used in the first murder was made by your father. You're an advocate of preserving your Native culture and defending your ancestral hero's reputation. There's nothing inherently wrong with that, but I don't believe for a minute that you're innocent in this whole affair. Someone is killing people with ancient Native weapons for some reason we haven't figured out yet, but eventually we will. So until then, you're on our radar until you start telling me what you really know. Are you getting my message?" Sam asked, his voice hardening with resolve.

"Loud and clear. And here's a message for you," Little Hawk said quietly. "Don't get me riled, buddy."

"Are you threatening me?" Sam asked quietly.

Little Hawk stayed silent, his face dark and brooding. "Be very careful, sir," Sam warned. "You're furious about a number of things I couldn't even begin to guess at. My message is just another perceived insult." They stared at each other for a long moment.

Little Hawk pointed his finger at Sam's chest, his nostrils flaring. "Get off my property. You're no longer welcome here," he snarled.

Sam held up his hands. "Fine. I'll go, but I'll be back with a warrant. And when I come back, I'll find out what you're hiding,

Little Hawk. It won't go well for you if you've been holding out on us."

Without speaking, Little Hawk thrust his arm toward the driveway. Sam thought he looked strangely regal and authoritative like his ancestor, Blackhawk. *Funny how genetics works*, he thought. He climbed into the Jeep, turned around in front of the cabin, and slowly drove out the driveway onto the gravel road.

18

Lori Lifto drove down the field road to the open pasture on her father's West Salem farm, where she'd set up a practice field. The plywood target with its three concentric circles was at the far end of the pasture close to the woods but not close enough to lose an ax if she missed the plywood board. She smiled. *Not likely,* she thought. *I never miss.* Then she wondered if she'd become overconfident. She shrugged to herself. *If you're good, you're good. I guess my practice is starting to pay off.*

She stopped her VW Passat wagon when she got closer to the practice area. Climbing out of the car, she opened the hatchback where a leather pouch lay securely tied shut. The air was cool, but the sun was struggling to shine through the thin cloud cover—a good day for some target practice.

She'd already driven by the detective's house on Cliffwood Lane beneath Grandad Bluff in La Crosse and checked out the duplex. Her plan would get Birkstein's attention—make him nervous, worried, skittish. The only problem was she'd lose her ax in the process, but what was one ax compared to the thrill of hassling a cop? Besides, she had over fifteen axes in her collection. Sacrificing one of them was minor compared to the message she wanted to send Birkstein:

Don't accuse me of criminal activity when you have absolutely no proof.

The whole incident in the alley that night was absurd. How could anyone conclude she'd killed someone based solely on her ax-throwing ability? Of course, she did have an attitude, and Little Hawk had warned her about aggravating a cop. But she couldn't forget the cop's swaggering bluster when he questioned her in the alley. Then she remembered his hazel eyes and curly mop of hair. Despite his obvious physical attractiveness, the guy was also a real jerk—a typical cop.

She stood behind the car thinking about her plan. Her accuracy with an ax was like any other athletic endeavor—you had to visualize the end result in order to be a winner. And you had to practice a lot. She could almost hear the whirring of the ax rotating in mid-air and the dull *whack* when it hit its target. She imagined the stunned disbelief of the cop when he realized what she'd done. He'd know right away it was her. But proving it would be almost impossible. After all, anyone could throw an ax. Lori smiled. This was going to be so good—almost as good as sex. Almost.

She opened the leather pouch and took out her Woods Chogan tomahawk. It felt good in her hand, light but deadly accurate and extremely sharp. She stroked the steel handle, then ran her finger very lightly along the precision blade. A thin ribbon of blood appeared on her index finger. Walking through the wet grass to her practice field, she went through her mantra before heaving the ax: Dominant hand on top, thumb up. Other hand at the bottom, thumb up.

Rock forward. Rock backward. Place the ax all the way over the top of your head.

Rock forward again and release just above eye level.

Just think of the child's rocking horse. The motion was very similar. Rock forward, backward, forward, and release. *A piece of cake*, Lori thought, her green eyes glowing with anticipation. *This is gonna be great.*

☐

Trent Willow fidgeted as he waited in the interrogation room at the La Crosse County Law Enforcement Center. He wished he still smoked. He could use the calming effect of a cigarette right this minute. All he had was a bottle of water and a stick of gum. He unwrapped the gum and stuffed it in his mouth, chewing desperately, trying to relieve his growing anxiety. He took a gulp of water. He was sick and tired of this investigation into LeMar's death. And now Tanya. Were the police really making any headway? It didn't seem like it. Just then he heard voices outside the door. Was it those two detectives, the Black woman and the tall guy with the funny-colored hair, who interviewed him the first time? *Maybe it'll be someone else this time*, he thought.

The door opened, and two women entered the room.

"Hello, Mr. Willow," the Black woman said. "We've talked before. Remember?"

Trent smiled casually. "Sure I remember, but I'm sorry to say your name slips my mind."

"Detective Deverioux," she said, reminding him. Pointing to Leslie who stood against the wall, she said, "This is Detective Birkstein. We'll be conducting the interview today. We just have a few questions for you. Were you aware that you are entitled to have counsel present if you so choose?"

"Yes, I'm aware of that, but that won't be necessary," Trent responded dryly. He took in the lady standing by the wall—classy, dressed in a pair of gray slacks and a white blouse with lace trim. Pearls at her neck. Long blonde hair. Classic good looks. Stupid blonde jokes would not apply to her.

"Fine. Let's get started then," DeDe said. She leaned over to a shelf on the wall where the VCR was located. She pushed the lever down to start the machine. After the reading of Miranda rights and stating the date, time, and participants in the room, they got into it.

"Could you tell me where you were last night and who you were with?" DeDe began.

Trent sat back in his chair, his hands resting casually in his lap. "I was home alone until eight-thirty when Tanya Cadwallader called me from Piggy's Lounge. She wondered if I could come and have a drink with her, so I left my house at about nine. I was at the bar until eleven forty-five."

"Have you known Tanya long?" DeDe asked.

"About ten years. We don't socialize in the same circles, but once in a while we have lunch together. You know—realtor to realtor. Market talk, like that."

"So you weren't surprised when she called you last night?" Leslie asked.

Trent frowned and scratched his nose. "No, not really, although it was a little late. But like I said, we usually went out to lunch. In fact, I don't make a habit of drinking alone with single women." Then he added hastily, "Unless it's a formal date, of course."

"Were you aware she'd been attending AA meetings?" Leslie asked.

Trent looked balefully at the two women. "Yes. I felt bad that she'd fallen off the wagon again, but she'd relapsed many times before. I know the pattern; my father was an alcoholic for years. But I was hopeful if she stayed with AA long enough, she'd finally get sober." He leaned forward in his chair and placed his elbows on the table. He seemed genuinely sad at the loss of another real estate friend. "I didn't think being a real estate agent could be so dangerous. Maybe I should rethink my career choice." He let out a snort of disdain.

Watching Trent carefully, Leslie asked, "What did you talk about last night while you were together?" Her stomach was a little unsettled today; whether from the concussion or the pregnancy, she wasn't sure. She crossed her arms in front of her waist as she listened.

"Well, we talked real estate, and we talked about her daughter. She was worried about Felicity's prospects with men. Wondered if she'd ever find the right one," Trent said, thinking back.

DeDe and Leslie waited. When they didn't comment, he continued.

"After some small talk, she brought up LeMar Burke's murder. She felt really bad about it. I did a lot of listening and tried to slow down her drinking. I even ordered her a hamburger from the restaurant, but obviously that didn't work. She got sloshed anyway." He turned his mouth down in regret.

"Did she talk about Terry Waite at all?" DeDe asked.

"Yeah, she mentioned what an SOB he was. She was pretty disgusted with him. He *is* an arrogant piece of work. Almost everybody agrees about that."

"Where did she come down on the Waite property?" Leslie asked. "Was she still pursuing a listing with Terry, trying to convince him to sell?"

Trent shook his head. "My impression was she hadn't had any contact with Waite for a couple of months, but she was pretty drunk, so I could have misunderstood. Or she was lying, although I always thought she was pretty honest. Selling that property would have really put her on the real estate map around here. Her agency stood to gain a lot of notoriety if that property sold. In recent years, because of Tanya's embarrassing drinking incidents, her business reputation has suffered. Her agency stood to gain a lot if that transaction had gone through, and it would have patched up her reputation around town, too. She was definitely disappointed when everything fell apart, but I don't know if she'd made any overtures with Waite recently. My guess is not. But she could have had some kind of private agreement with him, I s'pose."

"Do you think any money was exchanged?" DeDe asked. Trent look puzzled. "Would she have been paid under-the-table money by LeMar to continue her efforts with Waite to convince him to sell?"

"I don't know, but I doubt it," Trent answered. "Besides, that's unethical—"

"And illegal," added Leslie.

"Did she seem anxious about anything?" DeDe asked.

"Well, she was drinking," Trent said, "but she didn't need much of an excuse to do that. I didn't sense there was anything that was upsetting her particularly. She just seemed like she needed someone to talk to."

"And what state was Tanya in when you left the bar?" DeDe continued.

"Oh, she was hammered. I offered to take her home, but she said she was going to call her daughter or call a cab. I left it at that. I didn't want to create a scene."

"Do you have any idea why she might have been murdered?" Leslie asked.

Trent thought about it for a moment and finally said, "No. Whatever thoughts I have would be pure speculation. And you're probably more interested in hard, solid facts. Witness testimony. Stuff like that."

"No, not necessarily," Leslie said.

DeDe interrupted. "So speculate. Did you see or hear anything last night that would help us identify Tanya's killer?"

"No." Trent sat motionless, staring at the two women. "Like I said, we talked real estate, her daughter's dating prospects, and how demeaning and condescending Terry Waite was. That was it."

"So, where were you this morning between nine and eleven-thirty?" DeDe probed.

Trent's eyes widened at the insinuation, and his mouth fell open in disbelief. "Are you accusing me of having something to do with Tanya's death?" he sputtered, his eyes flicking back and forth between the two women.

"Not at all, Mr. Willow, but we've got to ask. We just need to establish your alibi to eliminate you from any suspicion. Your whereabouts this morning, sir?" DeDe asked again, her voice picking up an edge.

Trent blew out a frustrated breath. "I was at home until ten o'clock—you can talk to my housekeeper—and then I went to the Hmong Cultural Center to talk to the director there about a listing on the south side. After this interview, I'm headed to a Driftless Native Consortium board meeting in La Farge."

"Any witnesses who can corroborate your whereabouts?" Leslie asked.

"Sure. Got a piece of paper?" Trent asked, retrieving a pen from his suit coat pocket.

Leslie scrounged around the room and finally tore a half sheet from an extra log-in tablet that was laying near the VCR. She handed it to Trent.

He thought about people who'd seen him or were with him, wrote down their names and contact information, and pushed it over to DeDe without a word. They reviewed what he'd said, going over it again, looking for changes or discrepancies, but Trent seemed solid about what he'd seen and heard.

"If there's anything else you think of later, please feel free to call us," DeDe said.

Trent got up from his chair and walked to the door. Then he turned and asked, "One question. Do you have any idea who's doing this?"

"We're gathering evidence, doing a lot of interviews, trying to come up with motives," Leslie said, although her words lacked confidence.

"In other words, you got nothin'," Trent said rudely, holding the door open. He walked into the hallway, the door slamming loudly behind him. Leslie and DeDe watched his slow and ponderous departure down the hall.

"Well, that didn't end well," DeDe said, watching him disappear around the corner.

"Who said it's ended?" Leslie said, rubbing her stomach.

□

It was seven o'clock Wednesday evening, and DeDe Deverioux and Jude Delaney were standing in the renovated barn that was soon to be christened Si Bon, the newest fine dining establishment on the south side of La Crosse. The wooden wagon wheel chandeliers glowed romantically, and the wide plank floor and stacked limestone fireplace added a casual ambiance that DeDe found comforting and inviting. She could imagine the buzzing conversation of hungry patrons filling up the dining room, having drinks, ordering from the menu, their laughter and pleasure filling the barn as they enjoyed their meals.

"Oh, JuJu! It looks so fabulous," she said, hugging him around the waist.

"It does, doesn't it?" Jude said as he watched her expression of wonder at all that had been accomplished in just one week. He'd been unbearable with the carpenters, electricians, and plumbers, bugging them about all the details, checking and double checking with them every couple of hours. He just about drove them all crazy with his fastidious attention to detail, but in the end, his natural charm and easygoing humor won them over. The upshot of the past two weeks was that construction was on schedule. Everything was looking great. They'd all put in a lot of extra time and effort, and it showed in the final product. The other bonus—they hadn't killed each other.

"How's the kitchen looking?" DeDe asked, grabbing his hand and heading toward the kitchen.

He bowed deeply and said, "Let me escort you, madame." She smiled and followed him into the depths of the barn through the swinging doors into the spotless, stainless-steel kitchen—his cooking kingdom in just another month.

"Well, whaddya think?" Jude said once they were in the spacious kitchen. He held out his arm as a tour guide might when one entered a prestigious museum. DeDe's eyes wandered over the gigantic stoves and coolers, the walk-in refrigerators and freezers, the granite countertops, the pots and pans hanging from the racks above the stove, and the Amish-built cupboards lining the pantry.

"Wow! You sure didn't spare any expense."

Jude's expression fell, the excitement withering like a leaking balloon. "Honey, world-class kitchens are not cheap. Don't worry about the money. I made a killing on the sale of my restaurant in New Orleans."

He watched her face for some dark sign, hoping they wouldn't end up in a fight. He'd sacrificed his life in New Orleans with the hope that they could have a new beginning here in Wisconsin. And he understood DeDe's insecurity about finances. Poverty had a way of leaving deep and lasting scars on a person's psyche. After all, they'd both grown up dirt poor. But it frustrated him that DeDe still struggled with the price tag of almost everything, although he understood where that came from.

"I know. I know." She waved her hand flippantly as if dismissing the expense. "I guess it's just my simple childhood. I'm not used to all this upper-crust stuff."

Jude felt his temper flare, but he checked his attitude, knowing if he lost it, all the progress they'd made would disappear. He was tired of starting over. He just wanted to move on with DeDe from a place of trust.

"This isn't upper crust, baby. Believe me, I've worked upper crust and this is a long way from that. This is going to be a neighborhood place that people can come to and have a great meal, be with their friends and family, and feel like they belong here. A welcoming place. A place that pays homage to everything that's good and right and decent about the Midwest." Jude waited for her to say something, but she just stood there in the massive kitchen looking at the gleaming surfaces now in a state of limbo until the drama of opening night.

"I've done my homework, honey," he continued, trying to reassure her. "This place is pure Midwestern hospitality and friendliness. The old barn, the wagon wheels, the fireplace, the polished wooden floors. It's all going to work together to send the right message. And we ain't even talkin' about my food yet."

DeDe's face softened with emotion, and a few tears glimmered at the corners of her eyes. *Oh, boy. Here it comes*, he thought. He realized he'd tensed up, and he twisted his neck from side to side in an effort to relax. In the silent moments that followed his little speech, he waited patiently for her response and was mildly surprised when she spoke.

"I'm just so proud of you," she whispered. "You've worked so hard, and everything looks so fantastic."

Jude came up to her and kissed her gently on the lips. "I'm doin' this for us, baby. I could have taken the money from the sale of the restaurant and gone on a long, long vacation. But I want a family, a real family, and this is the first step." He wrapped his arms around her.

Slipping into her low country Carolinian drawl, she looked up at him and said, "A family, huh? Well, ain't we be workin' on that?" His gentle brown eyes softened. "You gonna keep de wife pregnant and down on de farm singin' 'Hambone'?" DeDe teased.

Jude rolled his eyes when DeDe broke into a gentle dance, her hips undulating in a seductive sway as she broke into the familiar Gullah song.

"Hambone, Hambone, where you been? Round the corner an' back agin. Hambone, Hambone, where's you wife? In de kitchen cookin' rice." DeDe's voice echoed softly in the silence of the spotless kitchen.

"As a matter of fact, Mrs. Delaney, we've been workin' hard on this family idea. And it's been damn fun, too. You're about wearin' me out these days," Jude said as DeDe threw her arms around his neck, smiling seductively. "Guess we can't go up in the hayloft no more and make love. The loft's gone."

"Well, the love ain't," DeDe whispered. "Let's get outta here and go home," she said, taking his hand. They walked through the restaurant to the front entrance. Jude flipped the lights off and locked the doors. The night air was warm with the promise of green grass and budding trees. In the distance, the river glowed with a golden wash of sunset colors. A few boats, out on the early spring evening, bobbed like corks, the bluffs dark and hunched over the shoreline on the Minnesota side.

"Never thought I'd be livin' this far north," DeDe said softly. "Grandma Hettie wouldn't believe it if she saw us now."

"I can hardly believe it, either. But it's good, isn't it?" Jude said softly, holding her hand.

"Yep, it is. It's real good."

☐

Bedtime had come, but Lillie was having none of it, not until her issues were resolved. Carol had tucked Henri in bed. Now she sat in the Amish rocking chair in the corner of Lillie's bedroom listening to the conversation.

"You said you'd find her, Bapa," Lillie whispered as she lay snuggled under her quilts, her eyes misting with tears.

"I tried my hardest, but I didn't know where the lady was, sweetheart. I didn't even know her name," Jim said, begging off responsibility for the death of Tanya Cadwallader.

"Some detective you are," Lillie pouted. "Isn't that what detectives are supposed to do? Find people?" Her lower lip quivered as she tried to comprehend the terrible injustice of the situation.

Carol leaned forward. "Hey, that's not fair, honey," she said softly. "Your daddy is a great detective, but sometimes criminals get ahead of the good guys."

Jim looked over the rumpled bed covers at Carol, and then he focused his attention back on Lillie. "You asked me to try and find her. But I was too late. Sometimes that happens, Lillie. I'm sorry."

"Does that mean I have to forgive you? Because Sister Mary Jo says that if we don't forgive those who sin against us, then God won't forgive us when we sin. Is that true?" Her blue eyes were like pools of sapphire with flecks of gold.

"Is that a trick question?" Jim asked, hiding a smile.

Lillie slowly shook her head. "You shouldn't joke about God stuff, Bapa," she said seriously.

Jim closed his eyes briefly. "You're right. I shouldn't. Sister Mary Jo is absolutely correct," he said. Jim grabbed Lillie's small hands in his large ones and looked directly into her eyes. "Really, Lillie, I'm terribly sorry I couldn't find the lady in your dream. There just wasn't enough time and information." An image of Tanya Cadwallader's lifeless eyes floated back into his memory, her brains splattered on the floor and wall of the wayside restroom. He squeezed his eyes shut in an effort to erase the images from his mind. "Can you forgive me?"

Lillie lay silently in bed studying Jim's face. She sighed, sat up, and scooted her compact body into his arms. "Well, I guess I'll have to forgive you," she said into his shirt, "because if I don't, then God won't forgive me for breaking the garage window yesterday when I threw a rock at Henri and missed."

"What?" Carol exclaimed, her eyes wide with shock. "You threw rocks at Henri?"

"Sorry, Mom. He was being a royal shit."

"Language," Carol said tersely. "And saying sorry doesn't mean there aren't consequences, young lady," she finished sternly.

"We'll talk about that tomorrow," Jim said, tucking Lillie back under the covers. Jim and Carol kissed Lillie good night, closed the door softly, and stood in the hallway.

"Jim, you're too soft on her," Carol said in a fervent whisper, her brown eyes firing up.

Jim laid a finger across her lips. "Shhh. I'll deal with it. But she does have a unique way of presenting the truths of God, doesn't she?" He let a grin slip across his face.

Carol's expression hardened. "Jim, this is not funny. She threw rocks at Henri."

"And you never threw rocks at Vivian? Come on, honey. All siblings do stuff like that. I remember one time, I picked up this big clod of black dirt at the edge of a plowed field and chucked it at Dave. Hit him right—"

Carol held up her hand in a stop motion. "Don't," she said, then leaned into his chest. He kissed the top of her head.

"I suppose I could give you the quote from the movie *Love Story*," he said softly.

"What's that?"

"Love means never having to say you're sorry."

Carol's head jerked up, and her brown eyes blazed. "That's a bunch of bullshit, Jim. Don't tell Lillie that one. You'll never hear the end of it."

"You got me there. Let's have some tea," he said, chuckling softly.

20

THURSDAY, MARCH 28

Grandad Bluff towered six hundred feet into the muted sky above Cliffwood Lane, leaving the street and houses below in dawn's gray shadow. As the sky lightened, permutations of rose and maize and peach swirled together and crept along the horizon like the pattern in a kid's kaleidoscope. The minutes flitted by, and with each passing moment the sky brightened. At exactly 5:48, the sun rose above the treeline. The flagpole on the bluff of the city's famous landmark sent shafts of light racing in a thousand directions. The sandstone precipice that had been dark in the ambient grayness of dawn just a few minutes ago now shimmered with golden brilliance in the diffused sunshine.

Below on Cliffwood Lane, most residents were still hunkered down in their beds trying to catch a few more z's, but a couple of early risers wandered outdoors to their front porches to retrieve the *La Crosse Sentinel* or the *St. Paul Pioneer Press*. The newspapers could be found on the porch, the shrubbery, or the sidewalk—depending on the delivery boy's aim or his mood.

Sonny Fields, Sam and Leslie Birksteins' neighbor, was an early bird. He never used an alarm clock. He rose at five o'clock every day. The habit was a throwback to his days on the farm when he'd milked cows and fed the hogs and chickens.

He stood on his porch, the *Sentinel* in his hand, and glanced up and down the street, looking for Paco, Birksteins' black lab. That dog was a born winner with an electrifying personality. And besides all of that, the pooch was a real decorated war hero, and he had the commendations to prove it. Leslie had shown him the certificates that hung proudly on her living room wall.

The dog liked to come over and crap in his yard when he wasn't looking. It drove his wife nuts, but Sonny thought it was comical. He loved his visits with the big brute. All the dog asked for in return was a pat on the head, a thump on his side, and a doggie treat from an ice cream pail he kept hidden behind the lattice by the back steps. If Stella knew he was actually *rewarding* the dog for his daily dumps, she'd blow a gasket. Still, Sonny couldn't hate the dog, even though he left piles along the woods at the back of his lot.

But what really tickled Sonny's funny bone were the dog owners who walked around with little bags to pick up the poop. He stifled a grin every time he saw them stooping over and collecting turds. *What would they do with a spreader full of manure?* he chuckled to himself. Of course, if they didn't pick up the dog piles, there would be a major problem in the neighborhood. He laughed out loud when he thought of Jed Clancy, the banker next door, who'd stepped in a huge pile of steaming dog doo in his yard last week, the shit squeezing up the sides of his leather wingtips. While that comical thought occupied his mind, Sonny stood smiling for a few moments by his front door, but Paco was nowhere to be seen today. He picked up the newspaper, went back in his house, and closed the door quietly behind him.

A half hour later, a forest green VW Passat wagon rolled slowly down the street, stopping in front of the duplex on Cliffwood Lane. Lori Lifto dipped her head as she gazed through the passenger window. She studied the Birkstein duplex again. It was the one on the right—the one with the big expensive door. Earlier in the week, she conducted surveillance of the place and formulated her plan, visualizing her execution. *The whole practical joke should take less than a minute*, she thought. In the passenger seat, her tomahawk lay folded inside a bath towel. She unwrapped the towel and flexed her fingers around the familiar handle. She could feel the tension in her chest as her heart ramped up. *Ready for a little payback*, she thought. *Leave the car running. This won't take long.*

With the ax in her right hand, she climbed out of the driver's seat and quietly closed the front driver's door until it softly clicked. The smell of earthworms and a hint of baking bread wafted on a gentle breeze. Holding the ax steady against her right leg, she approached the front door and stood on the sidewalk. She looked up and down the street. Nobody was around.

Three steps led to the front door, which was nestled under a small overhang that served as a tiny porch. Lori visualized the ax ripping through the air, catapulting end over end until it delivered an ear-splitting wallop in the wood. She gripped the ax, rocked forward, rocked backward, and then forward again, releasing the tomahawk at the perfect moment. As soon as its heft hurtled into space, she knew it was spot on.

Whack! When the ax connected with the wooden door, it sounded like a gunshot. The blade sank into the wood, its handle pointing downward. Perfect execution. Lori stood there for a few moments, reveling in her formidable talent. *Am I good or what?* she thought with an inward glow. She turned to head back to the car, but that's when everything fell apart, unraveling at incredible speed.

Inside the duplex, Sam Birkstein was standing in his boxers and T-shirt by the bathroom sink brushing his teeth. The sound of the ax hitting the front door undid his peaceful morning routine.

Leslie had been sleeping, but the jarring reverberation startled her awake. She jumped out of bed, not really sure why she was standing up. She knew she'd heard something loud, but she didn't know what it was. The closest thing that floated upward in her consciousness was a gunshot.

"Sam! What was that?" she yelled.

Paco barked excitedly, a deep-throated woofing, his protective instincts coming alive. Sam ran across the living room in his underwear and T-shirt, threw the deadbolt aside, and whipped the door open.

When the front door flew open, the huge canine dove from the front porch, clearing the three steps as he soared through the air, practically knocking Sam over. Landing on the sidewalk, Paco gained purchase on the rough surface of the cement, his muscles rippling with power, his attention riveted on the intruder who was hightailing it to a Volkswagen parked on the street.

"Paco! Paco! Come back here!" Sam yelled. Then his eyes wandered to the door.

"What the—" he sputtered. "Who—" His mouth fell open as he gawked at the ax embedded in the door, but by then, he realized if he didn't stop Paco, the woman who was running down the sidewalk to the street would be seriously injured.

Lori Lifto looked over her shoulder and realized something was wrong. *Very* wrong. She must have miscalculated. In the growing confusion, all she saw was a huge black blob moving fast, saliva spraying, teeth bared. She felt the impact of the growling, snarling dog high on her back between her shoulder blades. The beast was incredibly strong. Paco tackled Lifto and brought her face-to-face with the cement sidewalk. On impact, her front teeth tore into her upper lip, and she heard the crunch of bones when her nose and chin hit the cement, all in fast-forward motion. A salty stream of blood began pouring from her nose and mouth, forming a bright red puddle beneath her head. At the same time, she felt a steady, intense pressure on her right leg, something that felt like a vise grip. She cursed, then screamed. At the same time, intense pain and the taste of blood in her mouth filled her with unbridled panic. She screamed again and began spewing profanity.

Launching himself down the stairs, Sam ran barefoot to the spot where Lori Lifto was detained in the jaws of Paco. *Serves her right*, he thought, his anger building.

"Get that dog off me!" Lori bellowed, looking over her shoulder. Sam grimaced at the sight of her face, and for an instant, he felt sorry for her.

"Paco! Down, boy!" Sam said, grabbing Paco's collar. The dog growled ominously. "No! Down!" he ordered again. Paco released his hold on Lori's leg but continued to stand over the woman, his teeth glistening in a feral snarl, his sleek, muscular body in a defensive stance.

Leslie appeared on the front porch, hastily pulling her robe closed.

"Sam? What's going on?" she yelled, her hair disheveled, her eyes wide with surprise.

Sam looked over his shoulder at Leslie as Lori Lifto rolled on her back, covering her eyes with her arm. She began to cry and shake, the shock of the incident penetrating her tough, overconfident exterior.

"The door. Look at the door," he said loudly, pointing.

Leslie slowly turned, and her eyes widened at the sight of the embedded tomahawk. "Sheesh!" she said softly.

Sam continued talking to Leslie in a commanding voice. "Call down to the station and get a squad car over here," he said calmly, still holding onto Paco. "Then bring me some ice and a roll of paper towels."

He reached over to assess Lori's injuries, lightly touching her arm, but she jerked angrily away and shouted, "Don't touch me!"

Sam pulled his hand away, still kneeling next to her, grappling with the anger that was boiling to the surface. "Can you sit up?" he asked, although he was tempted to lay into her with a good cussing out—like it would do any good.

"Get your dog away from me!" she said, her words jumbled, blood still pouring from her nose and mouth.

"You might feel better if you lay on your side. The blood won't go down your throat," Sam said casually. "If you swallow too much blood, you might puke."

By this time, Leslie appeared next to Sam with a bag of ice in one hand and a roll of paper towel in the other. She took Paco by the collar and led him into the house. Then she slipped on a pair of jeans and a sweatshirt, returning to the scene outside. Paco barked excitedly inside the house. Neighbors began appearing on their porches and front yards, wondering what all the commotion was about.

In a couple of minutes, a city police car arrived. Lori was sitting up with the ice and a towel pressed to the lower half of her face, her green eyes frosty with anger and humiliation.

The cop, Jason Marcus, walked over to the threesome. "Whoa!" he said, eyeing the embedded ax in the front door and the bloody woman sitting on the sidewalk. "Sam, Leslie. What happened here?" He squatted down next to Lori and rested his arms on his haunches.

"I'm arresting her, and you can take her downtown," Sam said brusquely, his hazel eyes dancing with anger.

"Wanna tell me what happened first?" Marcus asked, meeting Sam's gaze.

"Lori threw an ax at my front door. And my dog," he stopped and corrected himself when Leslie gave him a dirty look, "*our* dog, knocked her down and held her here until I got outside."

Leslie shook her head. "Always a mistake to mess with Paco," she said nonchalantly.

Lori came alive. "That damned dog tried to kill me. He tackled me and held me down! This is total bullshit! He's a killer! He oughta be put down!" Her words were garbled through the paper towel, but her disdain was obvious. She leaned over and spit blood into the grass.

"Okay. Let's get to the bottom of this," the cop said firmly. He looked at Lifto and pointed. "And I might add, if you don't want to get tackled by a dog protecting his property, then you shouldn't go around throwing axes at people's front doors," Jason said, unclipping a set of cuffs from his belt. "That tends to upset homeowners and their pets. Let's look at your injuries."

Lori gingerly pulled the towels and ice away. The bridge of her nose was turning an ugly dark purple, and blood continued to seep from her nose and upper lip where her teeth had sliced into the flesh.

Jason grimaced. "That's nasty. Looks like you've been in a bar fight."

As if she didn't hear him, Lori continued to blubber. "I think I broke my nose. Oooh! It hurts!" She fell in a heap on her side and began crying again.

In a brief exchange with the officer, Sam explained his encounter with Lifto and Little Hawk in the alley behind The Aimless Ax earlier in the week to the current scene in which an ax was stuck fast in his front door. Listening to the account, Marcus lifted his upper lip in disgust and shook his head. Then he helped Lori to her feet, cuffed her hands in front of her, and walked her to the squad car.

"Hey, my car is still running," she said, pointing toward her VW.

"I'll shut it off and bring the keys to the center," Sam said.

"You're really going to cuff and stuff me over a practical joke?" Lori whined as the blood dripped from her chin. "Who got injured? It sure as hell wasn't that killer dog!" She spit into the grass again and swiped her chin with another sheet of paper towel.

"Really? Are you serious?" the cop said as he strapped her in the back seat. He looked back to Sam and Leslie standing on the sidewalk. "They just keep gettin' weirder and weirder. But this is a first, I gotta admit," Jason said. "I'll need a statement from you down at the jail sometime this morning."

"Sure. I'll be there in less than an hour," Sam said. "She might need to be looked at. I think her nose is broken, and she probably has some contusions on her leg where Paco held her down."

"Yeah. I'll run her over to emergency first," he said. "Damn, that dog is tough, huh?"

"He's trained in detecting IEDs and taking down enemy combatants. He was decorated for his service in Iraq," Leslie said. She raised her eyebrows and tilted her head toward Lifto sitting in the cruiser. "Does she qualify as an enemy combatant?"

"I'd say when you fling axes around, you'd be considered an enemy combatant," the officer said. Then, glancing at Lori, he said to her, "Guess you picked the wrong address to bury your hatchet."

"Whatever. Just shut up and get me to a hospital," Lori mumbled, resting her head on the back seat.

"Hey, some respect," Sam growled. Lori flashed him a belligerent stare.

Leslie and Sam watched as the squad car slowly departed the scene. They could hear Paco inside the house barking up a storm, still agitated by the incident.

"What was that all about anyway?" Leslie asked Sam as he started up the sidewalk.

"I don't know for sure. Maybe payback for questioning her in the alley?" Sam said, shrugging his shoulders. "I don't think she needs much of an excuse to create mayhem. According to Little Hawk, she has a very bad temper that she's never learned to control."

"Throwing axes at people's doors does get attention, doesn't it? Is she just stupid?" Leslie asked sarcastically. Sam stopped at the front door and, with considerable effort, jerked the ax from the wood.

"No, she's not stupid," he said, entering the living room with the hatchet dangling in his hand. "But she does have a sense of entitlement and a very high opinion of herself and her talents—if you call throwing an ax a talent."

"Seems to be a talent. Wait 'til Higgins hears this one," Leslie commented. "He's not going to believe it."

☐

Jim was sitting at the dining room table in a pair of jogging pants and a long-sleeved T-shirt, finishing his bowl of oatmeal. Carol was in the shower, and Lillie was crunching on a piece of toast.

"She did what?" Jim asked loudly when Sam called him at seven o'clock.

Lillie's eyes widened at the tone of his voice. Henri threw a Cheerio at her, and she lobbed it back at him. Jim waved at them to stop.

"She buried an ax in my front door this morning about six-thirty." Sam heard a groan.

Jim slumped in his chair and covered his eyes with one hand. "And she did this because?"

"I have no idea," Sam said. "Apparently, she doesn't need a reason to intimidate. She acted on impulse or a misguided sense of self-importance, or she's a narcissist who can't help herself? Take your pick."

"You seem pretty calm, considering what happened. I'll talk to her when I get there. Call down to the jail and make sure they keep her. I want to interview her."

"She's in the ER at St. Francis right now. Paco did a number on her. Hit her from behind and smashed her face into the sidewalk. Probably broke her nose, chipped some teeth, cut up her lips. She's a mess." Jim grimaced when he heard the tale. "She'll be booked for assault with a deadly weapon and willful destruction of property— maybe a hate crime. I'm at the office right now, so I can take care of it," Sam said.

"What about Paco? You might get some pushback about him," Jim said grouchily.

"She can file charges against us if she wants, but I doubt it'll stick. Besides, it could be argued that if Paco hadn't tackled her, we'd be spending a lot of time, effort, and money hunting her down, so the way I see it, our pooch saved us a lot of hassle and overtime pay."

"Maybe. But you're going to have to try to rein in his protective instincts," Jim reminded him.

"He flew out the door before I could stop him," Sam complained loudly. "His training and instincts run deep. What can I say?"

"Whatever. I'll see you in an hour."

By the time Jim had showered and dressed, he was running late. He grabbed a cup of coffee, kissed everyone goodbye, and headed down Chipmunk Coulee Road. When he got to Highway 35, he turned left and headed for the Tip Your Hat tavern in Genoa. The spring morning was warm, but winter still hung at the fringes. The snowbanks had diminished to dirty piles of lumpy gray ice along the roadside. Sullen clouds hung in the sky like a batch of dingy laundry, but every once in a while, the promise of blue peeked out between the clouds.

Jim thought about what they knew so far, even though they hadn't collected enough evidence to prove anything. Other than the two ancient ball clubs used as weapons, the tie to realtors and cave petroglyphs was tenuous at best, and then there was the ornery university professor with an attitude. Now they had people flinging axes through the air in residential areas. How weird was that?

Jim was convinced Trent Willow wasn't involved. Paul had discovered some substantial cash withdrawals made by one murder victim, LeMar Burke, but that seemed to be a dead end, although the pile of cash found in Tanya Cadwallader's desk needed an explanation of some sort. The renegade Ho-Chunk group couldn't seem to get their act together, and after talking to Stephanie Decorah at the Tomah museum, no one seemed to take the group seriously. However, Little Hawk was a conundrum. Was he involved? Hard to tell at this point. The discovery of the ball club in Waite's cave by Bobby Rude could be crucial. That was the third club found in the vicinity of the murders. But what else were they missing? The only light at the end of the tunnel was Lori Lifto and her tenuous relationship with Little Hawk. And what about this high-power electricity line being built in the near future? More investigating would have to be done there. Maybe some of the players were getting nervous, making mistakes. Things might open up.

The ax-throwing stunt by Lori Lifto left Jim incredulous. Apparently, the gall of some people knew no bounds; it took little to provoke them into performing incredible acts of stupidity. To Jim, it seemed like everyone now lived for a dare and the next big thing, whatever that was. People were so easily offended, and they got their dander up about the dumbest things. *What did Lifto think would happen when she started throwing axes at people's houses?* Jim thought.

Despite the seriousness of the incident, he chuckled when he thought about Paco ramming through the door and tackling Lifto. What he wouldn't have given to be a bystander on the street corner when that played out.

He rolled into Genoa, a tiny fishing village on the banks of the Mississippi. The power plant sat next to the river in the morning sunshine, its buildings like a bunch of upended children's blocks. Huge pitch-black mountains of coal were piled beside the plant, waiting to be hauled inside and burned to create the electricity used by the region's population. Twenty years ago it had been converted from nuclear to coal, but Jim had recently heard the rumbling threats to shut down the plant and purchase electricity from Canada. Jim shook his head. The power companies were pitted against the environmentalists who were marching their agenda forward. Jim wondered if the environmentalists understood the amount of energy that would be needed to replace all the coal and nuclear power plants in the United States. He doubted it.

Traffic on 35 was steady. Workers were arriving at the plant, school buses were delivering kids to St. Ignatius Catholic School, and commuters were traveling into La Crosse to their day jobs. Semi-trucks hauling heavy cargo rumbled down the highway along with a few tractors pulling planters and plows.

Jim rolled into the parking lot of the tavern. Inside, the dark atmosphere and smell of booze and cigarettes further dampened his mood. Jed Klumstein was wiping down the bar, and he glanced up when Jim walked in.

"Morning," he said, a cigarette hanging between his lips. "You want to talk to Bobby? He said you'd be stopping by."

"Yep. That's why I'm here," Jim explained.

"Just go up the stairs," Jed said, pointing to the left in back of the bar. "He's gettin' ready for school and havin' breakfast."

Jim climbed the stairs and knocked quietly on the door, letting himself in. The apartment opened into a large, spacious living room and a smaller kitchenette and dining area with a round oak table and four chairs. A hallway led off to the right, where Jim assumed the bedroom and bathroom were located. The apartment was surprisingly clean and homey. The living room was furnished with an oversized brown leather couch, two recliners, a wide-screen TV, and numerous river landscapes, some by well-known local artists. A large decorative rug covered the wooden maple floor. On one wall, built-in shelves held a variety of books, family photos, and a collection of Red Wing pottery that Jed had accumulated over the years. The view of the river from the front windows was fabulous—one that Jim loved.

He heard a shower running in the back, so he pulled out a chair and sat at the small table in the kitchen. The morning edition of the *La Crosse Sentinel* lay on the table, the headlines of the Black River murder screaming across the top in big, bold letters—another reminder that nothing had been resolved. He read the article. It was pretty accurate. After a few minutes, he heard someone coming down the hall. When he looked up from the paper, Bobby was standing next to the table, barefoot with wet hair, dressed in jeans and a Logan High School sweatshirt.

"Hey, Bobby," Jim said politely. He could see the stress lines on the teen's face. His eyes were downcast, and his shoulders drooped, but his expression brightened when he saw Jim.

"Hi. Thanks for coming, Lt. Higgins," he said softly.

"How ya doin', kiddo?" Jim asked.

Bobby shook his head. "Not so good," he said, pulling out a chair and plopping down. Jim waited as the teen gathered his thoughts. "I thought every day would get better after my dad died, but I really miss him, even though he was hardly ever home, and when he was home, he was drunk." His voice broke off on a bitter note. He averted his gaze and stared out the window toward the river. Tears misted along his eyelids.

Jim's heart constricted with sympathy for the distraught teen. "Don't hurry things along. Grief is a process," he said tenderly.

"You've got to take one day at a time. You're going to be sad for quite a while, but pretty soon, one day you'll realize you've turned a corner."

Bobby's dark eyes studied Jim's face and then zeroed in on his blue eyes. "Is that how you felt when your wife died?" he asked softly. Jim met Bobby's gaze candidly. He supposed Sara had shared the death of Margie with her students, and that's how Bobby knew about it.

"Yep, I was sad for a long time, but there's nothing wrong with that. That's how you feel when you lose someone you love."

They talked a while more. Bobby told Jim how he loved to explore the bluffs around Genoa, where his favorite fishing holes were, and that he was perfectly capable of living alone now that his dad was gone. He had no intention of staying with Jed forever.

"I mean, Jed's a really good friend, but I don't want to live here. I don't even have my own room. Where am I supposed to put all my fishing stuff?" he complained with typical teenage angst.

Jim listened patiently for ten minutes, but time was slipping away.

"So tell me about Terry Waite's cave," he said, turning the conversation in a new direction.

Bobby told Jim about his hike to the cave and his discovery of the ancient ball club on the rock ledge. As he told the story, his demeanor changed. He spoke with fevered excitement.

"Boy, it freaked me out when I saw that ball club wrapped in a deer hide," Bobby said wide-eyed.

"Did you put it back where you found it?" Jim asked.

"Oh yeah. I got kinda worried when I remembered the stuff about the murder behind Jed's bar. There were some bigger footprints outside the cave. Somebody else was there besides me."

"The professor, maybe?" Jim guessed.

"Well, it's his cave, so that would make sense. But I got the feeling it was somebody else. I just don't know who."

"You didn't see anyone else on your way out to the road?" Jim asked.

"Nope. I guess I was kinda lucky, huh?" he said. His dark eyes locked with Jim's.

"Yes, you were very lucky," Jim said seriously. He leaned toward Bobby, rested his elbow on the table, and fixed him with a somber stare. Bobby recognized the serious expression on his face. It reminded him of another criminal incident they'd shared near Goose Island when Bobby revealed the lagoon where a murder weapon had been tossed.

"Listen, Bobby," Jim continued. "I want you to stay with Jed until we get this whole mess cleared up. Always let Jed know where you're going, and no more visits to that cave on your own. Understood?" His baritone voice was layered with an authoritarian quality.

"Yep. I understand." At that moment, Bobby looked very forlorn, and a thought popped into Jim's head.

"Hey, Sara is coming home this weekend. We're having dinner at our house on Saturday night. Would you like to come? Around five?" Jim asked.

"Sara? You mean Miss Higgins?" Suddenly Bobby's eyes seemed brighter.

"Yeah. Miss Higgins," Jim said, smiling.

"Well, sure, but I'll need a ride. Jed gets pretty busy on Saturday nights. He won't be able to bring me."

"I'll call you and have someone pick you up. How's that sound?"

"That'd be great," Bobby said, and he smiled for the first time that morning.

"I've got to get to the office. Thanks for your help, son." They stood up, and Jim rested his hand on Bobby's shoulder. Somehow Bobby seemed more solid than he expected. "Remember, you're on a journey. Don't expect too much of yourself right now," Jim counseled. "Things will get better over time."

"Yeah. I hope so. Thanks, Lt. Higgins."

Jim turned to go, then stopped. "One more thing," he said, holding up his index finger.

"Yeah? What's that?" Bobby said.

"Remember, it's okay to cry."

Bobby hung his head. "Sure. I'll try to remember that," he said softly.

Jim walked back downstairs, through the bar, and back to Jed. "This whole deal with the murder behind your bar isn't over. Bobby knows some things that could put him in danger, so if you could keep an eye on him, that'd be great," Jim said.

"I've never been a parent. I'm not sure he really wants to be here right now, but I'll keep tabs on him," Jed promised. "He's safe with me."

As Jim drove north on Highway 35 and then through the south side of the city, his thinking shifted to the upcoming family dinner Saturday night with his older children, John and his wife, Jenny, and Sara and her fiancé, Jerome, the former priest. Somehow Jim couldn't quite get used to the idea of Father Jerome Knight in a conjugal relationship, especially with his daughter, but facts were facts. Might as well not fight it. Besides, he really liked Jerome. He was good-looking, intelligent, friendly, and, best of all, he actually had some moral fiber. At least Jim hoped he did. After all, he *had* been a priest. That should count for something.

Carol had been fussing most of the week about the menu for Saturday night's dinner. When she brought it up again, Jim suggested they simplify everything and go out to eat. But that went over like a lead balloon.

"Jim, I can't believe you would suggest that," she said, her irritation piqued.

"Well, I was thinking of you when I said it." He lowered the *Wisconsin State Journal* a notch, looking carefully over the top of the paper. "You're a great cook, honey, but you're busy working and taking care of the kids. We could make a reservation at Piggy's. The kids would do fine there. It's not too fancy, and you'd actually get to enjoy the night instead of slaving away in the kitchen."

Carol shook her head. "No, no, no. That will never work," she said, holding up her hand in an emphatic stop gesture that brought the discussion to a screeching halt. She leaned forward from her position on the couch to make her point. "Jim, think about it. Jerome is being welcomed into our family. You can't scoot him off to a restaurant like he's a vacuum cleaner salesman. We have to make him feel welcome, and that means a home-cooked meal. It's the only way to go." She leaned back and waited for his response.

"Okay. I'm flexible," Jim said, tamping down his impatience about the whole hullabaloo. "So if that's the case, then let's keep it simple, honey. I can grill some steaks and make burgers for the kids. You can make a nice salad and a few sides. How's that sound?"

After a few moments of consideration, Carol said, "I think that might work, but what about dessert?"

"Simple. Pie from Gladys with vanilla ice cream."

"Oh. That's a great idea. Gladys makes great pies," Carol said, smiling. "What kind should we order?"

"Something light and summery? Lemon, maybe? Coconut creme? Blueberry? Gladys can make any flavor you want."

Carol rolled her eyes. "You've got to be kidding. Since when does a man care what kind of pie it is just as long as it's pie?"

"Well, you're the one who asked the question," Jim said impatiently, putting the newspaper in his lap so he could see her.

"Okay, okay. I'll just decide," she said tartly. She flipped her hand in the air as if she were waving a wand. "Lemon and blueberry. How's that sound?"

"I'll call Gladys today and order it. But then we should invite her over, don't you think? That all right with you?"

"You know it is. The kids will be so excited to see her. She's the only grandma they've ever known. You'll take care of it?"

"Absolutely."

"Mr. Responsibility. One of the reasons why I married you," Carol grinned.

Jim chuckled. "Well, that's not very romantic."

"You've met my ex. Being responsible carries great weight in my book, especially after my marriage went up in smoke."

"So that's a compliment, then?" Jim asked, confused.

"Absolutely. Matt was irresponsible, drank too much, was a womanizer—" Carol started.

"Got it, honey," Jim interjected. "But there must be a few other reasons you married me."

"What? You want me to say you're a real stud? You're dynamite in the sack? Well, I won't lie. You do deliver." Carol's eyes flashed with humor.

"Really?" he said, peeking around the paper. "Any chance we can work on that tonight?"

"There's a distinct possibility that all this talk could turn into some major action."

□

Jim approached the south side Kwik Trip, thought about a cinnamon roll but hurried by when he looked at his watch. Fifteen minutes later, he rolled into the law enforcement center's parking lot. He hurriedly locked the Suburban, walked across the pavement, and ran his ID card through the security scanner at the back entrance of the building. Stepping off the elevator on the third floor, he greeted Emily.

"Sam's in your office," she said as he hurried down the hallway.

"Hey. What's up?" Jim asked as he got to the office door and strolled in.

Sam was slouched in an upholstered chair, his foot resting on his knee, his phone in his hand. He was madly texting someone. He'd dressed casually today in dark Levi's, a blue shirt, and a yellow tie with little champagne glasses printed on it. Jim glanced at his feet— Dockers loafers with black dress socks. *Huh, wonder where he got those shoes?* Jim thought. *And the socks. Better than his yellow Nikes or those black and white wingtips. Must be Leslie's influence.*

Sam began his report. "While Leslie's been home, she did a little research on Lori Lifto. She has an interesting background. Grew up around West Salem on her dad's dairy farm as an only child. During high school, she was an average student, nothing outstanding, decent grades, participated in track and field. I wouldn't have pegged her as military material, but after high school in 2008, she enlisted in the army. She eventually tried to enlist in the Rangers, but she couldn't pass the physical qualifications, but that's not unusual. Only about twenty women have ever been able to qualify for that part of Ranger training. However, she did distinguish herself on the shooting range. She has formidable skills with rifles, according to her records. Quite a few citations and awards." Sam looked up from his notes and swiped his chin with his hand. "Maybe we're lucky she only threw an ax at our door. She could have opted for something a whole lot more deadly."

"So what has she been doing since getting out of the military?" Jim asked, hanging his jacket on the back of his chair. He sat down at his desk.

"After her honorable discharge, she returned to La Crosse. Had a couple of speeding tickets over the years and apparently was suspected of dealing drugs, but nothing criminal was ever filed with the police, although she was under suspicion for a while. Straightened herself out and got an entry-level job at Kwik Trip, moved up the ranks, and now she's the manager of the night crew at the bakery."

Jim noted the drug dealing. He wondered how many people who were in successful positions today had at one time used drugs of some kind. He guessed it would be a significant number. "Anything else? Friends, associations, acquaintances, clubs?" Jim asked.

Sam shuffled through the papers Leslie had sent by email.

"Nothin'. If you just read this stuff, you'd think she was an upstanding young woman. But everyone I've talked to, including Little Hawk, says she's unpredictable and hard to please. A narcissistic streak along with a bad temper, which she's never learned to control," Sam replied.

"So, let's set up the interview for this morning," Jim suggested.

"She just arrived downstairs," Sam said. "They've fingerprinted her, and she's been informed of the charges against her, so I'd say we could do the interview in about an hour."

Jim sighed. "Any possibility Leslie could help with the interview? She has a military background, which might be helpful in establishing some camaraderie," Jim suggested.

"I'll call her. An hour?"

Jim glanced at the clock. "Let's make it eleven o'clock."

"Got it." Sam texted Leslie. In a few minutes she texted back, and the interview was set.

"In the meantime, I want you to go visit the Kwik Trip bakery crew. Talk to her boss, people who work the night shift. Find out who her friends are, where she hangs out. That kind of thing. Sounds like she's something of a loner. Leslie and I will handle the interview."

"Sure. I can do that." Sam got out of the chair and walked out of the office.

Jim's phone buzzed.

"Higgins," he said crisply.

"Lt. Higgins. This is Amy Sandler, one of the crime scene techs working on the Cadwallader murder up in Black River Falls. You wanted to know what we found at the wayside."

Jim leaned forward, his elbows on his desk. He pulled a yellow legal pad from the corner of the desk and twirled a pen above the paper, waiting for the information. "Yeah, go ahead, Amy," he said.

In a crisp, even tone, Amy began. "There were two sets of prints on the door: one on the handle and one on the upper surface of the door frame near the edge. They match, but they're not Cadwallader's, and they were fresh that morning. As for the murder weapon, we had Ryan Blake look at it. He recognized the maker's mark—a guy from Illinois, but we're not sure who actually had the weapon in their possession at the time of the murder. We're still trying to trace the ownership of it."

"What about the injuries from the club?" Jim asked.

"The injuries to the brain and skull of Ms. Cadwallader were catastrophic—penetration of bone, massive bleeding, obvious damage to brain tissue. Cadwallader didn't die right away, but she was unconscious until she passed on. That's a blessing, I guess. You get the drift."

"Yeah, I sure do. It sounds very similar to the first murder down here. Anything else?"

"We were able to lift a relatively good shoe print from the sandy soil just outside the wayside toilet. We made a cast, so when you're asking for a warrant, you'll want to include shoes. I'll send you a photo of the cast. To me it looks too small to be a male, but I suppose some guys have very small feet."

"So the print is small—more like a woman's size?" There were a few seconds of uncomfortable silence.

"Yes. I'd say a woman's five and a half or six size."

"All right. That's something. Anything else?" Jim asked.

"DNA is nil except for Cadwallader's, of course. So the prints on the door and the shoe cast are what we have, but I suggest you call Sheriff Walsh. They've found out some more stuff on their end," Amy said tentatively.

Jim picked up the waffling in her response. "You sound like you're not supposed to be telling me that. Am I right?" Jim asked.

"No ... it's not that." She hemmed a bit. "It's just that Walsh is something of a perfectionist and control freak. He's worried about things leaking to the general public, so we have strict orders to only share what our team specifically found at the scene. I think there's some other stuff that he discovered that may have some bearing on the case, but he wants to tell you about that."

"And your point is?" Jim asked, confused.

"You know as well as I do, Lt. Higgins, that politics comes into this. Walsh is up for reelection in the fall, and he doesn't want this case botched so he looks incompetent, but you didn't hear that from me, if you get my meaning, sir."

Jim understood the point Amy was trying to make. The resolution of crimes and the crime rate had unmistakable ramifications when it came to a sheriff's reelection. The sheriff relied on good press and a consistent record of criminal apprehensions to keep the public's approval on the favorable end.

"Got it. Thanks for the heads up. I'll handle it. If anything else comes up or you have other ideas, let me know."

"I will, sir. Talk to you later."

Jim had no sooner hung up than his cell buzzed again. This time it was the antique dealer who'd handled the sale of the ball club, a man named Scott Pelligree, who owned a store called Wausau Antique Mall in Wausau, Wisconsin.

Scott said, "I'm returning a call from an investigator in your department, DeDe Deverioux. She asked about the sale of a replica 1840 ball club. Something about a murder? I did a little digging and came up with the information you want. A private collector named Trygve Swiggum purchased the club from my business last December. I just talked to him. He no longer has the club, but he's more than willing to talk to you. Do you want his phone number?"

Jim plucked a pen from behind his ear. "Yeah. Go ahead." He jotted the number on the yellow pad, hung up, and then dialed.

"Swiggums. May I help you?" a friendly female voice said.

Jim identified himself and asked to talk to Trygve. There was some shuffling and muffled sounds, and then a gruff, raspy voice answered.

"This is Trygve."

"Jim Higgins from the La Crosse Sheriff's Department. We're trying to track down an 1840 ball club replica that was sold to you in early December. Can you tell me about that?" Jim asked.

"Sure. I got an offer that was too good to pass up. I resold it two weeks after I bought it. Doubled my money."

"To whom?"

"Little blonde gal from La Crosse. She said she was purchasing the club for a friend of hers. She paid in cash. She wasn't interested in the provenance of the weapon. She seemed to be in a hurry. Just laid the cash down and left."

"Can you describe this gal?" Jim said.

"Well, like I said, she was blonde, small, maybe weighed about a hundred twenty pounds, but she was in shape, if you know what I mean. More muscle than anything. Must have been one of those workout freaks. Not really friendly. No small chitchat. All business. Counted the cash, took the club, and left."

Lori Lifto, thought Jim. "Did you notice the car she was driving?"

"Some foreign thing. Maybe a Volkswagen, but I'm not sure about that. But I do know it was dark green."

"If I send a detective over this afternoon, could you look at some photos to see if you could identify her?"

"Sure. I'll be home all afternoon working in my yard."

"Great. You can expect Paul Saner, a detective with our department, between two and three o'clock."

After the call to Swiggum, Jim got up and walked down the hall to Paul's cubicle. Paul was studying some papers at his desk.

"Paul?"

"Hey. What's up?"

"Get some photos together from our files—petite blondes who look similar to Lori Lifto—and include her picture in the bunch. I want you to drive over to Wausau this afternoon to this address," Jim said, handing Paul a slip of paper. "The weapon that killed Cadwallader was sold to a woman who sounds like Lori Lifto. The guy who sold it thinks he can identify her from a group of photos."

"Well, that's something," he said hopefully. Jim turned to go. "By the way," Paul continued, "I've been studying these phone records of LeMar Burke's. He made repeated attempts to reach Terry Waite during February and March. Some calls apparently weren't returned, but on March 16, they had a forty-minute conversation about something. That might be important since Waite claims he couldn't stand the SOB. So what were they talking about?"

"No idea, but it feels like things might be breaking loose," Jim said hesitantly. "I'm heading downstairs to interview Lifto in half an hour. Contact Terry Waite. I want him down here at five o'clock this afternoon. No excuses. If he refuses, we'll send a squad car to pick him up if we have to. Make sure he understands that. Maybe by that time, we'll know more about the club in the cave if I can get a search warrant from Judge Monroe."

Jim turned to go.

"One more thing," Paul said. Jim stopped again and turned around. "I happened to pick up a brochure at the Tomah Ho-Chunk Museum. Guess who's on the board?"

"Terry Waite?"

"Right and—"

Jim's phone buzzed. He lifted a finger. "Hold that thought for just a minute," he said briskly. He answered his phone.

"Jim. Sheriff Walsh up in Black River. Got some CCTV that I'm sending to your email. I think you might find it pretty interesting."

"Oh yeah? Who's on it?"

"You mentioned some professor that was giving you a hard time? Tall, scarecrow-looking guy?"

"Yes, he's a person of interest, but we have very little to go on," Jim explained. "Why? What did you find?"

"He was at Kwik Trip in Black River the day of the murder. We have him on camera fueling up his vehicle."

Jim's heart ticked up a few beats. "Really? That's something. Send it over."

"Sounds good. Talk to you later."

Jim clicked off.

"What now?" Paul asked.

"Terry Waite was spotted on closed circuit camera at Kwik Trip the day of the murder in Black River. The question is: What was he doing in Black River? Seems strange, doesn't it?"

"Well, that's what I was going to tell you. The museum's board of directors had a meeting at one o'clock that afternoon in Tomah. I checked it out. Terry was there."

Jim thought about that for a minute. "Doesn't prove he committed murder, but his presence in the vicinity is interesting. Something to dig into. A starting point anyway."

"Good luck on that. I'm outta here if I have to drive all the way to Wausau," Paul said, grabbing his coat.

Jim hurried back to his office and finished the paperwork for the warrant on Waite's farm south of La Crosse. He could feel the momentum of the case shifting in their favor. Things were coming together. He had probable cause to search Waite's premises based on Bobby Rude's discovery of another ball club in the cave on his property. How many ball clubs are just lying around in a cave? *Not many*, Jim thought. Maybe only one.

Back in his office, he summarized the investigation of LeMar Burke's murder and the similarities to the Cadwallader murder in Monroe County, linking them together with the unique murder weapons and the cave petroglyphs, although that seemed weak. But he included it anyway. He also mentioned the need to look for shoes at Waite's residence in the hopes they might match the cast of the footprint at the Black River murder scene. With Terry Waite's presence in Black River the day of the murder, Jim was zeroing in on him as a prime suspect. Finishing the warrant application, he emailed it to Judge Monroe's secretary. Then he sat down and began composing a list of questions to ask Lori Lifto.

☐

Leslie arrived at the law enforcement center at ten-thirty and went straight to the interrogation room on the first floor. She purchased three bottled waters from the vending machine in the hallway, put a box of Kleenex on the table, and laid out two yellow legal pads and two sharpened No. 2 pencils. Then she took the elevator upstairs to the third floor.

Higgins was in his office talking on the phone, staring out the narrow window that overlooked

Vine Street. He finished the conversation and turned in the chair. Leslie was standing near his desk.

"Ready for the interview?" he asked, looking at her carefully. She seemed healthy, but he could see a shadow of anxiety on her features—a tightness across her lips, a tension around her eyes that was hidden just below the surface. *The pregnancy or the effects of the accident?* he wondered. *Maybe a little PTSD?*

"How're you feeling?" Jim asked casually.

"That's a loaded question, Chief." She smiled tentatively. "I know you and Sam have been plotting my work duties, and I appreciate your concern—"

"You are one lucky woman to have Sam going to bat for you," he said, pointing his index finger at her as he leaned over his desk. "We did discuss your condition, and Sam has every right to be concerned. Whenever you're ready, we'll talk about it and work out a schedule you can live with. Fair enough?"

"Yeah. I can handle that, I guess."

"You didn't answer my question," Jim said. "How are you feeling?"

Leslie crinkled her nose. "A little queasy, but I guess that's normal in the first trimester."

"Have you told the grandparents yet?"

Leslie shook her head. "No, but there'll be a tsunami of emotion when that day comes. Sam's mom is going to shit a brick."

"Ouch! That's an unpleasant word picture," Jim said, squelching a grin.

"I can't imagine the ways she will spoil this child. Words are not adequate," Leslie said as she rolled her eyes toward the ceiling, a long sigh escaping into the stuffy office.

"That's what grandparents are for, kiddo. Spoil the baby silly, and then give them back to their parents so they can deal with the fallout." Leslie's eyes opened wide. Jim grinned. "It's the truth, so you better get used to the idea."

"Guess I'll have to. Are you ready to head downstairs?" Leslie asked.

Jim looked up from a form he'd been working on, stuffed it in the corner basket on his desk, and grabbed his suit coat off the back of the chair. "Let's do this," he said tersely.

Leslie noticed his careful ensemble: lightweight wool navy slacks, a crisp Michael Kors gray linen blend shirt with the classic MK logo imprinted on the pocket, and a charcoal-blue striped tie overlaid with a gray Italian knit blazer. Leslie had noticed the inside label: Bonobos. *Someday I might get Sam's taste elevated to that level,* she thought. Then she smiled. *Probably not. Besides, we couldn't afford it.*

"I set up the room. Any particular direction you want to take during the interview?" she asked.

Jim thought a moment. "Yeah. Let's focus on Lifto's whereabouts on the days of the two murders and her possible association with Terry Waite. Also her relationship with Little Hawk."

"I think she might be a tough nut to crack, sir," Leslie said as she flicked off the light switch. "According to Sam, she's a piece of work." Leslie remembered Lifto's fiery green eyes and belligerent attitude toward Paco outside the duplex earlier that morning, but then, when she thought about it some more, she pitied anyone who thought the black lab was a pushover. Lifto had discovered it was a bad idea to mess with Paco.

As they descended to the first floor on the elevator, Leslie continued her evaluation of Lori.

"Sam says Lifto's not stupid despite her actions this morning with the ax," Leslie said. "After putting together her biographical information, I called her dad and talked to him about a half an hour." She paused, remembering the exchange. "He was pretty honest, I think. He told me she's had trouble making and keeping friends since her mother died when she was ten. After his wife's death, Lori turned inward, isolating herself. The few friends she had were usually boyfriends who projected a tough image—big bruisers, fighters, guys who challenged the system. She thrives on agitation and controversy. She likes to get people riled and then stand back and look innocent—and enjoy the show. I'm not sure my presence will bring out the more feminine side of her," Leslie said, "or get her to confess anything."

"Probably not, but you're perceptive. Just jump in whenever you feel it's appropriate. Her ties with Little Hawk make sense if what her dad says is true. But does she seek out these guys for protection, or is it a game with her to see if she can control them somehow?" The elevator dinged and the door opened. They stepped off and began walking down the narrow hallway to the interrogation room.

"You mean like mind games? Or sexual conquest? Like that?" Leslie asked.

"Both, maybe. I should've talked to Vivian about that, but we'll have to wing it. Ready?" Jim asked, standing in front of the door to room number two. His tousled good looks and expensive clothes had thrown many perps into thinking he was a pushover or some trendy glamour boy. Nothing could be further from the truth, as Lori Lifto was about to find out. Leslie gave him a confident head nod.

"Let's hit it. We're three minutes early," Leslie said, glancing at her phone.

"You military types—always watching the clock."

"Training runs deep, sir," Leslie said as she opened the door.

They stepped into the interrogation room, a tight eight-by-ten-foot space with bare beige walls, a video camera mounted in the corner, and a rectangular table and three chairs. The air inside the room was always stuffy and smelled vaguely of human sweat and cigarettes. Today was no different than any other day, and the stale smells reminded Jim how many times he'd been in this room before.

Lori Lifto sat in a molded plastic chair in the cramped room, slouched backward, her head resting on a rolled-up towel that had been tucked under her neck. An ice bag lay over the bridge of her nose, and when Jim and Leslie walked in, she carefully raised her head, grimacing with pain.

Jim couldn't help but notice the purple bruises spreading across the swollen bridge of her nose, creating the raccoon-looking dark mask around her eye sockets. Her swollen upper and lower lips had been stitched together where her teeth had torn into the flesh when she crashed on her face in front of Sam and Leslie's duplex. However, that didn't diminish her smoldering green-eyed stare as the two detectives entered the room.

Lifto carefully laid the ice bag on the table and crossed her arms over her chest, sullen and standoffish. Despite her injuries and Jim's initial pity, he could see Lifto was poised for the interview and their questions. Her defiant and surly attitude was on full display, like the hostile demeanor of a junkyard dog. Even though she was small in stature, she gave the impression she might vault over the table and grab one of them by the throat. *She's gonna be tough*, Jim thought. Leslie was having similar thoughts. She'd often seen attitudes like this in interviews with captured Iraqi insurgents during her stint in the Gulf War.

"Ms. Lifto, I'm Lt. Jim Higgins." Then turning to Leslie, he said, "This is Detective Leslie Birkstein. I believe you met her earlier this morning at her residence on Cliffwood Lane."

Jim and Leslie sat down at the table across from Lifto and settled in. Lifto gazed at Jim wordlessly, taking in his expensive threads, his handsome, serious face. His dimples barely showed when he talked, but they were on full display when he smiled widely. Lifto exchanged a brazen stare with Leslie.

"We meet again," Leslie said nonchalantly. "I understand you spent some time in the 32nd Infantry Brigade out of Camp Douglas. Is that right?"

"Yes," Lifto said without elaboration. "That's correct."

"Ended up in intelligence with the 232nd Military Intelligence unit?" Leslie continued.

"Yes."

"Tell us about your duties with that specific unit," Leslie said, clasping her hands in a relaxed pose on the table.

"We assessed threat levels to the nation's security using computer and surveillance technology, mostly in the Midwest," Lifto said.

"Pretty standard stuff since 9/11. I also did a three-year tour of duty in Afghanistan.

"How'd that go?" asked Leslie, tipping her head slightly.

"I might be overstating the case, but I enjoyed military life, although that might be considered politically incorrect nowadays." She shrugged her shoulders, waiting for a response, then went on. "I excelled at nighttime surveillance. I had an eye for detail and a great memory ... and the ability to sneak up on the enemy," Lifto said with a hint of pride, locking eyes with Jim. "The dark isn't really dark with night vision goggles. But my stealth is what qualified me for the unit in the first place."

Jim tucked that piece of information away and leaned forward. "Before we get too far along here, you do know you have the right to counsel at any time during the interview. Do you understand that?"

"Yes, I'm well aware of my rights," Lifto said in a short, terse manner. She swallowed nervously. "I won't be needing counsel."

"Your choice. We're also recording this interview, so let's get started," Jim suggested. He stood up and walked over to the camera and pushed the start button. After he was seated again, he recited the Miranda rights and then began.

"LeMar Burke, a realtor for Hathway Industries in New Orleans, was killed with an ancient Native American ball club sometime during the evening hours of March twenty-first. He was found in a snowbank in the rear parking lot of a bar in Genoa, Wisconsin, on the morning of the twenty-second. We're trying to find his killer. Where were you that evening?" Jim's blue eyes scanned Lifto's battered face, but he was feeling no pity now.

"You think I'm a killer?" she scoffed, leaning forward in disbelief. "That's kinda far-fetched, isn't it?"

"Well, for someone who throws axes at people's doors, you do open yourself up to suspicion," Jim said, tamping down his annoyance. "But believe me when I say that most killers look like the average Joe on the street. Somebody you'd stand next to in the checkout line at the grocery store," Jim informed her. "So—back to my original question—where were you on the evening of March twenty-first?" he repeated, more impatiently this time.

Lifto tilted her head upward toward the ceiling. "Mmm. That was about eight days ago, right? During the big snowstorm?" she asked.

Jim almost laughed at her wide-eyed act of innocence. Then he bit off his impatience and said, "Yes, that's right. The big snowstorm."

Lifto paused, remembering. She twisted uncomfortably in her chair. "The snowstorm was a Wednesday night." She paused a moment, thinking. Her index finger tapped the tabletop. "I remember now, because a lot of my crew at the bakery couldn't get in to work. The roads were terrible, so I had to take a shift on the line since we were pretty shorthanded. So to answer your question, I went to work at seven and was at work until about seven the next morning."

"Fair enough. We'll follow up on that. Tell me about the confrontation you had with Sam Birkstein in the alley behind The Aimless Ax this week," Jim said.

Lifto's green eyes flickered with antagonism. "He interrupted a perfectly rational discussion I was having with a friend of mine out in the alley."

"You mean Little Hawk?" Jim asked.

Lifto rolled her eyes, her petulant mouth turned downward. "Yes. We were settling some stuff between us, and Mr. Sherlock walks up and starts asking questions. Who does he think he is? Dr. Phil? What about privacy? Is that a thing of the past?" Lifto asked, her temper flaring. "Nowadays, you should be able to have a discussion with a friend without some cop trying to butt in."

Jim rested his hands on the arms of the chair, relaxed and calm. "He was concerned. He thought your discussion was escalating. Things seemed tense. He wanted to make sure you were safe."

Lifto gazed at Leslie. "And you're married to that guy?" she asked. Leslie lifted one eyebrow but said nothing. Lifto shook her head. "Good luck with that," she continued. "Although he is nice to look at, especially his—" Lifto cut off her comment when Leslie leaned forward across the table. Lifto tried to smile, but it hurt too much. Instead, a slight frown creased her forehead.

"How did you learn to throw axes?" Leslie asked.

"About three years ago," Lifto said, "a friend introduced me to the sport."

"You like it?"

"Yeah, I do."

"Why?"

"It's a challenge. Someone told me once that women weren't suited for it. I took offense at the comment and set out to prove them wrong." Lifto paused for effect. "And I did. I proved them all wrong."

"You throw competitively?" Leslie asked.

"I used to, but now I just throw for the fun of it."

"When you ruined our front door this morning, was that fun?" Leslie asked, her tone suddenly icy.

"An eye for an eye. Your husband harassed me, and I thought he deserved some payback."

"You do realize you'll be spending some time in jail for that, don't you?" Leslie rasped.

"It was worth it, except for that damn dog."

Leslie wagged her index finger back and forth. "Language. Paco resents being the object of animosity and profanity," Leslie said. "So do I. He's a hero. He's saved my life more than once," she smiled icily, "and he has the commendations to prove it."

Jim cleared his throat. He was losing patience with the direction of the conversation. "Do you know Professor Terry Waite?" he asked, steering the interrogation in a different direction.

Lifto locked eyes with Leslie, then flicked her attention to Jim when he asked the question. "Terry who?" she asked, squinting and lifting her lip in a sneer.

"Terry Waite. He's a professor of history at the university," Jim said.

"I don't know him," Lifto said flatly. "Never met him. Not a fan of history."

"In December, did you travel to Wausau and purchase a replica of a ball club from Trygve Swiggum?"

For the first time in the interview, Jim noticed a flutter of anxiety in Lifto's eyes, like the sparkle of a fishing lure in a cold trout stream. Her mercurial temperament suddenly seemed more subdued. Less smart-ass, more caution. Jim thought he'd hit a nerve.

"Yeah, I did. So what?"

"Do you still have it?" Jim asked.

"No. I gave it to someone as a gift."

"Who'd you give it to?" When she stayed quiet, Jim asked again with a little bite. "Who received the gift of the ball club, Ms. Lifto?"

Lifto sat up carefully. She put her hands in her lap. At a spot just under her jawline, the skin pulsed with the steady rhythm of her heart. "What I do with my possessions is my own business," she said rudely, rubbing her neck.

"Answer the question, Ms. Lifto," Jim said brusquely.

"Okay, Okay." She let out a frustrated sigh. "I gave it to Little Hawk for Christmas."

"How did you find out that Mr. Swiggum had a club for sale?" Jim asked.

"On the internet. You can find practically anything on the internet if you look long enough," Lifto said, recovering her cool.

"Where were you on Thursday of this week between nine and eleven in the morning?" Jim asked.

Lifto thought for a minute, her index finger tracing invisible circles on the table. "I got home from work about seven, showered, then read the *Sentinel* and had breakfast. I talked to my dad for about ten minutes and went to bed," she recited.

"You didn't travel to Black River Falls to do reconnaissance work for Little Hawk that morning, did you?" Jim noticed her eyes open a little wider. The question was a total stab in the dark, but Jim had discovered that sometimes a daring question could turn things in a new direction.

"What?"

"You heard me. Answer the question." Jim's voice had hardened. His eyes turned cold like the blue of an icy glacier.

"No. You listen to me," Lifto began, and her index finger started poking the empty space between them. "I don't know what you think you're doing here in this little interview but—"

Jim's hand slammed down on the table causing Lifto to jerk in her chair and pull back from the table. Her eyes grew wide. "No, *you* listen!" Jim said loudly. His hand stung from the slam on the table which fired him up. "Two people have been clubbed to death with ancient weapons. You have admitted buying a club from a dealer in Wausau which you then claim you gave to Little Hawk as a gift. Whoever killed these people has a talent for hitting their targets with enough power and brute force to deliver a fatal blow. The weapons were left lying next to the victims, something Little Hawk claims is done as a symbol of an honor killing. Somehow I find it hard to believe that you are innocent about these murders when you admit you gave Little Hawk a weapon very similar to the ones used in the killings. Someone else might be fooled by your pretentious attitude, but that would not be me." By now Jim's eyes were blazing. He tugged at his tie, a sure sign he was infuriated with Lifto's attitude. Pointing his finger at Lifto, he said, "Don't try to placate me with some off-the-wall responses, and *don't* tell me how to do my job." They locked eyes in a death stare.

Finally, Lori Lifto tilted her head back and studied the ceiling for a moment. The room was deadly quiet. Jim waited as he exchanged a glance with Leslie, his blue eyes dancing. Finally, after a few tense moments, Lifto focused her attention back on Jim with a deadly calm.

"What was the question?" she asked.

"Did you follow Tanya Cadwallader to Black River Falls on

Thursday morning?" Jim asked again, controlling the tone of his voice.

"No. I told you, I went home to bed. You can check with the UPS guy who lives downstairs. He talked to me as he was leaving for work. He saw me go into my apartment."

"Have you ever met Tanya Cadwallader?"

"No."

"Was Little Hawk acquainted with Tanya?"

"I don't know," Lifto said icily.

"Are you aware of Little Hawk's focus on protecting land that was lost by attrition during the Indian wars, particularly under Chief Blackhawk's leadership?" Jim asked. He had a sudden thought, not exactly an insight but something close to it. What was the history of ownership on Terry Waite's farm? Had it ever been claimed by the Sauk tribe? He scribbled a reference to it on the yellow legal pad. *Later,* he thought.

Lifto shook her head and closed her eyes briefly. "Little Hawk is a passionate person, but some of his dreams are a little out in left field, if you know what I mean. I'm not saying he's unhinged or anything, but he does have some goofy ideas about getting delayed justice for his people." She looked at Jim and Leslie. "I don't get it. I never pretended to get it."

Jim persisted. "Did Little Hawk ever reveal plans for some kind of revenge on realtors in the area—perhaps those who were interested in the selling of land that was once held sacred by the Sauk tribe?"

"No, not to me," Lifto said brusquely.

"Has he ever mentioned LeMar Burke's name in your conversations?"

"Not that I recall."

"To your knowledge, has he ever been to Terry Waite's farm?"

Jim stared at Lifto. She had suddenly become quiet and pale. He waited. "Ms. Lifto, did—"

"I heard you. Is that the guy with the cave?" she asked, scrunching up her face.

Jim felt a stab of hope. "So you do know him?"

Lifto shook her head slightly. "No, I don't know Waite personally. I know *about* him only because Little Hawk talked about some cave he goes to so he can renew his commitment to his people and his vision. It's got some ancient prehistoric drawings in it, or something like that, and he says he can hear the voices of his descendants giving him strength for his mission." She waved her hand dismissively. "He says there's power in the drawings, and it helps him stay focused." She rolled her eyes theatrically. "It all sounds like baloney to me. Anyone who believes that is a little off upstairs, in my opinion."

There was a quiet knock on the door of the interrogation room. Jim frowned. Everyone in the building knew that you didn't interrupt an interrogation unless it was an absolute necessity.

"I'll get it, sir," Leslie said, standing up and walking to the door. She stepped out into the hall. Jim could hear some intense conversation. The door opened again, and Leslie said, "Sir, I think you'd better talk to Emily."

When Jim saw Emily, he knew something was up.

"What's the matter now?" he asked sharply, stepping into the hall and closing the door.

"I would have called you but you must have shut your phone off," Emily said, her green eyes shining. "Bobby Rude is missing. Someone named Jed Klumstein called your office from his cell phone. He's pursuing someone he believes abducted Bobby," Emily said. She handed Jim a sticky note. "Here's his cell number. It's not a good situation. You better call him right away, Chief," Emily said carefully.

Jim rubbed his hand over his eyes. "I don't believe it," he complained. "I was worried this might happen."

Emily pivoted and walked briskly toward the elevator.

"Thanks, Emily," Jim shouted after her. He started down the hallway, then suddenly turned and addressed Leslie, who was standing in the hall outside of the interrogation room.

"Finish up with Lori and take her back to jail. We may have to interview her again."

"No problem," Leslie remarked. "What are you goin' to do now?"

"Gotta try and find Bobby before he gets hurt," Jim said over his shoulder as he turned around and jogged down the hall to Sheriff Davy Jones' office. Jones looked up when Jim barged into his office and began speaking immediately in rapid-fire style.

"Sorry to interrupt," he said, "but somebody grabbed Bobby Rude down at the Tip Your Hat tavern in Genoa. We don't know where the guy is headed, but, according to Emily, Jed Klumstein is following him through town. I'm leaving now. I'll need you to coordinate things and arrange backup once I figure out where this bozo is taking the kid. I'll stay in touch," Jim said as he turned and left Jones' office. He ran out of the building and was just about to climb into his Suburban when Sam drove in the lot. Jim flagged him down. "Get in!" he ordered loudly, his hand waving in the air. "Quick!"

While Sam parked his Jeep, Jim climbed in the Suburban and dialed Jed's cell. Sam ran around the front, opened the passenger door, and jumped into the front seat. Jim floored the accelerator and fishtailed out of the parking lot while Sam buckled his seat belt and listened intently to the one-sided conversation.

"Where are you right now?" Jim asked loudly, laying the phone on the seat and switching to speaker.

"I'm coming up to the stoplight on 35 and Ward just beyond Hass Park," Jed said. "I'm about three car lengths behind the guy. I'm pretty sure it's that Little Hawk guy. He's in a Sierra 1500 crew cab, red and white. So far, I don't think he knows I'm following him. I drove like a bat outta hell to catch up to him once I realized he'd snatched Bobby from the back parking lot at the bar. That son of a bitch!" Jed's voice had grown more desperate as he recounted the incident. By now Jim was weaving in and out of traffic, racing south along Losey.

"What kind of vehicle does Little Hawk drive?" Jim asked Sam.

"A crew cab pickup, I think," Sam said.

"Red and white?" Jim asked.

"Yeah, from what I remember," Sam said.

Familiar landmarks were flashing by: a Catholic church on the right, Oak Lawn Cemetery on the left bordered by a Kwik Trip convenience store, and farther down the street, the old, abandoned Kmart. Jim jerked across a couple of lanes of traffic and pulled into the deserted Kmart lot.

"Okay, Jed. You're going north and I'm coming south. Stay calm, and stay back," Jim said soberly. "Don't try to signal him in any way or let him know you're following him. We'll hook up with you at the abandoned Kmart parking lot. Just stay on your phone and tell us where you are. Little Hawk's probably heading over to his place near Cashton, so he'll take 33 up over the ridge. Once we get him in our sight, you can pull over and we'll take it from there."

"The hell you will!" Jed shouted, his voice scratchy with anxiety. "You told me to take care of Bobby and that's what I'm gonna do!" This was followed by a string of expletives.

Jim slumped in his seat at the sound of Jed's desperate voice. *What are we gonna do now?* Jim thought to himself.

Sam touched his holstered pistol tucked beneath his jacket. He couldn't believe Little Hawk had whisked Bobby Rude away from the Tip Your Hat tavern. Where he was headed and what he had in mind was anybody's guess. Watching the vehicles slow at the traffic light, Sam touched Jim's arm lightly and pointed. Little Hawk's crew cab truck approached the stop light on Losey and State Hwy. 33.

"There he is," Sam said softly.

They watched as the traffic came to a stop. Little Hawk was behind a pickup with a Century Fence decal on the side, and Jed was two cars behind him. Jim noticed a dark head of hair on the passenger side and a large man with long black hair at the wheel of the red and white F-150 truck. He reached over and unlocked his glove compartment and took out his Sig Sauer P226 pistol, checked the safety, and laid it on the seat.

"Yeah. That's Little Hawk with Bobby," Jim whispered. Talking into his phone, he said, "Jed, we have them in our sights. The traffic will thin out now when you climb up the ridge. He may spot you, so try to stay back quite a distance. We'll follow you. Don't try to confront Little Hawk. We're armed. If there's any gunfire, we don't want you involved. Understood?"

There was silence on the other end. Jim repeated, "Jed, do you hear me?"

Traffic began moving and finally Jed grumbled, "I heard you." Jim wasn't sure he would follow orders. "I got my 22 behind my seat. I could give you some backup."

Jim shuddered when he thought about what would happen if a civilian got involved— especially if things went haywire—which they usually did. With the ramifications of a situation like that, Jim could lose his job, or at the very least, be put on administrative leave.

"No, Jed. My job would be the line if you were involved. I really need your cooperation on this," Jim said. He was imagining Jed's anguished disappointment at failing to keep Bobby safe.

"I'm already involved, don't you think?" Jed snarled. "God, that poor kid." A few moments of silence passed. "I could help. I've broken up more fights than you'd care to know about at the bar."

"I know, and I understand how you feel. I asked you to keep an eye on Bobby, but it's not your fault that Little Hawk decided to grab him. Sometimes things happen that we have no control over. This situation can still work out peacefully, but we'll all have to use our heads and not get jumpy," Jim lectured. Silence followed. After several seconds, Jed returned.

"Yeah, I s'ppose you're right," he grumped. "But I sure as hell don't like it."

Jim continued following Jed carefully from about a hundred yards. A few cars turned in and out of traffic in front of him. As they drove through the east side of the city and began climbing out of the river valley, the traffic thinned considerably. They drove a couple more miles and after a long silence, Sam leaned toward Jim.

"You better hope Jed backs out of this, or your ass is gonna be grass," he said casually.

Jim rolled his eyes. "You think I don't know that?"

Suddenly up ahead, Jed's beat-up Ford Escape turned right on a gravel road. Jim picked up the phone that he'd tossed in the seat and dialed Jed's number.

"What?" Jed snarled.

"What's up, Jed?" Jim asked.

"I'm headin' home, I guess. Good luck. I hope nobody gets hurt. Let me know how everything turns out." The phone clicked off.

Jim breathed a sigh of relief and glanced at Sam. "Thank God. We don't need a civilian involved in this whole mess."

"I wouldn't count on Jed going home. That's just what he wants you to think," Sam said, looking in the side mirror as Jed turned and rumbled out of sight.

Up ahead, State Highway 33 unfolded like a flat black curving ribbon along the high exposed ridge. On either side of the ridge, the land dropped off into steep rolling hills and peaceful valleys, the bluffs of the river receding in the rearview mirror. Up ahead, Little Hawk slowed and drove carefully around a tractor pulling a disc.

When they reached the outskirts of Cashton, Jim turned on a side street and slipped into a peaceful neighborhood on the edge of town.

"Fire up the GPS on your phone and figure out another way to arrive at Little Hawk's cabin. I can't follow him much longer without him knowing it," Jim said. "It'd be great if we could arrive at his place before he gets there."

Sam looked at him. "And then what?"

"I don't know yet. We'll have to figure it out on the fly," Jim said quietly. He gripped the steering wheel harder, his knuckles turning white. "On the other hand, we could just use our noggins and your knowledge of the area since you've already been to Little Hawk's place," he said impatiently.

They made their way through the countryside, Sam using his memory of the area and his excellent sense of direction, weaving through Amish settlements. Horses and buggies carrying Amish passengers clopped down the blacktop roads. The white houses and red barns seemed to appear and disappear with surprising regularity until Jim felt like they were traveling in circles. Sam guided them in a northwesterly direction toward Little Hawk's residence.

"We're close now," Sam said when they crested a long steep hill. "Little Hawk's driveway is down the road about five hundred feet on the right." Jim slowed down. "What do you want to do now?" Sam asked. He could feel little rivulets of sweat running down his rib cage. His unease had grown as he thought again about Little Hawk's formidable skill set and his imposing physical strength.

Jim pulled over to the side of the road and stopped to think. "Let's find a field road, dump the Suburban, and walk around to the back of the property. We can approach the cabin from there and make a plan."

"If we cut through these woods," Sam said pointing north, "and then backtrack down the hill we should come to his land," Sam said, trying to remember the layout of the property. "Shouldn't take too long to hike in. Sound good?" Sam asked, turning to Jim.

Jim nodded. "Sounds like a plan. Let's do it," he said.

Parking the Suburban on the edge of a field, they climbed out, and Jim locked the truck.

"I'll follow you," Jim said, pointing along the edge of the woods.

Sam skirted the edge of a thick stand of bare deciduous trees interspersed with some massive white pines. When he'd gone about two hundred yards, he turned and walked into the woods. The ground beneath the trees was carpeted with a thick layer of fallen leaves and pine needles which absorbed the sound of their footsteps. The musty smell of rotting vegetation and an occasional burst of pungent pine wafted in the air. The afternoon weather had leveled out, and although it was overcast, the temperature was a moderate fifty degrees, perfect for hiking, but still wet in the fields and woods from the recent heavy snow. Here and there patches of deep snow lay in shaded areas. The sky was steel gray; the low cast clouds drifted like shifting fog.

Jim looked down at the J.M. Weston black leather loafers he'd bought on his honeymoon in Paris with Carol. Mud and leaves were squishing up the sides, muck stuck to the bottom.

When Sam looked back to check on his progress, he caught Jim inspecting his pricey shoes. He turned away before Jim could see his grin. *Mud's better than dog shit*, Sam thought, squelching a chuckle.

They continued walking through the woods, heading northwest, climbing over a few barbed wire fences, hiking through open areas beneath the trees. Sam slowed his pace and came to a stop when he saw Little Hawk's pole shed in the distance. He held up his hand. Jim stopped. Sam pointed to the shed.

"This is the back of his property," Sam said quietly. "The buildings are a little farther that way." Jim stood next to him, huffing a little bit. They looked around some more while Jim took out his cell and dialed Sheriff Jones. He talked for a few minutes. There were some yeah's, got it's and other noncommittal remarks. Then he hung up.

"Jones sending in the troops?" Sam asked.

"He will if we need it. They'll be at the bottom of Norwegian Hollow Road." Jim looked around again, noticing the layout of Little Hawk's buildings. "Let's find a vantage point and get our bearings before we go in. Maybe behind the shed?" Jim suggested.

"Sounds good," Sam whispered.

They worked their way around a few clumps of sumac and elderberry and finally snuck up behind the pole shed. A service door was located near the front of the building on the north side of the shed. Sam sidled along the perimeter of the shed and slipped through the door into the interior. Jim followed. When they were inside, they heard the rumble of a truck engine coming up the driveway, and then the slamming of doors.

"Just in the nick of time," Jim whispered. With only one small window, the men's eyesight adjusted to the dimness inside the shed. They crept cautiously through a collection of farm machinery and other agricultural junk toward the front of the shed. Jim picked up the scent of oil and gasoline and the faint dusty smell of chicken feed. They strained to pick up any conversation, but all they heard was the wind whistling through the pine trees. Little Hawk and Bobby walked onto the porch and entered the cabin.

"I guess we'll just have to walk up and knock on the door and tell him to hand over Bobby," Sam suggested.

"Well, that's one option," Jim said casually, raising his eyebrows.

"You got a better idea?" Sam whispered heatedly.

"Nope. I don't. I'll take the lead," Jim said, stepping out of the side door. But just as he began walking up to the cabin, Jed's rattletrap SUV bored up the driveway, coming to a grinding halt on the gravel. Jim and Sam watched Jed climb out of the vehicle.

"Bobby inside?" Jed asked impatiently. Jed's expression was a mixture of regret, fear, and anger. A bad combination in anyone's book. A combination that could drive a person to do something desperate and stupid.

Jim tipped his head back and stared at the sky thinking, *Great. This is gonna turn into a real shit show.*

Little Hawk heard all the commotion and glanced out the window. The curtain flicked back in place, and it became quiet again. Jim's anxiety ramped up when Jed reached into the Ford Escape and grabbed his 22.

"Put the gun away, Jed," Jim said, his voice suddenly taking on a quiet commanding tone, his face like chiseled granite.

"Who the hell does this guy think he is?" Jed said loudly, his index finger pointed at the cabin. "You can't just walk up and grab kids off the street!"

"I agree. It's against the law, but people still do it." Jim stood tall, not giving an inch. "The gun. In the truck, Jed," Jim said pointing at it. "Now."

Suddenly the door opened, and Bobby walked out onto the porch. The three men turned and looked toward the cabin. Bobby seemed unharmed, although his lips had taken on a white, waxy appearance, and his eyes were wide with apprehension.

"Lt. Higgins! What are you doing here?" he asked. He was a good actor, but Jim could see he was scared. Jim crooked his finger at him as Sam stepped forward next to Jim. Bobby walked silently down the three steps of the porch and approached the men. Jim pointed the teenager toward Jed. Jed's face softened with emotion when Bobby came close. Jed gently put his arm around the teenager.

While he kept his eye on the cabin, Jim said, "Jed, I want you to take Bobby and go to the bottom of Norwegian Hollow Road. Sheriff Jones should be there. Tell him what's happened, have Bobby tell his side of the story. Then tell the sheriff we're talking to Little Hawk."

"Right. Gottcha," Jed said. Bobby climbed in the SUV, and Jed carefully backed up and drove down the lane through the woods. After they'd driven off, Jim and Sam stood in the driveway wondering what their next move should be.

"Are we still on plan number one?" asked Sam, glancing at Jim.

"Is there a plan number two that I don't know about?" Jim asked. "I guess we don't have anything better. Let's go." He climbed the three stairs and knocked on the door of the cabin, then stepped away with his back against the cabin wall.

"Little Hawk? Come on out so we can talk," Jim said loudly.

As the minutes passed, it remained ominously quiet. Finally, Sam stepped up and pounded his fist on the door.

"Little Hawk? It's Sam Birkstein. Come on out. We need to talk. Bobby's gone and he's safe. We just want to know why you took him in the first place. Let's get this settled."

The silence that followed was foreboding. Jim shuffled his feet, then ran a hand through his short, cropped hair. He stared at the wooden planks of the porch, hoping that some kind of peaceful resolution could happen. Sam was about to knock again, when the door slowly opened. Little Hawk stood in the doorway, unarmed but clearly perturbed, his face dark with anxiety. His shoulders were coiled with energy, his eyes burned with frustration. He stood with his hands on his hips as the two detectives turned toward him.

"Hey," Sam said softly. "What's going on?"

Little Hawk dropped his hands to his side. He inspected the two detectives on the porch and finally focused his attention on Sam.

"I just wanted to see what the kid knew about the cave on Waite's property," he started saying. "He got in my truck voluntarily—you can ask him—and it turned out he's been using the cave as a kind of retreat."

Jim was watching Little Hawk carefully. Since they hadn't talked to Bobby yet, the suggestion that Bobby Rude had voluntarily cooperated with Little Hawk was suspicious, to say the least.

"What about the ball club he says he discovered in the cave? Is it really there?" Jim asked.

Little Hawk's dark eyes flashed. The image of Chief Blackhawk floated into his memory, and he marveled that after several generations, Little Hawk looked surprisingly like his ancient ancestor—the proud warrior in Jim's dream.

"It was there the last time I was at the cave," Little Hawk commented. He stepped forward and closed the door behind him.

"When was that?" Jim asked.

Little Hawk squinted and looked out at the bare trees that surrounded the cabin. "About four days ago."

"Where'd you get it?" Jim asked.

"Christmas gift from my friend, Lori Lifto," Little Hawk responded.

"So the club belongs to you?" Sam asked.

"Yeah. That's not a crime, is it?" Little Hawk said, his voice edged with sarcasm, his eyes sparkling with challenge. Jim's thoughts were racing. *If the club in the cave belonged to Little Hawk and was still there, then the club used in Cadwallader's murder was a different weapon.*

"No," Sam continued calmly, "but you have to admit it looks suspicious, especially when two people have died from blows to the head with ball clubs, and you admit you have a club hidden in a cave." He cocked his head to one side, waiting for Little Hawk's response. "I mean, really. How many people own ball clubs? You get my point?"

Little Hawk silently shook his head. "Point taken."

"How well do you know Professor Terry Waite?" Jim asked, interrupting the exchange.

"We've been friends for a couple of years," Little Hawk offered.

"Friends? That seems a little intimate to me. From all indications, Professor Waite is a pretty independent, solitary individual. Can you describe your relationship with him?" Jim asked.

Little Hawk leveled a gaze at him, a strange look of condescending arrogance. Jim recognized the look—the same one he'd seen when suspects were questioned about their possible involvement in a crime.

Pursing his lips, Little Hawk said, "I got to know him when I took his Wisconsin Native American history course. We had some fascinating discussions, and I discovered we shared some commonly held beliefs."

"Like what?" Jim asked.

By this time, Little Hawk had relaxed a little and was leaning on the door frame, his muscular arms crossed over his chest. "That all people deserve dignity and respect, for starters."

"A noble principle, but it's all pointless if it means people who differ with you in some way end up with a caved-in skull—like LeMar Burke and Tanya Cadwallader," Jim said tightly, crossing his arms over his chest.

"Are you suggesting that I had something to do with those murders?" Little Hawk asked, suddenly standing straight, his posture tense and rigid like a boxer poised to throw the first punch.

His impressive height and keen athleticism gave Jim pause. He began assessing their chances of taking down Little Hawk if he got violent.

"Did you kill LeMar Burke and Tanya Cadwallader?" Jim asked quietly.

"No! No, I did not!" Little Hawk hissed intensely.

"Did Terry Waite kill them?"

"How would I know that? I haven't talked to Terry in over a month. I have no idea what he's been doing. You'd have to ask him," he said. Little Hawk's eyes had changed; they glowed like little hard black marbles.

"What about Lori Lifto? Could she have killed them?" Sam asked. Little Hawk let out an exasperated sigh. "I. Don't. Know."

"But you admit that Lori is a highly trained individual who has formidable skills in shooting and surveillance," Jim remarked calmly. "And then there's her ax-flinging escapades."

"Lori has a temper problem. I've been on the other end of her fits more than I care to admit," Little Hawk confessed. "Whether she killed anybody, I don't know." He glared at Sam and Jim. "Are we done here?"

Jim stared at the porch floor for a moment. Then he said, "Right now, I'm taking you into custody for abducting a minor. You'll be taken to the sheriff's department in La Crosse to give your statement. You may be charged with kidnapping, depending on what Bobby says. Those charges might stick—a very serious matter, I might add."

"I would never kidnap someone! Especially an innocent kid!" Little Hawk shouted. "He came with me voluntarily!" He took several deep breaths, his chest heaving as he tried to regain control. Jim and Sam waited him out. Finally, in a quieter voice, he repeated, "I told you. Bobby and I had a conversation in the parking lot. I asked him to go with me for a ride to talk about the cave and the petroglyphs. He agreed and jumped in my truck. What can I say?" Little Hawk held his hands out at his sides, palms up.

Jim shook his head. "You should have had more sense than to take a minor in your vehicle without checking first with a supervising adult. No matter how you slice and dice it, that doesn't look good."

They stood silently in a tight threesome on the porch, the tension mounting until Jim said calmly, "So, just so we're clear. I'm going to call Sheriff Jones, who's waiting at the bottom of Norwegian Hollow Road, to take you to the law enforcement center in La Crosse. You'll be questioned. So will Bobby, and depending on that conversation, we'll see what happens." Jim took out his cell and called Jones. In the meantime, Little Hawk glowered threateningly and continued his desperate conversation with Sam in low, hushed tones as he tried to negotiate his way out of a trip to jail. When the police cruiser arrived, Little Hawk was read his rights, cuffed, and placed in the back seat.

As the squad car drove slowly down the driveway, Sam and Jim walked down the gravel road away from the cabin to the Suburban. Jim's mind was racing with possibilities. They still had no one in custody for the two murders, and if Little Hawk was telling the truth, he hadn't been involved either.

Jim stopped abruptly as they walked up to the truck. He turned to Sam.

"Somewhere there's another club. So does that mean another murder is being planned? What's your take on this whole deal?" Jim asked.

"I don't know, Chief. What I do know is that most perps, especially those who have killed someone, aren't going to confess easily. Little Hawk isn't an innocent bystander, but Terry Waite is beginning to look like a stronger suspect." He thought a little more. Holding up his index finger, he said, "Maybe all three—Little Hawk, Lori Lifto, and Terry Waite—are involved somehow. But what's the motive? That's what I can't figure out. We don't have a motive. You don't go around killing real estate agents just because they want to buy a piece of property that's not for sale." Sam shook his head as if it were full of cobwebs, which is pretty much how he felt. "Right now, it's all pretty much a crap shoot, don't you think?" Sam gazed at Jim for a long moment. "I know what you're going to say. Sex, money, or power, right? In a murder it usually boils down to one of those three."

Jim's blue eyes, normally friendly and candid, flashed with anger. "Correction: it's not a crap shoot. This is a murder investigation, and it's just a matter of taking the information we have, evaluating the people involved, checking their alibis, and reducing the whole ball of wax to a probable motive and a probable suspect. Someone has already killed two people, and now Bobby's discovered a third club. But you're right. Our motives are still fluid—and weak." *More like nonexistent*, he thought to himself.

They walked to the Suburban, and Jim unlocked the doors.

"You got any ideas who the killer might be?" Sam asked, his elbows resting on the hood of the truck as he stared across it at Jim.

"Not sure yet, but the fog's lifting," Jim said as he opened the Suburban and hopped in the cab. Sam jumped in beside him.

"Terry Waite's involved somehow in this whole thing," Jim continued. "And you might be right about Waite, Little Hawk, and Lifto working together. Maybe Paul discovered something in Wausau this afternoon that we didn't know before. I've got DeDe working on tracing the ownership of Terry Waite's land down at the courthouse, and Leslie's following up with the protesters at Scenic Rivers corporate office. There's something still mysterious about this whole land ownership deal and the death of these real estate agents. We're missing something important." He glanced over at Sam, who was slouched against the passenger door, his forehead crinkled in frustration.

"I think my mind has turned to mush," Sam said despondently.

"God, I hope not," Jim said. "I need every brain cell on this team firing on all cylinders if we're going to figure this out."

21

By the time Jim and Sam had driven back to the law enforcement center, it was already late afternoon. The team met in the classroom down the hall on the third floor. Everyone looked beat, having spent the day on road trips, carrying out interviews, and, in the case of Jim and Sam, conducting a wild goose chase that landed them back where they started with little to show for it.

"So where are we in this investigation?" Paul asked, an edge of frustration in his voice. His tie hung like a wet noodle around his neck, and his long-sleeved shirt was wrinkled. He chewed slowly on a stale chicken sandwich. A piece of lettuce fell out of the sandwich and stuck to the front of his shirt. He didn't bother to pick it off.

"Lotta loose ends which we're going to try and tie together right now," Jim said. Everyone suddenly became quiet.

The whiteboard was plastered with photos of the two murder victims, the ball club murder weapons, crime scene photos, maps, postmortem reports of the two victims' injuries, and other germane information. Although the board was an inanimate object, Jim felt as if it had anthropomorphized into a monster that was poking him in the chest with a bony finger, teasing him to find a common thread among all the clues and evidence the team had collected.

He began reviewing all the information from each member of the team: the interview with Lori Lifto and her association with Little Hawk, Paul's trip to the weapons dealer in Wausau to confirm the purchase of the second ball club, Bobby Rude's discovery of another ball club in Terry Waite's cave on his farm, Sam and Jim's arrest of Little Hawk for the abduction of Bobby Rude, and Sam's interviews with the Kwik Trip bakery crew earlier that morning. In the meantime, Leslie and DeDe had inquired about protests happening at the Scenic Rivers Energy Cooperative corporate office, although, at the moment, Jim couldn't figure out what connection it could possibly have to the case.

"Just so we're all on the same page, Little Hawk convinced Bobby Rude to ride to his farm so he could pump him about the cave on Terry Waite's land," Jim started. "Bobby agreed, which was a poor decision, but that's pretty typical for a thirteen-year-old. As Bobby said, 'I didn't mean to cause such a ruckus.' But he sure did. However, for the record, he did go voluntarily, so Little Hawk is off the hook on the abduction and kidnapping charges. He's still in the running for the murders, though, at least in my book," Jim said, looking wilted and tired. He popped open a bottle of water and took a swig, then took a bite from a granola bar. He continued talking as he chewed thoughtfully. "So we know that Lori Lifto purchased a ball club from Trygve Swiggum," Jim started. "Have I got that right?" he asked, looking at Paul.

Paul temporarily lowered his sandwich and swallowed. "Yes, Swiggum identified her from a group of twelve petite blondes. Pointed directly to her and said, 'That's her, one hundred percent,'" Paul explained, swallowing a bite of sandwich. "We're still waiting for the dealer from the Eau Claire gallery who's tracing the ownership of the first club."

"Great. And Little Hawk admitted the club was a Christmas gift from her. Whether Lifto's involved in the murders remains to be seen, but we'll keep her in the loop for now," Jim said. "Considering her cocky attitude, given enough time, she may do something else that's incredibly stupid."

"She still in the slammer?" Sam asked.

"As we speak. Judge Monroe is holding her for forty-eight hours not only for her attack at Sam and Leslie's duplex this morning but also for further questioning in connection with the two murders," Jim said. "Sam, what about the interviews of the bakery people at Kwik Trip?"

"Well, everyone at Kwik Trip likes Lori as a boss," Sam started. "I talked to four people who said she's fair. But she has little tolerance for absenteeism, even if it's a good excuse. Her employment record is spotless. Always gets to work on time, delivers on her production goals, seems to understand her team's idiosyncrasies, and encourages them to go above and beyond the company's expectations," Sam said. He scowled and let out a huff, "I guess I'm one of the few who find her disagreeable to the extreme. But maybe—"

"She finds you attractive despite her hatred of the police," DeDe interrupted, smiling disarmingly. Leslie's eyes widened with concern. Sam made a rude sound and waved her off, his cheeks reddening with embarrassment.

"Exactly what happened at that bar the other night, Sam?" Leslie demanded, her eyes flashing.

Before things got totally off track, Jim interrupted and redirected the discussion. "Forget that petty bullshit. Let's get back to the facts, people. Sheriff Walsh up in Black River found some CCTV from Kwik Trip that shows Terry Waite filling his gas tank about noon the day of the Cadwallader murder. He attended a board meeting of the Ho-Chunk Nation Museum in Tomah that afternoon at one o'clock. Puts him in the vicinity of the murder."

"Has he been interviewed yet?" Leslie asked.

"Nope. I moved the interview up to five o'clock tonight," Jim informed them. "I have a list of questions as long as your arm." He stopped, stared at Paul and Sam, and flicked his finger back and forth at them. "I want you both there, by the way."

DeDe spoke up. "FYI, people. Waite came by the ownership of his property by perfectly legal means. He inherited it from his sole uncle on his mother's side. Waite was the only living nephew. Your suspicions about it belonging originally to the Ho-Chunk Nation were well-founded. It's one of many sites of ancient Oneota villages, highly valued for the artifacts found there. Second, you better ask the professor about the high-power electrical transmission lines that are scheduled to be constructed adjacent to his property by the Northern Alliance for Energy in 2024. From what we've discovered, the first public hearing held in January of this year was rife with opposition from Native and ecological groups throughout the Upper Midwest."

Jim leaned back in his chair and crossed his ankles. He loosened his tie, his face creased with concentration. Sheriff Davy Jones had mentioned the demonstrations that took place at the Scenic Rivers Energy corporate office earlier. *How'd I miss that?* he thought. Since then, DeDe and Leslie had been trying to connect with some of the protesters.

"Is that what Jones was talking about when he mentioned the protests at Scenic's central office?" Sam asked, verbalizing Jim's thoughts.

"Tell us more," Jim said. "This could be the kind of thing that could send Terry Waite off the rails," he said.

"I agree. It probably could," Leslie said. "They're the only demonstrations happening right now in the city. They've been relatively peaceful. Hopefully they don't get hijacked by more radical fringe groups, which seems to happen more often than we probably realize," she said. "I talked to several of the staff at the Scenic office, and they said other than the hassle of walking through a bunch of picketers every morning and listening to some dude banging on a drum, the demonstrations were low-key—so far."

"What's their beef with the transmission lines?" Paul asked. "Are the demonstrations just about that?"

"No. It's more, much more," Leslie said. "We talked to the chief organizer of the protests, a Gary Bellows. First of all, he told us no environmental assessment of the area has been done, as surprising as that sounds. This area is rich in biological diversity. Plus, there are large tracts of land that have been given back to the local Ho-Chunk tribe. It sounds like environmental watchdog groups and the Ho-Chunk Nation are going to force the hand of the power company, the DNR, and other local environmental agencies to do an environmental impact study, which will stall the project for at least a year. The Native protesters are concerned about Indian burial sites, ancient village remains, and the sustenance they get from the land through hunting, trapping, and fishing."

"What are they suggesting be done besides the assessment?" Jim asked.

DeDe took over. "They want the public educated about the threats of the high lines to the area through a series of forums. They're advocating for the land rights of people who are living in the immediate corridor of the high lines. That would include Terry Waite. Their ultimate goal is to stop the purchase of electrical power from Canada while promoting local wind and solar energy development instead," she explained.

"Sounds like an uphill battle," Sam commented sourly.

"It is, and these environmental issues can become highly charged and polarizing," Paul commented. "Just look what happened in South Dakota with the protests over the Bakken pipeline. It's not unusual for bribes and under-the-table payoffs to be involved somehow."

"So what are you thinking?" Jim asked.

Paul's lips turned downward as he thought. "Is it possible LeMar Burke was using some of his personal wealth to influence local power company officials, and Terry Waite found out and eliminated him?" Paul asked.

"It's possible. Anything's possible, but is it probable?" Jim asked.

Paul cocked his head to one side. "Burke's ecological philosophy certainly would not come down on the side of the Natives or citizens with environmental concerns."

Jim looked pensive, deep in thought for a moment. "You know, that's really a good connection we haven't thought about." He leaned forward resting his elbows on his knees. "To take it a step further, would protecting petroglyphs and ancient Oneota sites from exploitation be another factor in this whole power line controversy?"

"Could be," Sam said. "You can justify all kinds of criminal activities when you're trying to protect special interests."

Jim raised his eyebrows. "True," he said, pausing. "So, hang with me for a minute. Imagine this scenario. Terry Waite finds out LeMar Burke's been paying off local zoning officials or power company executives who pull some weight, especially those who have the responsibility for securing the power grid for the Driftless Area in the future. In other words, an entity that benefits from the construction of new lines from a new power source," Jim started. "Namely, Scenic Rivers Energy Cooperative."

"Whoa! Whoa! Whoa! You don't have any proof of that, Chief," Paul reminded him. Jim sat up straight and lifted his hands palms up toward them.

"I know, I know. I'm just thinking out loud. Theory building," Jim said, giving Sam a sideways glance.

Paul shrugged and mumbled, "Okay, theory building. Whatever. Go ahead."

"Anyway," Jim continued. "Waite finds out about Burke's payoffs and threatens to blow everything wide open. Burke offers Waite two million for his land to shut him up—the ultimate payoff—but Waite is too principled to accept the offer, and, in a fit of rage, Waite does Burke in."

"Or Waite accepts the offer for his property, and then, feeling guilty at caving to the money, decides to eliminate Burke before anyone can find out? Sounds a little canned," Sam said, his arms crossed over his chest. "We have no evidence they met on the day of the murder during the blizzard. It'd be pretty hard to prove."

"You got a better idea?" Jim growled.

"No. Other than an outright confession by Waite, I don't," Sam said calmly.

"What about Tanya's murder? Any theories about that?" Jim asked, inspecting his fingernails.

He threw a conspicuous frown in Sam's direction. "I'm all ears."

Paul jumped into the fray. "Tanya knew a lot of people in the real estate business. Maybe she knew about the two million dollar offer that LeMar Burke made to Waite. That's some powerful knowledge that could be used to her advantage. Or maybe she might have stumbled across paperwork or a conversation about payoffs. Or in her real estate dealings, she might have heard rumors of blackmail or collusion. Maybe *she* was blackmailing Waite."

"What about Trent Willow?" Leslie suggested, leaning back, gazing out the window at the thick gray weather. "Did Tanya confess something to Trent when they had drinks the night before her murder?"

Paul jumped in. "Drinks? She was flat-out drunk on her ass. She could have let something slip and didn't remember she'd ever said anything. So ... yeah, Trent might know something if she spilled the beans," Paul said, staring at the ceiling tiles with a preoccupied look. "Maybe Waite decided to eliminate Tanya, too, since she knew enough to blow the whistle on the whole shebang."

"Possible," Jim said, admiring the ingenuity of his young team. "Maybe Trent Willow's not as innocent as we seem to think. We may have to talk to him again. He seems to be straight up, but everybody has their secrets. Of course, right now it's all pie-in-the-sky bullshit," he said sourly. Everyone thought about that for a minute, but Jim continued thinking out loud.

"But we do have a whole new lead in this case with the power company tie-in and the proposed controversial high lines." There was a break in the conversation as everyone thought about that. Jim continued. "The chessboard just got more interesting and complex," Jim said as he glanced at the clock on the wall. "Sam and Paul, we have fifteen minutes until the Waite interview. Let's head downstairs."

He stood and stretched backward, reaching his hands to the ceiling in a yoga-like pose. After his stretch, he turned to DeDe and

Leslie. "Ladies, I want all the paper you can get on the top-shelf management at Scenic Rivers Energy Cooperative—who's in charge of external affairs, public issues, securing the power supply for the future. Stuff like that. People who have some influence with this line project. Got it?"

DeDe nodded. "Sure, we can do some research, but the corporate office is closed now. How fast do you want this?"

"Do the background sometime this weekend," Jim said, "and Monday morning we'll hit it hard and see what shakes out."

"Got it, Chief," Leslie remarked.

Jim, Sam, and Paul continued conversing as they walked down the hallway, leaving DeDe and Leslie slumped in their chairs.

"Why don't I feel confident that we're moving forward?" DeDe asked Leslie, who was sitting next to her.

"In my limited experience, about the time you think you've hit a dead end, that's the time everything can blow sky high," Leslie said.

22

Professor Terry Waite folded his angular body into the uncomfortable molded plastic chair. He'd been escorted into the interrogation room by a city police officer. Squirming restlessly, he swiped his hands through his thinning salt-and-pepper hair, then plopped them in his lap in defeat. The humiliation he felt was like sour bile that rose from his gut into his throat. He swallowed uneasily. Sitting in the law enforcement center waiting to be questioned like a common criminal was the highest personal insult he had ever experienced, and, over the years, he'd endured plenty of them. Just another affront from a long list of simpletons who didn't appreciate his razor intellect, verbal acuity, or insatiable curiosity.

Here he sat like a two-bit criminal. He thought back to the interview he'd had with that smart-aleck detective about a week ago. The police were nothing but a bunch of gun-toting morons who existed only because right-wing radicals funded their worthless pursuits—all in the name of law and order. Total hypocrisy! A complete disgrace! As far as he was concerned, the country was rapidly descending into a police state. Thank God—or some higher power—for the Second Amendment right to bear arms. He might need a gun sooner than he anticipated, although the thought of firing a weapon made him shake in his boots.

He heard low voices rumbling outside the door, and despite his iron self-control, his anxiety bubbled to the surface. He took a deep breath in and slowly exhaled, whispering his yoga mantra—

I am enough. His lip curled in a subtle smirk. *And ... I am enough*, he thought smugly. *I'm all I'll ever need.* Somehow during this travesty, he had to appear cooperative and in control—kiss ass, as some of his college students would say—even though he despised everything the police stood for.

The door opened wide, and three men entered the room, each one looking bone-weary. Limp ties, wrinkled shirts, rumpled slacks. In the case of Higgins, a pair of very muddy, though obviously expensive, shoes. *Typical Keystone Cops*, Waite thought. *What a joke.* After a flurry of arranging chairs, turning on the recording equipment, introducing themselves, and reading the Miranda rights, the interview got off the ground.

Best to get on top of the guy right away, the professor thought. His eyes traveled up and down the tall man who appeared to be in charge. *Looks like he's going to a fashion show instead of an interrogation*, he thought.

"Mr. Waite—" Jim began, but the professor leaned forward and spoke curtly.

"I prefer *Professor* Waite," he said in a clipped tone, tipping his nose slightly upward to meet Jim's gaze.

Jim dipped his head in deference to the professor's taste like the gentleman he was. "Very well." He started again. "Professor Waite, could you tell us what you know about Hathway Industries?"

Waite looked bemused. "Hathway Industries? I don't know anything about the company other than it was LeMar Burke's place of employment. In my opinion, they seem to have money up the ying-yang with very few scruples. Of course, that's just an opinion. I have no facts to back up my claim."

"So you have no knowledge whatsoever about the inner workings of the company?" Jim continued. "You've never had any business dealings with them?"

"No, none. Why would I?"

Jim ignored the retort. Sam spoke up. "You mentioned LeMar Burke. Could you describe your relationship with him?"

Waite's eyes shifted to Sam. He took in the young detective's youthful face—a mixture of confidence, decency, and innocence—and his swarthy good looks. The professor leaned forward and placed his arms on the table. Clasping his hands together, he assumed a condescending attitude. His hair looked like sun-dried straw, similar to the scarecrow in *The Wizard of Oz*.

"My relationship with Burke was antagonistic and confrontational. But you already know that from my previous interview with—" He glanced at Paul. "Sorry, your name slips my mind."

Paul glared at him. "Saner. Paul Saner," he said, feeling small and insignificant. The irritation of confronting Waite's arrogant superiority a second time within a week made his mouth suddenly go dry. He felt his face heating up. *Did some people deserve an uppercut to the chops?* he thought. *This might be the moment.*

"Oh yes, that's right," Waite continued, snapping his finger. "I remember now, Officer Saner. How could I forget that disparaging insult that hung in the air when you left my office the last time we talked? When you accused me of murder?" Waite asked, a nasty little grin turning up at the corners of his mouth.

Paul refused the bait and moved on. "On March sixteenth, you received a phone call from LeMar Burke, which lasted over forty-five minutes," Paul said. "It hardly seems reasonable that you would chat with someone you supposedly loathed for such an extended period of time. What did you talk about?"

"Ah, I see you've been checking up on my personal habits, especially my digital footprint. I remember the search warrant passing over my desk. All part of the job of being a crack investigator, I presume?" Waite said caustically, his eyebrows lifting in feigned surprise.

"Answer the question, Professor," Jim said calmly, although his eyes were dancing with irritation. He groaned wearily and loosened his tie. *All this hostility, and we're only a minute into it,* Jim thought. *This is going to be like pulling teeth—without novocaine.*

Professor Waite's expression hardened, his grin disappearing. "So, we're back to Mr. Burke, are we?" He sighed loudly, leaned back, and crossed his legs. "Well, Burke believed his innate Southern charm was irresistible. However, no amount of charisma, Southern or otherwise, was going to make me change my mind about selling my land. The man failed to comprehend a couple of simple words—no thanks. As the saying goes, 'What part of no don't you understand?'"

"So your entire conversation with Burke was focused around the offer on your land and your refusal?" Paul asked, his gaze fixated on the austere professor. "Doesn't seem like that would take forty-five minutes."

"Well, the conversation took a turn," Waite responded hesitantly. He swallowed, and his protruding Adam's apple bobbed up and down.

"I'm sure with your excellent verbal skills, you can answer our questions succinctly so we can move this along," Jim said. "What else did you discuss, Professor?"

"We argued about the high-voltage electrical transmission lines that are being proposed by Scenic Rivers Energy Co-op in preparation for purchasing Canadian electricity when the Genoa coal plant is closed in 2025," Waite said sourly. Then he sat silently like a cat who had just swallowed a mouse.

"And why would that be a concern of yours?" Sam asked.

"Oh, come now, detectives," Waite said, the sarcasm dripping from his voice. His eyes deliberately connected with each man. "If you've done even a minimal amount of investigating, then you already know that the high-voltage power lines will be constructed on the border of my property. I can't think of a bigger eyesore to the beauty of the area than to have skeletal metal towers hovering over us like huge, inanimate insects—like something straight out of an Orwellian novel. It's worse than anything Big Brother could have dreamed of, to say nothing about the damage it will do to precious Pre-Columbian village sites and petroglyphs in the area. And the impact of high voltage on human health is still being studied."

"Are you talking about the petroglyphs on your farm?" Sam asked dryly. Waite nodded his head.

"George Orwell wrote about Big Brother in his book *1984*. Is that correct?" Jim asked.

"Are you familiar with his work?" Waite asked, anxious to turn the interview into a philosophical exchange.

Jim waved him off. "Doesn't really matter. How did your discussion about the transmission lines go with Burke?" he asked.

Waite licked his lips, pondering his answer. "I vowed to fight it tooth and nail; he vowed to use his influence to help it come to fruition. It's no surprise that we were on opposite ends of the ecological spectrum," he said. *That's a concept much too sophisticated for your simple minds*, he thought scornfully. He leaned back in his chair, shifting his body weight back and forth as if he were sitting on a pincushion.

"Have you been involved in the protests that have been taking place at the Scenic Rivers corporate office these last few weeks?" Jim asked.

"What they're doing is admirable, but my university schedule doesn't allow me that luxury. I just don't have the time," Waite answered bluntly.

"You don't really expect us to believe that you ended your conversation with Mr. Burke on good terms, do you?" Paul asked.

"No. I told you earlier, Officer, that I disliked Burke immensely. That doesn't mean I had anything to do with his untimely death."

"Most of the murders I've investigated have at their very core a strong dislike of a person, usually bordering on hatred," Jim said, his eyes steely. "Are you telling me your emotions and feelings are above suspicion?"

Waite's voice, normally thin and reedy, became laced with bitterness, and his cheeks took on a pink hue. "Burke was abysmally uninformed about the current condition of the global environment, cared nothing about the state of the cosmos, and saw his role as one of beneficent overseer in the name of corporate greed and power. He was a fool. I had no time for him when he was living, and I have less time for him now that he's dead."

The room suddenly became very quiet. The three detectives stared at Waite, the room humming with pent-up tension. Jim finally responded after several moments of uncomfortable silence.

"I'm shocked at your disregard for the deceased, Professor," Jim said, his voice smooth and well-modulated. "Isn't human life at the apex of your ecological value system, or are we just organic organisms on the same level as the centipedes and snails wallowing around in the muck?"

Waite looked at Jim with renewed interest. "Well, I've finally met a police officer who seems to be well-read and articulate. Perhaps my opinion of your lot will have to be modified from thugs and bullies to something a bit more civilized."

Jim stared at Waite, a tiny muscle rippling in his jaw, his blue eyes blazing. "Frankly, Professor, I could care less what you think about me. As an officer of the law, I'd hoped to appeal to your sense of decency and fair play. Isn't that what we expect from those who educate our youth?"

Waite tipped his head slightly. "Turning the tables on me, I see. What was the question, Lieutenant?"

"Did you kill LeMar Burke on the evening of Wednesday, March twenty-first, and deposit his body behind the Tip Your Hat tavern in Genoa, Wisconsin?" Jim waited, his stare fixated on the professor's intense green eyes. The atmosphere in the room seemed to swell with humidity and sweat, and the odor of stale aftershave permeated the air. An angry fly buzzed incessantly against the frosted windowpane.

Waite closed his eyes briefly and gritted his teeth. "No. I did not kill LeMar Burke, or anyone else for that matter."

"Why should we believe you?" Paul asked out of the blue. Jim looked at the floor and smiled. Paul seemed so genuine that Waite was momentarily thrown off balance.

"What about truth? Do you believe in the truth?" Sam asked.

Recovering, Waite commented, "Truth? Belief? My, my. We are pulling out all the stops, aren't we?"

"Enough!" Jim interjected loudly. Waite jumped involuntarily. "I want some straight answers. Enough philosophical fluff." Jim's face was dark with anger.

Everyone stared at him. Waite looked pleased that he'd gotten the conversation derailed, but Jim pressed his advantage.

"Tell me what you knew about Tanya Cadwallader," Jim said sternly, folding his arms across his chest. Like a disciplined school child, Waite sat up straighter when Jim gave him an icy stare.

"She was the real estate agent who brought LeMar Burke into my life—much to my chagrin. I didn't care for her, but I would never have harmed her."

"Murdered," Jim said softly, deadly serious.

"Excuse me?" Professor Waite mumbled, leaning forward across the table.

"She was murdered," Jim said, continuing to stare at Waite. "How do you explain your presence in Black River Falls on the day of her death?" Jim noticed Waite's furtive glance at the clock and the fine sheen of sweat that appeared on his forehead. *Maybe we're finally getting somewhere*, Jim thought.

"I drove through Black River Falls to a board meeting at the Ho-Chunk Museum in Tomah that afternoon."

"Time?" Jim asked.

Flustered, Waite answered hurriedly, "About eleven in the morning, as I remember."

Jim felt a flicker of satisfaction when Waite admitted he'd actually been in the city that day. But he knew he was lying. The CCTV recorded him filling up his tank at about nine-thirty. He decided to pour it on. "But before your meeting, you followed Tanya Cadwallader to a client's property near Glen Falls, and when she left there, you followed her to the wayside where you clubbed her over the head …"

Waite sprung out of his chair and shoved a clenched fist in Jim's face. Jim stood suddenly, his chair scraping the floor. He towered over the table in a defiant stance opposite Waite. When Waite raised his fist and shook it in his face, Sam leaped to his feet and held up his arm in a protective gesture in front of Jim. Sam glared at the professor. Waite paled significantly but refused to sit down.

"That is a preposterous and utterly false accusation of magnum proportions!" the professor yelled, his finger jabbing up and down perilously close to Jim's tie. "I had nothing to do with a murder! Not Lemar's or Tanya's! The very thought—"

"Shut up and sit down, Professor!" Jim shouted, leaning forward until he was practically nose to nose with Waite. Waves of anger rolled off the two men as they stood across from each other. Finally, Jim turned to Sam. "It's okay, Sam," he said as he placed a hand on Sam's arm and straightened his tie. "Sit down, Professor," he said more calmly. "Please."

Collapsing into the uncomfortable chair, Waite asked weakly, "How did you know I'd been in Black River Falls?"

Jim shrugged. Trying to maintain control, he said roughly, "Nowadays there are very few places you can go where you aren't recorded on a surveillance camera of some kind. You filled your car with gas at the Kwik Trip by the I-94 freeway exit that day," Jim said as he glanced at his notes and tamped down the hostility in his voice. "Since you were a person of interest in the LeMar Burke case, the police noticed you when they reviewed the CCTV tape," Jim said. He let that sit a while. Then he asked, "Where did you get the ball club that's hidden in the cave on your property?"

"How do you know about that?" Waite asked softly, his eyes large with surprise. Suddenly he seemed disoriented and strangely submissive. *Maybe I have to give the cops more credit than they deserve,* he thought.

"I have my sources," Jim said.

Waite slapped his hand down hard on the table, his indignation firing up again. "So you've been trespassing on my property!" he said, his voice loud and blunt. "That's illegal since my land is posted. You need a search warrant for that."

Jim told him the truth. "I haven't set foot on your property, sir," he calmly reassured him. "So how did the ball club get in your cave?"

"I discovered it early this spring when I did my semi-annual visit to the cave. I was surprised to see it there myself. I don't know how it got there, and I sure as hell don't know how you found out about it."

Jim ignored the barb. "Have you ever had any association with D'Marius Blake or Lori Lifto?"

"The names aren't ringing a bell, but maybe they attended one of my classes. I don't know."

"You might know D'Marius as Little Hawk," Jim informed him.

Waite's eyes brightened. He pointed his index finger at Jim. "Oh, yes. Little Hawk. He's taken some of my classes and added some valuable insights to our class discussions about Native Americans."

"Have you ever associated with him outside of the university setting?" Jim asked.

"We've had a few beers together at one of the local bars on Third Street," Waite offered.

"Would you say your philosophies about the downtrodden, mistreated people of the world dovetail at times?" Sam asked.

The professor threw Sam a demeaning glance. "Yes, and you police officers would do well to take a few courses in human relations and the subcultures in American society. You could learn a lot from their credos. It might make you more responsive to their beefs about racial inequality and injustice—often delivered at the hands of law enforcement."

"Point taken," Jim said, going on without batting an eye. "So you admit you've had a friendship with Little Hawk outside of the university setting."

"Yes," Waite said reluctantly.

"What about Lori Lifto? Know her?" Paul asked, his arms crossed over his chest.

"Only that she's Little Hawk's friend."

"Since we're in the sharing mood, anything else you want to tell us?" Jim asked, trying to keep the sarcasm and frustration out of his voice.

"No, I think the mood for sharing is gone."

"Let me tell you one thing, sir," Jim said, his voice gritty with determination. "I'm not sure of your involvement in the murders that have been committed, so right now, you're free to go, although I'm requesting that you remain in La Crosse. I will tell you flat out that you are a person of interest in the deaths of LeMar Burke and Tanya Cadwallader." When Waite's mouth fell open in obvious surprise, Jim held up his hand in a stop motion. "Save your outrage for someone else. We may be contacting you again with more questions as the investigation moves forward," Jim said, standing.

Waite abruptly pushed his chair back and prepared to leave. "You mean this farce is finally over?"

"You're free to go," Jim said simply.

Waite gave the group one final contemptuous glance and marched from the room, his head held high, his clothes fluttering like bat wings on his bony frame.

"Well, your description didn't disappoint, Paul," Jim said quietly, watching Waite's spindly frame recede down the hallway.

"He's a piece of work, all right," Paul responded, rubbing his unshaven cheek.

"I'd like to deck him right between the eyes," Sam hissed, his hazel eyes bright with anger.

"A soft answer turneth away wrath," Jim said quietly.

"Proverbs 15:1," Sam replied. "Are we done for the night, Chief?"

"Yes, for tonight," Jim said. "Keep in touch if you hear anything. By the way, the search on Waite's property is set to begin at eight tomorrow morning. The warrant was on my desk when we got back from Cashton this afternoon. Waite knows nothing about it, but I'll be there. You're going to be there too. I'm sure it'll be quite a show," Jim said quietly.

By the time Jim headed south along the Mississippi River on U.S. 35, it was already past eight o'clock. Despite the frenetic activity of the day, there didn't seem to be a lot of forward movement in the case, but he was used to that in his profession. However, there were very few cases in which he'd failed to gather enough evidence to prosecute a perpetrator. His mouth twisted in a grimace at the memory of those dead-end cases. He knew every detective had them, although he didn't like to admit it. He held onto the hope that something would be revealed that would move this whole mess forward.

Turning on Chipmunk Coulee Road, he gunned the Suburban through the twisting curves toward his home. Although the sun had set behind the stark skeletal trees, the horizon was still ablaze with a kaleidoscope of swirling reds, pinks, and golds. The damp air was warm and held the promise of rain. Hues of green peeked out here and there in the open fields, and a few trees were beginning to display some leaf buds—all of it an inkling of the spring season soon to unfold.

Jim drove into the garage, and when he walked into the back hallway to hang up his coat, Carol met him and kissed him tenderly.

"Tough day?" she asked, her brown eyes warm and sympathetic.

"Yeah. Long and frustrating," he said gruffly as he sat down on the bench, leaning over to take off his shoes.

"What happened to your shoes?" she asked, looking at his favorite loafers caked with mud. "What've you been doing?"

"Chasing Little Hawk through the woods," Jim said dejectedly, dropping a muddy shoe on the tile floor. "Think they're ruined?" he asked, turning the other one over dejectedly.

"I don't know," she said, crinkling her nose at the muck that clung to them. "Boy, they were expensive, too. Did you catch him? Little Hawk?"

"Yeah, but not before he grabbed Bobby Rude at Jed's tavern down in Genoa," he said.

Carol's eyes widened with concern. "Oh, no! Is Bobby all right?"

"Everything's all right," Jim reassured her.

Over the past few years, Carol was beginning to grasp the frustrations and dangers of police work. But despite her fear that he'd be harmed, she continued to support her husband in countless ways, although sometimes Carol didn't always feel appreciated for her compassion.

Jim stood and pulled Carol toward him, burying his nose in her hair, taking in the warm concern that seemed to be at the very core of her being.

"Where are the kids?" he asked.

"In the living room watching *Little Mermaid 2*."

"Could you make me a sandwich and bring me a beer?" he asked, stroking her back.

"Absolutely." She started down the hall, but Jim caught her hand and pulled her back. He looked into her brown eyes and squeezed her hand. Suddenly he felt bone-tired—the kind of tired when your brain feels like mush, and you wonder whether you can put one foot in front of the other.

"Are you okay?" she asked, searching his face, her brown eyes soft and warm.

"How'd I get so lucky to find you?" he said tenderly, leaning against the wall. He remembered the stark loneliness that had confronted him when he came home to an empty house after Margie died. The depression had threatened to squash him like a bug.

"God orchestrated it, I believe," Carol said calmly. "And don't feel it's your duty to hold up the wall. In fact, if you don't sit down, I think you'll fall down." She pointed her arm down the hall. "Go. Get in the living room. Watch the movie, and cuddle the kids. I'll bring you a beer and a roast beef sandwich with Swiss on rye."

"Mustard and mayo?" Jim suggested.

"You got it," Carol said, walking through the dining room to the kitchen.

A half an hour later, Jim was snuggled up with Henri on his lap in the black swoopy chair while Lillie lay sprawled on the couch with her favorite blanket engrossed in the movie. Jim was half-dozing when the doorbell rang, his mind sifting through the facts of the murder cases. His frustrated groan at all the dead ends they'd encountered startled little Henri from his drowsiness. The little tyke jerked, his eyes opened, but Jim cuddled him deeper into his chest, and he went back to sleep.

After a muffled conversation in the foyer that Jim couldn't decipher, Carol appeared at his elbow. She looked down at him and said softly, "Lydia Alberg is here to see you, honey. She apologizes for the lateness."

Jim moaned softly. Henri was fast asleep, so Carol leaned over and plucked him from Jim's arms and carried him to his bedroom. Lillie stirred on the couch.

Worried, she asked, "Bapa? Where are you going?"

Jim knelt on one knee by the couch and fingered her fine blonde curls.

"Nowhere, I hope. If I have to go, I'll let you know, okay?" he said. He kissed her cheek tenderly.

Lillie scowled. "Is this another lady that's in trouble? Does she need your help, too?"

"You're too little to be wondering about that. That's my job, toots," he said, standing up. "You finish watching the movie, and then I'll tuck you in."

Jim walked swiftly from the living room through the dining room and arrived at the front entry where Lydia Alberg stood waiting, her face lined with worry. She was dressed in jeans, sneakers, and a dark maroon UW–L sweatshirt. She smiled tentatively as Jim stepped toward her. He extended his hand, and she grasped it, a little too desperately for his liking.

"Lydia. What brings you out here tonight?" he asked politely, disengaging from her intense handshake and stuffing his irritation at her intrusion into his personal life.

"I'm so sorry to bother you," she started, sweeping her hand dramatically through her long black hair. Jim thought, *But not sorry enough to wait until morning.*

"So what's up? Jamie get himself in some kind of scrape?" he asked, fighting to hide the sarcasm that was lurking just below the surface.

"I hope not. He gets off work at four o'clock, and now it's almost nine-thirty, and I haven't heard from him. Do you think he's in trouble?" Her face scrunched in panic. Jim understood where the mild autism came from. Lydia was adept at hiding her disability, but occasionally the condition surfaced. *Nothing's changed in four years,* he thought. *She's still flying the helicopter around her son, looking for a place to land so she can spy on his every move.*

Jim did nothing to hide his frustration. "Well, listen, Lydia. He's an adult. Maybe his plans changed, and he joined some friends for a beer and a pizza."

"He doesn't drink anymore. He gave up alcohol after he discovered that cave with the gold and got pushed into the river."

Jim pursed his lips at the memory of his first encounter with the Albergs when Jamie became involved in a dangerous murder case involving an impressive cache of lost gold treasure. He'd nearly drowned when the killer tossed him into the Mississippi River.

"Okay. Well then, maybe a girlfriend?" Jim suggested diplomatically.

"He's come a long way in that department, but he's still socially awkward. You remember that, don't you, Lieutenant? How awkward he is?" Her brown eyes had a pleading quality to them that made Jim feel uncomfortable, like he was being backed into a corner.

"Yes, but a girl can have a strange effect on a guy. Especially if she comes on to him with determination."

Lydia huffed, and her face grew dark. "Are you suggesting that Jamie is out prowling around for an unsolicited sexual encounter?"

"Might be. Happens quite a bit in the college crowd." Jim shrugged. *What planet does this woman live on?*

"Really, Lt. Higgins. You surprise me. I wouldn't have believed—"

"Listen, Lydia. I'm going to be straightforward here," Jim interrupted rudely. "Please don't take offense at what I'm about to say. Maybe you need to back off a little with Jamie. He's an adult. He needs to learn to manage his own life, make his own mistakes, savor his own successes, without any interference from his mom." Jim sighed, the weariness engulfing him. The day was at an end. His old shoulder wound ached, he needed a shower, and he was looking forward to one of Carol's great back rubs.

Lydia slammed her clenched fist against her leg in a gesture that reminded Jim of a spoiled teenager. "You sound just like my husband." She stopped suddenly and held up her index finger. "Correction— former husband. He was always telling me I was hovering. Doing the helicopter thing."

Jim felt something grab his pant leg.

"Bapa? Can you tuck me in? The movie's over," Lillie said, clinging to his leg. Jim laid his hand tenderly on her shoulder.

"Is this your daughter?" Lydia asked, forgetting her tirade. She leaned over, resting her hands on her knees as if she were viewing a display in a museum. "Oh, my! She's adorable!"

Lillie gave Lydia a haughty stare. "I take advanced classes in Math and Social Studies even though I'm only in the second grade. I'm a better-than-average reader, and I play piano and write music, too. Sometimes I help Bapa solve crimes. I'm not just another pretty face," she finished, crossing her arms over her chest while her toe tapped the hardwood floor.

"That's my Lillie. She's a force to be reckoned with," Jim said, trying to hide his amusement at the amazed look on Lydia's face. Mrs. Alberg slowly straightened to her full height. "And she hasn't seen much of me lately," Jim continued.

Lydia didn't seem to get the hint, so Jim gently herded her toward the front door. "Listen, if Jamie doesn't show up by morning, call the police and tell them what's happened. They'll try to keep an eye out for him. Until then, go home. Take a long, relaxing bubble bath. Try to stop worrying. Maybe say a prayer," Jim suggested as he opened the front door and guided Lydia outside. She walked toward her car and then turned toward Jim, her dark eyes liquid with the start of tears.

"Do you think he's okay?" she asked again.

"I'm seventy-five percent sure he's just fine," Jim said. "And he's very smart. If he gets in a jam, he'll have to think his way out of it or put up his dukes and fight his way out of it." Lydia's eyes widened at his suggestion. "Most young adults have to do that at some point in their lives. Good night, ma'am," Jim said. He grabbed Lillie's hand, stepped back into the foyer, and locked the door.

"Bapa, did that lady need your help?" Lillie asked, slipping her hand into Jim's.

"More help than you can imagine, sweetie," he mumbled wearily.

23

SATURDAY MORNING, MARCH 30

Braxton Lewis, who served on the executive staff at Scenic Rivers Energy Cooperative, was the first vice president of power delivery and a liaison to the External and Member Relations staff. He strode across the nearly empty parking lot at the corporate office complex on the south side of La Crosse on Saturday morning after working on various matters that had demanded his attention. It was a thankless job. The hours were grueling, but his six-figure salary seemed to make all the trade-offs worthwhile. At least, that's what he told himself.

Lately, all he'd gotten accomplished was quelling the protests of the Native people of the area and the environmental factions that had come out of the woodwork to protest the development of the high-voltage power line project, which would eventually deliver electricity from Canada to the Upper Midwest.

Nowadays, when it came to the environment, there was little room for negotiation. Usually the protesters adopted an all-or-nothing stance, which left few viable alternatives for consensus. Unfortunately, it was his role to try and subdue the uneasiness that was growing within the community and still deliver an acceptable contract that met the future needs of the power company. The negotiations had already broken down twice. They were starting talks again next Tuesday. Trying to come up with realistic solutions that everyone could live with wasn't working, although he was proud of his team for developing creative possibilities as opposed to scrapping the entire project.

He wished he still had LeMar Burke's influence on the project. When he'd gotten wind of Burke's five-star complex development south of La Crosse, Braxton had used the opportunity to invite LeMar to address the Scenic Rivers Energy Cooperative board of directors early in January. That had only been possible through his contacts in the community, namely Trent Willow. Burke's support of the high-powered lines had gone a long way in convincing the board that the project was vital for the future growth and economic opportunities it would provide for the Tri-state area.

The violent death of the Louisiana tycoon left Lewis feeling vulnerable and exposed. Now he was left to his own devices, and Lewis realized the support for the project was disappearing just like the industrial big shot. He wondered if the project would survive the scrutiny of the public. He thought about Burke's mysterious death and wondered how much the police had uncovered about his connections to the high-line project and his interest in the land owned by Terry Waite. He'd followed the murder investigation in the *Sentinel* and on the local TV stations. Some guy named Higgins was in charge of the investigation, but things were moving slowly. However, it was only a matter of time before they discovered the money Burke had sifted into Braxton's private savings account in Holmen. *I've got to move that money offshore soon*, Braxton thought. *Things are starting to get complicated.*

The early morning weather had produced a chilly fog, but now, thanks to a warm breeze from the south, the temperature had risen significantly. The fog was burning off, and the day promised to be beautiful. As Braxton walked across the paved parking lot whistling a mindless tune, he removed his suit jacket and slung it over his shoulder with an air of nonchalance.

He noticed the white puffy clouds in the azure sky, and his heart grew lighter. He was looking forward to his twelve-year-old daughter's soccer game at Carroll Field on Isle La Plume near the Gundersen Lutheran Hospital. His daughter, Elyse, was center in the starting lineup. She had worked hard to improve her leadership and soccer skills. He remembered her glowing face when she'd been elected captain of her team this year. He was so proud of her. He breathed in the fresh spring air and thought, *What a great day for a soccer game.*

The gunshot sounded like a Fourth of July firecracker. The bullet struck Braxton in the center of his chest, entered his heart, and blew out his back between his ribs. He was only about twenty feet from his car. At first, as he stumbled and fell to the ground, he thought he'd been careless. *Did I trip over my own two feet?* he thought. But immediately following that thought, a pain radiated from his chest outward—a pain so intense it took his breath away. And then the wash of blood soaked his shirt and began to pool beneath him on the pavement. *Am I dying?* he wondered.

Flashes of his wife, Cheryl, and their daughter, Elyse, passed through his confused mind. Their smiles. Their laughter. Their love of life. Suddenly he was hovering above the earth looking down at himself awkwardly sprawled on the pavement. His face was pale and ghostly white, his lifeblood seeping in a puddle around him in the parking lot. Then in the next instant, he was flying through a narrow tunnel and at the end was a brilliant white light. A warmth spread throughout his body, and he was enveloped in a lovely cocoon of peace. He felt safe. His breathing became erratic, finally slowing to a stop. His heart continued to beat slowly for a few more seconds until it finally stopped, too.

Braxton Lewis was dead.

☐

Jim got up early Saturday morning. He'd slept well despite the thoughts swirling in his head about the murders when he'd gone to bed. Carol's luxurious backrub had relaxed him and sent him into a deep rest as it always did.

The coffee pot gurgled noisily on the counter. Jim placed two slices of whole wheat bread in the toaster. He rummaged through the refrigerator searching for the raspberry jam that Gladys Hanson had sent over a few days ago. Then he grabbed two hardboiled eggs to eat with his toast.

He sat at the dining room table staring out the window leisurely sipping his second cup of coffee. He'd scheduled the search at Terry Waite's property for eight o'clock this morning. Sam and Paul and a couple of other officers from the sheriff's department would meet him at Waite's farm and begin the arduous task of going through the house and outbuildings. He hoped they'd find something that would lead to a breakthrough—a clue or a vital piece of physical evidence that would confirm or negate the connection between Terry Waite, LeMar Burke, Tanya Cadwallader, and the power company. At any rate, it seemed like a huge task that might not yield much, but he didn't know what else to do.

He slipped back into the bedroom quietly and chose a navy pair of dress slacks, a gray pinstriped shirt, and a maroon Nordic tie with navy checks woven into the fabric. He finished the ensemble with a dark gray wool suit jacket. He was sitting in the wingback chair by the bedroom window putting on his socks when Carol rolled over and sat up. She watched him with sleepy eyes.

"You'll be home to cook the steaks, I hope," she said tentatively, her voice groggy with sleep.

"Should be, but you never know. If things break open, it could be an all-nighter," Jim said. "I'm sure Jerome can cook steaks if he has to."

"Really? An all-nighter? You're that close to solving this whole mess?"

"No, not yet. But sometimes things happen that accelerate the situation. Kinda like high school chemistry."

Carol frowned. "Huh?" she said confused. After a moment she said, "Did I miss something?"

"You know—like those experiments when one chemical causes a chain reaction," Jim explained. "Like that."

"Like an explosion?" Carol suggested, her eyebrows wrinkled together.

Jim suddenly had a vision of a mushroom cloud in the sky over La Crosse. "No, not necessarily an explosion," he said hastily, feeling foolish. "Maybe that was a bad comparison, but things are starting to come together ... I think."

Carol flopped backward in bed. Jim got up and leaned over her, kissing her quickly. "I'll see you later. I'll be in touch. What time are Sara and Jerome getting here?"

"Not 'til this afternoon. Be careful," she warned. "And promise me you'll make every effort to be here?"

"Absolutely. Love you," he said softly as he retreated from the bedroom.

☐

The search at the farm progressed slowly after the initial objections of Professor Waite, who ranted and waved his arms in a wild tirade. He railed about a police state, badgering and harassment by law enforcement, and the infringement on his Fourth Amendment rights—all to no avail. Jim stood in front of him taking the verbal blast with as much dignity as he could muster.

"I have the right to be secure against unreasonable searches!" Waite screamed in Jim's face.

"Mr. Waite, you have received a copy of the warrant which describes what we may confiscate," Jim said as he began ticking off the items on his fingers. "One—ball club weapons, two—any clothing with traces of blood, three—a specific pair of shoes whose tread pattern is included in the warrant, and four—any other materials including paper documents that might relate to the murder cases of LeMar Burke and Tanya Cadwallader." Jim finished in a reasonable voice, although he could feel the blood pressure pounding behind his eyes. Throughout the house, drawers and closet doors were opening and shutting as officers methodically searched through the contents of the house. The scent of mothballs floated in the stagnant air of the house.

"I'm contacting my lawyer!" Waite said belligerently. "You cannot get away with this!"

"I'm afraid we can," Jim responded. "The U.S. Constitution at work, sir." Jim hardened his voice and took a step toward Waite. "Listen carefully, Professor Waite. You are welcome to watch us conduct the search and call your lawyer, but under no circumstances will I tolerate your interruption of my officers' duties here. You will remain orderly and quiet. You will not interfere with their work as they carry out this search."

"Or what?" Waite sneered.

Jim leaned in, the intensity of his blue eyes causing Waite to back up a few steps. "Or I will have you arrested for obstructing justice. Are we clear?"

Waite swallowed. His hollow-cheeked appearance and limp, baggy clothes made him look like someone who might have been living on the street, but the glint in his eyes reminded Jim that Waite had a deep-seated intelligence and tenacious stubbornness.

"Are we clear, Mr. Waite?" Jim repeated, his voice impatient.

"Yes, but I will be registering my protests in an official complaint drawn up by my lawyer." He stuck his chin out in defiance, staring into Jim's eyes.

"As is your right, sir," Jim said. Then, with a flick of his hand, he said, "Now, make yourself scarce, Professor Waite, so we can do our job."

Waite spun on his heels and exited the house, where he continued to pace on the small front porch. His footsteps echoed ominously on the weathered floorboards as Jim watched him fume and frantically text on his phone.

The police officers continued their work, combing through Waite's drawers, closets, and several file cabinets of documents and papers. The house was surprisingly spartan except for a few pieces of good quality furniture, one or two oil paintings by obscure artists, a couple of expensive wool rugs, and other small items like coffee tables and nightstands. The only thing that seemed extravagant was his collection of books. Still, in the final analysis, the overall effect of the home was one of an ascetic who lived a joyless existence. No family photos or mementos. *Why am I not surprised?* Jim thought. *The guy lacks any kind of social graces that would attract anyone to him.*

As the morning wore on, Jim and his team doggedly rifled through the possessions in Waite's home. They confiscated some financial records and other documents that would take many days to read thoroughly and digest. Somewhere in those documents, there might be a motive. A payoff by Burke? Maybe. Waite's cell phone records had already been looked at, especially his activity with Tanya Cadwallader's real estate agency and his conversations with LeMar Burke earlier in the year.

When they moved to the small, detached garage, things started heating up. A pair of Red Wing work boots were found in the trunk of Waite's car. The treads looked like the pattern of the shoe prints left at the murder scene at the wayside in Black River Falls. With the boots, a lightweight jacket was found. Crime scene would look at it for blood spatter.

They were about to head to the cave to search its contents when Jim's cell pinged.

"Higgins."

"Jim. Davy here. We've got another murder," he said unceremoniously.

"What?" Jim asked frantically. "Who? Where?" He walked into the warm sunshine near the garage and stood on the driveway with his cell phone pressed to his ear.

"An executive at Scenic Rivers Energy Co-op named Braxton Lewis. Shot in the chest right through the heart. Looks like a long-range shot with a high-powered rifle. He didn't have a chance. He died in the parking lot at the office this morning around nine o'clock. We're searching for witnesses. His secretary discovered his body lying about twenty feet from his car half an hour ago." Jim heard Davy sigh, and he imagined his anguished features.

"So what do you want me to do?" Jim asked, regaining his composure.

"Get over here with Sam. I've got some of my men searching the buildings in the area. We might get lucky and find the roost where the shooter was. We know he was shot from the east in the direction of the bluffs based on the entry and exit wound. Luke's already here. I need your take on this, Jim. You'll have to leave the search at Waite's to Paul and the other officers you've got on the scene. See you in fifteen minutes."

The line went dead. Jim tipped his head back and closed his eyes, his cell phone still in his hand. He slowly put it in his suit jacket pocket.

Sam noticed Jim's bewildered expression and walked over.

"Chief? Everything okay?"

"No. There's been another murder," Jim said quietly.

"What?" Sam asked, mirroring Jim's confusion and disbelief. "When?"

"Braxton Lewis, an executive at Scenic Rivers Co-op, was gunned down in the corporate parking lot this morning. No witnesses at this point."

"Holy moly."

"Well, there's one thing we do know," Jim said, meeting Sam's disbelieving stare.

"What's that?" Sam asked.

"This is one murder we can't pin on Terry Waite. He was here with us the whole morning."

Jim and Sam raced north into La Crosse and arrived at the scene of the shooting. Crime scene crews were moving around in the parking lot bagging any evidence they found in and around Lewis' car and in the general vicinity. Police cars had cordoned off adjacent neighborhoods, and a sea of blue uniforms swarmed in and around the energy company's main office. Directly behind the building, the Mississippi River flowed deep and silent, a few fishing boats anchored about a hundred feet out from shore, the occupants intent on their casting.

On such a beautiful spring day, the flashing red and blue lights of the squad cars seemed incongruous and terribly sad. Jim's heart grew heavy, the familiar malaise of death filling his chest, evaporating his sense of well-being. He could feel the weight of another murder on his spirit. The man was only forty-two, in the prime of life. Probably had a wife and children. Now his mutilated body lay under the cover of a white sheet as he was loaded into the medical examiner's van. Jim's anger flared, but he tamped it down, knowing it would only distract him from the task at hand. He walked up to Luke Evers, the La Crosse County coroner.

"Has the world gone nuts, or is it just my imagination?" Luke spat bitterly.

"You mean you're just first noticing now? It's been nuts for quite a while," Jim said with a feeble smile. His weak stab at humor did nothing to lighten the atmosphere. He lifted his chin and met Luke's angry gaze. "What's your take on this?"

Luke watched wearily as the ambulance crew loaded the victim into the back of the van. "Shot with a high-caliber rifle. Whoever did it knew what they were doing. I think the perpetrator could be someone with sniper training—military, maybe. But a competent hunter with a high-powered scope and big-caliber rifle could have done it, too." Luke tilted his head at Jim, then averted his gaze to the bluffs opposite the parking lot. "What a damn waste," he said disgustedly.

As Luke gave his assessment, Lori Lifto popped into Jim's mind, but he kept that thought to himself. They'd held Lifto for forty-eight hours, but she'd been released from jail late last night despite Jim's protests. Jim followed Luke's gaze to the distant bluffs overlooking the city. "You're not thinking someone shot him from a couple of blocks away, are you?"

Luke shrugged his shoulders. "Can't tell yet without a thorough examination of the victim's wounds."

Sam piped up. "If he was hit from long range, we're dealing with someone who probably had a spotting scope and was familiar with the problems of wind, distance, and atmospheric conditions."

"Caliber comes into consideration, too," Luke said.

Jim analyzed the situation, his thoughts zeroing in on the scenario. *Was this a conspiracy that was tied together with the other murders? A hit list? If so, were there more killings planned?* "Man, this just keeps getting worse and worse." He briefly closed his eyes, hoping that when he opened them, this would all be some big, bad dream. When that didn't happen, he said, "Well, what're we doing? We need a plan."

Davy Jones walked up, overhearing Jim's comment.

"We've got a plan. Here it is. Our team is scouring the area within a radius of five hundred yards in every direction. We'll start searching and go farther out if we have to."

"Sounds good. In the meantime," Jim said, "where do you want us?"

"Why don't you and Sam take the industrial area southeast of the office?" Davy said, pointing in that direction.

"Sure, we can do that," Jim said. "We'll get started."

Davy Jones nodded, then walked toward another officer who asked a question and pointed to the distant bluffs.

Turning to Sam, Jim said, "As soon as we know the trajectory of the bullet, we can begin to zero in on possible shooting sites— buildings and the tops of them, trees, shrubbery, hillsides—but we'll start with the buildings now. The trouble is, a lot of them are closed on Saturdays."

"So, does that mean we should look at buildings that have access to the roof even though they're not open or occupied?" Sam asked.

Jim turned his lips down at the thought. "That could be a possibility." Turning to Luke, he continued, "As soon as you know the angle of the shot, call me. Trajectory will determine whether the shooter was on an elevated site like the top of a building. We'll be going over in that area," he said pointing east toward the bluffs, "to look for possible shooting sites. Maybe find some witnesses who might have seen something. Just call me on my cell." He began walking toward the Suburban with Sam. They climbed in the vehicle, then sat silently. The overwhelming silence inside the cab was all-encompassing. The red and blue lights of several squad cars flashed rhythmically in the distance, reminding them of the gruesome circumstances.

Jim sagged against the seat. "Do you believe this?" he finally asked, staring out the windshield. He leaned his head on the headrest and closed his eyes briefly.

"Well, yes and no. The circumstances surrounding this shooting are totally different than the ball club murders," Sam started, thinking out loud. "But you can't deny the connection of the power company, the high lines, and Waite's property. It seems like a big ball of—something."

Jim leaned over and started the truck. "Contact DeDe and Leslie and get them working on Braxton Lewis' background. I want to know everything from the kind of coffee he drank to the size of his BVDs."

"Right, Chief," Sam said as he pulled his cell from his pocket and began texting.

☐

By noon, every available officer from the City of La Crosse and the sheriff's department were combing the buildings and neighborhood in a five-hundred-yard radius from the Scenic Rivers corporate headquarters, talking to whoever they could about possible sightings of unfamiliar people in the neighborhood.

Jim and Sam ran into one man, dressed in Carhartt jeans and a gray sweatshirt, who seemed certain about seeing a small individual hanging around an old, abandoned furniture store in the vicinity. The man's bushy hair and overgrown beard bristled from his face like a used Brillo pad, but his demeanor was friendly. He was headed to the river carrying a fishing rod and a tackle box.

"So, tell me about this person you saw," Jim began as Sam took notes. "Could you identify any facial features or distinct habits, like their walk, for instance?"

"Well, the person was small, almost feminine in their proportions. The sway of the hips seemed like a woman," he began.

Jim felt a thrum of excitement. "Yeah, I know what you're saying. Anything else?"

"Whoever it was wore a hooded sweatshirt, and it was pulled forward far enough that I couldn't see their face, plus they wore a billed cap underneath the hood." He leaned back and looked upward at the sky, remembering. "Wore a black sweatshirt, I think, and a pair of insulated camo coveralls." His eyes flicked back to Jim's face. "Sorry. That's about it."

"What time was this?" Sam asked.

"Early this morning, about six-thirty," the bushy man said.

"What were you doing over here that early?" Jim asked.

"I went over to my buddy's house for breakfast. We do that every Saturday. Then I go fishing."

Jim nodded. They took his contact information and watched him slowly continue his walk to the river.

"Well, that was something," Jim said, glancing at Sam.

Sam's face crinkled. "Yeah, something, but we've got a long way to go."

They decided to split up and meet at Jim's Suburban after an hour of searching for other potential witnesses who might have seen something.

The neighborhood reminded Jim of an anthill. It seemed like every time he looked up and down another block, a squad car rolled up and officers piled out, ready to take the search to the next level. The area was crawling with police. Jim had been combing the surrounding neighborhood, talking to anyone he saw, knocking on doors, rousting people out of their Saturday morning comfort zones, trying to find witnesses who might give them a clue about the shooter. He finally took a break and called Carol at one o'clock.

"Hi, honey. What's happening there?" he asked.

"Well, the kids are having quiet time in their rooms, and I'm straightening the house for the umpteenth time today. How're things on your end?"

"You heard about the shooting?"

"Yeah. What's up with that?"

"If you could see this place right now, you'd swear La Crosse has been invaded by guys in blue and brown. I've never seen anything like it, frankly."

"Any results?"

"Not yet. Zilch."

"What are your chances of being home for dinner?"

"Right now, with all the officers here, if we don't stir something up, I should be home about four," he explained. "But I may get called out again later if something heats up. You know the drill."

"Unfortunately, I do. Whatever happens, stay safe ... and I'm hoping you'll be home to grill steaks about six." She chuckled softly.

"Thanks. I'll call if I can't make dinner."

Jim hung up. He recognized a familiar silhouette jogging toward him, with Sam following close behind. He jumped out of the Suburban as Jamie Alberg stopped in front of him. Sam brought up the rear, panting and sweating. Jim put his hands on his hips, wondering where Jamie had come from.

"Where the hell have you been?" Jim demanded angrily, giving Jamie a parental scowl. "Your mother was at my house last night at nine-thirty worried sick about you."

"Not my problem," Jamie puffed, trying to get his air.

"Yeah, well it's not mine either, buddy, but your mom sure seems to think it is," Jim said, feeling like he was having a déjà vu moment with his teenage twins.

"Never mind that, Chief. Some officer over by the crime scene thinks they found something," Sam said.

"Where? What'd they find?" Jim asked, the tension rising in his voice.

Sam turned and began jogging south along the tree-lined street. "Come on. It's this way," he shouted over his shoulder.

The trio went down the street to the nearby corporate parking lot, which was now mostly deserted and empty. Sam trotted around the back of the Scenic Rivers office complex to a copse of thick deciduous trees with some evergreens mixed in.

Jim stopped jogging to catch his breath. "What are they looking at?" he asked Sam as he watched a number of officers clumped around a small patch of brown grass. One of the cops walked up to them.

"Don't disturb those footprints," the cop said to Sam. Jim stepped forward as another officer walked over and began explaining what they'd found. Jim and Sam followed him toward the river and walked a little way along the bank to the north. The cop stopped, pointing to a stake pushed in the ground. Jim knelt beside him.

"See right here. Someone tied up a boat. The stake's still in the ground. There's a lot of footprints. We think it may have been the shooter. Probably cruised along the shoreline in a small boat. Docked it here and tied it up. Walked into that small thicket of woods and waited for Lewis to emerge from the building. Shot him as he walked to his car." Jim met his gaze, but he had serious doubts about the officer's conclusions.

"That's a good theory," Jim said, "and the physical evidence might be an explanation of what happened, but the medical examiner might not agree with you. He thinks the shots came from across the street toward the east, over by the bluffs or possibly from the top of a building," Jim said. The officer shrugged. Jim continued. "We won't know until we get a full report from Luke Evers. But it is possible the assassin came here by boat. Good work," he said. "Until we talk to Luke again, you concentrate your efforts here. Look for the spent bullet, and we'll go back across the street. How's that sound?" Jim asked.

"Okay by me," the officer said.

The trio walked back the way they'd come. Once they were out of earshot, Jim turned to Jamie.

"You still haven't told me why you're in this neighborhood. What're you doing here anyway?" Jim asked Jamie. The irritation in his voice was matched only by the aggravation written all over his face.

Jamie met Jim's harassing comments with a cool stare. "For your information, when I heard about the shooting, I volunteered to help search. I know a lot of the city police force," Jamie said.

"And that would be because ... ?" Jim asked, his glance focusing on the taller buildings in the vicinity.

"I volunteer every year to help organize their city-wide Crime Stoppers picnic in my neighborhood. It's a great way to put a face to a uniform ... and meet some nice girls."

"Really?" Jim said, rolling his eyes at Sam. They walked a little farther.

Sam led them across the street into an industrial neighborhood where there was a wholesale steel outlet, two or three metal fabricating businesses, a carpet cleaning service, some electrical and plumbing services, and several HUD apartment houses mixed in.

"Where you goin', Sam?" Jim yelled.

"There's an old three-story abandoned furniture store over here," Sam said walking beneath the tall, bare maple trees that lined the street. "The one that guy mentioned. It might give a shooter a good vantage point of the Scenic Rivers lot."

They walked across another empty lot littered with abandoned semi-trailers. The blacktop was cracked, and potholes littered the worn-out surface like a bunch of empty eye sockets. A few dead sumacs were at the edge of the pavement. Jim turned and looked back at the office parking lot. They were at least three hundred yards away from the scene of the shooting—a long way if you're aiming to hit somebody in the chest. Jim knew in the world of long-range shooting, three hundred yards was not that far. With the current high velocity and caliber of rifles today, anything greater than 1,200 yards was considered a real long distance by the experts. A skilled deer hunter could be farther away than three hundred yards and easily kill the animal with one well-placed bullet, but even at that distance, the shooter would have to be experienced and accurate.

Sam stopped in front of a tall, deserted brick structure. The large glass windows along the front of the store had been broken out long ago and replaced with pieces of plywood that had turned gray and moldy. A steel entrance door between the windows seemed to have kept intruders out so far. The building was three stories high and had at one time churned out a line of moderately priced furniture for the average homeowner. Black letters on a faded signboard above the front door were cracked and peeling, the brick facade stained green with moss. Standing in front of the building, Jim recalled visits here with his parents when he was a kid. It was easy to see that it had been abandoned for years.

Sam disappeared around the corner of the building, and Jim and Jamie followed him. The back side had a three-story fire escape that zigzagged up the brick wall, and a metal ladder continued from the top of the fire escape to the roof of the building.

"You think the killer went to the roof to shoot?" Jim asked, wondering about Sam's assumptions as he stared upward at the fire escape.

Sam shrugged. "Don't know, but it would sure give you a good view of the parking lot where Lewis was shot. Did Luke call with the trajectory of the bullet yet?"

"No, he's probably still examining the body. But we should know pretty quick after the postmortem is completed," Jim commented.

"Well, it's worth checking out, don't you think?" Sam asked Jim, tipping his head upward, gazing toward the top of the building. "So who's going up first?"

"That would be me," Jamie said over-confidently, poking his chest with his thumb.

Jim opened his mouth to protest, but then he remembered the lecture he'd given Lydia about letting Jamie make his own decisions. He silently prayed the kid wouldn't fall off the fire escape or tumble through rotten roof boards to an early demise.

"Go for it," Jim said calmly.

"Really? You're not going to try and stop me?" Jamie asked, his eyes wide with surprise.

"Nope. You're an adult. Put on your big boy pants and go for it," Jim drawled, trying to hide a grin. Sam stared at him, then turned to Jamie.

"Listen. Be careful," Sam said, giving Jim a quick, disgusted look. "That fire escape is probably a hundred years old, and the roof boards and shingles could be rotten. Tread lightly when you get up there," he counseled.

"Aren't you coming, too?" Jamie asked, suddenly unsure of himself.

"I'll be right behind you," Sam assured him, making a cradle with his hands to boost him up onto the fire escape.

Once Jamie had started climbing, Sam turned to Jim and hissed, "Chief! What the hell are you doing? What about not letting civilians get involved in official police work? What if he falls through the roof and breaks his neck? What then?"

"Every decision has a consequence. I'm sure your parents taught you that, didn't they?" Jim asked, giving Sam a brazen stare. Jim thought of his daughter Sara probably driving into his yard right now with a renegade priest in tow. Had he taken time to really teach his kids about the consequences of their decisions? He hoped so, but when it came to his daughter, he wasn't so sure. As if reading his thoughts, Sam blew out his breath in a huff.

"Kinda like Sara running away? Like that, Chief? Seducing a priest into marriage? How are those consequences workin' out for you?" he asked, his jaw set in a determined expression.

Jim's temper immediately flared into a red-hot poker. "She's free to make her own decisions. She's an adult, after all," he said sharply, biting down hard on his back teeth. "I haven't interfered with her choices." Sam noticed the muscles rippling along his jawline.

"Right."

"What's your problem?" Jim asked gruffly, his blue eyes hot with anger.

"I don't have one." Sam paused a moment in a death stare with Jim. Finally, he said, "So—are you going to give me a lift so I can get up on this fire escape?"

Jim gripped his hands together and gave Sam a boost.

Several minutes later, while Jim paced the perimeter of the building, Sam finally leaned over the side of the roof and peered down at him.

"Chief, looks like someone was up here recently," he said, holding out a leather glove. He let go of it, and it floated down and landed at Jim's feet. He leaned over and stared at the glove. It appeared to be small, perhaps a women's size. He slipped on a pair of latex gloves and shoved it in a baggie.

"We're comin' down," Sam yelled over the side.

When Jamie and Sam were safely on the ground again, Sam described what he'd seen on the roof.

"Some of the grit from the shingles has been disturbed. Then there's that glove. That must have been left accidentally. The view of the Scenic Rivers office is perfect. The trajectory could work. Of course, Evers would have to validate that. But the killer could have easily shot Lewis from here, climbed down, hiked to a car in the immediate vicinity or that boat over by the river, and escaped from the scene undetected."

Jim grunted. "Well, let's get this glove to crime scene and get them over here to take a closer look. Other than that, there's not much to go on. No CCTV cameras that I can see."

"Chief?" Jamie interrupted.

Jim turned. "What?"

Jamie shifted uncomfortably. "I should have called you last night, but I was ... well ... occupied at the time."

Jim tried to imagine Jamie in a sexual encounter. The kid had a certain innocence that could appeal to the right kind of woman: the curly hair, his soft hazel eyes, an obvious gullibility. But Jim shook his head and gave up those thoughts as he waited for him to continue.

"I didn't go home last night because I was staked out at Terry Waite's farmhouse," he said matter-of-factly.

"What?" Jim exclaimed, his eyes popping with surprise.

"I decided to check out the activities of the professor. I hiked across the bluff before sunset, then dropped down into the valley behind his farm. There's a small rise behind his house, and I sat under the cover of a big blue spruce in my sleeping bag." Jamie stopped his narrative abruptly when he noticed Sam and Jim staring at him with gaping mouths. "Well, Lieutenant, you mentioned him as a person of interest ... and I got *interested*."

"Words fail me," Jim said softly. "And what did you observe from your hidey hole under the pine tree in your sleeping bag?" He couldn't imagine what Jamie was going to say.

"Waite had visitors—Little Hawk and Lori Lifto—and they were all drinking, laughing, and smoking cigars out on the front porch. That Lifto. She's a piece of work. Cocky and bold. Unfortunately, I was too far away from them to understand the drift of their conversation, but they all seemed to be having one hell of a time, excuse my French. Personally, I didn't understand what there was to celebrate. After all, two people they knew were dead. Now Braxton Lewis is dead, too."

Jamie stopped talking briefly. Sam and Jim remained stock-still and mute. Jamie continued.

"All I really found out is they all know each other—pretty well from the looks of it. And they seemed to be celebrating something, or they were enjoying some kind of cosmic joke."

Jim was astonished. He finally found his voice. "Jamie, if I'd have known what you were up to, I'd have kicked your butt all the way home. But seeing how it's too late for that … I guess I won't waste my time. You didn't happen to snap any photos or video with your phone, did you?"

Jamie smiled broadly. Jim had to admit the kid had a winsome personality despite his obvious quirks.

"Yeah, I did. Flipped my phone to night mode and got some good pictures and a video about a minute long. I could have taped longer, but my battery was low, and I didn't want to get caught without a way to call 911. You know, in case they noticed me and came after me." As he spoke, he whipped out his phone and began scrolling through his photos as Jim watched. He stopped suddenly and handed the phone to Jim. "I think there's about four or five shots," he said. "And the video's right there, too, although it's pretty short."

Jim grabbed the phone, and Sam sidled up to him. The pictures, though far away, were clearly the infamous trio enjoying more than just a cigar.

"Something of an esprit de corps, wouldn't you say?" Jamie asked, tipping his head, his eyebrow lifting in suspicion.

"Ya. They seem really friendly," Sam whispered. "What now, Chief?"

Jim pursed his lips, deep in thought. "Let's see the video." Jamie reached over, found the video, and handed the phone back to Jim. The video was slightly blurred but definitely revealed a friendly camaraderie among the group. After a few minutes he said, "Jamie, can you send these photos and the video to my email? You know my address?"

"Yeah, I do," Jamie said as he took his phone from Jim and began the transfer of the photos and video.

Jim pursed his lips, deep in thought. "Gotta be careful. If we spook 'em, we'll lose 'em," he said.

"On the other hand, this may be the perfect moment to call them downtown and question them separately," Sam suggested. "See if their stories line up."

Jamie interrupted. "Just remember, Chief, they'll have an attitude. If they act anything like they did last night, they're not going down easily. You know the old saying? 'We must all hang together, or most assuredly, we shall all hang separately.'"

Jim frowned. He doubted any criminal he'd ever known would have heard of the saying, let alone quote it.

"Ben Franklin, sir," Jamie clarified. "His thoughts about the signers of the Constitution."

"Whatever," Jim said with a surly tone. "Let me think on this for a minute." He glanced at his watch. "It's already three o'clock. Sam, call Paul and Leslie and DeDe. I want each one of you to contact one of the four—Waite, Lifto, Little Hawk, and Willow. Arrange for them to come to the center at four this afternoon for another interview. Put them all in separate rooms. We'll meet in my office in a half an hour to discuss our strategy."

"What are you going to do?" Sam said, whipping out his phone.

"Go back to my office and re-read the interviews we've already conducted and study those photos and the video Jamie took. We're missing something. I just don't know what it is."

Jim turned to Jamie. "Thanks for your help, Jamie. This group looks like they're in bed together, but we won't know for sure until we discover a solid motive. We'll let you know how everything comes out."

"So I'm being excused from the case?" Jamie asked plaintively. His hazel eyes searched Jim's face for a sign of hope that he wouldn't be thrown out on his ear.

"Sorry. You're out of it now," Jim said. "But thanks for your help." The finality of the words hit Jamie in the chest like a fist.

He huffed an exasperated sigh like a leaking balloon. "What a crock of shit," he said softly to himself. He turned and began walking back to his car, mumbling incoherently. Although he'd been stymied, a plan was forming in his mind.

"Don't do anything stupid, Jamie," Jim called after him.

"You better not count on that, Chief," Sam said softly in Higgins' ear, leaning in, his eyes fixed on Jamie's back. "You know how he is."

Higgins pulled away from Sam and whispered, "Yeah, don't remind me."

Jamie walked away. He waved his hand indifferently over his head and thought, *Something stupid, no. Something risky, yes.*

24

Jamie left Jim and Sam standing in front of the abandoned furniture warehouse, waiting for the crime scene crew to arrive. He crawled into his Jeep and eased his vehicle away from the curb, thinking deeply about his next decision. It was fraught with danger, but he'd been in sticky situations before, and somehow he'd always managed to escape relatively unscathed. Still, beneath all his bluster, he realized his plan could go terribly wrong.

Over the last ten days, he'd been monitoring Lori Lifto's Facebook page. Lori had friended him, and they'd exchanged a few meaningless texts after he'd commented on her ax-throwing abilities. As Jamie followed her exchanges, her posts seemed harmless enough; after all, she'd had a successful career as an army officer. But if you knew about the two murders in La Crosse, Lori left some pretty tantalizing clues about her ability to use a variety of weapons, including an ax. *And couldn't those skills be put to use in throwing ball clubs?* Jamie guessed her ego needed regular strokes, but her comments seemed to vacillate between expertise and bluster. She hinted at her participation in high-risk activities—physical surveillance that required top body conditioning, hiking and climbing, staying undercover, utilizing sharp observational skills, and tolerating changing weather conditions. To Jamie, it seemed like she *wanted* to plant the idea that she was capable of murder in her Facebook followers' minds. Was she just flirting with a dangerous idea, or was the talk of murder something she'd actually done? Jamie found it difficult to separate Lori's tantalizing tidbits from actual reality. Where did her imagination stop and her experience start? Was she trying to lure him in through her narcissistic bluff? Should he abandon his idea of forcing a confession out of her?

Jamie had been involved in other criminal cases with Lt. Higgins in the past. From those experiences, he'd learned you couldn't pigeonhole criminals in the same category as archaeologists. Archaeologists were egotistical yet practically minded, intense, and sensitive. They usually carried shovels, picks and chisels, not loaded guns, axes, or ancient ball clubs. Criminals were totally different dudes. Lots of them were stark raving nuts. *You'd have to be deranged to kill someone, wouldn't you?* Jamie thought. Messing with a criminal—a murderer—would be dangerous and might result in a very bad ending.

Before he could put his plan into action, Jamie decided to go home and reassure his mom that he was safe. There'd be hell to pay for his all-nighter under the pine tree on Waite's property. However, his mom would never know that's where he'd been. He mumbled under his breath. He loved his mom, but she was just too much sometimes— too much drama, too much anxiety, too much control—just too much of everything.

Jamie drove up the driveway to his boyhood home and parked his Jeep under the huge maple tree that towered over the front yard.

Entering the side door from the garage, he yelled into the interior of the house.

"Mom! I'm home!"

After a few moments, he heard stomping feet somewhere upstairs, and then the thumping footsteps descended the stairway. His mother, Lydia, appeared in the living room where Jamie was sprawled in the recliner, the TV remote in his hand. He flipped casually through the channels and met her inscrutable gaze with a look of indifference.

He'd put his parents through the wringer with his antics and accidents, getting sideswiped on his bike by a furniture truck, being abducted and thrown in the Mississippi River, and enduring several injuries while skiing and playing hockey. Furthermore, his hobby as a treasure hunter, which took him on excursions throughout the Upper Midwest, had produced some relationships with quirky, peculiar enthusiasts like himself. Then there were the wild nights barhopping in Cairo, Egypt. Luckily, his mom knew nothing about that. But each incident had sent his parents, particularly his mom, into a full-blown tizzy.

"Where have you been, young man?" she asked accusingly, her face rigid with tension.

"In case you hadn't figured it out, Mom, I don't need to answer to you about where I've been. Jeez, I'm twenty-one, for Pete's sake!" He could see his mom gearing up for a dramatic overreaction; her hip was cocked at a funny angle, her jaw had that familiar determined look, and her eyes blazed with irritation. Jamie gave her a cool stare, his voice calm and well-modulated. "Adulthood has arrived, in case you hadn't noticed."

Lydia took stock of her son slouching in the recliner. Letting out a theatrical sigh, she replied, "Well, if it doesn't matter where you've been, then why are you here? Like you said, you don't need to report to me anymore. So, to what do I owe the honor of your presence?" Lydia crossed her arms, waiting. Her eyebrow cocked up like a jaunty question mark.

"I live here, Mom, remember? Temporarily anyway. I'm going out of town for a few days, and I just wanted to let you know so you wouldn't worry. And *pa-lease*, don't go reporting to Lt. Higgins about my whereabouts. That's not necessary. All you do is get him riled up."

She flicked her wrist at him as if he were a pesky fly. "Fine. Go. Be happy. Explore some more damp and depressing caves ... or whatever it is that you do these days," Lydia said gruffly, fighting the panic rising in her chest.

"Okay, I will," he snapped. Then his voice softened. "But first, could you make me something to eat?"

Lydia's lips turned up at the corner ever so slightly. "Sure. Fried egg sandwich with ham and cheese?"

"Beggars can't be choosers," Jamie said, smiling, stretching out in the recliner.

☐

Little Hawk sat sulking on the couch in his cabin near Cashton, his legs crossed and his bare feet propped on the edge of the coffee table. He alternately chewed his fingernails while flashing dagger stares across the room at Lori Lifto. With her feet tucked up under a quilt, she scrolled through the text messages on her phone. As prickly as she was about her relationships, he found it surprising she had anyone to text. She must have some friends he didn't know about. Who was she texting, and what was she planning?

Lifto remained silent, her thumbs madly tapping her phone. He continued staring at her with hooded eyes, his dark hair swept away from his face in a long ponytail. Lori was a woman he wished he'd never met, but it was too late for that now. He was up to his neck in her subterfuge. Things were rapidly becoming very complicated. Higgins and that other young detective were starting to figure things out. So was he.

Little Hawk was sure that Terry Waite and Lori Lifto were complicit in the murders of Burke and Cadwallader—had probably killed them—although *he* was totally innocent. He realized the cops might not look at it that way, though, especially since the weapons had such a direct link to his famous father. After the meeting last night at Waite's farm, where the booze and cigars had flowed freely, he was shocked to hear about the money that had exchanged hands with the power company executive, Braxton Lewis. Apparently, LeMar Burke had a slush fund worth millions that was used to buy influence and power in the corporate world.

Little Hawk's blood boiled when he realized the group had hijacked his interest in his Native heritage to carry out their deadly plan. Not only that, they'd exploited his passionate belief in his people and their dignity for their own twisted ends. After all, he was the one who had introduced them to the effectiveness of the ball club. Over the years, he'd learned all about the beauty and power of ball clubs from his father. But hiding a club in Waite's cave had been a big mistake, especially when it attracted the attention of that nosy kid, Bobby Rude.

Whoever had actually thrown the ball club at the two victims was up for grabs, but Little Hawk had a crawling sensation of horror that the woman he thought he loved was the murderer and that she had been well-paid to carry out the killings. As for the man who'd been shot earlier that morning, Lifto was a trained sniper—you didn't have to be a rocket scientist to figure that one out. As far as Little Hawk was concerned, it was all damage control from here on out.

As if sensing his uneasiness and distrust, Lori looked over at him and held his stare.

"What's the matter now?" she snarled.

"Who're you texting?" Little Hawk asked quietly, lifting his chin toward her.

Her smile sent a chill up his back. Her eyes were like an iceberg, gray and cold. Her petulant glance made Little Hawk think *shark*, and his heart slipped into a faster rhythm.

"You know better than to ask a question like that. I'm not playing that game," she said, shaking her head. "I've maintained my independent lifestyle throughout our relationship. We always agreed each of us would go our own way, and I'm not changing that now. Besides, you don't tell me who you're texting, so why should I tell you? You're not getting nervous about our little business deal, are you?"

"I thought I loved you, but I'm beginning to see I was wrong. The meeting last night with Waite. How long have you been sleeping with him?"

Lori sputtered and choked, then let out a muffled chuckle. "You've got to be kidding! I don't have to sleep with a scarecrow to get what I want. There are other methods at my disposal to convince him to cooperate."

"Like what? Blackmail? Death threats? A boatload of the money?"

"Sorry. No can do," she said with a subtle smile, wagging her finger at him. "Off limits."

She rose from the recliner and came, crouching in front of Little Hawk, her tight sweater revealing the swell of her firm breasts.

"Don't be mad at me. You have just as much riding on all this as I do. We'll both have enough money to live very comfortably. We can move out West somewhere and get lost in the anonymity of a good-sized city. Besides, I've enjoyed our time together, and I can't say that about too many of the men I've dated." She leaned into him and kissed him on the mouth.

Little Hawk pulled away, then scrambled out from under her and walked out the door. He rubbed his lips, trying to get the taste off. *It's like kissing a snake*, he thought.

Lori watched him leave, her eyes slits of malice. She had plenty of problems to deal with, but she didn't want to eliminate Little Hawk yet. She needed him just a little bit longer.

□

Jamie Alberg sat in his Jeep at the south side Kwik Trip parking lot on Mormon Coulee Road, absentmindedly watching customers pump gas and walk into the store to pay. A middle-aged couple was arguing next to their car, and the woman was getting heated up. Jamie scratched his cheek, his mood pensive. He kept watching the couple. Their altercation reminded him of his parents' arguments before the divorce—the yelling and swearing, the accusations flying through the air like lead shot. His thoughts turned to Higgins and Birkstein. The looks they'd given him when he told them about the clandestine meeting were priceless, the surprise on their faces enough of an incentive to continue with his plan. He just hoped it would work out the way he anticipated.

He'd texted Lori Lifto as soon as he'd left the abandoned furniture factory, and now he was nervously waiting for her response. Although he had no solid proof, he was sure she was the mastermind behind the killings of LeMar Burke and Tanya Cadwallader—probably had killed them herself. And the shooting death of Braxton Lewis certainly had all the hallmarks of her expertise. She had the capability and the aloof mindset to plan it and carry it out. All of those surveillance tactics she'd perfected in the military had been put to good use. She'd bragged about that on Facebook, too. Bashing out someone's brains would have been a display of her athleticism and skill—something she hinted at in her posts.

His phone beeped. He looked at the text. His stomach rolled over, and he thought he might puke: "5 tonight @ Waite's cave. Come prepared for action. I can use your help. LL"

☐

The smell of charcoal wafting in the cool evening air made Father Jerome Knight's mouth water. His stomach turned over with a rumble of hunger. He carried the thick T-bone steaks to Higgins' back porch and carefully placed them on the grill over the red-hot coals. Shutting the lid, he picked up his beer and took a sip. He was still hoping Lt. Higgins would be home in time for dinner. Sara was so excited to tell him the news of their engagement she'd been acting like a lovesick teenager all afternoon.

On the drive down from the Twin Cities this afternoon, she'd chattered incessantly. "What do you think Dad will say?" The diamond on her finger sparkled in the afternoon sunlight. Without waiting for Jerome's response, she continued. "We've hardly talked in the last couple of months. What do you think?"

"I don't know your dad well enough to predict how he's going to react. He's probably still trying to wrap his head around the idea of a Catholic priest going for broke, giving up his vow of celibacy and poverty to ask his daughter to marry him." He looked over at her. "And … since I made that move, I'm now officially unemployed. I guess I'm fulfilling the poverty part of my vows. But the whole thing would probably send any red-blooded American dad into cardiac arrest."

A frown clouded Sara's forehead. "Well, thanks for the reassurance, honey," she commented sullenly, rolling her eyes. "So you're hopelessly in love, with no job prospects, and kicked out of the Church. What a reality check, huh?" Jerome could still see the disappointed expression on Sara's face.

A sudden peal of laughter from inside the house startled Jerome back to the present. He lifted the grill lid and checked on the steaks. Sara appeared at his elbow. She had dressed carefully for the big announcement—a beautiful silky blue dress with colorful embroidery at the neckline and a loosely tied sash around her small waist that hinted at a curvaceous body beneath. She wore a necklace of cultured pearls, a gift from her mom. Her outfit was accentuated with a pair of tall, brown leather boots. Her blonde glossy hair was wrapped in a casual bun at the nape of her neck, and her complexion glowed with joy. *She looks fabulous*, Jerome thought.

"How're the steaks?" she asked, giving him a quick peck on the cheek. "Carol wanted me to check."

"Just got them on the grill. It'll be another fifteen minutes at least."

"No problem. I'll just visit with Bobby and Gladys a while longer." Sara disappeared into the house again.

Truth be told, Jerome was feeling anything but confident. Higgins had a reputation around town. He had a stiff moral backbone and a sense of decency that some found repugnant in this day of anything-goes morality. People had mistakenly labeled him a dandy and a do-gooder. But beneath his friendly exterior, Jerome knew he could be steely and purposeful. His leadership at the sheriff's department had turned a group of independent and bull-headed investigators into a highly efficient team who'd solved some pretty convoluted crimes. Higgins was tough, tenacious, and intelligent. When it came to defending his sometimes-unconventional methods, his team was loyal and committed to his leadership, wading through the smoke and fire together.

How will I stack up? he thought. *I don't even have a job.*

Higgins couldn't possibly imagine how hard he'd tried to resist Sara's charms. From the first day he'd arrived at St. Ignatius Parish, she was friendly and made him feel welcome and needed. Caring and sensitive, she was an extremely effective educator. And her deep, abiding faith was another bonus. Maybe that was what had been so attractive to him in the first place. And then there was her natural physical beauty. No matter where she went, men's stares followed her.

When Sara was abducted by a lunatic drug dealer last year and held captive for several days, Jerome feared he would never see her alive again. After her rescue, Jerome spent several months counseling her back to a place of trust and faith in God while agonizing over the vows he had taken as a priest. Vows of poverty, chastity, and obedience to the Church, all the while falling more deeply in love with her than he'd ever intended. Jerome's worst fears materialized before his very eyes: he might never get another chance to live a life with the woman he loved. If that happened, he'd never forgive himself. The sincerity of his priestly vows was real, but so was the desire to write his own love story. He fought the inclination furiously. He prayed and fasted and would have whipped himself as Martin Luther once did if he thought it would keep him faithful to his promises. But in the end, he couldn't deny his overwhelming love for Sara.

How will I explain that to Higgins, he thought? He bit his lower lip as he considered the ramifications. *Well, he's a man. He's been married twice. Surely he must understand love, the desire to share your life with someone, and the sexual attraction that eventually comes in any serious relationship.*

Jerome sighed. He lifted the lid on the grill and flipped the steaks over, their tantalizing aroma filling the air. He looked off in the distance; the wooded area around the house was just beginning to awaken to signs of spring. Silently, he prayed this family would welcome him as he hoped they would. He desired Higgins' blessing, and he knew that Sara couldn't be happy without her father's approval.

25

Jim sat in his office after returning from the old furniture shop. He twisted in his chair, absentmindedly running a hand across the back of his neck as he reread the interviews with Terry Waite, Lori Lifto, and Trent Willow. In the transcripts, they'd all had a conflict with LeMar Burke's ecological philosophy. But now, in light of the recent shooting of Braxton Lewis, that seemed less important. Something else more sinister was working beneath the surface. He thought about it. *Sex, money, power? Which ones were at work here?*

Waite, in particular, was the strongest candidate as a suspect for the murders. His hatred of Burke was open and bitter, and he made no effort to hide his disdain for the man and what he represented. Willow, on the other hand, seemed anxious to placate the investigators. Jim wondered if the familiar tactic wasn't an effort at deflecting attention from his involvement in the crime. Little Hawk seemed attached to Lifto by puppet strings. Was their relationship purely sexual? Or was Lifto getting her kicks from controlling and using Little Hawk? Maybe a combination of both. Lifto left nothing to the imagination. Surly, antagonistic, egotistical, and extremely proficient in the use of axes and guns, she was a perfect candidate as the killer, but hard, physical evidence was frustratingly absent. Still, she was stupid enough to get caught throwing an ax at someone's front door and tackled by a dog in the process. If she couldn't even pull that off without a hitch, then she'd mess up again somewhere down the line.

What about Tanya Cadwallader? Obviously, she'd had some information that the group didn't want to come to light. Was she eliminated because she was a threat, or was it more complicated than that? Was she involved in the Burke murder and then gotten cold feet and wanted out? Jim leaned forward and huffed an exasperated sigh just as his phone beeped.

"Higgins."

"Jim, Luke Evers here," the coroner said crisply. "I've got a preliminary handle on the Lewis shooting. You ready?"

"Go ahead."

"He was shot from quite a distance; I'd say at least a range of three hundred to five hundred yards. The trajectory of the shot was downward at about a forty-degree angle," Luke explained.

Jim interrupted. "Like being shot from the top of a building?"

"Yeah, I'd say the physical evidence would line up with that. He was most likely shot from an elevated position of some kind. The path of the bullet had a definite downward trajectory, entering the body in the center of the chest and exiting in the lower left quadrant of the back. Whoever did it knew what they were doing. Had to have a high-powered scope. Someone with obvious training, or at the very least, an experienced marksman, so my theory about the shooter being military is still a possibility."

Jim nodded silently. Being a deer hunter, he was familiar with long-distance hunting rifles and scopes. He had a couple of them in his gun safe at home.

Luke went on. "One of the officers located the spent bullet in the grass on the edge of the parking lot. That was incredibly lucky, but we need all the luck we can get. It came from a Remington 223—a standard hunting rifle. The bullets are easy to purchase and cheap.

As for the wound itself, the bullet blew through the front outer wall of the chest and breastbone. A direct hit to the heart and exited the lower back, blasting through the kidney. Perfect aim. From there on out, it was basically over. Massive internal bleeding from a high-velocity weapon doesn't leave you with a very good chance of survival."

"That's awful," Jim said bleakly. "Anything else?"

"Nope. I just wanted to get the trajectory to you."

"Thanks, Luke."

Jim had no more than hung up when his phone buzzed again.

"Higgins," he said despondently.

"Jim, it's DeDe."

"Yes. Have you got something?"

"Yes. The weapon from the Blue Earth/Copper Moon Gallery in Eau Claire was purchased by none other than our favorite professor—Terry Waite. The guy at the gallery described him to a tee. There's no doubt it was Waite."

"Any in-store CCTV?" Jim asked.

"No, it's been erased, but he does have a signature for the purchase."

Jim's heart rate ticked up. "Go ahead," he encouraged.

"The distinct way he crosses his T's and makes his W's leaves no other conclusion. Waite purchased the club at the gallery."

"Well, that's something," Jim said.

"I thought so, sir. I'm still running down protesters who've been at the corporate office this week. Nothing conclusive yet, but I'll keep at it," DeDe finished.

"Great. Thanks," Jim said. The phone clicked off.

In the silence that followed, Jim wondered about Braxton Lewis' last thoughts. Cradling his head in his hands, he rested his elbows on his desk, thinking about Lewis. He had to have known he was dying. Although Jim had been shot a couple of times in his career, fortunately, they were not life-threatening events, but any gunshot wound was considered serious. He could only imagine the horrible panic and terror that engulfed someone when they realized they were at death's door.

Jim picked up his cell phone from his desk and scrolled until he found the photos and video that Jamie had taken while he was hiding under the pine tree on Waite's property. The drinking and callus attitude suggested they shared a level of comfort and familiarity that fired up Jim's anger and frustrations.

"Damn you all," Jim whispered at the phone, his face like flint. "I will figure this out if it's—"

"You say something, Chief?" Paul asked, standing in the doorway of Jim's office, crunching on a bag of Cheetos as he leaned casually on the frame. His dress shirt was wrinkled, and his slacks hung limply on his tall frame. Jim gave him a blank stare. "I thought I heard you talking to someone," he said, licking off a finger, "but there's no one else here."

Slamming his fist on his desk, Jim stood abruptly. Paul's eyes widened. "Lifto, Waite, and Little Hawk all know each other, contrary to their testimonies so far," he began angrily. "These photos Jamie took, specifically the video, show a level of affinity that none of them ever admitted in their interviews." He held up his phone with the screen facing Paul. "They all lied—every one of them." Jim's eyes blazed, and he pointed a finger at Paul. "We've been buffaloed like a bunch of rubes, and that ticks me off!"

"Most criminals do lie, Chief. What are you gonna do about it?" Paul asked calmly, grasping another Cheeto between his fingers, stopping midway to his mouth. He sensed Jim was about to go off the rails when Emily ducked around him and walked briskly into his office.

"Sorry to interrupt, Jim, but Mrs. Lewis is on the phone." Emily raised her eyebrows and tilted her head. When Jim looked nonplussed, she continued. "The widow of the victim this morning? She says she has important information that's for your ears only." Emily raised her eyebrows and tilted her head. "Line 1."

"Thanks. I've got it," Jim answered. He picked up his landline as Emily retreated from the office. "Mrs. Lewis. This is Lt. Jim Higgins," he said in a serious voice. "I'm so sorry about what's happened. How can I help you?"

Jim heard muffled crying on the other end. He waited, and after a few moments, Mrs. Lewis began speaking.

"It's bad enough to lose your husband in broad daylight to some kind of nut—shot to death with a high-caliber rifle—but then to find out he's been hiding things from you. Well, that's just unbelievable! We've never had any secrets. At least I didn't think we did."

The words spilled out of Mrs. Lewis like a torrential gushing stream. Jim decided not to interrupt. "I was going through our finances a couple of days ago, and I uncovered some very unpleasant information I knew nothing about. I intended to confront Braxton about it, but now he's dead."

Jim swallowed. His throat felt dry and raspy, and a visceral cramp tugged in his gut. He threw Paul a wide-eyed stare and held up his hand in a stop motion.

"And what was that, Mrs. Lewis?" Jim asked. Paul straightened up from his slouching position against the door frame, picking up on Jim's serious tone.

"Apparently, Braxton was receiving considerable sums of money from someone over the last year, which he squirreled away in a private account. He had a personal safety deposit box at a bank in Holmen filled with certificates of deposit. Why would he do that?" she asked indignantly. Jim heard the confusion and outrage through the line.

"How much money are we talking about?" Jim asked quietly, his blue eyes holding Paul's stare.

"The certificates of deposit are for about half a million dollars. The deposits were made in installments over the last year or so. All of the money is now in a separate account at the Holmen bank in Braxton's name. I thought all of our accounts were at First Federal in La Crosse," she said in a clipped, crisp voice, "but obviously I was deceived." The distraught widow had disappeared, and in her place was a very angry, betrayed wife.

"Well, you're right about one thing. That's a substantial sum," Jim said, his heartbeat quickening. He flicked his finger at Paul standing in the doorway, then covered the phone with his hand. "It's Mrs. Lewis, the widow of the shooting victim this morning," he whispered. Paul sat down in the nearest chair, his attention riveted on Jim. "Do you have any idea where he got that kind of money, Mrs. Lewis?" Jim asked.

"How would I know?" Mrs. Lewis exclaimed shrilly. "I didn't even know it existed until today."

"Are we talking about money that wasn't part of his regular salary at Scenic Rivers?" Jim asked. "Maybe he was socking away part of his salary for—"

Mrs. Lewis rudely interjected, "Bullshit, Lieutenant. You and I both know that if he had a personal safety deposit box with certificates for half a million dollars in it, he didn't want me to know about it. In the first place, I know where every penny goes in this household, right down to the money Braxton spent on his socks and underwear. He hid this from me. It's as simple as that. The question is why? Do you have any ideas about that?"

"Yes. There might be two possible scenarios that would explain it," Jim suggested. "My guess is he was being blackmailed by someone to keep quiet, or he was paid off for some kind of influence he might have had."

There was a break in the conversation that you could have driven a Mack truck through. Finally, Mrs. Lewis said, "Blackmailed? Paid off? You can't be serious."

"Yes, I'm serious."

"But why? I don't understand." Her voice quivered with emotion. Jim could imagine her tear-stained face full of disbelief, not only shocked by the murder of her husband but also by the exposure of his hidden financial dealings. But deeper than that was the trust that had always been present—a trust she thought was immutable. And now that trust was broken beyond repair with no way to fix it.

Jim said, "I'm not totally sure about all the connections yet, but I may be able to answer your questions more clearly after I talk to your lawyer. Would you release this information so we can use it in our investigation? Are you willing to do that?" Jim asked.

"Absolutely. Have at it," she said indignantly. "Go for it." She started to cry again. "Why did this happen to Braxton?" she whimpered. "What was he thinking?"

Jim took a deep breath and dove in. "Mrs. Lewis, I believe your husband was assassinated because of his involvement in some kind of cover-up at the power company. He may have been bribed into using his position to influence the board of directors to approve the construction of new high lines being proposed from Canada, or he may have been bribed to keep silent about it. I'm not sure yet. It's most likely one or the other, but right now, that's just a theory. However, with your cooperation, we may be able to identify the other participants in this deal and bring your husband's killer to justice." There was a long silence.

"I'll admit that I don't understand this, Lt. Higgins, but I will cooperate fully with your investigation. I just have one question," Mrs. Lewis said.

"Sure. Go ahead," Jim responded.

"How am I supposed to explain my husband's murder to my daughter?" And the line went dead.

☐

Lori Lifto looked around her apartment at the chaos she was leaving behind. Closet doors and cupboards had been rifled through and stood open, the contents in disarray. The bed was unmade, the dirty dishes still piled in the kitchen sink. No time to straighten it up. She had to get out. After answering Jamie Alberg's Facebook message, she came back to her place to pack some essential things she would need on her getaway out of the country. She had two loose ends to tie up before she ditched the scene—Jamie Alberg and Terry Waite. Despite her hostile intentions, she couldn't bear to hurt Little Hawk. She usually didn't care if someone was offended by her callous attitude, so it surprised her when empathetic thoughts about Little Hawk pushed their way into her brain. Maybe she was capable of love after all.

Lori stood in front of the couch and hurriedly evaluated the contents of her duffle bag. She had carefully packed it with a few pieces of essential clothing, a picture of her dad, a pair of good running shoes, her Smith & Wesson 9mm handgun, and of course, the money—lots of money all bundled together—over one hundred thousand dollars. She buried the rest of the money in a Cortech plastic mesh strong box on her dad's farm where she could get to it later when things calmed down.

She hastily zipped the bag, then stood in the quiet apartment, her mind spinning with the dangers that lay ahead. After several moments, Lori shook her head and slung the bag over her shoulder. She locked the door, descended the stairs to her car, and began the drive across town to Professor Terry Waite's farm.

26

The interviews that Jim had planned at the law enforcement center in the late afternoon on Saturday went awry. Trent Willow, according to his housekeeper, was out of town on business in Milwaukee and would not be returning to La Crosse until mid-afternoon on Monday.

No one could locate Lori Lifto. She had disappeared. When her supervisor at Kwik Trip was contacted, he admitted that she had hurriedly applied for and was granted a week's vacation. Her father did not know where she had gone and was unaware of any vacation plans she might have had.

Little Hawk showed up at the center at four-thirty. Paul talked to him. He claimed he was unaware of Lifto's plans and emphatically insisted he knew nothing about her whereabouts.

Little Hawk slumped in the chair like a pouting child, filled with dark, ambivalent feelings—torn between his love for Lori and the cognizance of her dark deeds.

"Have you talked to Lori recently?" Paul questioned.

"Yeah. I talked to her this morning," he said in a flat voice. His response aroused Paul's suspicion.

"So, what did you talk about?" Paul jabbed.

"It's none of your business, as far as I can see," Little Hawk said icily. "It's private."

Paul wondered how Little Hawk expected him to continue to believe the things he said.

"May I remind you, sir, that this is a murder investigation," Paul said. "You haven't exactly been forthcoming with information about the crimes that have been committed."

Little Hawk scooted his butt back in the chair and pushed his shoulders back. "Well, that's because I don't know anything about the murders."

Paul dipped his chin in disbelief, his eyes widening.

"That's the truth!" Little Hawk retorted. In Paul's experience as a detective, the truth could be a mighty slippery thing.

"You and Lifto are both suspects in these murders," Paul said, "so what you discuss in private is not privileged. You lost that freedom when you decided to associate with people like Lifto and Waite." Paul stayed quiet, but Little Hawk refused to budge. "So, what did you talk about this morning with Lori?" he asked again, more impatiently this time.

Little Hawk stared at the wall for several moments, then flicked his eyes to Paul. "We had an argument," he said simply.

"About what?"

"Trust."

"What's that supposed to mean?"

"I can't trust her anymore. That's all."

"Why?"

"She used me and betrayed my people for her own ends."

"How so?"

"I don't know exactly," Little Hawk said, his shoulders slumping as he leaned forward and placed his elbows on the table. "All I can tell you is I taught her how to throw the ball club. That was probably my biggest mistake." He groaned and looked briefly at the ceiling. "It's all such a big mess. I wish I'd never gotten tangled up with her."

"I need you to tell me what's going on," Paul insisted, sitting down across from him. "What you know about Lifto and Waite could help move this investigation forward to a conclusion, and what you know could be instrumental in preventing the deaths of other people." He leaned across the table and caught Little Hawk in an intense stare. "Three people are dead, and I'm sure Lori Lifto had something to do with that."

Little Hawk covered his eyes with his hand and leaned back in his chair, considering his options. He knew this moment would come— the moment when he ratted on Lifto and extricated himself from this whole disastrous mess.

Paul watched Little Hawk carefully. He seemed to be wrestling with his conscience. Paul pulled his cell phone out of his pocket, scrolled until he found the video and pictures of the meeting on Waite's front porch the night before, and reached over and gave his phone to Little Hawk.

"What's this?" Little Hawk asked warily, his dark eyes flitting back and forth from Paul to the phone. "Is this some kind of trap?"

Paul shook his head. "Nope. Just look at the pictures and video, and then tell me what you think."

As he viewed the video, Little Hawk's expression became defiant, and he grimaced. When he looked up at Paul, a resignation passed across his features. "Where'd you get this?" he asked softly.

"That's not important. What's important is what you talked about last night at Waite's place. So tell me, what were you celebrating?"

"Lori and Terry were celebrating. I was just along for the ride."

"Do you expect me to believe that?" Paul asked brusquely. His question was met with silence.

Finally, Little Hawk sighed and leaned forward. "I have no proof of this, but I believe Lori was involved in all three murders, probably did all three. But she had help. Waite was involved, too. Since she's disappeared, it's all a crock of shit, wouldn't you say?"

Paul felt lightheaded. Was Little Hawk privy to information about Lifto's whereabouts during the Burke and Cadwallader murders? He steeled himself, then asked, "Do you have any proof that she committed the crimes you mentioned?"

"No," Little Hawk blurted, "not really." His demeanor had changed from surly to a victim who'd been betrayed. "But she's been lying to me about everything else, so go figure."

"Did you help her commit the murders?"

"No! Absolutely not! Like I said, the only mistake I made was teaching her how to use a ball club." He hesitated. "That, and falling in love with her." He hung his head in shame.

"On the night of the blizzard, did you have any contact with Lori?" Paul asked. He wasn't sure where he was going with this by rehashing ground he'd already covered, but he was beginning to doubt everything the impish woman had told them during their interviews, including the fact that she swore she was working the night shift during the blizzard when LeMar Burke had been killed.

"The night of the blizzard?" Little Hawk asked as if coming out of a trance.

"Yeah, the night of the blizzard." Paul continued emphatically. "She claims she was called to work in the early evening around seven and was at the bakery until seven the next morning."

Little Hawk felt a chill spread across his chest, and his eyes widened with a sudden realization. "She didn't go to work until about midnight. She stopped at my place about eleven and left a half hour later." Then, as if anticipating Paul's next question, he asked, "So where was she until eleven?"

Paul pointed at Little Hawk's chest. "That, my friend, is the million-dollar question."

☐

Jamie Alberg lay shivering on the floor of the cave on Terry Waite's farm. He was bound hand and foot with duct tape. His stomach muscles ached where Lifto had sucker punched him, catching him off-guard. In the moments following the first punch, he endured repeated kicks and well-aimed blows to the face, chest, and stomach. Despite his valiant efforts to fight back, she manhandled him. Any chance he had of putting up a reasonable defense had been destroyed by her lightning-quick reflexes and considerable physical strength.

In the pitch-black darkness, with his feet bound and his arms taped behind his back, he continued to wiggle along the cave floor, painfully making his way toward the back entrance of the cave. It helped that he had been in the cave before when he'd explored the cavern for MVAC. Still, he felt like a lowly worm trying to escape through a maze. The low ceilings and damp floors were littered with sharp, unforgiving rocks. He still had his cell in the pocket of his jacket. His plan was to get his cell phone out of the pocket somehow so he could call Lt. Higgins for help. But that seemed to be an outlandish idea and, at the moment, comically unrealistic.

Lori and Jamie met at the cave at five o'clock. Jamie mistakenly thought he could force a confession out of Lori Lifto. Lori had shown up to meet this upstart kid, but it soon became evident he had no idea who he was dealing with. Jamie didn't get the chance to question Lifto about her involvement in the murders. The closest Lifto came to a confession was to remind Jamie he had to be eliminated because he was beginning "to put it all together." Lifto's eyes glowed eerily in the light from her cell phone. Her elongated shadow flickered on the cave walls, making her seem larger than she really was. She stared at Jamie for several minutes.

"Are you going to kill me?" he'd asked calmly, although inside he was petrified. *How did I get myself in this predicament?* he thought.

"Do you have any idea how many people I've actually killed?" she asked in a tone that sent chills down Jamie's spine. *Don't antagonize her*, he thought.

"Not a clue," Jamie commented innocently, but his heart was in his throat.

"More than you could count. And the United States government paid me to do it." Her green eyes blazed with hatred. She clenched her fist and pumped it in front of Jamie's face. As she talked, his eyes widened in alarm. "This," she swept her hand from her head to her toes, "is what you get when the army is done with you—when they've taken away your humanity and created a monster of tactical expertise and efficiency!"

"Killing is always a conscious choice, wouldn't you say?" Jamie asked, lifting his eyes to meet her gaze. "Nobody made you do it, did they?"

The slap across his face was swift and hard. Jamie groaned with pain as blood began to run from his nose and drip off his chin.

"Shut up!" Lifto shouted. "You don't have the faintest idea what I'm talking about, and I don't need you to act as my conscience. And for your information, I'm not going to kill you. I'm just going to let you die in this stupid cave all by yourself when you're only a few miles from help. Somebody will find you—or your skeleton someday. But it won't be anytime soon," Lifto spat.

□

Jamie stopped crawling and struggled to sit upright along the cave wall. He leaned against the cold rock. Sweating profusely from his efforts, he pulled his legs up and scrunched them against his chest. He could feel the phone moving inside his jacket, pressing against him—literally so close and yet so far out of reach. He kept wiggling, thinking he might dislodge it somehow, but after five minutes he gave up.

"The only way I'm going to be able to call Higgins is to get my hands free," he said softly to himself, "so I can get my phone." He felt the sharp stones along the wall and began to rub his bound wrists against them. It seemed futile, especially when he thought about how strong duct tape was, but after a half hour, he could feel the tape weakening. Finally, the tape broke when he jerked his hands downward suddenly.

With shaking fingers, he fumbled in the front pocket of his coat and retrieved his phone. Flipping it open, he quickly composed his message to Lt. Higgins and then began removing the tape from his ankles.

While Paul questioned Little Hawk, Leslie Birkstein tried to reach Professor Terry Waite to set up an interview time. His phone had repeatedly gone to voicemail. After talking to Leslie, Jim finally drove out to Terry Waite's farm. He stopped briefly in the narrow one-lane driveway and strapped his shoulder holster and pistol beneath his suit coat. He thought about his approach. Waite was a prickly character, probably a killer. Jim wasn't going to take any chances. He jerked when his phone beeped.

"Higgins."

"Jim. Paul here. We've got some more info on Lori Lifto, courtesy of Little Hawk," he said brusquely.

"Oh, yeah? Like what?" Jim asked gruffly. "Like she's flown the coop?"

"I'm not sure, but that's a strong possibility. But listen to this. Little Hawk claims Lori didn't get to work until midnight on the night of LeMar's murder. I looked back in the notes of the interview you did with her. She told you that she went to work at seven that evening. That's not true."

"I thought somebody checked on that," Jim said, feeling stupid that something so straightforward could have slipped by without a simple confirmation with a phone call to the bakery. "How'd that happen?"

"I don't know, a lotta irons in the fire, I guess, but this puts a different spin on our original assumptions. I also stopped back and talked with the gal who was manning the front desk of The BonBon during the blizzard. When I showed her a photo of Lori, she recognized her. Lifto was in the hotel in the early evening. The desk clerk thought it was around eight o'clock. If what Little Hawk says is true, then Lori Lifto is *the* prime suspect in the Burke murder." Paul explained. Jim heard some rustling of paper in the background. "And one more thing ... crime scene called. The DNA in the wine glass in Burke's room at The BonBon wasn't Terry Willow's; it was Lori Lifto's."

Jim closed his eyes and softly pounded the steering wheel with a steady beat. "For Pete's sake! How could we have missed something so simple?" he asked.

"It happens. Don't get hung up on it, Chief. We need to find Lifto. We just left the hotel, and Little Hawk and I are on our way to her apartment," Paul said. "I'm heading out to her dad's farm if we can't find her in town. Where are you?"

"I'm driving down Waite's driveway as we speak." *He's probably dead, too,* Jim thought.

"Be careful," Paul warned. "I know he's a scrawny dude, but even scrawny dudes can do stupid and desperate stuff like shooting you in the gut. Should I send Sam your way?"

"Yeah. That'd be good—the sooner the better. Talk to you later." Jim dropped his cell on the seat.

The day had flown by in a blur, and now it was six-thirty. The blue and cloudless sky was being swallowed by low inky clouds that darkened the western horizon. A cloud bank was rapidly gathering at the horizon, racing in from the west, trampling the orange and golden colors of the sunset beneath it.

Driving slowly down the one-lane gravel path, Jim gripped the steering wheel firmly. The bare trees lining Waite's driveway set him on edge, making his nerves jangle like a live electric wire. Was Lifto the murderer of all three victims? Jim could certainly imagine that, but you couldn't convict on gut feelings. Still, the evidence was mounting up. Lifto's presence at The BonBon Hotel the night of the blizzard was interesting, and the DNA gave them some much-needed solid physical evidence that Lifto had visited the victim. As far as the other victims, Jim had no doubts she had the stealth to surprise Tanya Cadwallader in the roadside toilet near Black River Falls, then slip away undetected. Furthermore, her army record testified to her shooting capability. Jim was convinced that Braxton Lewis had been eliminated with one well-placed shot—the characteristic of a confident and proficient assassin. Maybe the glove Sam found on the roof of the furniture store would be another piece of evidence that pointed to Lifto. Hard physical evidence was gelling around Lifto. Despite the cool temperatures, tiny beads of sweat broke out on Jim's forehead as he pulled up to Waite's dark farmhouse.

Stopping in the driveway, he parked the Suburban and stepped out of the vehicle. He listened to the quiet. Except for the twittering of a few birds, the silence was thick. A light breeze prickled his skin and sent a chill down his arms. He always hated these moments in policing when darkness descended, and he was alone with no backup. He didn't have a clue what he might find in the shuttered dwelling.

Jim walked slowly to the house, his footsteps crunching on the gravel. A crisp pine scent floated in the air as he mounted the stairs to the overhanging porch. He stopped briefly, his nerves grating like fingernails being dragged over the surface of a blackboard. A crow squawked loudly from a nearby tree, startling him. His footsteps echoed on the weathered floorboards of the porch. He stopped in front of the faded door and knocked loudly.

Nothing. Silence. He turned the doorknob and was surprised to find it unlocked. He stepped into the kitchen.

"Professor Waite?" he hollered loudly, flicking on the light switch. He thought he heard a groan. *Just my imagination,* he said to himself as he walked into the living room. The smell of mothballs and stagnant air wafted in the house. *Waite lived here,* Jim thought, *but he was like one of the vases on a shelf. No warmth or the feeling of a family's love existed within these walls.* Terry Waite was a man who was utterly alone in his own home.

Continuing down the hall, Jim walked into the nearby bedroom and flipped the light switch near the door. The sudden brightness made him blink. That's when he saw a shoe sticking out the side of the bed on the floor next to the wall. He walked over and looked down at Waite lying on his side next to the bed. Jim knelt down and checked for a pulse—weak and erratic. Waite seemed unable to answer his simplest questions. Jim looked for visible wounds but didn't notice any. Poison? A medical issue? Heart attack or stroke?

He didn't know.

He reached for his cell, then remembered he'd thrown it on the front seat of his vehicle. He ran out quickly to the Suburban. Standing in the darkness, Jim called 911. Once the ambulance was on its way, he returned to the bedroom. Waite was still unconscious.

Through the bedroom window, Jim noticed a Jeep approaching the farmhouse. Sam was kicking up mud along the narrow driveway. He roared to a stop by the house. Jim walked out to the kitchen and waved weakly in Sam's direction from the front porch. At that moment, his cell beeped—a text. He squinted at the phone as Sam jogged to the house and stepped on the creaking floorboards of the porch.

"What's goin' on?" Sam asked, stopping in front of him.

Jim frowned at the garbled message on his phone. "Waite's in the bedroom unconscious. I'm not really sure what's wrong with him, but I called an ambulance," he said.

The wailing of the siren reached their ears, and Sam pointed toward the highway, "Should be here in a few minutes from the sounds of it," he said.

Jim turned and opened the kitchen door. "Let's wait inside while I try to figure out this crazy text," he suggested.

"What text?" Sam asked.

"Look at it," Jim said, pushing the phone into Sam's hand. Jim leaned against the kitchen counter as Sam rapidly read the garbled text: "HLP SOS CAV AT WAIT BCK ENT JA"

"Oh, brother," Sam groaned. "I told you Jamie couldn't be trusted. What the hell did he do now?"

Jim frowned at Sam's suggestion. "You figured out the text already?" he asked.

Sam looked up at Jim, then back to the phone. "JA? That's gotta be Jamie Alberg. SOS? That's the universal code for help, isn't it? If I'm right, then Jamie is in some kind of trouble." He glanced at Jim, who was looking over Sam's shoulder at the cell phone screen. "He must be in Waite's cave. BCK ENT? I don't have a clue what that means."

"What's next?" Jim said as he rolled his eyes and shook his head. "This is probably another pathetic attempt to get our attention." Red flashing lights blazed through the skeletal trees lining the driveway. Jim glanced out the kitchen window as the ambulance approached the farmhouse. It rolled up and two EMTs hopped out.

"Let's take care of Waite, and then we'll deal with Jamie," Jim said.

"Jamie's been actively involved in the case despite our attempts to discourage him. Maybe Lifto got to him?" Sam suggested, his brows arching over his hazel eyes. "Lifto's the one who's been whacking the victims, Chief. I'm convinced of it."

"Well, so far, the evidence is scarce," Jim snarled. "The crew this morning didn't find the club that had been stored in the cave. Seems to have disappeared. So now we have another club floating around somewhere. What else is going to happen before this is all over?" he asked, his voice gritty and rough. His eyes were bloodshot, and he was beginning to feel exhaustion seeping in at the edges of his consciousness.

Jim stepped back out on the porch and waved the EMTs inside.

"He's in the bedroom," Jim said over his shoulder as he led the way into the home. While the crew prepared Waite for a trip to the hospital, Jim and Sam wondered about the message.

"Why would Jamie be at Waite's cave?" Jim asked.

"No idea," Sam said, scrunching up his face in thought. "But when he left the old furniture store, he was angry because we called him off the case. Maybe he rendezvoused with Lifto somewhere. Kinda stupid, but Jamie doesn't have a big reservoir of common sense." His face darkened. "If Jamie's with Lifto, he's in a world of hurt. He has no idea who he's dealing with. Her skills in reconnaissance and hand-to-hand combat reduce his chances of survival to just about zero."

While they were standing in the kitchen, a cell phone rang. The ring was muffled, and Sam and Jim began scouring the kitchen, opening cupboards and drawers, trying to find the phone. Eventually, Jim noticed a kitchen drawer that was open a crack. The ringing continued. Jim pulled the drawer open. The ringing stopped just as Jim grabbed the phone, which was muffled by some kitchen towels.

Sam crowded next to Jim.

"Waite's phone," Sam said. "Let me have it," he said as he took the phone and cradled it in his hands. He played around with it, punching apps. Jim watched in frustration.

"Find anything?" he asked.

"It's just a wild hair, but I'm going to check and see if he recorded any phone calls. Finding this phone in a kitchen drawer seems like an evasive move. Who keeps their phone in a place like that?"

Jim waited, the tension mounting.

Sam stiffened. "There's one here from this morning at 11:28." He thumbed an app and waited.

"I need my money," a female voice said in a quiet but threatening tone.

"I paid you for what you did. Mission accomplished. Isn't that what they say in the military?"

"You wanted your problem solved. I solved it," the female said.

"This one wasn't something I told you to do. That's on you, not me." Jim and Sam recognized the voices of Terry Waite and Lori Lifto. Waite continued. "I suggest you get out of the area as soon as possible and don't contact me again. Our business dealings are over."

The call ended abruptly.

Jim looked at Sam. "That's it, Sam. Waite and Lifto. Proof of collusion and murder for hire. It's there." Jim slipped the phone inside his jacket.

"Sounds like it. Speaking of murder, we better try and find Jamie, don't you think, Chief?"

"That kid is a cop's worst nightmare," Jim complained. "Come on, let's do this."

Jim stepped off the porch and walked to the Suburban. His mind was swirling with the ramifications of the recorded conversation. He stopped suddenly and turned toward Sam. "Lifto must have come over here after the phone call. Waite had enough sense to hide his phone before she came in the house. Most likely an argument took place, and something happened to Waite."

"Could be," Sam commented.

"You know where this cave is on the property?" Jim asked, sitting on the tailgate of the Suburban to change his shoes. Despite Jim's conflicts with Jamie in the past, he had a soft spot for the kid. After all, Jamie *had* given them some valuable information. He just hoped they wouldn't find him dead or seriously injured inside the cave. The thought prompted him to rummage in the rear of the Suburban and retrieve his first aid kit.

Sam looked past the garage to a wide meadow beyond, the darkness of the evening rapidly closing in. "I talked to Mike Leland this afternoon after they finished up the search when we were called to the Lewis murder. He described where the cave was on the property. It'll be tough in the dark, but I think I can find it," he said. "Let me get my flashlight out of the Jeep."

When Sam was ready, they walked down the driveway, opened the gate to the meadow, and began hiking across the open field. There was still just enough ambient light to make out the physical features of the land around them. After fifteen minutes, Sam stopped abruptly. He looked around, getting his bearings.

"We're close. I think it's this way," he said, pointing toward the south. "Come on."

Jim followed him through thick brown grass until Sam stopped again. His eyes scanned the landscape, searching for the slight rise in the land where the obscure entrance of the cave was located.

"Over here," Sam said confidently. But before they could arrive at the cave, Jamie appeared out of the shadows, limping and holding his side. Jim and Sam rushed toward him. When they reached him, Jamie collapsed on the ground, groaning.

"Jamie! What happened?" Jim asked, kneeling beside him.

The young archaeologist looked confused. "Lt. Higgins," he whispered. "Lifto beat the crap out of me."

"I can see that," Jim said, noticing the dried blood around Jamie's nose and the purple bruises that were darkening his face. "Where is she?"

"In hell for all I know," Jamie snapped, coming to life.

"That's not much help," Sam interjected. "Where is she now? Do you know?"

"No idea. She left me for dead. Said she hoped I'd die in the cave. What a witch!" Jamie spat angrily.

"Okay, let's get you up and back to the farm. We'll take you to emergency and put out an APB on Lifto," Jim said. Jamie grasped Jim's arm firmly. While they retraced their steps back to the vehicles, Jamie filled them in.

"She admitted killing lots of people over in Afghanistan, but she didn't actually admit killing Burke or Cadwallader or Lewis," Jamie said. "But she had opportunity, and she's certainly skilled in hand-to-hand combat." He rubbed his stomach gingerly. "I think she broke a couple of my ribs."

"Yeah, we can see you're hurtin', buddy," Sam said sympathetically.

Limping Jamie back to the farm, they laid him in the back seat of the Suburban. Jim called Gundersen Lutheran Hospital on the drive into La Crosse while Sam followed him in his Jeep. In less than ten minutes, they rolled up to the hospital's ER entrance. Two nurses appeared with a wheelchair and loaded Jamie into it. Jim and Sam looked on.

"You gonna call Lydia?" Sam asked.

"Do I have to?" Jim grumped.

"Yeah. You have to."

"Well, we sure didn't learn anything new about Lifto from Jamie—nothing we didn't already know."

"That is true," Sam said, tapping Jim's arm. "The phone call, Chief."

Jim made a wry face and pulled out his phone. "Yeah, I'm on it."

Once Lydia Alberg arrived, Jim and Sam checked on Terry Waite's condition.

"Are you family?" Dr. Larkin asked, "Because if you're not ..."

"Police," Jim said curtly, producing his ID. "Lt. Jim Higgins, La Crosse Sheriff's Department." Pointing to Sam, he continued, "Sam Birkstein, one of my associate detectives. We believe Mr. Waite is involved in a series of murders that have taken place in the area over the last few weeks."

Dr. Larkin's eyes widened. "Really? You mean those club murders?"

"Yes," Jim said brusquely. "What's his condition at the moment?"

"Well, let me tell you what we know so far," Dr. Larkin began. "Mr. Waite had a drug called Rompun in his system. Rompun is frequently used as a filler agent in cocaine or heroin. It's a tranquilizer typically used by vets to treat horses. It immobilizes the animal so they can perform surgical procedures. Fortunately, Waite didn't overdose, but his vitals were all over the board when he arrived. We can't really give him anything to counteract it. Over time the kidneys will remove the drug from the system, and he'll wake up, although he could have some permanent neurological damage and kidney dysfunction. At this point, all we can do is monitor his vitals and let nature take its course," Dr. Larkin reported. "He's not outta the woods yet."

"I need regular updates about Mr. Waite's condition," Jim said, pointing at the doctor's chest, his blue eyes intense. Dr. Larkin backed up a couple of steps. Listening carefully, the physician noticed the disheveled, expensive clothing, the harried expression, the fiery blue eyes rimmed in dark shadows. "He has crucial information about a suspect we believe has committed the murders. So at the first sign of consciousness, I need a phone call."

Dr. Larkin nodded. "Sure, I can do that. I'll inform the nursing staff of the situation," he promised, his eyes wide with concern.

"Good. And don't let him leave the hospital until we've talked to him," Sam instructed tersely as they turned to leave. "We'll post an officer at the door."

☐

Carol collapsed on the couch, her cell phone to her ear. She was bone tired. Although Sara had put on a happy face at the engagement dinner, beneath her lovely features was a sadness that broke Carol's heart. Another family event missed. Another crack in the troubled relationship between Jim and his daughter. Carol listened to the ringtone and hoped Jim would answer.

"Carol? Everything okay?" Jim answered on the third ring.

Carol could hear the weariness in his voice and his growing frustration about the unsolved murders. By now, it was almost nine in the evening, and she wondered when he would be home.

"Not the right question, honey," she commented. "Things might look all right on the outside, but somehow I think there's a price to be paid."

Despite his weariness, Jim tried to be reasonable, but the attempt crashed like a deflated balloon. "I can imagine. I'll be in the doghouse for months. I'm sorry—things just didn't work out," he sputtered weakly. He briefly explained finding Terry Waite unconscious in his farmhouse, the surprise recorded conversation on the cell phone, Jamie Alberg wandering around in a dazed state, and Lori Lifto's disappearance.

The silence grew when Carol didn't respond.

Finally, Jim asked, "So ... how *did* the dinner go?"

"Sara put on a happy face, but she was disappointed that you weren't here."

"I'm sorry I didn't get home, but I was swamped with this situation, and things spiraled out of control," Jim explained. "They'll still be here tomorrow, right?"

"Yes, although they may leave in the morning." Carol chewed at her fingernail, waiting for Jim's answer.

"We're still checking out a few things in West Salem but ... I'll be home in a while."

"I'll see you then," Carol said, and the phone went dead. She nestled under the afghan and turned down the TV. Soon, despite her attempts to stay awake, the day caught up with her, and she fell asleep.

27

Jim and Sam left the hospital and wheeled into the McDonald's on Losey Boulevard, where they grabbed a couple of burgers and coffees. Sam called Paul.

"We decided to head up to West Salem and talk to Lori's dad," Sam explained to Paul, "to see if he has any idea where she might have gone."

"Good luck with that," Paul said. "She's left her apartment in a shambles—apparently, she packed up in a hurry. I think our number one suspect is gone. I'm almost to her dad's farm right now."

"What about Little Hawk?" Sam asked.

"He said he was going back home. He's pretty sure Lori is on the run, possibly headed for Canada where she can get lost and survive until things calm down here."

"She know anybody there?"

"I have no idea, although Little Hawk says she texts with a number of her army buddies regularly," Paul said.

During the conversation, Jim chomped hungrily on a burger and mulled over the situation staring them in the face. He briefly thought about Sara's engagement party but decided he didn't have time to think about it now. He tapped Sam's arm.

"Ask Paul what the girls found out about the finances at the power company," he said.

Sam switched the phone to speaker and laid it between them on the seat. "What about the finances at the power company?" Sam asked.

"The girls are still digging into that as we speak, but they think Lewis was paid handsomely out of LeMar's slush fund to influence the board into approving the construction of the high lines from Canada. DeDe interviewed a number of the board members who confirmed Burke's visits to the facility. He also spoke at least once to the entire board to give his assessment of the economic impact the high lines would have on the La Crosse business community. Apparently, he was a very persuasive speaker. Shortly after his visit, the board approved the project." Paul explained. "The girls are going to get together with Mrs. Lewis' lawyer sometime tomorrow to investigate Braxton's account at the Holmen bank.

"What about the protesters?" Jim asked.

"Not much new there—at least nothing we didn't know before. No one is standing out from the crowd. DeDe hasn't been able to find any specific threats against Lewis from the protest crowd."

Jim interrupted. "So it looks like Lori is still our main suspect. You agree with that, Paul?"

"From the evidence we've uncovered today, I'd say she's the one," Paul said. "But who paid her to do the jobs?"

Sam smiled. Then he told Paul about finding the recorded conversation on Waite's phone.

"We're pretty sure that Waite paid Lifto to take out Burke and Cadwallader, although his conversation could be interpreted differently depending on what lawyer he hires. One thing we did learn—Lifto acted alone in killing Braxton Lewis.

"Well, we're finally getting somewhere," Paul said. "By the way, the boots that were found in Waite's trunk had some pine pitch residue on them and some grains of sand in the seams, but it'll be hard to prove they came from any of the murder locations. Although it's not out of the question that the stuff on the shoes *could* be from the Black River killing, it'll take more testing, including soil samples of the area. Crime scene techs in Black River are still working on it."

Sam coasted to a stop at a light in Onalaska. "We're on I-90 heading to West Salem. We'll be at the farm in twenty minutes," Sam said.

It was dark now. Jim was thinking about the evidence they'd discovered, but his instincts told him they were too late. From all indications, it looked like Lifto had already gotten out, headed for someplace unknown.

"Do you think Lifto's gone, Chief?" Sam asked as if reading Jim's thoughts.

"Probably. She'd be stupid to hang around here. Although when she buried the ax in your door, she proved she's impulsive and dangerous, so who knows? She might still be around. The APB is out, so hopefully she won't get too far."

"She's pretty sharp," Sam said. "Her dad might be helping her. He's our last hope of tracking her down."

Sam pulled over and punched in Harlan Lifto's address in the GPS. They drove in silence to West Salem. Sam woodenly followed the automated directions until they arrived at Bluff Sky Road. Turning left, he drove down a driveway lined with evergreens to a classic foursquare farmhouse complete with gables and a wide front porch. Paul's Ford pickup was parked in the driveway. Sam pulled up behind the truck. Farther down the driveway near the barn, Lori's VW Passat sat in the shadows.

Light blazed from a single room toward the front of the house. The stark beam shone eerily from the window into the dark farmyard. Jim thought it looked like an Edward Hopper painting. Jim noticed someone walk to the window and briefly look out when Sam drove into the yard. Sam and Jim waited inside the Jeep until Paul appeared on the front porch. He walked wearily toward the truck. Rolling down the passenger window, Jim said, "She's gone, isn't she?"

Paul's face was etched with worry. His shoulders heaved as he sighed, and he ran a hand across his chin. He was tired, and his old leg wound ached like an infected tooth. "Her car is here, but her dad says he doesn't know where she is, but we shouldn't leave here without a thorough search."

"Did he consent to a search of his property?" Jim asked, staring straight ahead.

"No, not unless we have a warrant," Paul answered.

"We don't need one!" Jim snarled, throwing the door open. "Lori Lifto is a major suspect in three murders. When we find her, we're going to arrest her. I'll talk to Mr. Lifto. We're searching the premises whether he likes it or not." He stepped out of the truck and looked at Sam and back to Paul. "Get your vests on," he ordered brusquely. "This bullshit stops right now. I'll be back in a minute."

Jim opened the truck door and jogged to the front porch, knocked, and let himself in. He was back in a couple of minutes. He started spitting orders.

"There are two outbuildings in addition to the house, according to Mr. Lifto—a barn and an abandoned chicken coop," Jim said. "Sam and I will do a quick once-over of the house." He pointed toward the shadow of the barn. "Paul, you stand watch out here 'til we're done in the house. Then we'll check out the barn, and you can check out the chicken coop. Remember Lifto and her surveillance training— and her penchant for drama." Jim struggled into his Kevlar vest and strapped on his shoulder holster and gun.

Sam followed Jim up the stairs of the front porch. They went into the house and were gone for about fifteen minutes. Finding nothing, they came back outside and stood in the driveway, fidgety and nervous. Apprehending a dangerous fugitive filled them all with anxiety. Sam chewed nervously on his lower lip. Jim thought of Carol and the kids at home sleeping peacefully in their beds. Paul remained silent and serious. The night was like velvet, thick with soft, hushed sounds. As the men stood in the driveway, a full moon emerged from behind a cloud bank and illuminated the farmstead with pale light. Suddenly, the kitchen light went out like a candle extinguished by the wind. The darkness of the home filled Jim with a sudden dread.

"We've done this before, Chief," Paul said quietly, but his face was like a frozen mask. "We know what we're doing."

"Yeah, I know," Jim said. "It's also gone wrong before, too, but I don't need to remind you of that, do I?" Paul shook his head and remembered another shootout near Avalanche, where he almost lost his life.

"Okay? Are we ready?" Jim asked.

"Let's go," Sam said, walking slowly and cautiously toward the barn. A security light next to the garage illuminated the south side of the house but left the outbuildings in dark shadow. Jim flicked on a flashlight. A slight breeze blew through the towering pines that bordered the driveway, and the gentle swish of pine needles accompanied their footsteps. The air was saturated with humidity. Jim wondered if a storm was brewing.

"Slow. Careful," he warned Sam when he opened the barn door. Jim watched Paul continue down the driveway toward the chicken coop.

Jim and Sam entered the barn and stood in the darkness of the vacant building for a few seconds listening for sounds. Gradually their eyes adjusted to the dark, and they began to make out the features of the old structure. The barn, in its former glory years, had been the place where a small herd of cows had come in to be milked each morning and evening. A wide cement aisle went down the middle of the barn and was bordered on each side by about fifteen stanchions. In front of the stanchions on each side was a feeding trough for grain and hay. A wide sliding double door at the end of the barn was closed tightly. Despite the years the barn had been uninhabited, the smells of manure and hay lingered in the air. Jim touched Sam's arm and pointed.

"Move slowly. Don't turn on your flashlight unless you absolutely have to. You go right, I'll go left," he whispered in his ear. "Meet you at the end by the double doors."

They crept along the walls in front of the feed aisles, stopping frequently to listen. As Jim's eyes adjusted to the darkness, he realized the moonlight through the barn windows provided just enough light so he could see Sam creeping along the other side of the barn's interior. They were almost to the end of the building when Jim heard a creak. He stopped, his heart in his throat. The idea that Lori Lifto might be waiting to lob a ball club or ax at them filled him with apprehension. At that moment, he was thankful for the darkness. His mouth was dry, and blood pulsed in his ears like a bass drum. After a few moments, he made a decision.

"We know you're here, Lori," he said loudly. "Come out and surrender. No one will get hurt."

Silence. He noticed a cobweb in the moonlight framed in a window.

Sam had stopped halfway along the barn wall. A ladder attached to the wall led to the hayloft above. Sam flicked on his cell flashlight for a second and made a gesture toward the loft, like, *I'm going up.* Jim nodded. Sam quickly turned the flashlight off again.

Jim strained to hear what Sam was doing. He heard the ladder creak softly, but he didn't know if it was his imagination or if it was real. He grimaced with frustration. After a few moments of painful silence, mayhem of some sort erupted upstairs, filled with grunts, scuffles, and thumps. Sam suddenly let out a howl, and another body tumbled through the hole in the floor of the loft with Sam right behind. They both landed with a thud in the cement feed trough.

Jim flipped on his flashlight, jumped over the gutter, ran across the aisle, and rushed up to Sam, aiming the flashlight at the bodies on the floor. Sam groaned and rolled on his side.

"Oh, Jesus. I think I broke my arm!" Sam groaned. The other body remained strangely silent, laying in the alley like a feed sack. Sam rolled toward Jim and came face-to-face with Lori Lifto. She'd been struck in the back of the head with something. Jim stared in disbelief at the massive wound. There was no second guessing—Lori Lifto was dead. *Another ball club?* Then another thought: *Whoever did it must still be in the hayloft.*

Kneeling next to Sam, Jim whispered, "Stay here. Don't try to get up, and don't go anywhere. I'm going to get whoever did this. They're still in the hayloft." Jim turned to the ladder and put his foot on the first rung.

"No! Wait!" Sam whispered hoarsely. "Before you go, get my phone out of my pocket." He gingerly sat up against the wall, his face tight with pain. Lifto's limp body lay in a heap where she'd landed, her head wound leaving a pool of blood on the cement floor. Jim dug around in Sam's jacket and found his phone. Sam took it and began texting. "I'll get Paul up here," he said.

"Yeah. I'll need all the help I can get," Jim said. "I'm going up." He turned and began climbing the ladder.

The hayloft was dark and cool, and a dusty smell permeated the air. When Jim was eye-level with the floor, he stopped, then looked and listened. What he'd expected was true; the hayloft was quiet, dark, and foreboding, but he could make out the structure of the barn roof above. He crawled through the hayloft opening in the floor and sprawled flat on his belly in some loose hay chaff, making himself less of a target. More listening. Still nothing moved. He heard his quick, raspy breathing and willed his heart to slow down. He got quietly to his knees, then stood next to the hole in the floor with his back toward the outer wall. Jim looked down and saw Sam scrolling on his phone, the blue screen lighting up his tense face. His thumbs flew over the keys. The light coming up through the hole below illuminated a switch next to the ladder on the wall in the loft. Jim thought for a moment and then made a quick decision.

"There's no way out of here except down this ladder," he said in a firm, determined voice, "and you're not getting past me." He carefully withdrew his pistol from the holster under his jacket. "So if you're planning on coming out of this alive, step forward. This needs to end now. I'm turning the light on."

Jim flicked on the switch. The brightness of the single bulb over the ladder made Jim squint uncomfortably; however, the corners of the barn remained in darkness. *Great*, he thought. *Now the killer can just finish me off, climb down the ladder, and escape.* Then he thought about Paul somewhere outside the barn. *Maybe not.*

From a far dark corner of the barn, Jim heard the soft thud of approaching footsteps. A figure moved slowly toward the pool of light. Jim could barely make out the silhouette in the gloom, but from the physicality and proportions of the person, he was sure it was Little Hawk. He waited. The person walked with stealth, the footsteps swishing through the loose hay. Little Hawk stepped into the light. He stopped ten feet in front of Jim. His dark eyes were moist with tears. His arms hung at his sides. Jim had seen a lot of angry, defeated criminals in his day, but he couldn't remember ever seeing one filled with such childlike regret.

"What's going on, Little Hawk?" Jim asked softly. "Why Lori? Why now?"

As he talked, Little Hawk's voice cracked with emotion. "I didn't want to kill her, but she would have killed Sam if I hadn't stopped her," Little Hawk said. He hung his head for a long moment. Jim waited. He was sure there was more to come. Little Hawk lifted his head and gazed into Jim's eyes.

"What went wrong, Lt. Higgins? When I first met Lori, she was so exciting. I'd never met anyone like her before. She was so confident, good at almost everything she put her mind to. We connected on a physical level, and then later found out we shared a lot of other interests."

"Did you teach her how to use the club?" Jim asked, interrupting Little Hawk's reverie.

Little Hawk shook his head silently. "Yeah, and the ax, but I didn't know that the whole friendship with me was orchestrated by Lori and Waite from the beginning. They were going to frame me if anything went wrong. I just didn't realize Lori was playing me all along. I thought she really loved me. I was so stupid."

"You're not the first one to be taken in by the beauty of a woman. Unfortunately, Lori was also a ruthless killer," Jim said. They stood looking at each other for a moment.

"What now, Lieutenant?" Little Hawk finally asked. "What happens now?"

In the distance, Jim heard the wail of a police siren. Down on the floor of the barn, Jim could see Paul kneeling next to Sam, talking to him quietly. He looked up and Jim caught his eye. "We're okay," Jim said. "We're coming down."

Turning back to Little Hawk, he said, "I'm taking you into custody for the murder of Lori Lifto. After you, sir," Jim said, flicking his wrist at the opening. Then he hesitated and held up his hand. "One more thing," he said. "How did you manage to hit Lori with the ball club when the barn was dark?"

Little Hawk smiled sadly. "I was waiting up here for quite a while. I parked my truck off the road about a quarter mile away and hiked to the barn through the woods in back. I guess my eyes must have adjusted to the dark, I guess. The dark isn't always as dark as you think it is." He turned and climbed down the hayloft stairs. Jim followed closely behind. When they reached the bottom, the West Salem police had arrived.

After several moments of explanation, Little Hawk was read his rights, handcuffed, and loaded into a squad car. Sam walked gingerly to the Jeep, holding his injured arm, and got in the passenger side while Jim situated himself behind the wheel. Paul leaned on the door frame talking through the open window. The CSI van from the La Crosse Sheriff's Department rolled quietly down the driveway.

"So what happened up there, Sam?" Jim asked.

"When I stood up, I heard someone rushing me. Then Lori suddenly fell against me all limp, and I tumbled down the hole with her and hit the floor."

Jim said, "Little Hawk was waiting up there. He must have known she was leaving the country and would come to say goodbye to her dad. I guess Lori wasn't as good at reconnaissance as we thought. The ball club is still lying on the floor of the loft. Tell the tech crew when they get here, Paul."

"Right. You taking Sam to the hospital?" Paul asked.

"Yep. He needs to be checked out," Jim replied.

"Want help?" Paul asked.

"Nope. Stay here and get the crime scene crew started. After that, go down to the center and file the charges on Little Hawk. We'll question him tomorrow. Then go home. While Sam's getting checked out, I'm going to pay a visit to Terry Waite."

Jim arrived at the ER in La Crosse a half hour later and helped Sam into the hospital. Then he went in search of the professor. Taking the elevator to the third floor, he wandered wearily down the hall to Waite's room, greeting the police officer stationed at the door.

The hospital room's lighting was dimmed, and the door was propped open slightly. Jim tapped quietly on the door and went in. Terry Waite lay sleeping in a standard-issue hospital gown under a light blanket. He looked more frail than Jim had remembered. Waite's eyes fluttered beneath his eyelids like he was having a bad dream. For all Jim knew, he probably was having some kind of nightmare. This whole affair had certainly caused Jim some sleepless nights.

Jim spoke his name softly. "Professor Waite? Professor Waite?"

After a moment, Waite's eyes slowly opened. He looked at Jim and closed them again. "What do you want this time?" he asked bitterly.

"Lori Lifto is dead," Jim said. There was a significant stretch of silence.

Waite finally opened his eyes and looked at Jim. A shadow of a grin appeared, then faded. "That's too bad, but she got what she deserved."

Jim's face hardened, and the muscles in his jaw rippled as he fought to control his anger. "What gives you the right to judge her, especially since you hired her to kill Burke and Cadwallader?" Jim said contemptuously.

"You have no proof of that, Lieutenant," Waite said. This time the cold smile froze on his lips and stayed there.

Jim fumbled in his pocket and pulled out Waite's phone. The professor watched, his eyes full of suspicion. The smile disappeared. Jim found the recording on the cell phone and began to play it. As Lifto's and Waite's voices filled the small hospital room, the professor turned a paler shade of white.

"Where did you find that?" Waite snapped, his senses coming alive. He grabbed at the phone, but Jim pulled it away from his reach. "How did you get my phone?" Waite pushed the button on the bed control and raised himself to a sitting position.

Jim stepped a few feet back and began his explanation. "After I found you unconscious and while you were being loaded into the ambulance, a phone rang. We hunted until we found it. For some odd reason, it was hidden in a kitchen drawer. Sam discovered the conversation you had with Lori earlier this morning. Apparently, you inadvertently recorded your argument with her. A technological faux pas," Jim said holding up the phone. "It's all here."

Waite's face darkened with anger. "I was under duress!" he spat, his angry words filling the hospital room. "Lori was threatening to kill me if I didn't pay her for shooting Braxton Lewis, but I had nothing to do with that. That's all on her. I had no idea she was going to eliminate him."

"But you planned and hired her to execute the murders of two people you disagreed with politically and environmentally. Isn't that correct?" Jim asked, staring at Waite.

"I refuse to answer without my lawyer present," Waite said piously, tipping his nose to the ceiling.

Jim sighed. His shoulder ached, and his stomach growled noisily with hunger pangs. He just wanted to get this over with and go home to his family. "What happened this morning?" he asked wearily. Jim waited. When he was about to give up, the professor began to talk. Unobtrusively, Jim began recording the conversation on Waite's phone.

"After our conversation this morning, Lifto showed up at my place about noon." The professor seemed to be resigned now to some form of truth-telling since the paid-for-hire killings were out in the open. With the discovery of the taped phone conversation, his acrimonious attitude softened. His shoulders slumped in resignation, and he leaned back and rested his head on the pillow as he talked. Jim sensed he was ready to come clean.

"I want to be done with this whole disastrous affair. Nothing turned out as I planned. I only hired Lori to shake up Burke—threaten him a little—but she got carried away. Her and that stupid Indian of hers. What possessed her to use that ball club is beyond me. Then Cadwallader contacted me and tried to blackmail me about what she knew about Burke and his offer on my land. I made the mistake of telling Lori about my conversation with Cadwallader, and she took the law into her own hands—again."

In the silence that followed, Waite picked at the corner of the sheet. Jim wasn't sure about Waite's version of the Cadwallader murder. He wasn't convinced that Waite hadn't killed Cadwallader himself, but the account of Lori's threat getting out of hand with LeMar Burke seemed to fit with what he knew about her disposition and training.

"So what happened today?" Jim asked. Waite looked up at Jim as if coming out of a trance.

"When Lifto arrived at my place, we had a shouting match. I made the mistake of turning my back on her, and she stabbed me with the needle and injected me with something that made me very dizzy. She must have thrown my phone in a drawer to prevent me from calling for help. As soon as she injected me, she took off. It didn't take effect immediately, but within a few minutes, I staggered back to my bedroom to lie down. I must have passed out and fallen on the floor."

"Yes, that's where I found you when I came to the farm at about six o'clock this evening," Jim said. "You're lucky to be alive. Of course, your luck ended when you recovered from the Rompun. Now you'll be facing a long prison sentence for the contract killings of LeMar Burke and Tanya Cadwallader. Professor Waite, you have the right to remain silent ..."

28

After the formal arrest of Professor Terry Waite was complete and a police officer was secured at the door, Jim called Leslie to the hospital where Sam was having his broken wrist set in a cast. Then he stumbled out to the parking lot and began the drive home to Chipmunk Coulee Road in a fog—a literal one. The cool April evening had given way to a thick, murky mist that settled along the curving roads of the valley where Jim lived. The drive took longer than usual, and Jim used the time to review the twists and surprises of the mysterious ball club killings.

As he turned in his driveway, he realized it would be weeks, if not months, before they could put together all the physical and forensic evidence that would send Terry Waite to prison for a long time. Lori Lifto had paid for her evil doings with her own life. That she was killed by the man who claimed to love her didn't surprise Jim. Possessive, jealous love was often the motive behind murderous intentions. *Vengeance and justice are mine, saith the Lord*, Jim thought. *Don't tread on God's territory.*

Walking into the laundry room, Jim sat on the bench and removed his shoes, hung up his coat, and walked through the dining room to the kitchen in his stocking feet. He took out a frying pan, found some eggs in the refrigerator, whisked them into a froth, and dumped them in a pan. He put bread in the toaster and found a beer in the fridge. He'd just popped the top off the can when Carol appeared in the kitchen in her robe.

"Hey," she said quietly. She walked over and wrapped her arms around him and held him.

"Hey yourself," he said, feeling the warmth of her against his chest. Dealing with miscreants of all kinds made the reality of normal life so precious. He felt a swell of gratitude in his chest.

She pulled back and leaned against the counter as Jim dumped his scrambled eggs on a plate and buttered his toast.

"Come and sit down so I can tell you what happened," he said, walking into the dining room. He plopped his plate on the table, sat down, and began wolfing down his eggs and toast.

"Beer and eggs?" Carol said looking over his plate, her eyebrows raised in distaste.

"Works for me," Jim said tersely. Carol tipped her head slightly.

"So tell me what's been going on," she said.

Jim began relating his account of the day's events. As he retold it, he felt himself relaxing, unwinding from the tension of the day. In a few minutes, a yawn crept across his face, his eyes began to droop, and Carol took his hand. She led him to the bedroom. He unbuttoned his shirt and took off his pants, then fell into bed, rolled over, and was asleep in an instant.

29

SUNDAY AFTERNOON

Jim had come to the conclusion early in his career that investigating violent crime like murder bled into your soul, and if you had no way of spiritually renewing yourself—cleansing your heart from within—you would die a slow death of callous indifference.

When he woke early Sunday afternoon, his soul was troubled by all he'd seen and heard. He lay in bed and stared at the ceiling, knowing he should pray, knowing he should find some way of removing the stain on his soul. *Father forgive them, for they don't know what they're doing,* he thought. Instead, he lay there like a piece of driftwood, stiff and straight and worn smooth by currents that were out of his control.

There was a click, and the bedroom door opened.

"Bapa? Are you awake now?" Lillie asked, creeping carefully to the bedside.

When Jim stared into her blue eyes, he felt tears of thanksgiving spilling over onto his cheeks. Lillie found Jim's hand and held it tenderly in hers.

"Bapa, you can't lay in bed all day," Lillie said quietly. Her eyes were like the deep blue of the ocean. "Come on, we're waiting for you. Can you get up now?" Her innocence struck him in a new and deep way.

Embarrassed by the tears on his cheeks, Jim rolled to the side of the bed and sat up. He was still exhausted, and his mind was fuzzy with the facts of Terry Waite's confession that rolled around in his head. His mouth tasted sour, and he could smell the sweat lingering on his clothes.

"I need a shower, and then I'll get dressed," he said.

"Okay, Bapa. We're getting ready to say goodbye to Jerome and Sara." Her eyes brightened and she said excitedly, "Hey, guess what? I get to be in their wedding. And Henri is going to carry their rings up the aisle."

"That's nice, Lillie," he said absentmindedly, wiping his cheeks with the back of his hand.

He got up and moved around, feeling overwhelmed by the normalcy of the day—the soft feel of the sheets on his skin, the sunshine that seeped through the sheer curtains of the bedroom, the unobtrusive sounds of everyday life going on outside his bedroom sanctuary. He stood and plodded to the bathroom. After a shower, he dressed in a pair of jeans and a sweatshirt and joined the family in the living room.

"Well, look who's entered the land of the living," Carol said softly when he made his appearance in the living room. Jerome, who'd been reclining in the swoopy black chair, hurriedly stood up as if he'd gotten an electric shock from a cattle prod. Sara rose and walked toward Jim.

He opened his arms, and she walked into them. To Jim, Sara felt solid but stiff with anxiety. He continued to hold her, and her stance softened until she pulled back to look at him, her cheeks wet with tears.

"Congratulations, sweetheart," Jim said softly, running his finger along her cheekbone. "Jerome will be a fine husband for you. Now I can quit worrying about what you're doing all the time." He grinned, and his dimple dented his cheek.

"Are you really happy about it, Dad?" she asked, her blue eyes reflecting trepidation at what his answer might be.

"I'm absolutely thrilled. And I'm sorry I missed all the hoopla last night," he added. "When's the big day?"

"Looks like June fifteenth in your backyard," Sara answered.

Jim looked over at Carol and lifted his eyebrows. Carol shrugged her shoulders. "Can't say no to such a beautiful bride and handsome groom," she said.

"We'll make it work," Jim said, and he began to feel a load of weariness lift. He turned to Jerome and shook his hand firmly. His blue eyes held the former priest in a marked expression of serious reflection. "Take good care of her," he said.

"I'll do my best to make her happy," Jerome said.

In half an hour, Jim, Carol, Lillie, and Henri were standing in the driveway on Chipmunk Coulee Road, waving goodbye to Jerome and Sara. As the car disappeared around the first bend, Carol hugged Jim around the waist.

"Feeling better?" she asked.

"No. Not really. I might need to talk to Vivian and maybe Pastor Bjornstad. This case has really wiped me out."

"You're probably suffering from some situational depression," Carol suggested.

"Happens in my line of work. I might take a few days off," Jim said trudging through the front door.

"You've got plenty of PTO," Carol said. Her face softened, and she turned to him, giving him a tender kiss. "Let's get away. Go somewhere."

"I need to recoup first," Jim said. "I'm exhausted."

"Sure. After the wedding?"

"After the wedding sounds good," Jim said, and he smiled for the first time that day.

30

THREE WEEKS LATER

T he tables at Si Bon glowed with flickering candlelight as the wait staff bustled efficiently among the crowded tables, delivering drinks and food. The detective team sat around a large oval table tucked in a corner of the refurbished barn. A white tablecloth, gleaming china, and sparkling glasses filled with a white Moscato lent an air of casual relaxation—something Jim's team needed after the arduous case of the ball club murders.

Terry Waite was sitting in the La Crosse County jail awaiting his initial hearing in two weeks. His murder-for-hire scheme involving LeMar Burke and Tanya Cadwallader was gelling each day around the physical evidence that was piling up. Forensic investigators had amassed an impressive amount of fingerprints, DNA samples, clothing, shoe casts, and soil samples, placing Lori Lifto at the scene of both murders. In addition, Jim's team continued to gather financial records of payoffs and bribes associated with the crimes. The taped phone conversation between Lifto and Waite was pivotal, as was Waite's taped confession as he lay in the hospital. Mrs. Lewis' financial records of her husband's savings account added credence to the theory that collusion and kickbacks had occurred between Lewis and Burke over the high lines scheduled to be constructed in the future by Scenic Rivers Energy Cooperative.

Little Hawk was released on his own recognizance with a little help provided by his dad in the hefty sum of fifty thousand dollars bail. His trial was scheduled to begin on June 5. However, his lawyer argued that the homicide charge be dropped since it was justifiable when Little Hawk killed her to prevent the murder of another police officer, namely Sam. Jim had his doubts that it would stick, but time would tell. It was all on the lawyers' turf now.

Sam stood at his place and raised his glass.

"A toast. To my beautiful pregnant wife," he said, looking at Leslie, "and a crack investigation team that put away some unsavory thugs. May the ball club be forever put to rest."

"And the hatchet," Jim said under his breath as everyone lifted their glasses in a toast. Carol reached under the table and squeezed his hand. Jim leaned back, put his arm around her, and pulled her to himself, kissing her on the temple.

"As usual, you're the loveliest woman here," Jim whispered in her ear, looking deeply into her brown eyes.

"Nonsense, Jim. Look at Leslie. She's got that beautiful pregnant glow, and DeDe looks so happy now that Jude is on his way to a great start with the restaurant," Carol whispered back. "Ruby is always gorgeous and—"

"Just say thank you," Jim interrupted smugly.

"Thank you," Carol said, looking into Jim's eyes. She could still see traces of anxiety and exhaustion when she looked at him this closely. She'd been worried about his mental state, but Jim assured her that his sessions with Vivian were helping.

"Did you talk with Pastor Bjornstad yet?" Carol asked quietly as the bustle of celebration and conversation swirled around them.

"Yep, had a session with him yesterday," Jim commented casually.

"And?" Carol waited.

"He reminded me of the words of Elisha when he was surrounded by the horses and chariots of the enemy. 'Don't be afraid, for those who are with us are more than those who are against us.' Second Kings 6:16. That's a paraphrase, but you get the drift, right?" Jim's eyes seemed particularly blue as he gazed at his wife.

Carol ignored his question, opting for one of her own. "Were you afraid, Jim?"

Jim paused, not sure how much he should tell her. "People were getting whacked by ball clubs so ... yeah, I was afraid we wouldn't be able to figure out who was behind it."

"And now?"

"Now I'm not afraid, just sad and angry that four people's lives were wasted."

"I want you to remember something, Jim," Carol said. The serious tone of her voice made him sit up a notch. He turned and looked at her. "You," she laid her hand on his chest, "are a fine police officer, a wonderful husband, and a fantastic father. When you took those thugs off the street, Lillie and Henri are safer, and their future is brighter. In the tough times, I want you to remember that, my love."

Jim swallowed conspicuously and took a sip of his wine. "Okay, I can do that."

"One more thing," Carol said quietly.

"Go ahead."

"I love you forever and always," Carol said, and she leaned over and kissed Jim long and fervently. Jim pulled away after a few intense moments. "When are we going to Charleston?"

"I'm ready when you are, baby," Jim replied softly.

Carol smiled widely, tears shimmering in her eyes.

THE END

ABOUT THE AUTHOR

Sue Berg is the author of the Driftless Mystery Series. She is a former teacher, and enjoys many hobbies including writing, watercolor painting, quilting, cooking and gardening. She lives with her husband, Alan, near Viroqua, Wisconsin.

The Driftless Mystery Series set in the beautiful Driftless region of the Upper Midwest does not disappoint. With complex characters, intriguing plots, and surprising twists and turns, this series will delight you with its ability to entertain while upholding the values we all treasure; love, faith, loyalty, and family. It is destined to become a beloved and enduring legacy to the people and culture in this unique part of the country.

COMING IN MAY 2025

JIM HIGGINS' ADVENTURES CONTINUE...

Look to the next page for an excerpt from *Driftless Identity*.

THURSDAY, AUGUST 28

A SIMPLE TEST TO FIND OUT
WHETHER YOUR MISSION IN LIFE IS FINISHED:
IF YOU'RE STILL ALIVE, IT ISN'T FINISHED.
YOUR MISSION GOES ON.

SUE BERG

1

The heat during the last few weeks of August had been stifling and unrelenting. The trees wilted in the hot sun for lack of water; the grass had turned brown and crackled underneath your feet. A dusty haze in the air left a fine grit across the surface of everything. Farmers were worried about their crops. Golf courses were pumping water on their lawns and greens. People were crabby and short-tempered. Where was the rain?

Late Thursday evening, lightning flashes streaked across the sky in brilliant blue fingers of incandescent radiance. All day the humidity had been building, and now it seemed about to smack its big fist across the landscape. The air smelled of ozone and moisture.

Leslie Birkstein draped her hand across her swollen belly and restlessly tucked her feet under the afghan. The air conditioning was turned too low again. Her husband, Sam, who was scrunched in an awkward position on the couch, sat up suddenly when a growl of thunder rattled the windows of their hilltop cottage on U.S. Highway 35 along the Mississippi River south of La Crosse, Wisconsin. The light from the TV bathed the room in a blue hue. Sam got up, walked to the large window, and watched lightning bolts dance on the horizon of the Mississippi River bluffs on the Minnesota side over two miles away.

"Hey, will you go to Gas & Go and get me some maple nut ice cream?" Leslie asked, trying to keep the whine out of her voice.

"Another craving?" Sam asked. He turned and looked at Leslie. "It's almost eleven, hon. I was thinking about going to bed."

Leslie smiled shyly. "Yeah, I know what time it is, but just think, in another couple of months, all these cravings will be gone, and then you'll have to listen to baby Birkstein fussing and crying. You might even be walking the floor, trying—"

"Okay, okay. When you put it like that, I guess I can indulge your cravings."

"You're a good man, Charlie Brown," Leslie said, walking up to him and hugging him around the waist. Paco, their black lab, got up from the rug and stretched in a lazy movement reminiscent of a yoga pose. He let out a groan accompanied by a huge yawn. Then he stood and wagged his tail, looking expectantly at Sam.

"No, Paco. I'm not taking you with me. You have to stay with Lez," Sam said, holding up his hand in a stay position. Paco's tail drooped like a flag being lowered to half-mast. Sam walked to the entryway and grabbed his rain jacket off the hook. "Be back in a half an hour," he said.

The door slammed shut. Leslie stood by the window and watched Sam back the Jeep out of the garage into the rain that had just begun to fall. He headed down the steep bluff driveway toward the gas station in Stoddard, seven miles north on the Great River Road.

In the quiet cocoon of the Jeep, Sam could barely hear the threat of the rumbling thunder. He thought back over the events of the last six months. So many things had happened, the first being their surprise pregnancy, which they'd found out about in April. Now Leslie's expanding abdomen was a taut ball of muscle and growing baby.

Sam was fascinated with the pregnancy, frequently laying his hand on Leslie's belly to feel the active life within her. He read about the baby's development, poring over a medical nursing textbook he'd bought at Goodwill. The only thing he found scary was the delivery, although taking childbirth classes with Leslie had helped alleviate some of his anxiety.

Then another surprise development landed in their lap—Bobby Rude's childhood home, perched beneath the precipice of Warner's Bluff in Genoa along the Great River Road, came up for sale. Bobby, now a junior at Logan High School in La Crosse, had gone to live with Jerome and Sara Knight after his alcoholic father had died in April at the Tomah Veteran's Hospital. Bobby had been instrumental in gathering crucial evidence in a couple of tough cases facing the investigative team at the La Crosse Sheriff's Department. His dream was to become a cop—more specifically, a detective.

Sam and Leslie hadn't planned on purchasing a home, but they were tired of city life and wanted a place in the country to begin raising their family. The house was situated on the top of a steep hill beneath the sandstone bluffs that rose above the tiny river town of Genoa, whose buildings were scattered like pebbles on a sand beach beneath the ridge of rock just south of the house. The view of the majestic Mississippi from their front window was worth every penny they'd paid for it, although the house had fallen into disrepair over the years and needed substantial improvements.

They purchased the riverfront property for a modest sum, but the dwelling was small and needed new plumbing, electrical work, and a roof. In the process of remodeling, they decided to add an expansive wing to the north: an art studio for Leslie and two bedrooms with a master en suite bath above it on the second floor. Sam revamped the kitchen with new appliances, IKEA cupboards he purchased online, and granite countertops. The rest of the house was freshened with paint and new flooring.

Despite the responsibility of a mortgage, Sam and Leslie enjoyed the panoramic views of the river from their home every day. The wide, silent waterway flowed south while barges ferried their cargo throughout the seasons when the river was open. The variety of wildlife passing through their backyard never failed to amaze and delight them: white-tailed deer, turkeys, foxes, coyotes, and multitudes of birds, including their favorites, bald eagles and red-tailed hawks. Sam had discovered several mountain biking trails in the area, which gave him and Paco some much-needed exercise and recreation. Their daily runs alleviated the stress of Sam's detective work at the La Crosse Sheriff's Department.

Things at the law enforcement center on Vine Street had been slow throughout the summer. The investigative team was still gathering and organizing the evidence from the ball club killings, their last major case. Lori Lifto, the ax-wielding assassin of the victims, was dead, but the other perpetrators were alive and incarcerated in the La Crosse County jail until their trials began in the fall. In the months since their last sensational murder case, the investigative team had been busy with low-level crimes: cuffing and stuffing drug dealers, tracking down the perps of small-time robberies and house break-ins, and conducting interviews with victims of sexual assault and domestic abuse.

As Sam drove north on the Great River Road toward Stoddard, the wind and rain began to pick up, the thunderstorm building in intensity. Lightning crashed every few seconds, and the trees whipped in a circular pattern as if in a blender. Leaves and small twigs blew across the river highway in gusts of wind that rocked Sam's Jeep from side to side. Several cars pulled over on the shoulder of the road, waiting for the pounding rain and turbulent blasts of the wind to ease up.

Sam drove into Stoddard and parked along the Gas & Go building. When the storm showed no signs of abating, he pulled his hood over his head, opened the driver-side door, and dashed inside the store. A young teenage girl looked up when he entered. She smiled tentatively as Sam pushed his hood back.

"Nasty out there?" she asked, taking in his brown curly hair and hazel eyes.

"Yeah, you might say that," Sam said, shaking off the rain as it dripped on the floor. "What's the forecast anyway?"

The girl shrugged her shoulders. "Don't know. I get off at midnight, so I hope it settles down before then. That's all I care about," she said, disinterested in the weather.

Sam walked to the freezer section and pulled out a tub of maple nut ice cream. On his way to the front check-out counter, he grabbed a bunch of bananas and a gallon of milk. Sam set the items on the counter, paid for them, and waved to the clerk as he exited the store.

Back on the road, sheets of rain beat against the Jeep. Sam drove slowly, inching his way south on the deserted River Road highway, noting the absence of other travelers. Several miles out of town, his Jeep coughed and hiccupped. Sam eased the car over to the shoulder of the road, where the engine completely died. He tried to start it. Nothing. He groaned with frustration.

"What the Sam Hill is goin' on?" he rasped to himself. His eyes scanned the instrument panel, then fixated on the E of the gas gauge. "What! You've got to be kidding! How could I run out of gas?" he asked, talking to himself. He slammed his fist into the steering wheel, then slumped back into his seat. "I don't believe this!"

After a few moments, he made a plan. He reached for his cell, then let out another frustrated sigh. He'd left his phone on the kitchen counter. Now his options were fewer—none of them pleasant. He figured he was about a mile from home at the most. Trying to hitch a ride back to Stoddard in a raging thunderstorm was not appealing.

After a few more minutes, the rain seemed to ease up. "Guess I'll just have to walk back to the house," he said softly. "Lez will never let me live this down."

Sam decided to leave the groceries in the Jeep. Leslie would have to bring him back with some gas anyway so he could get his vehicle off the road before morning. He opened the car door in disgust and stepped out into the storm, locking the Jeep with his key fob. The wind whipped rain into his face, blowing his hood back. He grabbed it angrily and pulled it back on his head, tying the strings firmly.

Then he ducked his chin to his chest and started walking.

Sam had been in thunderstorms before while camping, hiking, and biking. Outside in the elements, the noise of the electricity passing through the atmosphere was deafening and scary. As he walked, he recalled an incident in Canada when his family was tent camping, and the wind and rain were churning the woods around them. He'd been terrified. Those memories always created uneasy feelings when thunderstorms and high winds barreled across the land.

During the lightning flashes, he noticed the wide river had taken on the look of a raging serpent, complete with whitecaps and sloshing waves. He was almost to the scenic turnout above Genoa when suddenly, without warning, a tree about a hundred feet in front of him was struck by a lightning bolt. The brilliance of the electrical current supercharged the atmosphere around the tree. The current traveled through the ground along the highway in a microsecond to where Sam was walking. He was blown off his feet, his shoes landing somewhere behind him. He tumbled to the ground face down, unconscious, his heart thumping in an irregular rhythm. The rain continued falling for fifteen more minutes until it slowed into a gentle shower.